LEAVING WHITE SANDS

JEFFREY FLAAT

DEDICATION

To Luddites everywhere.

TRANSACTION JOURNAL

ACKNOWLEDGMENTS

This book could not exist without the encouragement of several people.

In 1982 and 1983, Sue Stoner and John Horbacz introduced me to Literature in a way that made it a fascinating journey into different worlds and different times, not boring stuff written by old dead dudes. Without their guidance (and without Mr. Horbacz's insistence that I read "Waiting for Godot"), this book would not exist, and I likely would also not be a filmmaker. Whether they will ever know it, this book is their legacy more than mine. Good teachers change lives, and they were the best.

My kids. I would be incomplete without my kids. They inspire me every day to try to be a better person, even when I don't feel like it. I do it to try, in the smallest of ways, to influence the future to be a better one for them (and my grandkids).

Dana Skvarek II and Jolene Skvarek, through their processes of authoring their books, showed me that moving an idea from your head to paper is possible, though not easy. It is their encouragement to "just go write" that led me to start typing. I blame them as well for this book.

Finally, Ken Metcalf introduced me to some truly scary technology back in the day, and between that insanity and his brilliant explanations of how twisted today's technology can become, along with just a bit of paranoia and science fiction, this book exists.

There are many more people who inspired me and mentored me on my path to complete this fable. Without all of these people and their influences in my life in one way or another, I would have neither the story, the confidence to write this story, the motivation to do so, nor the experiences upon which it is loosely based.

To all of you, named or unnamed, I appreciate you.

Thank you for influencing me.

PREFACE

The beginning of the end was in 1950.

Credit cards have been in use since they were first introduced by Diner's Club in that year, followed by American Express who released their first card in 1958. Also in 1958, Bank of America introduced their credit card, originally called "BankAmericard" (later renamed to VISA and spun off into its own company). The first credit cards were printed on paper card stock and were typed. This required the merchant to fill out all of the information for the charge slip manually, which was time-consuming, and caused a great deal of errors. In late 1969, American Express changed to a plastic card with raised numbers, and also released the first manual credit card machine, which standardized the information transfer by placing the card and a charge slip in the machine, then manually rolling a press across the slip, which caused the card information to be transferred to the paper charge slip.

This technology remained mostly unchanged well into the late 1970's and early 1980's. Many new cards had been released by other financial institutions, including MasterCharge (later renamed to MasterCard in the United States, and Maestro in other parts of the world) and Discover Card. As an industry, the credit card issuers began printing booklets for monthly distribution to merchants around the world which contained card numbers that were invalid or fraudulent, and merchants would have to check the book to make sure the card that was presented was not invalid.

CHAPTER 1: FIRE TRAP

In 1982, Erik Torssen was working for Finland Global Finance Services, Gmbh (*Suomen Globaalit Rahoituspalvelut Gmbh*) ("Finland Global") as a computer engineer. Simultaneously, working from home in his spare time, Erik devised a method whereby a computer could validate a credit card transaction, store the information, and transmit the validation to the credit card company for storage in their systems until the charge slip was deposited and processed by the issuing bank. The process would also generate an approval code, which would be provided to the merchant.

Torssen, a particle physicist by choice but a computer engineer out of necessity, first presented the concept to his management team in October 1982. His direct management team liked the idea well enough that it was presented to the Board of Directors at their regular monthly meeting on October 29, 1982. The Board listened politely, thanked Torssen for his presentation, and promised to give it serious consideration.

On November 13, 1982, Erik Torssen was terminated by Finland Global for unspecified reasons, but was offered five years' severance pay and a non-disclosure non-circumvent agreement, wherein Finland Global claimed ownership of all of the intellectual property surrounding the validation methodology, and threatened Erik with financial ruin and criminal charges should he present the validation method in any form to any other entity within 20 years. Stunned and intimidated by the room full of lawyers, and facing financial ruin if he didn't sign the contracts and take the severance, Erik signed the agreement and moved back to his home country of Norway, where he continued to tinker with computers and the new global communications network released by the United States to certain government, educational, and financial institutions, his only companion being his burning hatred for Finland Global.

Erik Torssen continued his work in a small cottage in the tiny northern fishing village of Akkarfjord, Norway over the next five years. His design work managed to cover nearly all of his wall space in notes, process flow drawings, maps of the world, and lines of string of varying thickness connecting pinpoints on the documents. Erik spoke to no one but himself, except on the weekly trips across the street to the town's only post office and grocer for supplies.

Erik also permitted himself a cup of coffee and a short chat with the occasional fishing boat captain that may be in the shop at the same time, and eventually struck up a friendship with Captain Hans Rødtskjegg. Erik and Hans often discussed some of the new computer equipment that was beginning to be available to fishing boats, and Hans and Erik discussed possible ways to enhance the capabilities of the machines. During one such conversation, Hans explained to Erik an idea he had for vastly improving a depth finder to be able to show depths further ahead of the boats and farther out to the sides, but that he lacked the technical knowledge to build such a device. He also stated that he had discussed the idea with his brother, who was the Senior Vice President of Business Development for *Norges Nasjonalbank* ("Norway National Bank"). Hans' brother, Bjorn, stated that if a prototype could be produced and proven, that Norges could fund mass production of the new devices.

Erik and Hans spent the next three years on Hans' boat refining their prototype, and eventually dialed in the perfect combination of the technologies necessary to take a quantum leap forward in the technology of depth-reporting to ships' captains, for both small and large watercraft. True to his word, in February 1989, Bjorn Rødtskjegg shepherded the project and funding through the bank, and the product launched to fantastic success. Erik's royalties earned him riches beyond that which he could ever spend, but the happiness at the success was short-lived. His anger at Finland Global still burned in him, and his mood matched the seasonal darkness outside his cottage. Even months after the NuDepth project was completed, his walls were still covered with his transaction validation project. Erik ignored it as best he could, and even considered finally putting away the project, but the motivation to do so eluded him.

In late May 1991, Erik and Hans were enjoying a midnight lunch, sitting at a small table outside the grocery store and soaking in the summer sun.

"You seem glum, my friend." Hans pointed out. "You have more money than Odin! You should be the happiest man on the beach!" Hans roared with laughter, as Erik remained dour.

"I should," Erik replied. "I am just still haunted by the ghost of my past project. I just can't seem to put it away, and it still angers me."

"You have not told me of this project. Care to tell me?" Hans inquired.

"I'll do better, I'll show you." Erik offered. "But first, go change. I don't want my hut to stink like your boat for the rest of the summer." Both men laughed and finished their drinks.

A half hour later, a freshly changed Hans knocked on the door of Erik's cottage. Erik greeted his friend with a strong handshake and a quick sniff, then motioned for him to enter. Hans laughed, and stepped in, his expression immediately changing to that of shock.

"Odin's beard, what is this fire trap?" Hans asked incredulously.

"It was my idea for securing all of the credit card transactions for all of the world", Erik responded in a flat tone.

"...the whole world?" Hans stammered. "That's not possible. Bjorn and I have talked a bit about how credit cards are going to destroy the world, because there is no way to secure them. You're telling me you can do it?"

"In real time, yes."

Hans laughed again at the ridiculous arrogance of his friend.

"What you are saying, and what you have on the walls here, it's not possible to do."

"Yes, it is." Again, a flat and matter-of-fact response from Erik.

Hans' tone turned serious.

"You're sure?"

4

"Yes." Another flat response.

"Can you... can you make all of... this..." Hans gestured at the walls and clutter, "can you make all of this understandable? Understandable to someone who does not understand any of it?"

"Yes."

Hans turned towards the door and began to leave.

"Where are you going?" Erik asked.

"To the boat to call Bjorn." Hans said over his shoulder as he opened the door, then paused in the doorway. "You and I are going back to Oslo in a week to present this madness to Bjorn. And you, my insane friend, you are going to remake the world with this 'translucent validation' lunacy."

"'Transaction validation'," Erik corrected.

"Whatever word you call it," Hans laughed from outside the cottage, already jogging towards the dock.

"'Lunacy' is the more appropriate word," Erik said to no one, then sat down at his typewriter and loaded a fresh piece of paper. Across the top, he typed the phrase "REAL-TIME GLOBAL CREDIT CARD TRANSACTION VALIDATION". He returned the carriage twice.

"*Once more unto the breach, dear friends...*", Erik said to the typewriter. "*Once more.*"

CHAPTER 2: MADNESS

Bjorn Rødtskjegg sat in the chair behind his desk, his mouth slightly open in stunned silence. Hans sat in a chair on the other side of the desk, smiling, looking between Erik and Bjorn and back to Erik, who stood next to an easel with drawings supporting the typed presentation booklet that he had given to Bjorn. The silence was lasting too long, and Erik was growing more uncomfortable by the second.

"I told you, madness," Hans finally broke the silence with a laugh.

"This..." Bjorn stammered, finally closing his mouth and looking down at the book, then back at the easel and finally to Erik, "this could work." There was actual awe in his voice.

Erik was still uncomfortable, but less so now.

"As I said to Hans, yes." Erik answered.

"When did you first figure this out?" Bjorn asked.

"My first presentation to the Board was in late 1982," Erik said.

"Wait, what Board?" Bjorn now had concern in his voice.

"When I was working at *Suomen Globaalit*, I figured this out on my own time, and I presented it to the Board there, in late 1982, because I thought they'd want to use it, and maybe I could get a promotion." Erik explained. "But instead, they fired me and slapped me with a severe non-disclosure and non-circumvent contract and paid me a bribe."

"What is the duration of the contract?" Bjorn asked.

"Twenty years," Erik answered.

"So, you still have seven years left on that," Bjorn calculated.

"What if they didn't know?" Erik asked thoughtfully.

"These kinds of things are pretty iron-clad." Bjorn explained. "Anything we release like this could easily be considered industrial espionage, and they could destroy us in court. And you especially."

"But, what if they didn't know?" Erik asked again.

"How could they not know?" Bjorn was cautiously intrigued.

"What if all of the technology was contained inside a computer," Erik began, "and no one could access it at all. What if the software was loaded into the computer at the time we built it, and not just installed afterwards, and only the three of us in this room knew what it actually did? What if we just hooked up a computer to the connection network of the credit card companies, and all they knew was that a transaction went in, and either a decline or approval with a validation code came out? Just this black box like magicians use for their tricks? Besides, Finland Global isn't using my invention anyway."

Bjorn considered Erik for a long moment, then turned to Hans.

"You're right, Hans," Bjorn stated. "He is insane." Then Bjorn laughed loudly, followed by Hans. Erik could tell that the laugh was genetic.

"Here is what I will do," Bjorn stated, "I'm going to present your black magical transaction validation box to the Steering Committee. They meet in two days. You two stay at my house meanwhile. This idea of yours, Erik... it will either be a sea change in the financial industry, or we'll all be in jail for international financial fraud." Bjorn laughed again. "Come on, boys, let's get lunch."

CHAPTER 3: TYPEWRITER AND NOTES

Erik sat in the chair in front of Bjorn's desk, absolutely stunned. The Steering Committee had approved the project, despite the legal dangers. The legal department at Norway National Bank had considered the project, and agreed that the concept of the "black box" would provide sufficient cover for the "proprietary technology" contained therein, and had signed off on it, with the usual terms and conditions that any lawyer inevitably must add in order to justify their law license. Erik really was not sure what Bjorn had told the Committee to get it approved.

"Are you going to say something?" Hans asked after a bit.

"It's just that... all my notes," Erik began, "all my designs, hell, all my walls... It wasn't just a fantasy or useless hobby. This technology will change the face of the planet, and the name Torssen will be synonymous with Newton, Einstein, Rockefeller, Carnegie... I'll be famous, and I will buy Finland Global, and fire them all and bankrupt them, and close the company."

"Let's maybe build your magical black box first," Bjorn suggested.

"Of course, of course..." Erik snapped out of his fantasy. "I'll head home right now and get to work."

"Well, no," Bjorn stopped him. "Legal is completely adamant that all work be performed in a secure laboratory in the building here. You'll need to move to Oslo, and all materials and work products will be kept in your lab here. We can have a crew at your place tomorrow to start packing your possessions and get them moved here. We already have a flat purchased for you."

Erik considered the change.

"All I want is my typewriter and notes." He said after a moment. "Let Hans here use the cottage for his girlfriends." Hans laughed at that.

"Your typewriter and notes will be here tomorrow night." Bjorn stated happily. "For now, let me show you to your new laboratory and introduce you to your staff. After that, we will eat dinner, and then take you to your new flat."

All three men stood and walked out of Bjorn's office.

CHAPTER 4: CHIPS

Throughout the history of credit cards, fraud had become more and more rampant, costing merchants around the globe billions in lost revenue due to chargebacks. In the mid 1980's, a magnetic stripe was added to the backs of most credit cards, which contained unencrypted card information that could be read through a terminal at the merchant site. This terminal was connected to a telephone line, and when the merchant swiped the mag stripe of the card through the terminal and entered the transaction amount, the terminal would dial the credit card company, report the transaction, and return a confirmation code to the merchant, which the merchant would then write onto the credit card charge slip and deposit to the bank. While this functionality did reduce fraud, there were still many ways around the mag stripe / terminal methodology, and criminals were becoming more creative every day.

Meanwhile, MasterCard and American Express were considering more global solutions to the problem, and in early 1990 began testing a credit card with a semiconductor chip that contained both a microprocessor and memory. The chip had been successfully used in France since 1983 for use with pay telephones, and various companies around the world including Honeywell and Motorola had continued to advance the capabilities of the chip for use in various encrypted systems.

In November 1991, a French gift card issuer *Carte-cadeau France* began issuing reusable cards with the chip and PIN functionality which they branded *"Ma carte d'argent"* or MyMoney Card, which permitted holders to spend money and reload funds onto the card at their special terminals around France, thereby bypassing the banking and credit card systems completely. Banks and credit card issuers took notice at the explosion of popularity of the MyMoney Cards, and had various strategic and industry meetings on how to either combat the use, or to exploit the technology.

With that, the "chip card" became the new global standard.

CHAPTER 5: CARIBOU ON CAVE WALLS

The "Black Box Lab", as Erik's staff referred to the laboratory, was busy. Erik rarely slept at home, preferring to sleep on the small cot that he had stashed behind the mainframe. The room was usually dark, was kept at a constant 19C, the hum of the machinery drowned out any other noise, and the slight vibration from the cooling towers was comforting. His sleeping arrangements also had the added benefit of saving him the 15 minutes it would take to walk home, and when he was focused on a specific task or problem, he could work until he was exhausted, sleep a few hours behind the mainframe, and then get right back to work when he inevitably woke up with the solution. Actual restful sleep had eluded him since beginning work at *Norges Nasjonalbank*, but he was happy for the ability to finally build his dream system.

The Yule and Christmas decorations that he had permitted his team to spread across the laboratory provided a welcome splash of color from the usual black desks and white walls and floors. On this day, Erik was hunched over his desk and a scattering of papers, working on an algorithm to encrypt the bank transaction header. As usual, Erik was deep in his work, and was seemingly unaware of the people or room around him, so it was not unusual for him to not notice the person standing next to him. What was unusual was that the person was Bjorn. It was very rare for Bjorn to come down to the lab, and usually Erik had to take time away from his work in the fourth sub-basement of the *Norges Nasjonalbank* headquarters building to take the two-lift and 24 floor ride to Bjorn's office. Erik thought he could count on one hand the number of times he had been visited in the lab by Bjorn.

"God morgen, Erik," Bjorn finally said, after several long moments of

waiting for Erik to notice him, and finally realizing that time would never arrive. Erik startled.

"God morgen, Bjorn," Erik replied breathlessly from his small scare. "Is it morning? I don't notice time anymore… this lab is always daytime." Bjorn laughed the full laugh of his family, and Erik realized that he missed having breakfast with Hans, back… how long ago had that been?

A new realization dawned on Erik that he didn't really know how long he had been working on the project here, though it must have been five or six months, since the lab was decorated for Yule.

"How long has it been since you had a meal?" Bjorn asked. The confused expression on Erik's face was enough of an answer for Bjorn. "Come, my brilliant madman, I am hungry for a big breakfast."

Bjorn and Erik stepped out of the lift from the laboratory into the main lobby of the bank, and Bjorn started towards the main doors.

"Where are we going?" Erik asked, assuming they would just eat in Bjorn's office.

"I said I wanted a big meal, so we are going out." Bjorn answered, motioning towards the main doors, Erik noticed a limousine parked directly outside. Bjorn gave another easy short laugh and headed towards the door. After a few seconds, Erik followed, and joined Bjorn in the back of the car.

The men chatted about anything but work during the 20-minute drive. Erik had to ask what the date was, because he saw on the clock in the car that it was almost lunch time, but it was dark outside, so it must be winter. Bjorn had told him it was December 7. Erik realized that five months had passed since he had been working on this project. They talked about Hans, and how he had used his royalty money from the NuDepth project to buy five more boats and a cannery up north, and was having more fun, and working more, than he ever had in his life. Erik was happy to hear that.

They arrived at a very upscale-looking restaurant, and Erik became aware that he was vastly under-dressed for such a place. Bjorn noticed the hesitation and laughed. They were greeted by the hostess and taken to a private room, where what appeared to be an elaborate smorgasbord was already set up.

"Are we being joined by several more people?" Erik asked. Again,

Bjorn's laugh filled the room.

"No, I told you I'm hungry," Bjorn said, and they sat and began to eat.

An hour later, their meal complete, the two men traded a couple shots of *akevitt* and relaxed. Bjorn's expression turned dark.

"Too much drink on a full stomach?" Erik asked Bjorn, noticing the change of expression.

"No," Bjorn answered. "I have difficult news to tell you, and I have been avoiding it for the past week."

Erik steeled himself for the bad news. Had Hans died? Erik couldn't imagine what else it could be.

"The Board has decided to terminate your project." Bjorn said flatly.

The news hit Erik as if a punch to the chest.

"What? Why?" Erik managed to whisper.

"While you have been inventing the new global standard in our basement," Bjorn began, "*Carte-cadeau France* has begun shipping cards with semiconductor chips on them that can be used for storing money and assisting validation. The big issuers have taken notice, and they are going to begin issuing cards throughout Europe with these chips. The validation problem is solved."

Erik pondered the new information. He could not grasp how this little French upstart had managed to crack the real-time anywhere-in-the-world validation for any card issuer.

"How did they do it?" Erik finally asked out loud.

"What do you mean?" Bjorn asked.

"In order to do real-time global validation in any currency for any transaction," Erik explained, "all of the issuers have to use a centralized processor to make the validation decision. How did this little French turd convince American Express, MasterCard, Bank of America, and every other issuer on the planet to connect their systems together?"

Bjorn looked stunned, and took a moment to consider what Erik had just told him.

"They didn't." Bjorn answered finally. "The technology they are offering is just so the issuers can process even more securely within their own networks."

With that, Erik began to laugh. For a long time.

"Tor," Erik stated when he was able to finally speak, "they didn't solve the problem I'm working on, they just managed to solve the problem of the mag stripes not being secure. Their new 'technology' is just a faster way for them to paint caribou on cave walls." Erik laughed again. Bjorn still looked confused.

"Bjorn, this is what I'm saying," Erik explained further. "My black magic box will be able to take connections from *any* company that wants a transaction validated, whether between nations or banks or any other transaction that requires a validation, whether financial or something else, and say it's valid or not valid. Yes or no. On or off. Like a switch."

A slow smile crept across Bjorn's face. He poured both men another shot of akevitt.

"*Skål*, my brilliant friend."

"*Skål*," Erik agreed, and downed the shot.

Erik went right back to work after his lunch with Bjorn. He probably shouldn't have, he thought… that *akevitt* was good, and he was mentally fuzzy. His excitement wouldn't let him sleep now, though.

CHAPTER 6: CEASE AND DESIST

Erik and his team continued to perfect what the bank senior management had now come to call the "Switch". Since 1992, when the American government had begun making their new "internet", a new global computer network, available to the general public and commerce, Erik's team had analyzed the actual packet routing and structure each time the governing body released new updates. The challenges were no longer about making the Switch available to the global financial systems, the more important task was to hide the packets from all of the computers connected to the internet. Eventually, they devised a method, that should have been impossible, to hide the Switch outside of the normal internet; they gave the Switch an address that was outside the range of addresses available to computers on the internet. Every other computer would be physically unable to see the Switch or the packets it generated.

No one on the Board of Directors was able to understand the technical methodology. When Erik tried to explain that "the first octet of the IP address range that we use for the Switch starts with 256, which as we all know is a mathematical impossibility...", a Board member interrupted him to ask if there were not more than 256 computers on the internet. Erik gave up on that explanation completely. Then he explained the concept by using an analogy of someone standing outside of time in the minute in which we are living. They can see us and hear us, and maybe even get a word or two to us, but we can not access them. The Board seemed to grasp that concept, but then asked how the financial computers could interact with the Switch in order to retrieve validations. Erik explained it using a trope from spy movies.

"Consider when someone knocks on a door," Erik began, "and

someone on the inside opens a little sliding hatch on the door. The person outside says a code word, and the person inside gives a code word back. That's it. The person outside has no way in unless they are let in, has no idea what's behind the door, and can only get one of two answers: 'yes with code' or 'no'."

"But," countered one self-important Board member, "what if they use a battering ram to knock down the door? Then they can do damage."

"There's nothing behind the door," Erik answered. "Remember, what's behind that door does not exist in a manner that we can sense it at all. It's the same with any computers on the new internet; they can't see the Switch, because we are actually violating the laws of internet physics, as it were."

"Then how do we make updates to it or test it?" Another Board member asked.

"That's a great question, actually," Erik said, ignoring the glare from the previous Board member. "There will be exactly four plugs on the back of the Switch: one for connection to the mains, 2 for a fiber optic connection, and one serial port. It is through this serial port that we can physically connect another computer and access the Switch through a command console. The fiber connections will only be into our network, and those are behind that door that I spoke of earlier. Without a direct physical connection to the Switch, there is no way to do anything at all to it."

The Board was silent for a bit, then Bjorn recommended a recess. The motion was seconded and passed with unanimous consent. As Erik was packing up his easel, Bjorn approached him with a smile.

"You really have done it, haven't you?" Bjorn asked.

"Yes we have," Erik said quietly but confidently. "The Switch is configured, tested, loaded, and operational. All we need to do now is make a few test transactions from the real world, and then we can close the test port, and the sales team can go sell our service to the card issuers."

Bjorn laughed again and patted Erik on the back, then left Erik to finish packing up.

As Erik walked out of the room a few minutes later, he saw Bjorn, the Board Chairman, and two over-groomed men in three-piece suits with briefcases walking towards him. Bjorn looked furious.

"Dr. Torssen," one of the briefcases spoke to Erik. "Would you please remain in the room, we have something important to discuss."

The five men sat down at the table, Bjorn next to Erik on one side, and the other three directly opposite them.

"Dr. Torssen," Briefcase Number Two began, "we represent the legal department for Norway National Bank. This morning, we were served a Cease and Desist Notice by the legal team over at *Suomen Globaalit Rahoituspalvelut Gmbh.* They allege that you have a non-disclosure non-circumvent contract with them that does not expire for another three years." Bjorn dropped his head into his hands. "Further, they state that this contract specifically covers any and all work product or intellectual property, which they claim is theirs, regarding validation of financial transactions of any kind. Do you know anything about this?"

Erik sat in stunned silence. Someone had leaked his project, and someone back at Finland Global got wind of it.

And now they were going to shut him down again.

"Yes." Erik finally answered quietly.

"And you knew about this," the Board Chair directed his words to Bjorn. "And you understated the legal threat when this project was approved, didn't you?"

Bjorn just nodded.

"Then, security will escort you to your office to gather your personal effects. Your time with Norway National Bank is terminated effective immediately."

With that, two very burly security guards entered the room and stood behind Bjorn. Bjorn stood up, patted Erik on the shoulder, and left the room without another word. The Chairman continued.

"As for you, Dr. Torssen, you are to be escorted back to your laboratory, where you will gather your personal effects, and you will also be escorted from the building."

Erik could feel the rage building in him again. Not again... not a second time. They were going to take his concept away from him, again. And they would probably sign some kind of Joint Venture with *Suomen Globaalit Rahoituspalvelut Gmbh,* and both companies would rule the financial world for the next hundred years.

"The non-disclosure non-circumvent contract that you will sign with *Norges Nasjonalbank,*" Briefcase Number One began speaking, "will not have any financial offering like the one you signed with *Suomen Globaalit Rahoituspalvelut Gmbh.* What you have done, Doctor, is subject this organization to potential massive damages because of your lies and omissions. Our generosity is in not suing you."

"What about all my materials?" Erik asked, already knowing the answer. "What about all the hardware? What about the Switch?"

"*You* do not have any materials, Doctor." Briefcase Number One answered. "All assets of the project, including but not limited to all electronic devices, whether functional or not functional, materials, wires, drawings, chattel paper, and all other materials and intellectual property, tangible or intangible, now or hereafter identified are the sole property of *Norges Nasjonalbank.*" The lawyer rattled it off as if it was a contract. "But if you must know, part of our settlement with *Suomen Globaalit Rahoituspalvelut Gmbh* states that all of the materials must be delivered to them to be destroyed under observation by their representatives."

So, there it was.

Erik sat for a moment, his anger building. He became aware of two more security guards standing behind him. Briefcase Number Two slid a copy of their contact across the table to Erik. Erik quickly signed it without bothering to read it. Briefcase Number Two then slid the document to the Chairman, who looked it over briefly, then signed another copy of the document, and slid it to Erik.

"For your records," the Chairman said to Erik.

Erik retrieved the document and flung it violently at the Chairman.

"Shove it up your ass!" Erik, screamed at the Chairman.

Immediately, the two security guards grabbed Erik roughly by the arms and dragged him from the room.

CHAPTER 7: TURN THE PAGE

Erik opened the door to his cottage in Akkarfjord. The smell of old fish overpowered him. He swore a quick curse at Hans for not leaving his work clothes outside the cottage when he used it in Erik's absence. It occurred to Erik that he had been gone almost 3 years. It also occurred to Erik that he forgot to get his typewriter from the lab before they ejected him from the building. That thought angered him more, because it was probably among the "chattel" that was delivered to Finland Global for destruction.

Erik tossed his satchel onto his bed, then sat down heavily in a kitchen chair, thinking back over the events of two days ago when he had lost everything. Again. By the time the security guards had marched him into the laboratory, his entire staff was already gone. All of the computers, and even the mainframe, were off. The idiots had actually just turned off the mains, without actually shutting everything down correctly. He was sure there was damage to at least some of it. Even the Switch was powered down.

At that moment, the door slammed open, and Hans stormed in, his face full of rage.

"What did you do?" Hans screamed at Erik, and lifted him out of the chair.

"I don't know what you mean!" Erik screamed back. He really had no idea what had Hans in a rage.

"He is dead!" Hans screamed. "All of them are dead!" He shook Erik roughly with each word, as if punctuating his exclamations with the shaking.

"Hans!" Erik tried to slow Hans down, to bring him back to some calm. "Tell me what's happened! I don't understand!"

Hans paused, then let go of Erik, and stepped back. Erik fell back into the chair, and Hans sat down across from him.

"Bjorn," Hans began. "Bjorn and *your* team were all being flown to Finland. Bjorn told me it was to discuss some technology with some bank there after they were all fired from Norway National."

Erik was stunned.

"The plane was hijacked as soon as it entered Fin airspace," Hans continued, barely containing his rage, "and the military... Shot! It! Down! You were supposed to be on that plane, *not* Bjorn! You caused this! I should never have introduced you to him!"

Hans stood again and paced the cottage.

Erik digested the news that Hans had just told him. His entire team and Bjorn, going to Finland to talk to some bank? Erik knew what this was. Norway National Bank and Finland Global had made an agreement to ensure that no one ever knew how the Switch worked. But why leave Erik off the plane? And why have Bjorn on the plane? Bjorn didn't know how the technology actually worked. That's when it hit Erik: Hans was speaking literally when he said that Erik was supposed to be on the plane, and not Bjorn. Either Norway National or Finland Financial, or both, had probably assassinated the team and made it look like terrorism. Erik sat in stunned silence, attempting to grasp the enormity of what had happened.

"...*all of the materials must be delivered to them to be destroyed...*", Briefcase Number One's words flew into Erik's head. Did they actually also mean all the personnel?

Then he realized that only Hans knew that Erik was still alive.

"Hans, what did Bjorn tell you had happened in Oslo?" Erik asked finally.

"He said that he and you hid most of the secrets of your previous work from the legal team." Hans explained. "He said that somehow Finland

Financial found out the whole truth of what you and your team were doing, and that your project was ready, but that it got shut down, and you, your team, and Bjorn were all fired. But Bjorn was happy, because he said he was meeting with someone from a bank in Finland about the project, and they wanted to talk with all of the engineers. The Finnish bank was flying them all up there. Bjorn said he would come back for you, because he didn't know where you went. And now he is dead."

"My whole team was going to go to Finland… those bastards almost got me." Erik finally said. "They wanted to hide this from the world, and were willing to kill the whole team."

"I have to go. I have a trip to take." Hans started towards the door. "Don't leave town, we are *not* done talking about this." Hans marched out of the cottage. Erik just sat, listening to his footsteps grow quieter, contemplating it all.

After a few moments of thought, Erik nodded his head once, then stood up and walked to the fireplace. He pulled the two loose bricks from the hearth, and reached his hand into the dark hole. The bundles were where he had left them.

Retrieving the bundles of cash from the hearth, Erik tossed them all into his satchel, and walked out the door. He regretted that he could not say goodbye to his friend, but Hans needed to not know Erik's next steps.

CHAPTER 8: VERY FAINT WHIRRING

Bjorn Rødtskjegg sat on the veranda of his flat high atop the nineteenth floor of the building, overlooking an old-world courtyard in downtown Helsinki. The days leading up to today had been long, and some painful. He missed his brother terribly, but it was necessary to maintain the lie of his tragic death. He regretted the loss of some of the team members in the "terrorist hijacking", but there were only two engineers on the project that he trusted, so only they survived with him, here in Helsinki, in the the third sub-basement under the world headquarters of Finland Financial.

Bjorn took another sip of his *akevitt*. It wasn't as good as the Norwegian brand he usually drank, but it was passable. And it was only fitting that he celebrated today's victory with a Finnish brand anyway.

Today, the Switch went live. They even let him turn on the power to it after the engineers had hooked it up to the network and the mains. At the time, it struck him as to how little fanfare there was from the box as the power came on. He heard a fan start up, and a very faint whirring from inside, and then the two lights on the back began to flash, and that was it. One of his trusted engineers typed a few commands into his laptop that was connected to the back of the Switch, and a few lines scrolled by. The engineer turned to Bjorn and smiled.

"Gentlemen," the CEO of Finland Financial said to Bjorn and his team, "those first three transactions were your bonuses being deposited. Bjorn, yours went to your account in Mauritius, and Oleg and Phil, yours went to your accounts in the Cayman Islands. Please check your accounts to ensure you see the transactions. We are now live."

Oleg closed his laptop and unplugged it from the Switch. He then dropped it into the industrial shredding machine at the corner of the room, and after a few seconds of terrible noise, the only laptop with access to the testing port in the software was destroyed.

"*Ja,*" Bjorn said to himself, permitting himself a rare use of his native Norwegian tongue, "*i dag var en god dag.*" A good day, indeed. The Euros had appeared in his account in Mauritius, and had the promised number of zeroes on the right side of the amount. His future was bright.

CHAPTER 9: ST. PETERSBURG

In the year since the Switch had gone online, the sales team from Finland Global Financial had been very busy, quietly selling their next-generation transaction validation services to the top five global card issuers. Traffic through Finland Global's network had increased exponentially almost daily, and the network support team had been forced to increase the bandwidth and processing capability of their systems ten-fold. Through all of this, because of the relatively small amount of data that passed to and from the Switch, there had been little need to upgrade the Switch itself.

Still, the sheer volume of traffic hitting the Finland Global network from Europe, Russia, and the United States began to draw attention, and it was becoming more and more difficult to hide the Switch from would-be thieves and other malicious entities. The Board of Directors made the decision to commission the building and installation of a second Switch, to be installed in the United States, and have the load balanced between them.

After three months of waiting for the engineers to figure out how to accomplish the whims of the Board, very little progress had been made. With that news, the Board had decided to bring in outside contractors to assist with the development of the load balancing software and hardware. It was decided that the balancer would be installed in St. Petersburg, Russia, and the connections to the two Switches could be made from there.

This location solved several challenges. First, the Russian government could easily be motivated to keep the load balancer safe. Second, St. Petersburg was an easy train ride from Helsinki, so if any work needed to be performed on the hardware itself, it could be a one-day trip.

As there was no in-house talent to work on the balancer, management searched the world, and eventually located and recruited Dr. Keith vanGreig out of South Africa. Dr. vanGreig and his team had just completed secure work for the South African government on a similar project, and was hired to lead the balancer project. Within five months, the balancer was ready to go online, but there were logistical issues to be resolved first.

On the teleconference that morning, Bjorn had stated that they could not just unplug Switch 1, as it was now called, from the network and then plug it into the balancer in Russia. There would be at least a 15 minute disruption to service, and that would affect well over two millions transactions at current levels. Keith suggested that they plug in the new box, deemed Switch 2, first, make sure it's on, and then route all of the traffic from the balancer to Switch 2, and once verified, then unplug Switch 1. This would have the effect of making all the traffic suddenly flow to Switch 2, so they would have to make sure there was sufficient burst bandwidth supporting Switch 2 to accommodate the sudden increase, but there should be no loss of service. And then, when Switch 1 was connected to the balancer, the traffic would settle between them. The technical team in Helsinki agreed that Keith's method was the best way to move forward. Keith asked that Switch 2 be delivered to him in Durban so he could test and make sure it would work with the balancer. The question caught Bjorn off guard.

"We don't have Switch 2 built yet," Bjorn was forced to admit.

"Well, how soon can you have it built?" Keith asked.

"Let me get back to you after lunch," Bjorn bought time. He didn't actually know.

Keith agreed, and they all signed off. Bjorn turned to his team.

"How long will it take to build the Switch 2?" He asked his two engineers.

They didn't know. Oleg explained that Erik Torssen had actually built it, and they had the hard drive that stored the software for the original Switch, but they did not actually know how to build it.

"Can you look at the internal parts and figure it out?" Now Bjorn was beginning to panic. He had a treasure chest, but he had no idea how to open it.

"No," Oleg stated. Bjorn looked to Phil, who just shook his head.

"Get out." Bjorn growled at his two engineers, and picked up his phone.

"*Ja* man, I can build that," Keith replied.

"You're sure?" Bjorn asked. "The two engineers that actually worked on Switch 1 said the original designer built it, and they didn't know how he actually did it."

"Do you have the software that goes onto it?" Keith asked.

"Yes, we have that."

"Then let me fly up and take a few notes on the operating box, and get a copy of the software," Keith said in a very comfortable voice. "We should be able to build the new Switch in a few months, and I can make sure it works with the balancer while it's here. Where is this one going to be installed?"

Bjorn began to relax.

"Probably Los Angeles," he answered Keith.

"Bad idea, man," Keith's accent was almost too thick for Bjorn to understand. "See, when 'the big one', or even a moderate earthquake, hits Los Angeles, that Switch 2 is going to lose power, and by that time, you will have so much traffic going through the balancer that Switch 1 will suddenly lag and quickly fall over. Put Switch 2 somewhere else, still close to a port or large airport, but somewhere people won't think to look, and is not so much at risk of natural disasters."

Bjorn thought about it.

"Okay, we will give it some thought," Bjorn responded. "Meanwhile, send me your information so we can get your travel arranged."

"*Dankie*," Keith replied. "And remember, man, I don't fly coach." Keith disconnected, and left Bjorn to think.

CHAPTER 10: SERIAL NUMBER

Bjorn felt much more confident after Keith vanGreig's visit. He was a little worried when they had to actually open the case of the Switch 1 while it was operating, but Keith had been very careful with it. Keith took his notes, made a few sketches, signed his nondisclosure agreement, and took a hard drive with a copy of the software, destined to be loaded into Switch 2 when it was built.

Keith had expressed surprise and admiration at the simplicity of the hardware, noting that it was a marvel of engineering genius. Oleg and Phil had bristled at that, and Bjorn felt a pang of guilt, but he was also impressed yet again at Erik Torssen's engineering capabilities, and regretted his loss in the "terrorist attack" on the plane from Oslo.

"Have you ever seen anything like this?" Keith asked his lead engineer, Heinrich de Boer, as they both slumped over the photographs of the guts of Switch 1 that Keith had taken with the hidden camera installed in his glasses while in the server room in Helsinki.

"*Ja*, actually I have," Heinrich answered with a hint of melancholy in his voice. "I worked on this box."

Keith looked surprised.

"See that serial number on the main board?" Heinrich asked, indicating a set of numbers and letters in one corner of the board. "'ET' is for Erik Torssen. He designed this masterpiece. The numbers are irrelevant, he put them in to throw off anyone who may try to figure it out. 'ET' for Erik, 'BR', those are the initials for that manager Bjorn, 'OR' is Oleg Rostova, 'PM' is Phil Michum. Over here near the end is me, 'HB'. He did it wrong, told me I didn't deserve three letters when everyone else only had two. I was not one of the main engineers, but I did participate in some of the board assembly. 'HR' is Hans Rødtskjegg. Bjorn's brother. Erik always had a soft place in his heart for Hans, because Hans pushed Bjorn to take a chance. I heard that Bjorn Rødtskjegg was on that plane with Torssen. Interesting to see that he's still alive."

"Then we will add 'KG' to the end of the letters and put them on Switch 2's board, in memory and respect of those that were here before us," Keith stated. Then corrected himself. "Before *me*, I suppose. You were already here."

Both men chuckled.

"Well," Keith commented as they continued, "at least we know for certain that Bjorn can't be trusted, whether alive or dead. Wait, why are you alive?"

"I left the project before it ended," Heinrich replied flatly, and continued drawing the circuit map.

CHAPTER 11: ONE WEAPON

Doctor Amir Muhammed bin Salman had been living in Durban, South Africa for fifteen years, and had been working on Keith's team for the last ten years, and specifically for Heinrich for the past five years. More specifically, Amir had been the second in command on Heinrich's South African smart chip project for the past five years.

Other than Heinrich and Keith, no one knew more about the detailed capabilities and functionality of currency encryption on a smart chip and financial transaction encryption in general than Amir.

A native of Afghanistan, Amir left home in order to get away from the constant state of war that had enveloped his nation, and his family, for centuries. His grandfather had been killed in the battles against the Russians in 1982, and his father had been killed fighting the American occupation in 2003. He and his brothers had been radicalized, and all three of his brothers had died in attacks against American troops.

Amir, while believing that the Caliphate should span the globe, thought his family members, and the leaders of the various Islamic revolutionary groups, to be fools. America, like Russia before it, and the Zionists before them, could not be defeated in combat.

The seemingly unending supply of aircraft, artillery, ammunition, and bodies that their enemies were able to pour into any region where there was any progress by the Caliphate was insurmountable.

Amir thought differently from his people. Amir had a longer term view. And his view could easily build the Caliphate using the one weapon that the

United States, Russia, and China for that matter, were all slaves to, that was stronger than all of the armies and materiel of the world combined: currency. And Amir knew exactly how to steal all of the currency on the planet for himself, and install the Caliphate.

CHAPTER 12: LOOK AT ME

Bill Fibulee sat at the back of the crowded conference room and shook his head.

"Idiots." He said under his breath. Apparently, he didn't say it quietly enough, because it earned him an immediate glare from his boss on the other side of the room.

Bill reclaimed his right to remain silent, but still fumed, listening to the new CEO drone on about all the changes that he was making, in his attempt to impress the call center workers. This guy was incapable of running a lemonade stand; why the Board of Directors had hired him as the CEO of an internet advertising company was beyond logic. Bill realized he hadn't been listening.

"...it's like when I was directing Season One of 'Star Journey'," new CEO Jean-Pierre Jones droned. "We wanted to remain interesting, but also promote a future where happiness and harmony outweighed greed and avarice."

Bill wondered again how this guy could have been named CEO. And, his name… "Jean-Pierre *Jones*"? That was just pretentious. Oh, and why say "Season One" of that show? It was only on for one season. This guy just oozed pretension. The previous CEO had left because more and more of the Board of Directors had sided with Jones, who was merely a Board member at the time. Jones believed in a work environment where everyone felt happy and basked in the glow of the Universe in its most perfect form (he had actually said that at one Board meeting). The previous CEO, Jerry Millgrew, had laughed at him. Jones was offended, Millgrew didn't care.

Millgrew had a saying: "first rule of business is billing and collections, everything else is secondary, because without revenue, you have no funding for the rest". Jones, an avowed "utopian communist in the truest sense", bristled at that phrase, and began to actively campaign to have Millgrew removed, and to replace him himself. Jones had been successful.

Bill didn't like Jerry when he first stepped on as the CEO a few years prior. Jerry was a large man, a former championship football player in college, and still tried to live in that glory, but was also a brilliant businessman. Jerry was as likely to try to use his size to intimidate people as he was his guile. When Jerry and Bill first met, Bill was already ready to quit, because previous management had been worse than idiots, so when Jerry introduced himself, Bill blew him off.

It was during that first argument that Jerry learned that being a former college defensive lineman meant absolutely nothing to Bill. After Jerry changed his method of interaction with Bill, the two made an unlikely, if unholy, pairing.

Jerry would throw different ideas at Bill about making the call center applications and processes more efficient, and Bill, as the lead software developer for LookAtMe.com, would lead the team that wrote and fine-tuned the various systems. The software suite truly was a work of art, and Bill doubted that he would ever write a better one. But now, as he sat here in this all-hands meeting, listening to this idiot go on and on about how the comfort of the employees was his primary goal, Bill knew his life with LookAtMe would be changing, and not for the better.

"Can anyone here tell me," Jean-Pierre continued to bloviate, "how it can possibly be that we have 520,000 paying customers? Anyone?"

"Cartesian product?" Bill said to himself sarcastically. The other three database developers that worked for him all burst out laughing. *Busted.* Bill just grimaced, and didn't look up, but he could feel the glare from his boss upon him again.

"What was that?" Jean-Pierre asked from the front. Bill had no choice.

"I said, 'excellent design'," Bill lied.

"Fascinating!" Jean-Pierre said jubilantly. "Please explain 'excellent design' to us."

Crap! Bill thought to himself. *Now what?*

"Well, uh…" Bill stammered. "It's, uh… it's pretty technical… I'm not very good at translating technical terms into understandable explanations."

It was a complete lie, but he hoped against hope that Jean-Pierre would let it go.

"No, Bill, you're really good at it," Bill's boss, James Blorman, spoke from across the room. James Blorman was an ass-kissing little tyrant of a man. If his subordinates made a mistake, James was sure to chastise them loudly, and in the most humiliating method possible. When his team did something right, he took the credit. He also kept any department bonuses for himself.

"Okay, well…" Bill figured he'd just get it over with. "The systems that we have in place are the culmination of seven years of work and polishing and research by myself, my team, and Jerry Millgrew. We have that system dialed in, and it's because of that system that we are as profitable as we are. I look forward to maintaining that system and our profitability."

Bill avoided looking at either James or Jean-Pierre, because he knew they both could not stand Jerry, and they considered Bill to be his little minion. This would not be a good day, but for now, he was able to get that little dig in, spitting in the face of his tormentor.

"Thank you for that, Bill." Jean-Pierre kept his benevolent face plastered on. "I know you and your team are really busy today, so if you want to go back to work, you can do that."

"Thanks, JP!" Billed answered happily, knowing that Jean-Pierre hated that nickname. "We'll get back to it. Good talk!"

With that, Bill and his team headed back to their office.

Once back in the safe solitude of their windowless office at the back of the building, Bill's team roared again with laughter. Bill was pissed.

"Shut up!" Bill shouted at this team, who immediately fell silent. "I make *one* sarcastic comment, under my breath, and you guys point me out. What the actual hell?"

"Come on, Bill," Kyle Dobson answered. "'Cartesian product'? That was gold!" Kyle started to laugh again, as did the other programmers.

"Yeah well," Bill was still not pleased, "there are maybe 20 people on the planet that would laugh at the joke, and you lumps had to do it out there, with an audience of hundreds. Thanks for that. Anyway, you guys will not want to be here when James stops by after that meeting, so you should probably go to lunch."

His team didn't have to be told twice. They knew the shouting match that Bill and James would probably have, and Jerry wasn't around to protect Bill anymore.

James hated with a burning passion that Bill always seemed to get away with whatever he wanted, because Jerry claimed that "the systems would not work if not for Bill". James hated that man. And now, he was gone. And now, Bill couldn't just jump the chain of command anymore. And now, Bill would face the consequences of disrespecting James.

Bill saw the call center people starting to head back to their cubicles through his open door. He knew it wouldn't be long now. Within moments, he heard the stomping of petty little angry feet.

Here we go, Bill thought to himself.

James marched into Bill's office with a purpose and closed the door hard. He stood with his hands on his hips for a moment, glaring at Bill. Bill looked back innocently.

"Hi, James," Bill said.

"What the fuck is a 'Cartoonish product'?" James screamed at Bill, his face turning red, but his hands still on his hips.

You're a cartoonish product, Bill thought to himself, almost making himself laugh.

"If you mean 'Cartesian product', it means when a query result set contains…" Bill started to explain. James interrupted him.

"I don't care!" James screamed louder. "No one cares what any of your fucking database anything is!"

"Well, I think the shareholders would care when the systems I wrote don't bring in revenue anymore." Bill said, accenting the credit to himself.

"You think you're the shit, don't you?" James scolded. "You think you can fucking do anything you want to here, and just get away with it, don't you?"

Bill needed to slow this train down, otherwise it was going to get bad quickly.

"Listen, James, I know I accidentally angered you, but it was not intentional," Bill lied. "I would like to think that we can de-escalate this, find a common ground, group-brain this challenge, and embrace our success together." Bill tried to remember as many catchphrases from Jean-Pierre as he could.

James stood for a moment, still taking deep, angry breaths.

"You know what?" James said finally. "You're right, Bill. Let's see if Jean-Pierre can help us embrace our success together. Let's go, hot shot." James opened the door, and motioned for Bill to go first.

Bill felt all six hundred eyes in the call center follow his death march to Jean-Pierre's office, his little executioner James two steps behind. Bill intentionally took long strides to make James have to almost jog to keep up. As they were walking, Bill heard a text message ping in on his phone, and reached into his pocket to read the message.

"Don't you dare." James sniped. "Read your idiot messages on your own time."

Bill dropped his phone back into his pocket, and saw Jean-Pierre hanging new artwork in his office; the office that was Jerry's office two days prior. Jean-Pierre turned when he heard the two men approaching, and welcomed them into his office with great fanfare, then gestured them to seats around a round conference table in his office.

"Ah, Bill! Welcome to my space. I want you to know that I and the Board all appreciate the great leadership and ownership that you demonstrate with the system that brings in the financial life blood of this company." Bill mused to himself that Jean-Pierre should have been an actor instead of a director.

"But I also want you to consider," Jean-Pierre continued, "that *people* are as important as, and even more important than, money. Money can bring greed and arrogance, but human feelings and growth of the spirit, those are more important."

Bill decided to play along.

"I acknowledge your dialog, Jean-Pierre," Bill stifled a metaphoric gag while Jean-Pierre nodded acknowledgement of the phrase, "and I would like to share that I believe that we need to have the money to support the environment in which the growth of spirit can manifest."

"Oh, give me a fucking break," James barked.

"James!" Jean-Pierre admonished James. "These crimson words do not solve any challenges. Either join in the discussion and solutions, or please step out to your space to heal."

Bill was able to cover the laugh that escaped with a cough. James was clearly feeling physical pain at having to suck up to Jean-Pierre while simultaneously wanting to tear into Bill. Bill deemed it glorious. Today might be a good day.

"Bill, I would like to suggest a new way to accomplish goals of financial stability for the company and the spirit-nurturing environment," Jean-Pierre offered. "You and your team have lovingly gestated, birthed, and nurtured an amazing system. But as with every child, when the child is grown, it is time for the child to leave the parent."

Uh oh... Bill thought. Jean-Pierre continued.

"The Board has decided to outsource the software functionality of the company. The vendor that we have chosen likes your system a lot, and they have licensed the system from us to use for their other clients as well."

Bill felt his heart drop.

A slow, evil smile spread across James' face.

"So, effective first thing Monday, you will be our liaison to the new vendor, and will help them load and configure the system on their network," Jean-Pierre said with a flourish, as if giving Bill a promotion. "Obviously, your team will no longer be needed, but we will give them generous severance packages, and the vendor has expressed an interest in embracing them and absorbing them into their family."

Jean-Pierre looked expectantly at Bill. Bill looked through him, wondering what he would say to his team.

"Bill?" Jean-Pierre prodded.

"I um… I don't know what to say, JP," Bill replied, forgetting about the distaste for the nickname. Jean-Pierre let it slide.

"Well, no need to thank me, you really have earned it!" Jean-Pierre said with a clap.

"He sure has," James added, extra snark dripping from his voice.

That snapped Bill out of his fog.

"I'd like to be the one to tell my team what's happening," Bill stated.

"Of course," Jean-Pierre granted. "And you should be the one to give them their checks, too. Well, this has been, I think, very productive and healing and positive. Thank you for stopping by, Bill! The representatives from the new vendor will be here Monday morning at 10:00. You should all set up in your office."

With that, Bill stood up, avoided the hug from Jean-Pierre, and walked back to his office.

Bill plopped down in his chair, dreading what he would say to his team when they got back from lunch. They had worked together as a well-oiled machine for almost six years… Bill had selected them all… and now, Bill had to let each of them go.

Bill noticed a manilla envelope on his keyboard with no writing on it. He opened it to find three termination letters, one for each of his team, with accompanying severance checks. He looked at the amount of the checks; they were indeed generous.

That should help ease the shock, Bill thought to himself.

His team returned about ten minutes later. They walked in, all chatting their usual chatter. Kyle closed the door.

"So, how was that?" Eileen Chamberlain asked. Eileen. It was going to hurt the worst to terminate her. Bill had poached her from the call center when he found out she had a bachelor's degree in computer information systems. And she had become as much of a rock star developer as the other two in record time. And now, Bill had to fire her.

Bill looked into the envelope again and found that the envelopes containing the checks also had offer letters from the vendor for each of the team. He checked the offer on Eileen's letter. It was better than here.

Good.

"Bill?" Eileen asked again.

"Okay, listen up."

Bill broke down everything to his team of hand-picked experts. They were all shocked.

"They can't fire us!" Mark Stevens spoke up.

"Well, technically Marky, they can." Bill stated. "But, they can also offer good severance checks."

Bill handed out the checks. Whistles and gasps followed.

"Hopefully, those make it easier," Billed stated.

"Heck yeah, it does!" Eileen said softly.

"Also, in those envelopes are offer letters from the vendor." Bill continued. "I peeked at the offers, and they are good. And over there, you'd be working on this same system, so you're already the SME's. I won't get mad at any of you if you go over there. I can tell you that I will not be assisting in the transition of the software and data, so they will need you."

"I know a couple guys that work there," Mark stated. "It's not a bad place to work. And if I can go in there already a rock star, might be worth it. I think I'll go."

"You have my blessing, my son," Bill joked and made the sign of the cross at Mark, who bowed, then laughed.

"Now pack your shit and get out." Bill joked with Mark. Mark did so, hugged everyone, and left.

"Kyle? Eileen?" Billed turned his attention to his remaining team members.

"Do you want me to finish out the week?" Kyle asked.

"Nah, take a four-day weekend." Bill answered. "You're rich now anyway. But call Verve Software first and accept that job."

"Fo shizzle." Kyle joked.

Bill and Eileen helped Kyle pack his personal belongings, and after hugs all around, Kyle left.

Bill noticed that Eileen was trying very hard not to cry.

"There are no tears in database. I thought I taught you that." Bill said softly to Eileen.

Eileen laughed. Or sobbed. Bill figured it was a little of both.

"I'm not going to Verve." Eileen stated. Bill was surprised. "I was going to have to tell you this in a couple months anyway, so this works out. I'm pregnant. I have decided that I'm going to change directions and be a mom for a while. This is actually great timing."

"You're kidding! Congratulations!" Bill exclaimed. "You know you can do both if you want to, right?"

"Yes. Duh." Eileen responded, then softened her tone. "Thank you for believing in me."

"Thank you for proving me right... you know how much I like that." Bill responded.

"Shut up." Eileen laughed.

They packed Eileen's gear, one more hug, and she was gone.

Bill closed the door, and absorbed the silence of his now-empty office.

Bill tossed his phone on his desk, and noticed the flashing light on it. He remembered the message he had received a couple hours prior.

Bill opened the phone, scrolled to the message, and read it.

WHAT ARE YOU WORKING ON?

It was from Jerry. Of all people to text him today, Jerry. Bill typed in the response with his thumbs.

YUO WOULDNT BELEIVE MEE IF I TOL D YU

Bill looked at the unbelievably bad message, and wished for some way to have the typos be corrected automatically, and lamented his large thumbs and the tiny keyboard on his phone.

<beep>

DINNER TONIGHT?

YEES

CHAPTER 13: GLOBALFORCE

"Jerry," Bill answered. "You gotta know that I don't know how to use any of the development tools for a project like what you just tried to describe."

"I'm not hiring you as a developer, you're strictly project management on this." Jerry responded. "Oh, and Director of Operations."

"Yeah, no," Bill responded flatly. "I'm not Operations."

"Oh, sure you are." Jerry revved up his pre-prepared motivational speech. "Operations is the same as programming, you just get to program the way the company works, instead of the computer."

"No, it's not like that at all." Bill replied.

"Either way, you hate your job, we need you on this one, and there's nothing to keep you at LookAtMe."

He's got me there, Bill thought.

"You got me there," Bill answered.

"So, we'll see you Monday morning." Jerry stated.

"No," Bill corrected, "you'll see me 2 weeks from tomorrow."

"Unless they walk you out tomorrow when you give notice, then we'll see you right after that."

"Deal." Bill answered.

The rest of dinner was uneventful.

At 9:45 a.m. the next morning, after handing in his two weeks' notice at 9:30 a.m., Bill was walked out of LookAtMe.com. James was still screaming at Bill in the parking lot as Bill drove out of the lot, and across the street to the offices of GlobalForce, Inc.

As Bill parked, he could see James still in the parking lot, having watched Bill's 45-second drive to his new job. Bill waved across the street to James as he walked towards Jerry's office. James flipped Bill off and walked back inside. Bill laughed and walked into the lobby.

"Good morning, Mr. Fibulee," the suggestively dressed receptionist said with way too much friendliness in her voice. Bill wondered what this company was actually developing. "Mr. Millgrew is expecting you, I'll escort you to his office, right this way."

She stood up, and Bill noticed that the rest of her outfit was just as not-safe-for-work as her too-low blouse. And, did she have to use the word "escort"?

They arrived in Jerry's office. Jerry thanked her and flirted with her, and she laughed and went back to her desk. Bill closed Jerry's office door behind her, and went and sat at the very comfortable chair in front of Jerry's desk.

"Whadaya think?" Jerry asked with a wink.

"I think you're a dirty old man." Bill answered. Jerry laughed. "Is she even 21 yet?" Jerry laughed again.

"Of course she is." Jerry answered. "You remember that magazine model I dated ten years ago? Kandi is her daughter."

"I didn't know you ten years ago," Bill answered.

"Oh. Well, I dated her mom." Jerry said as if he was discussing a loaf of bread he bought and then threw away when it was slightly stale.

"Anyway," Bill got the conversation back on track. "My services are no longer required at LookAtMe. Give me my key, laptop, door access card, HR paperwork, and sign-on bonus check now."

"Key, door card, HR paperwork, and laptop are on your desk," Jerry verbally checked the items off, "and there is no sign-on bonus."

"Oh." Bill knew this game with Jerry. "Well, I have taken up enough of your time. Have a good day." With that, Bill stood and walked towards the office door.

"Did you have breakfast yet?" Jerry asked, ignoring the bluff completely.

"No, I kinda had a sour stomach this morning," Bill answered.

"Come on, let's grab breakfast," Jerry replied, standing from his desk. "I'll introduce you to your team after."

"Cool," Bill accepted.

CHAPTER 14: CURRENT PASSPORT

The three members of the technical team were already waiting at the table in the conference room. Bill could hear their easy conversation with each other all the way down the hall as he and Jerry walked towards the room.

"There are no secure conversations in that conference room, are there?" Bill quietly asked Jerry as they walked.

"Yeah, it's loud in this hallway." Jerry answered. "That's intentional. We have a separate room for secure discussions." Jerry didn't elaborate on why it was intentional.

Jerry entered the conference room a few paces ahead of Bill and greeted the technical team. They all responded positively.

They went silent as Bill entered the room, and simply stared at him.

"Everyone, this is Bill," Jerry announced, introducing Bill. "Bill, this is Taylor, Sienna, and Francis."

"Hi everyone," Bill said cheerfully.

No responses.

After a moment, they all looked back to Jerry.

"He is not a programmer." Francis stated flatly to Jerry.

"Uh, wait a…" Bill started to object before Francis cut him off.

"He is of no use to us if he is not a programmer." Francis continued.

Now Bill was pissed. Jerry began to speak, but Bill interrupted him.

"Listen, I don't want us to get off on the wrong foot here, so let me reset expectations," Bill stated, putting on his commanding tone.

"Team, Bill is the new Project Manager, and he has also agreed to take the position of Director of Operations." Jerry interrupted, attempting to regain the room.

"Francis, is it?" Bill addressed the one who had attempted to take a shot at him. "Francis, I was not hired to be a programmer, I was hired to be the Project Manager, as Jerry said. As far as your assertion that I am not a programmer, I won't get into a pissing contest with you about my skill set, because frankly, I don't need to defend it anymore at this point in my career. But with that said, I hope you can work for me, despite your willful ignorance about my capabilities. I'm sure you're a good developer," Francis bristled at the word, "but I need you and the rest of this team to work effectively on this project."

It was at that moment that Bill realized that he had no idea what the project was. All he knew was that it involved something to do with credit card data encryption.

"Well, now that that's all cleared up," Jerry chimed in, retaking the room, "we'll let you three get back to work, and I'll get Bill settled into his office. Do we still have the conference call in the afternoon?"

"Yes," Taylor called over his shoulder as the programmers exited the room.

"Come on, let's show you your office," Jerry said to Bill.

———————————

Jerry led Bill back to the far end of the hallway, near the main entrance, and motioned to an empty office there. Bill entered the office, taking in the over-decorated lavishness of the room, noticing that the chair looked comfortable. Bill walked around and sat in it. Yup, it was comfortable. He imagined he would take many naps in it.

"Like it?" Jerry asked.

"It'll do," Bill bluffed.

"Good, I'll leave you to it. Fill out your paperwork for HR. That office is across the hall from the conference room. The laptop is still pristine, so you can do whatever it is you do to a new laptop. Door card and administrator password book for the network, vendor accounts, and software subscriptions are in the top left desk drawer." Jerry said in his rapid fire way, and left.

It was a nice laptop. Bill switched it on, logged in, and appreciated it. It looked new. Bill realized they had planned ahead for today. He set himself to filling out his HR paperwork, and walked it down the hall. Upon acceptance of his HR paperwork, Connie the HR rep handed him an envelope. Bill checked it: it was his sign-on bonus, the check dated for the previous day. Bill smiled and headed back to his office.

Bill spent the rest of the morning getting his laptop configured. Jerry knew him well; the laptop had not had any of the applications installed on it yet, just the way Bill liked it. Nice, fresh operating system, untouched by the children in tech support.

Jerry popped his head in at about 12:15.

"Ready for lunch?" he asked.

"No. We just ate 90 minutes ago," Bill answered.

"Okay, I'll have it catered. We have a call at 1:00 with the head of the group in South Africa."

"Jerry."

"Bill?"

"Come in, close the door, and sit down," Bill demanded.

Jerry closed the door and sat.

"I need you to spend the next 45 minutes telling me exactly what it is we do here," Bill stated. "And I want to know all of the nations from which we have teams working. And I want to know anything else that I may not have asked about, because I want no more surprises. Except for surprise bonus checks… you can do those all the time."

"Okay, full briefing." Jerry began.

Bill listened intently as Jerry explained the entire operation to him. GlobalForce, Inc is a specialized technology development company that works with the largest two credit card issuers in the world. The project which Bill now commanded was to design, write, and build the prototype of a chunk of encrypted memory in the main memory section of the new chips that were being distributed on all of the credit and debit cards around the world, except for in the United States. The leading expert in chip card development on the planet, Keith vanGreig, lived in Durban, South Africa, and he had a small team that worked with him there. The remainder of the team of eighty or so developers and their project lead worked from their company offices in Johannesburg. While Keith was the head technician, he chose to work remotely from Durban, and only flew to Johannesburg when he had to. All of these people were working for Bill now, and they were close to getting the prototype working, but vanGreig and Francis had a disagreement, so now they were not making any progress. Bill, Jerry further explained, as the project manager for this project, needed to get the project moving again.

Jerry then asked Bill if his passport was current.

"It is, but why?" Bill asked.

"Because you leave Sunday afternoon. You'll fly from here to Heathrow, then head from there to Johannesburg."

Bill's head swam.

"What's the call at 1:00?" Bill asked.

"We'll be talking with Johan Smit's team." Jerry answered. "He's the owner of Simunye Holdings, the Joint Venture partner company down there. His company is the one that has all of the developers working for them, but they now take their direction from you."

"Hang on a second," something else struck Bill. "How long have you been working with GlobalForce?"

"About two years," Jerry answered. "You didn't think I only had one job, did you?"

Bill sat back in his really comfortable chair, taking in all that he had just been told. Then it dawned on him that he only vaguely knew where South Africa even was... he knew it was at the southern tip of the African continent, but he needed to see a map.

"How long is the flight?" Bill asked Jerry after a minute.

"About twelve hours from here to London, a few hours layover, then I think nine hours to Johannesburg. And they're eight or nine hours ahead of us."

Bill did some quick mental calculations.

"So, I'll get in..." Bill started to try to figure it out.

"About 4:30 p.m. local time Tuesday," Jerry answered for him. "They'll have a car for you, but you're going right to a meeting, so bring a change of clothes and change on the plane before you land."

Kandi popped her head in the door.

"Sorry to interrupt," Kandi interrupted. "Your food is here. Where do you want me to have them set up?"

"Secure room, please, Kandi," Jerry answered.

"Yes, sir," Kandi answered, and stepped back out of the office.

"We really need a more conservative dress code here," Bill stated to Jerry.

"Why?" Jerry asked.

"Because you're an old pervert," Bill replied.

Jerry laughed.

CHAPTER 15: NEXT TO BILL'S OFFICE

The "Secure Room" at GlobalForce was impressive. Bill took note of all the sound-dampening material on the walls and ceiling. There was a large conference table with a speakerphone in the middle of it, and two remote microphones at either end of the table. There were several monitors on the long wall, and a camera over each. Below each monitor was a computer. Bill was impressed.

A technician that Bill didn't recognize entered the room, sat at the middle computer, typed a few things while Jerry and Bill ate, and then looked up as a picture came up on the monitor above him. One by one, three squares filled the monitor screen with people, and the tech left the room.

"Good evening, Johan and team!" Jerry greeted them all warmly. They all greeted him back, talking over each other.

"Team, at long last, I would like to introduce Bill Fibulee," Jerry said, gesturing to Bill. Bill waved at the screen, feeling dumb after doing so, but then remembering that he was on camera.

"Ah, how's it, Bill," the person talking in a square labelled "Durban Tech" said. "Jerry has told us a lot about you over the past many months. Glad to finally have you on board, man!"

Bill made a mental note to ask Jerry about that later.

"Glad to be on board," Bill said warmly, trying to make a good impression, and hoping he could understand the accents well enough.

Jerry asked for an update on the status of the project. The guy in the Durban Tech box began to answer. Jerry slid a slip of paper to Bill, with the words "thats keith" written on it.

Keith went down a checklist of items that the team had been working on, and Jerry checked them off or made notes on his own list as Keith talked. The upgrades to Switch 2 went well, and it was functioning within normal parameters. The planned upgrades to Switch 1 were going to be delayed until early June, because there was a low traffic point identified in early June from historical traffic models. Jerry was not happy about the delay, but understood. Keith stated that the balancer had been successfully upgraded sufficiently in the last month to be able to expand to ten Switches if necessary, but noted that he could not think of a situation in which the planet could generate enough traffic to overwork more than three Switches. Jerry asked about the status of Switch 3.

"Well, about that," Keith started. Jerry looked up. "There is no connection into South Africa large enough to handle the traffic from the balancer to Switch 3."

"That's not what I asked," Jerry replied. "Let's try this again, what is the status of the build of Switch 3?"

Keith hesitated while he chose his words carefully.

"Building it is easy," Keith finally answered. "we just can't fulfill the part of the contract that states it needs to be connected in South Africa."

"Then get it built. Bill will be there on Tuesday. He is staying for as long as he has to in order to get that Switch activated."

"Got it, boss." Keith replied.

Jerry asked if there was any other business, and terminated the call.

Jerry looked at Bill. Bill looked at Jerry.

"The hell is a 'switch', and what do you mean I'm staying until it's active?" Bill asked.

Jerry explained that this "Switch", as it was called, was a completely secure black box that was operating in Helsinki. All of the major credit card issuers around the globe, and many banks outside the United States, subscribed to this service wherein they presented a financial transaction, like a charge on a credit card or a wire transfer, and this switch would either approve or deny the validation of the charge. They had overloaded it with too much traffic, so they built some box in Russia to split and balance the work between the "Switch 1" in Finland, and the "Switch 2" in the server room across from Bill's office.

Bill's blood ran cold.

"You wanna run that last part past me again?" Bill stammered.

"What? That Switch 2 he was talking about is installed here." Jerry acted like it was no big deal.

"So, half of the financial transactions *for the world*," Bill accentuated the last three words, "are running through the office next to mine?"

"Yes." Jerry answered flatly.

"And that doesn't scare the crap out of you?" Bill asked.

"No," Jerry was still not concerned. "Why would it?"

Bill began enumerating.

"First, we don't have a secure facility. Second, that's a regular air conditioner in that server room, and WE ARE IN PHOENIX! Third, our internet connection isn't special, it's a basic business subscription... I have a faster connection at home. Fourth, I didn't see a power backup stack or even a shitty battery backup in that server room. Fifth, there isn't even a lock on the server room door. Shall I go on?" Bill was ready for battle.

"First of all, calm down," Jerry said with a hint of annoyance in his voice. "Our facility met or exceeded all of the contractual obligations with Finland Global Finance, so we are fine."

"Oh, well then I guess everything is okay," Bill responded sarcastically, then asked, "when was this Switch 2 installed here?"

"About a year ago," Jerry answered. "And they were disappointed that you were not here to talk with them when they installed it."

"Sometimes I hate you," Bill said

Jerry chuckled.

Keith slammed his laptop shut.

"*Fok daai ou,*" he swore under his breath in Afrikaans, then turned to Heinrich and Amir, who were sitting next to him, listening to the call.

"I guess we'll get to work, hey?" Heinrich anticipated Keith's order.

"*Ja,*" Keith answered. "Can you do it by Tuesday?"

"We already have it built." Heinrich answered. Amir just grinned. Keith sighed with relief. "Just need to load the software and run a couple tests. But I still don't know where we are going to put it."

"Let that jarhead Yank figure it out," Keith responded. "Come on, boys, let's hit the pub. Tell me about the new encryption model over a few pints."

"Yep," Heinrich stated.

"I need to go home," Amir answered.

"Okay, cheers mate," Keith said to Amir, and pushed back from the desk.

The men stood and left, knowing that there was difficult work ahead, but not tonight.

CHAPTER 16: POSITIVE AND NEGATIVE

Keith liked to believe he was an intelligent man, and that he could understand technology pretty well. His multiple Ph.D.'s in various computer sciences and engineering specialties, and over one hundred fifty global patents, could be used to back that up, but this explanation that Heinrich was giving him for the new encryption was making his head spin.

"Hang on, mate," Keith tried to catch up with Heinrich, "I may have had one too many pints already, because I am not understanding this. Talk to me as if I know nothing about quantum physics."

"Do you know anything about quantum entanglement or quantum physics?" Heinrich asked with a hint of a grin.

"Pretend I don't," Keith bluffed.

"Fine." Keith began anew. "You know how, in normal physics, a particle can not physically be in two places at once, right?" Keith nodded his understanding. "Well, in quantum physics, it can, and it can be a vast distance away from itself and still exist in both places. And, a particle can have both a positive and negative charge at the same time, or neither, and that value changes depending on how you observe it." Keith began to glaze over. "Don't try to understand it, because no one does, just accept for a moment that such a state is possible outside our dimension of existence."

"For this discussion, I will accept that," Keith acquiesced.

"Okay, now, consider that you can use several of those quantum particles to do your computations for the encryption of the validation."

Heinrich watched Keith closely to see if he was still following, and it looked promising, so he continued. "Because these particles operate at speeds beyond what any of our current logic chips can accomplish, we merely load the decision processing onto these quantum particles, and because they don't really exist in our dimension, we can have them do the work much faster, with no heat generation, and at speeds trillions of orders of magnitude faster than anything that exists on this planet today, *combined*."

Keith glazed over again, but only for a moment.

"So, in theory," Keith was trying to consider possibilities without trying to understand the technology behind it, "we could make the encryption so far advanced, and so quickly, that no one on the planet would be able to crack it, even if they could intercept it, right?"

"Precisely!" Heinrich stated emphatically. "You know how that genius Erik Torssen designed the switches to operate outside the legal internet IP range? If we move the processing into quantum particles, it literally is taking place outside our dimensional space, and can not be accessed, except through our Switches."

"How much faster?" Keith asked.

"Think of it like this," Heinrich explained. "Right now, even the fastest computers on the planet would take about a hundred years to crack the highest forms of encryption available right now. If we used the quantum processors I'm building to do the same decryption work, it would take about five minutes. So, a lot faster."

Keith sat for a moment, looking for answers in his glass.

"And you think you can design this quantum processing capability for the Switches?" Keith finally asked Heinrich.

"Yes." Heinrich answered flatly.

"I hear Torssen was arrogant like that, too," Keith joked after another moment of consideration.

"I have all of his papers and notes in my head," Heinrich began passionately. "I have read, and understand, every single line of his source code. I understand his designs. I built that Switch 3 hardware in two days. I know how Erik Torssen thinks. This next-generation quantum 'Switch Q' that you and I are discussing will revolutionize the world for at least the next hundred years. No one else has anything like this."

"*We* don't have anything like this," Keith corrected.

"Keith," Heinrich was almost begging now. "Let me follow this through."

Keith looked at Heinrich for a moment. It was clear that Heinrich really did have a plan in mind.

"There is something you still are not telling me, I can see it," Keith said after a sip. "You tell me, right now, man. What exactly is it that you still need? And don't lie to me."

"Our team at CERN can make the quantum particles do the work individually, but they need a particle that can control a set and make them work together. They have not found the control particle, and without it, we are stuck."

"Stop fretting, my friend," Keith said with a chuckle. "The ANC is committed to making South Africa the next superpower, so the funding for the continued research is secure. Just keep the project quiet. And don't slip in front of that Yank next week and mention it... we don't want it to get back to his jarhead boss."

Heinrich nodded and went back to his pint.

CHAPTER 17: DON'T OVERTHINK IT

"I solved your problem." Jerry stated, walking into Bill's office.

Bill looked up from the incomprehensible technical specification docs for the new chip and PIN logic that were scattered across his desk.

"The fiber drops are being installed tomorrow, and the new cooling tower and backup power systems are being installed next week?" Bill asked sarcastically, already knowing the answer, but having no idea what Jerry was talking about.

"What? No." Jerry replied, slightly exasperated. "The connection problem for Switch 3. I solved it. Like I always have to. No one can think outside the box anymore."

Here we go, Bill thought to himself, and let Jerry get it out of his system so they could get back to pertinent content.

"Hey! Moving on!" Bill finally interrupted in order to get to the point. "Tell me the solution."

"Oh. So you remember Dave Conway." Jerry finally began. Bill didn't, but he played along. "Well, Dave's sister in law is old Russian royalty."

Bullshit, Bill thought to himself as Jerry continued.

"So, her father is head of the Russian government department that sources and outsources internet connectivity for the country, and for their global assets. Russia, it turns out, has a pretty impressive embassy in

Pretoria. So, see, it's solved."

"Let me see if I have this straight, despite having maybe a quarter of the pertinent information," Bill was frustrated now. "This guy Dave's brother's wife's father connected the internet to the Russian embassy in South Africa, so our connectivity problem is solved, right?"

"Yes." Jerry smiled.

"Cool." Bill said, sarcastically.

"Yup," Jerry said, and turned to leave.

"Hey!" Bill called him back. "That's not a full explanation. Get back in here and tell me the rest."

"You just said you understood it," Jerry was surprised.

"You really need to learn sarcasm." Bill said. "Now, how does the Russian connection to Pretoria help us?"

"Because," now Jerry was using his condescending tone again, "we can use that connection for Switch 3."

"How?" Bill prompted.

"Russia," Jerry continued, "has a black site that has a secure computer room. They kept calling it a 'server farm' for some reason. Looks like a shitty little office building on the outside, but it's a top security Russian 'server farm'. The Embassy in Pretoria is about ten miles from it. They have a cloth connection or something to that building."

"You can't be that technologically ignorant," Bill said with a sigh. "What is a 'cloth connection'?"

"I don't know, I'm not the tech, you are," Jerry responded. "Something about some kind of fibers in the connection."

"Do you mean a 'fiber optic' connection?" Bill asked, exasperated again.

"Yeah, that's it," Jerry answered.

"Okay, so," Bill said, mentally filling in some gaps, "do we have an agreement with the Russians yet to use their secure server farm for Switch 3? And has the State Department approved this?"

"The State Department has no jurisdiction, because this is an agreement between Finland, Russia, and South Africa, and the Russian docs are on the way," Jerry answered.

"In English?" Bill knew to clarify. Bill also knew that the bypass of the State Department would have to be clarified eventually.

"Yes, in English," Jerry answered.

"Wait, hang on," Bill thought of something else. "That's great that they have a fiber line between the embassy and the server farm, but as that guy from Durban said, there's no real speedy connections into South Africa from Russia. I checked the global connection maps."

Jerry hesitated for a moment, trying to remember some obscure term that he had never heard before a few minutes ago.

"What's an 'oh-see-twelve'?" Jerry finally asked.

"'OC-12' is a massive connection," Bill answered suspiciously. "There are only like five or six faster connections on the planet compared to that, and I'm pretty sure the faster ones are only theoretical. Why?"

"Vladimir said they have an OC-12 between their server farm in St. Petersburg and the embassy in Pretoria," Jerry explained.

"First of all, holy shit," Bill said in shock, looking back at the world map on his desk showing the larger internet connection cables across the planet, searching for an OC-12 cable from western Russia to Pretoria. "Second, the Russian guy you're talking with is named Vladimir?"

"Yes," Jerry answered.

"If you tell me his last name is Lenin or Putin, I quit."

Jerry laughed.

"No," Jerry brushed off Bill's obvious bluff. "He's Dave's brother's wife's father. Just relax."

"Whatever," Bill continued. "Anyway, there is no OC-12 connection between St. Petersburg, Russia and Pretoria, South Africa on any of the maps."

"Probably not." Jerry answered. "It's not official."

This just gets better every minute, Bill thought to himself.

"Wait," Bill realized with a shock, "where is that load balancer for the Switches?"

"In St. Petersburg," Jerry answered.

"In the facility where that OC-12 terminates, huh?" Bill pressed further.

"If you're asking if that's the building where Russia connects to that big cable you're talking about, then yes." Jerry clarified.

"Sooo," Bill finally had the full picture. "You are sending me into a Russian black ops server farm in Pretoria, South Africa to connect this unbuilt 'Switch 3' via fiber to a black-ops Russian OC-12 network. Is that the full picture?"

"Well, not exactly," Jerry was dancing now, and Bill knew it. "We're sending you to Johannesburg to meet with Johan and his team to make sure Switch 3 is fully tested and ready for prime time. Keith and his lead engineer will meet you in Johannesburg. Then you and Keith will be driven to Pretoria to install it and make and test the connection. Then they'll drive you back to Johannesburg, and you'll have a nice dinner."

"Just like that, huh?" Bill asked.

"Yeah, don't overthink it," Jerry answered, and left to flirt with Kandi.

"I'm meeting with Johan in Johannesburg, at the behest of Vladimir the Russian, huh? What could possibly go wrong?" Bill said to himself. "I wonder if I'll meet any other caricatures on this trip..."

CHAPTER 18: SPARKLING OR STILL

Bill's flight was only half an hour late arriving at O. R. Tambo, despite leaving Heathrow almost three hours late due to a fuel spill under his plane at the gate. Bill was well-rested despite the just under nine hours in the sky. He had never flown business class, and between the ridiculously comfortable seats and the spectacular service by the cabin crew on his British Airways flight, he felt great.

As he entered the Customs area, he saw a driver holding a sign with his name on it. Bill was a bit amused to see "The Honorable William Fibulee" written on the sign, but approached the chauffeur and identified himself. Bill was further amused when the man bowed to him. Bill tried to mirror the respect back. Oddly, Bill was escorted past the throngs of people amassed at the bottom of the escalator into the Customs area waiting to have their passport stamped, and was taken through a side door, where a very friendly official stamped his passport and very graciously welcomed Bill to South Africa. He then motioned with a wave of his arm, and a porter approached with Bill's luggage on a cart.

Bill knew now that something was not quite right. Almost all of the rest of his fellow passengers were still waiting to have their passports checked, and none of them was in this special office with him. He could see the luggage carousel for his flight beyond the windows of the office, and there was no luggage on that carousel yet. The official wished Bill a wonderful stay, then Bill, his porter, and his chauffeur left the office and were escorted to the waiting limousine. The official tipped the porter and chauffeur, then the chauffeur got into the front seat, and they pulled away from the airport. Bill's head was spinning.

"What is happening?" Bill said aloud to himself.

After a brief ride, the car arrived in front of a very busy hotel-casino resort. The chauffeur opened Bill's door, and Bill stepped out. The facility general manager was there to greet Bill, and said his luggage would be taken to his room for him, and that his party was waiting for him in the steakhouse. Bill said he would be keeping his laptop bag with him, but that he appreciated the help with the luggage. The manager then personally escorted Bill to the steakhouse and to his table.

Bill recognized several of the people from the teleconference last… week? Year? Lifetime? Bill realized he didn't actually know what day it was, then remembered that it was supposed to be Tuesday. Quickly he checked his phone, and saw that it was 6:15 p.m. He quickly shook his head to clear it. The members of the group all stood to greet Bill and shake his hand. He remembered Keith by name, but blamed the long flights for his inability to remember the other names. Bill eventually sat at the large table next to Keith, who had been saving his chair. A waiter approached Bill, and asked him something that Bill could not understand. Bill apologized and asked him to repeat the question. Bill still couldn't understand what the waiter had said, and felt a little panic. Keith said something that Bill also couldn't understand to the waiter, and the waiter shook his head and left.

"He wanted to know if you wanted water to drink, sparkling or still," Keith explained.

"*That's* what he was asking me?" Bill responded, exasperated. "I swear I had no idea what he was saying. Was he talking in a different language from English?" Bill inquired further.

"Not your kind of English," Keith laughed, "but yes, he was speaking English." Bill made a mental note to himself that he better learn to understand the three or four different dialects that he had already heard since getting off the plane an hour ago, or he was going to be in trouble on this trip.

For the rest of the evening, the team laughed and drank and told Bill lots of loud and apparently funny stories, of which he understood about a third of what they said, but he laughed with them and hoped no one caught on that he had no idea what they were talking about. They didn't seem to care. Only the guy sitting on the other side of Keith appeared to not care at all about the festivities, and he just sat quietly, nursing a few beers. As best as he could tell, the guy's name was Rick, because when he introduced himself, it sounded like "I'm Rick". Rick clearly did not like Bill. Bill hoped Rick didn't kill him with a lion or something while he was here.

Several hours later, after drinking a couple liters of "zteel" water, and a couple shots of passable vodka, and a couple hours at the Blackjack table, where he learned that American Blackjack and South African Blackjack have slightly different rules (and losing several thousand Rand), Bill headed to the front desk to find out where his room was and get the key. The hotel manager on duty escorted Bill to the lifts, swiped the key card, and handed it to Bill as the lift began to move.

"This is the key card to your suite," the manager explained. "It also gives you access to that floor of the hotel, which is restricted."

Eventually, the lift dinged and the door opened, and the two men stepped off. There were only two doors visible in the elevator lobby of this floor. The manager motioned Bill towards the door labelled with merely "A". Bill stepped to the door and swiped his card on the handle, and heard the lock disengage. He opened the door and stepped into the entrance hallway. Billed walked in and whistled. The suite was massive. Full bar, large seating area, two-story windows overlooking greater Johannesburg. Bill took it all in as the manager explained all of the amenities of the suite. Eventually the manager left, and Bill headed up the stairs to the main bedroom. It was equally impressive, as was the en suite, but Bill was too tired to fully appreciate it all at that moment.

"Dark," Billed called out into the room. The lights all dimmed and went dark. He hadn't believed the manager when he was told the lights and shower were all voice-controlled, but apparently, it was true. Bill slept.

CHAPTER 19: WORDS TO HIS GRANDFATHER

Amir was excited.

He just had to wait for the Switch 3 to go live, and when he was running the test transactions after Switch 3 was activated, he only had to insert one additional test line.

The irony that he would be using a facility that was installed in Pretoria by the former Soviet Union in 1979 made him smile whenever he thought of it, and each time, he would speak a few short words to his grandfather, who had died at the hands of those people so many years ago.

He sat at his computer, double- and triple-checking the command. Each test returned either the success message or the expected failure message. He was sure it was ready. And by the time someone noticed the problem and even started trying to back-trace the losses, there would be no tracking the actual origin of the transactions, because they would be lost to the oblivion of the Switch network. It was designed for ultimate privacy, and that was its greatest weakness.

The thought again thrilled him.

CHAPTER 20: BE NICE

Heinrich and Amir were not amused, and Keith knew it. Not just because their incoming guest worked for the hyena, but because he actually seemed to understand technology, and also seemed to pay attention and reason things through. That was going to be a problem sooner or later, because sooner or later, this Bill guy would understand the need for better and faster encryption, and they would not be able to hide the quantum work from him forever.

"Calm down," Keith said to them yet again. "He doesn't know enough to be a problem. Let's just get Switch 3 connected and operational, feed him one last good steak, and send him home. Done and dusted."

"Things are never that simple," Heinrich growled. "You know as well as I do the trouble these babies have had throughout the life of the projects. Every time it seems as if the project is about to have another great leap forward, something goes terribly wrong, and it gets delayed for years."

Amir nodded his agreement.

"This guy Bill," Keith countered, "is not 'something terribly wrong'. He is here at the behest of the American partner to fulfill the contract with Finland Global to connect Switch 3 in South Africa. Show it to him today, we hook it up tomorrow, he's back on a plane on Friday, and he is out of our hair. Switch 3 will cover the increased traffic from sub-Saharan Africa for at least five years, and by that time, the Finland-ANC-Russia quantum processing project will be ready to go live. By the time the rest of the world figures out just how advanced our switches are, the name de Boer will be synonymous with Newton, Einstein, Rockefeller, Carnegie, Torssen… And no one will be able to take it away from you."

"...again." Heinrich said under his breath to himself.

Amir bristled.

de Boer, Torssen, and vanGreig will be cursed for all of history for bringing this ruin to you all, Amir thought to himself.

"Anyway," Keith continued, "the Yank should be here momentarily, so be nice."

The only response from Heinrich was a grunt, and a disappointed scowl from Amir.

CHAPTER 21: BEYOND THE DREAMS OF AVARICE

Bill's limousine arrived in front of a glass office building well away from downtown Johannesburg. Bill was still unaccustomed to the service he was receiving from almost everyone with whom he had contact while in South Africa, and it was beginning to make him suspicious. As the chauffeur opened the door for him, a jubilant Johan Smit met Bill at the car, shaking his hand, and telling Bill how excited everyone was to have him here for this historic event. Bill played along.

Johan gave Bill a tour of the office, which actually encompassed the entire building, then escorted Bill to a conference room with a large table and about ten people waiting. Bill recognized Keith and Heinrich from the event the previous night. Everyone welcomed Bill, and Bill took a seat. Johan asked Keith to take the meeting.

Keith began the meeting by bringing Bill up to speed on the status of the Switch 3 project. Currently, the device was built, and was operating on the test bench well within normal parameters. There had been some hardware upgrades to Switch 3 over the previous two Switches, because of technology advances since the previous two had been built, so Switch 3 had a much faster CPU and more RAM, and therefore could handle more traffic, both in volume and processing speed, than the other two Switches.

"What's left to do with Switch 3, then?" Bill asked.

"Well," Keith answered after a moment of thought, "nothing. Not anything here, anyway. All that remains is to connect it to the rack in

Pretoria, console in and check a couple test transactions, and if they respond appropriately, that's it. Then we come back, take you to dinner, and wake up tomorrow and start the design on Switch 4." Keith finished with a laugh.

Everyone else in the room burst into laughter at the same time, except for Heinrich and one other guy sitting behind Heinrich. Bill took note, but didn't call them out. Johan then took over the meeting, thanking the team for all their hard work, especially Keith and Heinrich, and dismissed the meeting.

"Johan, if I may," Bill asked as the room was emptying, "may I keep the room for a few minutes to talk more with Keith and Heinrich?"

"Certainly." Johan agreed, and left the room. Keith sat back down, but Heinrich remained standing. Bill stood and closed the door.

"Gentlemen, I have a few more questions," Bill began. "Keith, specifically to you, why am I here?" Heinrich audibly scoffed at that. Keith shot him a quick glare.

"I presume," Keith began, "that it is because you are the project manager from the American partner on this Joint Venture, and as your company is the majority investor in the JV, that puts you in charge."

"Keith, I know your curriculum vitae," Bill said flatly, looking Keith directly in the eye, "and I feel like we may have begun to develop the tiniest bit of a rapport last night at dinner, but that is the most bullshit answer I have heard since I left Phoenix."

Keith began to laugh, knowing he was caught.

"Heinrich, why don't you give us a minute?" Keith said to Heinrich, who wasted no time or words on his way out of the conference room.

"Alright, mate," Keith began again. "No bullshit this time, you have earned that much. I believe that you are here to share the blame. That little argument they caused between me and Francis, that was for show, because they wanted you down here." Bill looked slightly surprised to hear that. Keith continued. "This new Switch 3, *if* it works, will bring exponentially more profits for Finland Global, and because of the fee structure the JV has with them, our companies, and you and I for that matter, stand to become rich beyond the dreams of avarice."

Bill liked the sound of that.

"But," Keith had to ruin it. "If this Switch 3 fails, it could damage the balancer, or worse send corrupted transactions through the balancer to the other two Switches, and that could disrupt all global financial transactions that flow through the validation network for days or weeks. If that happens, the world is going to want someone to punish. You and I, mate," Keith tapped his own chest, then Bill's, "you and I *will* find ourselves in The Hague, and we will not fare well. And your passport will mean nothing when you are arrested."

Keith stopped speaking and watched Bill, giving him a chance to digest everything that was just said. When he saw Bill's eyes focus again, Keith broke the silence.

"Lunch?" Keith asked, then opened the door and walked out, waiting for a moment for Bill to follow him.

"Yeah, but let me hit the restroom first," Bill answered.

CHAPTER 22: DIFFERENT BUILD

Bill waited with impatience for the call to connect. Finally, a sleepy Jerry answered the other end.

"Hello?"

"Are you fucking kidding me with this shit?!" Bill screamed at Jerry, not bothering with a greeting.

"Hey!" Jerry shot back, angrily. "Good morning to you, too! You want to slow down and tell me what's wrong? And what time is it there?"

"Oh, yeah, sorry, good morning, and it's just after noon here," Bill said with mock friendliness. "We are getting ready to head to lunch. Cool place, bro. They have me in a nice suite. I'm going to enjoy it a lot too, since I'll probably be *up on charges for crimes against humanity* in a year, thanks to you." Bill's tone turned back to his real anger as the "crimes against humanity" words came out.

"Well, it's 3:00 a.m. here, so I'm a little sleepy," Jerry responded. "Can we wait a couple hours to discuss whatever it is that you're overreacting to?"

"No," Bill was in full rage now, "we can't fucking wait a couple hours. We're supposed to turn on the Switch 3 this afternoon, and I just found out that if it fails, *I* could be charged in The Hague as an accomplice to a global financial meltdown. You can take a nap later."

"First of all," Jerry turned on his smooth voice again, "you're not going to be charged, you didn't do anything. Second, the Switch 3 isn't going to fail, because it's the same as the other two Switches. Third, there is no way to track anything to do with the Switch 3 back to you, because it's being installed at a black site. The location doesn't exist. And since it doesn't exist, you were never there. So, no problem."

"Jerry," Bill didn't think he could get madder, but found that he was. "Switch 3 *is not* the same as the previous two. They just told me that they 'made it better' than the previous ones. Faster processor, more memory. So, it can allegedly process more transactions faster than the other two. It's not 'the same'. We didn't know until today that they changed the build on the hardware, and we have no actual vision into what they built. How can we possibly turn it on now?"

Bill heard Jerry sigh.

"You are so narrow in your thought patterns, you need to take off your blinders," Jerry answered in his usual condescending tone that he used when lesser humans tried his patience. "If they did not follow the specifications, and if they did not inform us of that until after the hardware was installed, then there is no problem for us. They violated the terms of the JV. We can argue that they are 100% at fault, and even better, we won't have to pay them their portion of the fees we collect. So, either way, it's a win for us."

Bill was about to respond, but then heard a loud slam in the background on Jerry's phone, then a bunch of shouting, and Jerry hung up. Bill tried to call him back, but there was no answer. Bill sighed and dropped his phone into his pocket, washed his hands, and left the men's room where he had gone to have some privacy to call Jerry before he left with the team for lunch.

Keith and Heinrich were waiting outside for him, and he rode to lunch with them.

"When we get back from lunch," Keith was explaining the afternoon plans as they ate, "they will already have the Switch 3 loaded up into a lorry. We'll be driven to the site in Pretoria, where we will install Switch 3 in the rack, connect the mains and the network connections, and power it up. Heinrich will connect the laptop and run a couple test transactions from the console, and if they work, then he'll unplug the laptop, and we will all leave and be driven back. Should be there and back within about three hours."

"Wait," Bill needed clarification on something, "you said '*we* will'. Who all is going? I thought it would be you and Heinrich."

"And you." Keith finished.

"Not to dodge this," Bill started, "but why would I go? There's nothing for me to actually do on this."

"Because," Keith set down his sandwich and looked Bill in the eyes, "you are turning on the power."

"Uh…", Bill had no answer. He felt like he was about to kill the world, literally an executioner throwing the switch on an electric chair.

Keith finished his sandwich, downed his water, and stood up.

"Ready then?" He asked Bill.

CHAPTER 23: THE DRIVE

As they approached the loading dock in the back of the basement level, Bill saw four heavily armed guards standing around a black windowless van. Keith approached the leader of the men, and they spoke briefly, and then Keith introduced Bill to the leader, Vasily. The leader just nodded toward Bill. Heinrich walked off to talk to one of his team members, who's name Bill had learned was Amir, on the other side of the bay. Amir looked angry, and Heinrich had a short, quiet argument with him.

"Okay, let's load up." Keith said to Bill with a small laugh, then climbed into the open side door of the van and strapped into a comfortable seat. Heinrich joined them after walking away from his argument, and also strapped into his seat. Bill hesitated a moment, then shook his head and joined them.

The guard closest to the side door slid the door shut with a heavy thump, then the four guards all loaded into the van, and they rolled out of the loading dock and into the bright sunlight.

As they began the drive, Keith asked Heinrich what the argument was about.

"Amir thought he should be going and doing the final checks. I told him that was never the plan. He was pretty mad." Heinrich answered.

"Odd that he would think that," Keith responded.

Heinrich just nodded and looked out the front window.

The drive was uneventful, but Bill was filled with dread the whole way. Several worries filled him, including what he was about to do, and the strangeness with Jerry on the call a little over an hour previous. The van slowed and stopped, and Bill realized he had been asleep.

"Good nap?" Keith asked him with a laugh, as the side door slid open.

CHAPTER 24: NO ONE NOTICED

Amir was furious. It was always planned that he was to be the one to run the final check commands on Switch 3 once it was installed. For months, that had been the plan. And now, just like that, he was left behind.

After his argument with Heinrich in the warehouse, which ended abruptly and unresolved, Amir watched the lorry pull away, his carefully crafted plans disintegrating. Amir swore to himself, went back to his office, packed up his laptop, and left.

No one noticed him leave.

CHAPTER 25: UNDERWHELMED

They were inside another warehouse. Bill unbuckled his seatbelt and climbed out of the van after Keith and Heinrich. Bill noticed that two of the guards were carrying a large, unmarked Pelican case between them, and had headed towards a door on the far side of the room. Keith and Heinrich followed them, so Bill followed Keith and Heinrich, and was followed by the other two guards, who still carried their rifles. Bill resigned himself to his fate.

After entering the small office from the warehouse, they were escorted to a small closet. Bill wondered if that was where the server rack was located. One of the guards opened the door, and Bill saw that it was a cleaning supply storage room. Bill heard some clunking noises, then the entire closet slid into the side wall, exposing an elevator door. The doors slid open, and the guard who had been trapped in the supply closet stepped out of the elevator and motioned the rest inside.

The inside of the freight elevator was large. Bill wondered what kind of rip-off spy thriller he was walking through. When the doors opened again, they stepped off into an underground room, lined with rows of server racks, humming with what looked like hundreds of servers. About halfway down the main aisle, a woman in a white lab coat with her hair in a tight bun stood waiting for them. The two guards carrying the case walked to her, and set the case down in the aisle. They then stepped away, and everyone turned to look at Keith, Heinrich, and Bill.

Keith and Heinrich walked to the case, and opened it and began to pull rack mounting hardware from the case. Keith looked up at Bill as Heinrich began to assemble parts.

"You just going to stand there, mate?" Keith asked Bill.

Bill walked to where they were working and finally saw the Switch 3 in the case. It was literally just a black box, a rackmount 9U server with none of the usual electronic fanfare that he had seen on other servers, like color-scrolling logos and flashing lights all over the front. This was... boring.

The lab technician and a guard escorted Heinrich to the back of the rack, and he installed the slides into the rack as Keith installed the other parts on the sides of Switch 3. When it was ready, Keith stepped back, and a guard in the front worked with the guard in the back to load the Switch 3 into the rack.

Keith and Bill were then escorted to the back with Heinrich. Keith plugged in the fiber lines, then stood up. Heinrich plugged in a serial cable and tossed the other end through the rack to the front. He also stood up. Both men then just looked at Bill.

"What?" Bill asked. He had no idea what to do.

"Want to plug in the mains, mate?" Keith asked.

Bill felt stupid. He reached down and grabbed the power cable, and with a great flourish, plugged it into the socket on the back of the case.

"With this plug, I give thee... POWER!" Bill joked. Then he stood up and looked around. No one else was smiling. Bill sighed. A guard turned and started walking to the front of the case again, with Keith and Heinrich following. Bill just followed them. Once in front, they all looked at Bill again.

"Okay, seriously, you all have to stop doing this to me." Bill finally said, exasperated. "Just tell me what you want me to do. I don't know the game plan here."

"Turn the power on." Keith said flatly.

This is going well, Bill thought to himself as he reached down and flipped the little switch on the front from 0 to 1.

One small beep came from inside the Switch 3, then a quiet whirring that increased in pitch as the hard drive spun up, then silence. Heinrich knelt down and plugged the serial cable into the back of his laptop. Everyone watched as Heinrich typed a few commands and watched the results.

"All transactions verified." Heinrich said.

"Then we are finished here." Keith said.

Heinrich stood up and closed the laptop and disconnected the serial cable, then handed it to the lab tech, who took it and walked away. The guard still behind the rack pulled the serial cord back through the case, and one of the guards in front closed the rack.

"You did remember to turn off the testing port, right?" Keith asked Heinrich, who responded with a look that said *don't be stupid.*

"We go now." Said one of the guards in a thick Russian accent.

"*Da*, we go now." Keith answered. They all turned to walk back to the elevator door.

"Wait, that was it?" Bill asked. It seemed like there was a lot left to do for something so important.

"*Ja* man," Keith answered. "That was it. Switch 3 is on, is balanced, and is processing transactions. Nothing more to do."

"I am underwhelmed," Bill replied. Keith laughed and slapped him on the back as they walked towards the elevator.

The drive back to Johannesburg was uneventful, but Bill did not sleep. He kept waiting for the van to stop and the guards to execute him by the side of a deserted road and feed him to lions. When the van did stop, and the side door opened, they were back in the loading dock, and Johan was there to greet them and escort them to the celebration.

Switch 3 was online.

CHAPTER 26: RAID

"Give me a few minutes, guys," Bill said to Keith and Heinrich. "I need to call my office and get them updated."

Keith and Heinrich headed to Keith's office, and Bill sat alone in the conference room. Bill dialed the office number on his mobile phone, making a mental note to make sure to expense his phone bill this month.

"GlobalForce, how may I help you?" Kandi said at the other end of the call. She was definitely not sounding like herself.

"Kandi, it's Bill," he answered her. "What's wrong?"

Kandi burst into tears on the other end of the line.

"Oh, Mr. Fibulee," Kandi managed to get out in between sobs." They're going through his office, they lined us all up against the wall in the hallway and checked our ID's, then told us to get back to work, the programmers all left right afterwards." She was in a full panic.

Jerry, what did you do? Bill thought to himself.

"Okay, listen to me," Bill needed to get her to focus. "First, drop the formality, call me Bill. Second, take a deep breath, because I need you to be my eyes and ears right now." He heard Kandi take a deep breath. "First, tell me who is going through which office."

"Jerry's office," Kandi said, clearly still trying to hold herself together. "Some of their jackets say 'US Marshall' on the back, and some say 'US

Attorney' or 'FBI'. They're going through everything in his office, and boxing up a bunch of papers and stuff, and taking them out."

"Who is left in the office from GlobalForce?" Bill asked. He wanted everyone out of there until he could get home and see the rest of it.

"Just me and Connie," Kandi answered. She was starting to calm down.

"Okay, did they give you a piece of paper when they first came in?" Bill asked, wanting to know more details. "Should have said 'Search Warrant' at the top of it?"

"Yes," Kandi answered. "I have it right here."

"Perfect, read it to me please." Bill asked.

"By and for the district of Arizona..." Kandi started.

"Hang on," Bill interrupted her. He didn't need to hear the three paragraphs of preamble. "Just jump to where it says something about 'persons ordered to comply'."

Bill heard Kandi mumble as she looked for the relevant section.

"'Jerald Pertnoy Millgrew, and all documentation and articles relevant to Island Immunity Acres LLC' ... and a raid on their compound in Cuba?" Kandi read. "Who is Island Immunity Acres, and when was Jerry in Cuba?"

"I have no idea, but none of this has anything to do with us." Bill answered. He'd deal with Jerry later for an explanation on that, but for now, this could be managed. "Kandi, where is Connie?"

"She's in Jerry's office with them, making sure they don't take anything they shouldn't." Kandi answered.

Perfect, Bill thought.

"Perfect." Bill answered Kandi. "Connie is doing exactly what she should be doing. And so are you. Do you have your mobile phone with you?" Bill had a plan.

"Yes." Kandi answered.

"Okay, text Connie and tell her I'm on the phone." Bill began. "She has my mobile number. Ask her to call me as soon as those bozos leave, before she leaves the office. Then tell her that I told you to go home. I want you to change the answering service outgoing message to say that we are currently away from the office for a technology summit, and that we will be back in a week. Then go home. I know it is going to be difficult, but I need you to not tell anyone outside our immediate group what has happened. Follow me so far?"

"Yes." Kandi's voice had cleared up. She was thinking clearly now.

"Good," Bill had to think fast to get this under control. "How are you on cash? Are you good for a week, or do you need some to get through?"

"I don't need money, we got paid yesterday, so I'm fine," Kandi answered, her voice sounding stronger. "Is it okay if I go see my mom? She lives in Vegas."

"Actually, yeah, that's a good idea," Bill answered her. "Did the Marshalls tell you not to leave town?"

"No," Kandi responded. "After they looked at my license, they handed it back to me and told me I could 'resume my duties'. Assholes. Same with the programmers and Connie, but Connie told them that her duties were to make sure they didn't steal anything. The guy in charge got mad at her for that. Connie got back in his face, and they've been sniping at each other the whole time."

Connie just became Bill's new favorite.

"Good," Bill was glad they had cleared everyone else. "Yes, go see your mom, but drive, don't fly. And pay cash. I don't really want them to be able to track you if this thing gets weird. Do you know where Connie keeps the petty cash?"

"Yes." Kandi answered. "Why?"

"Go take $500 out of it, and use that for your trip to Vegas." Bill didn't want anything else to go wrong. He knew Feds tended to indict first and ask questions later. No point in letting innocents get caught up in whatever new stupidity Jerry had done. "And keep your receipts."

"You sure?" Kandi sounded unsure.

"Yes." Bill responded with faux firmness in his voice. "If you're to spend company money, you always need to have receipts."

Bill heard Kandi laugh on the other end of the phone. *Good*, Bill thought. *She's calming down.*

"Thank you, Bill." Kandi finally said.

"Thank you, Kandi," Bill wanted to make sure the reassurance stuck. "You've been really helpful. Did you send the message to Connie?"

"Yes." Kandi answered. "And I know she read it, because I saw her look at her phone, and then she winked at me."

"Okay then. Please change the voicemail message, take the petty cash expense money that I told you about, and go." Bill finished. "One of us will contact you within a week. I'll be on the plane back tomorrow, but it's like a day and a half long trip."

"Got it, boss," Kandi answered.

"Boss?" Bill thought. *Where did that come from?*

"Take care," Bill answered her. "Keep your head down, and enjoy your time with your mom."

"Will do." Kandi responded happily and disconnected the call.

Bill sat for a moment, collecting his thoughts, then headed to Keith's office.

"Ready for dinner?" Keith asked as Bill entered his office.

"*Ja!*" Bill responded, trying to sound like a local.

Keith erupted in laughter, and even Heinrich smirked.

"We'll make you a *Suid Afrikaans* yet!" Keith laughed, heading towards the door.

Bill had no idea what that meant, but at least he got Heinrich to stop scowling for a minute, so it was a good day.

CHAPTER 27: DOCTOR FIBULEE

Bill was not sure he could take any more surprises on this trip.

At dinner, it was just Bill, Keith, and Heinrich, until a fourth man joined them. Keith introduced him as M'Bulu Mabusa. M'Bulu enthusiastically shook Bill's hand and sat in the empty seat. Keith explained that he and Heinrich had been working on projects with M'Bulu for a few years, and that M'Bulu's group had some other projects they needed done, but they couldn't find any talent within South Africa to build the systems. Heinrich continued to grow more and more withdrawn and angry during the conversations.

Bill asked M'Bulu to explain what they were trying to accomplish. M'Bulu explained that there was a project underway to update the South African national ID card, and add a chip to it, like the credit card companies were doing. Heinrich choked on his water when M'Bulu said that. Keith shot him a look. The government wanted to be able to encrypt the information about the card holder on the chips, as well as their picture, a fingerprint, and other non-text information, and wanted to be able to store money on the chip, without requiring the holder to actually use a bank.

So far, everything that M'Bulu had mentioned for technical requirements were all functions that GlobalForce's application on the chip was capable of. Bill stated as much.

"But that is only a small part of it," M'Bulu continued. "I also want to build a system that will track everyone in the nation. From the time they enter my borders until they exit my borders, I want to know where they went, who they interacted with, what they talked about or whispered about, what they purchased, how they purchased it including serial numbers on the bills, how they got here, how they left, and what they wore. I want to know everything, and I want to track everything, and I want to store everything."

Bill's American blood ran cold, but his inner database developer danced at the possibilities.

"M'Bulu," Bill started. He was at war with himself. "What you're asking for in the tracking database system is technically possible. You would have to pull together several disparate systems, but it's still technically feasible." M'Bulu smiled and nodded. "But, the real challenge is that the significant invasion of personal privacy of every person, citizen or not, in South Africa is staggering. They wouldn't let you do that."

With that, M'Bulu erupted in laughter. Keith chuckled and shook his head. Heinrich sipped his beer. Bill got annoyed.

"I must have missed the joke," Bill said flatly. "Why is that funny?"

"Mate," M'Bulu finished laughing, wiped his eyes, then leaned forward, all of the humor having left his face, "your privacy begins and ends where I say it begins and ends."

Bill realized that this guy must think he's the king. Or he was drunk. Or both.

"How's that?" Bill asked, not backing down.

"Because," M'Bulu answered, sitting back and returning to his light-hearted method of speaking, "that is what I do."

Bill still wasn't following. He looked at Keith, who simply nodded. Heinrich sipped his beer again.

"You'll have to forgive my ignorance," Bill needed to figure this out. "I mean no disrespect by asking this, but I am apparently missing some vital information here, and I can't help you design your system until I understand it. How do you have the absolute authority to spy on every person in South Africa?"

"It's not spying, mate," M'Bulu maintained his easy conversational tone. "And it's not disrespectful, we have not given you all of the information, so your confusion is refreshing. I laughed, because your American ignorance of the real world is amusing. I hope you don't take offense at me saying that."

"Fair enough," Bill laughed in response. Bill really did feel completely ignorant at the ways the world worked outside of the American borders, especially after being plucked from his safe little filtered reality and dropped into what had been basically a Third-World country just a few decades prior. "But I still don't understand how you can make those kinds of decisions."

At that, Keith cleared his throat, and stood.

"Doctor Fibulee," Keith spoke formally. Bill caught the title change. "It is my honor to introduce you to the Minister of the Department of Home Affairs of South Africa."

Oooohhh, shit! Bill thought.

"Minister Mabusa," Keith continued, "may I formally introduce Doctor William Fibulee, Chief Operating Officer of our Joint Venture partner in the United States. You already have his CV, so you know his background."

With that, Minister Mabusa stood and bowed to Bill, who awkwardly stood and returned the formality.

"Dr. Fibulee, it is my great honor to finally meet you." M'Bulu stated in a formal tone. "I have been looking forward to this moment for very many months."

What in the hell has been going on at GlobalForce for the last year? Bill thought. *How have all these people already integrated me into their project plans a year before I even knew about it?* Then he answered his own question: *Jerry.* Bill filed that away for later.

"Minister," Bill began. M'Bulu interrupted him.

"Doctor," M'Bulu chuckled, back in his informal, easy tone. "Please call me M'Bulu. I find that formalities tend to interfere with actual progress. I already know your technical background and personal history, so I already know that you are imminently qualified to lead the team on my department's projects."

Bill digested this information. The South African government had a dossier on him. So many questions for Jerry when he got home.

M'Bulu continued.

"I also know that the nature of your work at home may be changing after the events of today, am I correct?" M'Bulu maintained his easy tone, but his eyes betrayed a more serious topic.

"You have me at a disadvantage," Bill danced.

M'Bulu laughed again, breaking the tension. Bill looked at Keith, who was conspicuously looking at the floor. Heinrich just continued to look at the table and sip his beer.

"Let's clear up a few things," Bill needed to slow this train down. "First, I'm not a doctor, I have not even finished my bachelor's degree yet. Second…"

"Ah," M'Bulu interrupted. "My apologies. I have something for you." M'Bulu retrieved his briefcase from under the table, opened it slightly, retrieved a large, thick envelope, and handed it to Bill.

Bill looked at the envelope. In neatly typed lettering on the label on the envelope, read "Dr. William Fibulee, Ph.D.". M'Bulu closed his briefcase and slid it back under the table.

"Open it." M'Bulu prompted Bill.

Bill opened the envelope, and slid the one heavy sheet of parchment from within. Bill read to himself: "University of South Africa, Pretoria Campus, *Philosophiae Doctor*, Computer Science and Engineering, awarded to William McKay Fibulee." Bill then noticed that it was dated the previous Thursday, which was the day he had officially stepped on at GlobalForce.

"I feel like I'm in a Tom Clancy novel." Bill said quietly.

M'Bulu and Keith roared with laughter. Heinrich did not.

"Don't be so dramatic, Doctor," M'Bulu continued to laugh. "The work you have done over the last twenty-five years of your career, both in database design and development, project management, business, and business management, makes you qualified. Accept the degree, and let's move on, shall we?"

M'Bulu had a point. Bill slid the sheet back into the envelope and set it behind him on the chair.

"What was your other point?" M'Bulu asked Bill.

Bill looked confused.

"You said that you were not a doctor, and we have cleared up that misunderstanding," M'Bulu clarified. "What was your next point?"

"Oh, right." Bill said, recovering from his surprise. "Second, please call me Bill if we are going to maintain our informality."

M'Bulu nodded in acknowledgement.

"Actual second point," Bill continued. "Even if it is true that you, *specifically* you, M'Bulu, can..." Bill paused and chose his word carefully, because "dictate" was not the word to use at this moment, "*define*, the personal privacy rules for the nation..."

M'Bulu began to laugh again. Bill just looked at him; this was getting annoying now with this humor about personal privacy rules.

"You almost said 'dictate', didn't you?" M'Bulu asked through his laughter.

Bill let out an exasperated sigh.

"I mean no offense, *Minister*," Bill said with a hint of anger in his tone, looking M'Bulu directly in the eyes, "but I am having a very difficult time with your flippant attitude about personal privacy."

Bill was already in way over his head, so he didn't bother to try to swim anymore.

M'Bulu's laughter stopped, and he matched Bill's tone.

"I am not taking offense at your anger, *Doctor*, because I am sure that, as a fervent American 'Ronnie Ray-gun'-supporting patriot, the personal privacy concept I have explained is as foreign to you as our accents, which you have done a tremendous job of learning to understand. But, *Bill*,"

M'Bulu de-escalated back to the informal, "if you are not going to be capable of setting aside your petty American sensibilities, and embrace the prodigious technology project which I have presented to you, then I fear I have significantly misjudged you."

Bill processed M'Bulu's words, and the significant meaning behind them. M'Bulu was right. His "petty American sensibilities" were unique among Americans in comparison to the rest of the world. And he was even more right about this being an amazing project for Bill, as a recently former database engineer, to manage.

Bill realized a few minutes had passed. He looked around the table. M'Bulu was watching him, but with a benevolent look on his face. Keith was eating. Heinrich was scowling and sipping his beer.

"Um," Bill began. "Minister... I mean, M'Bulu," Bill corrected himself, not intending to be formal. M'Bulu merely nodded his head once, accepting the correction. "I need to think about this. You're not wrong about how I feel about this as a tech, especially now that I am a doctor of tech..." M'Bulu laughed, as did Bill. "But you're also right about my 'petty American sensibilities'. I do hold them very tightly. Please give me a few days to process it and justify my decision to myself. I will have plenty of time to think on the plane tomorrow, and we should be able to talk Monday."

"That's a fair request," M'Bulu answered. "I know you have a few pressing issues to deal with at home. In order to reduce your worries about that, we have dispatched a security team to fortify your office, under the directives that Switch 2 is in that suite, and needs heavy protection. We have also provided personal security for the three members of your technical team, as well as your director of human resources, the Chairman of your Board of Directors, and for your receptionist, both at her apartment and at her mother's home in Nevada."

Bill was really stunned at all of this information. He also realized that he had never met anyone on the Board of Directors yet.

"That seems like a bit of an overstep, Minister," Bill again felt the need to gain some control of his situation.

"Not at all, Bill." M'Bulu stated flatly. "The personnel most closely associated with Switch 2, and the American partner that is maintaining it, have been put at risk. Not directly, but this issue with Mr. Millgrew is troublesome, and until you can get home and secure the company and the facility, you need our assistance. Your joint venture partner here, who has a contract with my department, has a substantial interest in making sure that GlobalForce is unaffected by this issue with Mr. Millgrew, and I need your attention here for a few days to discuss my new tracking system. So, it appears to be in the best interest of us all for my department to help secure the Switch 2 and your office, and your key people. Does it not?"

M'Bulu wasn't wrong, and Bill knew it.

"You're not wrong, M'Bulu," Bill agreed, switching back to the informal. "But my flight is tomorrow."

M'Bulu responded with only a smile.

"Apparently, my flight is not tomorrow," Bill accepted the realization.

M'Bulu's smile increased.

"So," Bill tested the waters, "if I were to agree to work on your project, *Minister*, what would the terms of the contract be? Hypothetically, of course…"

M'Bulu's smile grew even larger.

"We will discuss those terms tomorrow afternoon in my office, *Doctor*," M'Bulu answered happily, then he toasted Bill with his water glass.

Bill returned the toast with a laugh.

M'Bulu laughed.

Keith laughed.

Heinrich did not.

I really need to figure that Heinrich guy out, Bill thought to himself.

CHAPTER 28: STATUS UPDATE

It was almost midnight when Bill got back to his suite. He was exhausted and realized that he would be able to sleep late in the morning, because he didn't have to get on the plane yet. He didn't have to be ready to go until 11:30, which was when the car would pick him up and take him to M'Bulu's office in Pretoria.

Bill mused to himself that he was spending an awful lot of time in Pretoria on this trip. He wasn't sure why it was funny, but he chuckled at the idea. He made a mental note to call Connie in the morning and let her know that he was staying for another week.

"Oh crap! Connie!" Bill exclaimed out loud.

The events back in Arizona came flooding back into his mind. He hadn't heard from Connie yet. Bill was fully awake now. He tried to calculate what time it was back home. He was pretty sure he was nine hours ahead. He made the decision to risk it, and dialed Connie's mobile number. Connie answered on the first ring.

"Bill, how are you?" Connie asked with some concern in her voice.

"I'm fine," Bill waved off her concern for him. "How are you? How is everyone? What happened?" Bill's questions came rapid-fire, then he realized he needed to stop so she could answer. Bill apologized and asked her to go ahead.

Connie explained that the search warrant the Feds had served on the office had been for Jerry's office only, specifically to look for documentation and other items for another company that Jerry was involved in. There wasn't anything related to it in his office at GlobalForce, and the only things they took were personal items like Jerry's calendar from his desk and a few of the little statues he kept in his office. Right after the earlier call with Bill, Kandi had changed the outgoing message on the answering service, took $500 from petty cash in Connie's office (Connie pointed out that she had left a note saying "$500 for Bill's trip to Las Vegas"), and left. Connie had talked to the programmers and told them that they were on paid leave and not to worry because the company was fine.

"Connie, I have no words," Bill gave a heavy sigh of relief. "You are an oak, thank you so much for taking care of this."

"You have enough to worry about on your end," Connie brushed off the praise. "Call me when you land Saturday, and let's meet up to coordinate."

"Well, about that," Bill had to break the news. "The Minister of the Department of Home Affairs has opened negotiations with GlobalForce, er, well, with me, as the representative, for a massive development project. It'll be worth tens of millions of dollars to the company over the next few years. The Minister has asked me to stay another week to hammer out the details of the contract."

Connie was silent. Bill wondered if he had lost the connection.

"Connie?" Bill checked the line.

"I'm here," came the immediate response.

"It's midnight here, Connie, please just say what you have to say." Bill appealed to her mercy.

"I am not happy about this," Connie finally replied. "But if you can promise me that the company is going to remain in business, and the security teams that I assume the South African government is paying for will remain at least until you get back, I'll just make sure the lights stay on and the bills get paid. And I'll keep the employees pacified. The Board of Directors is already working with the legal team to prepare any necessary paperwork to ensure that GlobalForce is unaffected by Jerry's follies."

"Thank you, Connie." Bill was grateful. "I'll make this up to you."

"I know you will." Connie responded with a hint of humor in her voice. "I'm taking a week-long trip to a spa when you get back, and the company is covering it. Also, the Board Chairman would like to talk with you, if you can fit him into your busy schedule. I told him that you would reach out to him when things are settled down there. I'll have him email you."

"Fair enough," Bill laughed. "Keep me updated with text messages as new events happen, and I'll do the same. I'll check in with you tomorrow afternoon your time. Thank you again."

"Welcome, be safe." Came Connie's reply, and she disconnected.

"And now," Bill said to the bed, "I sleep."

Bill flopped onto the bed and began to relax, then realized the lights were still on. Then he noticed something hard under his cheek. He lifted his head and found a mint stuck to his face. He peeled it off and threw it towards the bathroom sink. He made a mental note to ask the front desk to have the cleaning crew leave the mints on the nightstand instead.

"Dark!" Bill hollered to the room.

The lights dimmed and turned off, and Bill slept.

CHAPTER 29: WRAPPED GIFT

Amir typed into his phone.

GIFT IS IN CAPITAL, BUT STILL WRAPPED

He set his phone down. He had never expected to have to send that message. He waited for the response.

PRAISE BE THAT IT HAS ARRIVED. WHY WRAPPED?

Amir knew this would not be received well.

I WAS UNABLE TO DELIVER IT PERSONALLY

Amir did not know if the next response would be his last or not.

GO TO CAPITAL, BE WITH GIFT, UNWRAP IT AS SOON AS POSSIBLE

Now Amir had to find the Switch 3. His next task was to secure a job at the Russian Embassy somehow, but that was for tomorrow.

For today, he packed his belongings into his backpack, and headed for the bus station.

CHAPTER 30: DEFINITIEF NIE

"*Definitief fokken nie!*" Keith yelled into the phone. "I told you that I am not leaving Durban! You agreed to that! There is no way I am moving to Pretoria!"

"Keith," Johan tried to calm Keith. "Will you please hear me out? The project has been reclassified. Only you, your two assistants, and the Yank are permitted to work on it now. I got off the phone with the Ministry of Home Affairs just before I called you. I'm not happy about this either, because we stand to lose a lot of money from the lost work, but they promised to contract us for some other unclassified project to make up for the lost income. But that is all contingent on you and your team in Durban moving to Pretoria for this project. They have provided secure flats for all three of you."

"Two," Keith corrected. "I don't know what happened to Amir. He was pretty pissed that he could not go with us to Pretoria with the Switch 3, and he appears to have gone off in a huff somewhere."

"Unfortunate," Johan replied. "Can you do the work without him?"

"*Ja*," Keith answered. "It'll just be a little slower. Let me go break the news to Heinrich. I'll call you back later." Keith disconnected the call.

He knew Heinrich would take the news even worse than he had.

"Sounds good to me," Heinrich answered.

Keith was gobsmacked.

"You're actually okay with this?" Keith asked, still incredulous.

"*Ja*, man, think about it," Heinrich explained. "We need the ANC funding to continue this project, we need the Russians to continue giving us technical support, and being that close to their embassy and Switch 3 would make it easier for us to make tests or upgrades as needed."

"Switch 3 is not at the embassy," Keith corrected him. "You know that, right?"

"*Ja*," Heinrich answered quickly, "I know it's not at the Russian Embassy, but the *Russe* working there know where it is, and it is in their best interest, and ours, to let us have access to it occasionally."

"You're deranged," Keith answered after a moment. "Just like Torssen was."

"You say 'deranged', I say 'brilliant'," Heinrich answered with a grin. "When do we leave?"

Keith was stunned. He didn't remember ever seeing Heinrich smile. The world made no sense in this moment.

"We fly tomorrow," Keith answered. "They'll have a car waiting at the airport for us, and they'll take us to our flats. We're staying in 'visiting dignitary housing' or something like that, but don't get too comfortable. I want to be gone soon."

"That works for me," Heinrich answered, and left to go pack his personal items for the trip the next morning. "See you at the airport."

Keith sighed, and set about doing his own preparations for the trip the following day.

CHAPTER 31: BLUE LIGHT BRIGADE

Luckily, someone had asked the front desk to wake Bill up at 9:00, because he hadn't set an alarm. Bill hung up the phone from the wake-up call and rubbed his face. The activities of the previous day came flooding back. He marveled at how much had happened in the span of eighteen hours... Jerry getting arrested by the US Marshals, the Switch 3 being activated, and then dinner with the Minister of Homeland Security, or whatever they called that department in South Africa, and now Bill was staying in Johannesburg for another week to discuss terms and deliverables for a project that would take up at least the next three years of his life, if he was realistic about the scope of such a project, and definitely would violate his sensitive little American sensibilities if he actually worked on the project.

Bill realized he was starving. An odd thought struck him...

"Can I get a ham and Colby cheese four-egg omelet, four pieces of sourdough toast with butter, and a large glass of fresh-squeezed orange juice?" Bill said to the room.

"Of course, Doctor." The room answered him.

Bill couldn't figure out exactly where the sound was coming from, but now he knew the room was bugged, so he would have to be careful what he said on the phone when he thought he was in private in his room. Then he thought about it... if what M'Bulu had said was true, even talking on his phone somewhere that was private wouldn't be private, and Bill's new system would make that possible. I can't work on this system, Bill thought.

Bill heard a knock on the main door of the suite.

He pulled on a really soft robe, walked downstairs, and looked through the peephole. A porter waited there with a room service cart.

Bill opened the door and the overly friendly porter rolled in the cart, and set up the food on the table next to the main windows overlooking the city. Bill signed the check for the food, and as an afterthought, wrote on a 500 Rand tip. The porter thanked Bill profusely and took his cart and left.

I wonder who's paying for this? Bill again wondered to himself.

Bill took a bite of the omelet. It was magnificent. Bill mused that all of the food he had eaten in South Africa had been amazing, and a stray thought crossed his mind about the possibility of actually moving here. He quickly batted that away and ate his breakfast with a vengeance.

Just before 11:30, Bill threw the strap for his laptop bag over his shoulder and headed to the elevator. As he opened the door to his suite, he was startled to find his driver waiting for him just outside the door.

"Good morning, Doctor Fibulee," the driver greeted him. Bill noticed that the driver was now up to speed on his title change too. Bill then remembered that he had left the diploma on his chair at the restaurant. That might be a problem.

Bill and the driver entered the elevator and rode down the long trip to the main level. The doors opened and Bill followed the driver to the main doors. As they approached the doors, Bill could see the limousine parked immediately out front, but as they got closer, Bill noticed police cars surrounding it. Now what?

The driver approached one of the armed police officers standing next to the limousine, who then walked back to his car after barking orders to the other officers. The driver opened the rear door of the limousine for Bill and waited.

"What's going on?" Bill asked the driver as he got into the car.

"That's your motorcade," The driver explained, and closed the door.

Soon, Bill's motorcade was speeding along the N1 highway to Pretoria.

Bill really wanted to look at the scenery, but the limousine was comfortable, and very soon, he slept.

Bill became aware that his car was slowing, and he began swimming up through what had been a very relaxing, if short, nap. When he opened his eyes, he was still surprised to see the motorcade escort vehicles, their emergency lights flashing, in front of and behind the limousine.

The driver opened his door after a moment, and Bill stepped out and looked at the building. The front of the building was a low dark facade with "Department of Home Affairs, Home Office" in white letters across the front. The main building behind the lobby was a dark, imposing 25-story building covered in windows. Bill looked up and took a deep breath. What have I stepped in? Bill thought to himself. Two assistants for M'Bulu greeted Bill at his car and escorted him to a private elevator, which took them directly to M'Bulu's office on the twenty-fifth floor. The door opened to a surprisingly modest office. Bill had expected marble and a large ornate desk and a flock of various aides, and at least a few wild animals as pets, but the office was only about two hundred square meters, with a nondescript desk, a few chairs, and a round conference table for four people.

M'Bulu stood with a large smile and greeted Bill. He then dismissed his aides and invited Bill to sit at the conference table with him. The two men sat and exchanged a few pleasantries, then M'Bulu got down to business.

"How did you enjoy your blue light brigade?" M'Bulu was fully chummy now, and not at all acting like the Minister of Home Affairs.

Bill had no idea what M'Bulu was talking about.

"My what?"

M'Bulu laughed quietly.

"You Yanks call it a 'motorcade'," M'Bulu explained through his chuckles, then got down to business. "So, tell me, man, have you decided to come work for me?"

"Work for *you*?" Bill replied with an easy laugh. "I'm not sure that's exactly legal..." Bill stopped as he heard his own words and saw the smirk on M'Bulu's face. "Yeah, I know, you decide what is legal for immigration, but I have responsibilities in the United States. Plus, I'm not sure that, as an American citizen, I can work on a project like this for a foreign government, even if you are an ally."

"We can work all of that out later," M'Bulu brushed away Bill's concerns. "The responsibilities in the United States will be covered for you. I'm not asking you to move to Pretoria yet, I just want you here for one or two weeks every quarter."

M'Bulu's eyes showed that he was the Minister again.

"Before I answer you," Bill countered, "what is the new schedule for my return flight?"

"You depart early Thursday afternoon, one week from today," M'Bulu answered, rising to retrieve Bill's travel plans from his desk, then returning and handing them to Bill, "and you arrive home on Saturday early afternoon local time there. You will have a driver in Phoenix now, and your security team will remain on duty at the company as well. You and your team are valuable assets, Bill, and we need to keep your team there protected and focused while you help my team here with the National Secure Citizen system."

There it is, Bill thought to himself. They already had a name for it. And they probably already had a team.

"I personally approve all technical leads and key personnel on this project." Bill looked directly at M'Bulu as he made his demand.

"Agreed," M'Bulu answered.

"My compensation package is going to be greedy," Bill began. "So, let's negotiate that now."

M'Bulu laughed and turned his notepad to a clean page, picked up his pen, and looked at Bill.

The two men spent the next fifteen minutes defining the terms of Bill's contract. M'Bulu called to an aide, who walked in, took the paper from M'Bulu, and went off to type up the contract.

"I'll need whatever documentation is necessary to legally work in South Africa," Bill said, remembering that he was not technically legal to work in

South Africa yet.

"Ah yes, thank you for reminding me," M'Bulu answered, opening another file on the table, and handing Bill a Permanent Resident Permit. "You are legal. This is valid for five years from today. Do not lose it."

"So you knew I would be accepting this gig, then?" Bill asked, knowing the answer.

"No, actually." M'Bulu answered flatly, surprising Bill. "I believed that your American patriotism would overwhelm your desire to help make South Africa a safer country. But, I wanted to be prepared in case you did."

"Okay then," Bill accepted the answer. "Show me to my office."

M'Bulu laughed loudly.

"Right this way," M'Bulu stated happily. "I know you're going to love what we have done with it."

CHAPTER 32: STUNNING BLANDNESS

M'Bulu opened the door to Bill's office, then stepped to the side to let Bill go in first. Bill looked around and absorbed the stunning blandness of the room. Like M'Bulu's office, it was about 200 square meters, a mid-sized desk, a docking station for his laptop with 2 additional monitors, a round table with four chairs, and a wall of windows.

Bill decided it was perfect. This office would have the same underwhelming image from which to launch the death of personal privacy that the fanfare-less action of turning on Switch 3 had provided. Bill then realized that the other three walls of his office were actually white board walls. Bill decided that this was a perfect room for designing the system.

"This will do," Bill stated finally to M'Bulu.

A warm smile crossed M'Bulu's face.

"I am glad that you approve," M'Bulu answered. "Ah, before I forget…"

M'Bulu opened the office door and retrieved a frame from an assistant. He crossed to the desk and handed it to Bill. It was Bill's Doctorate diploma in the frame.

Bill was touched.

"Thank you, M'Bulu," Bill said with a smile. "I will get some hardware tonight and get this hung tomorrow."

"Nonsense," M'Bulu answered. "Just decide where you want it, and it will be there before you arrive here tomorrow morning.

"Fair enough." Bill knew where he would be working tomorrow as well.

He decided to get to work.

"M'Bulu, I'd like to discuss the Switch project before we get started on your 'NSC' project," Bill started right in. M'Bulu walked to the conference table and sat. Bill joined him.

"What is your question?" M'Bulu asked.

"You have led me to believe that the Switch network is vital to the South African government," Bill began.

"No," M'Bulu corrected. "It is vital to the economic future and security of the people of South Africa. But either way, it is vital to South Africa."

"Why?" Bill actually caught M'Bulu off guard with the question.

M'Bulu opened his mouth to answer, but then stopped and considered his next words carefully, as though wrestling internally with two different responses. He finally spoke after a moment.

"Doctor Fibulee," M'Bulu was speaking as the Home Affairs Minister now, so Bill paid very close attention to the words. "You and your company are negotiating a contract with the Government of South Africa to assist with the development of a project meant to secure the safety and economy of South Africa for at least the next one hundred years, are you not?"

"That is correct, Minister," Bill matched the gravity and formality of the conversation.

"And tell me, Doctor," M'Bulu continued, "how seriously do you take nondisclosure agreements?"

"You know the answer to that, Minister," Bill continued. "You know that I hold them sacred, and that is why it took me as long as it did to read the NDA you presented us with before I agreed to it."

"I do know that," M'Bulu nodded. "I just needed you to say it for the room."

In his own special way, M'Bulu had just confirmed for Bill that his office was indeed bugged and monitored. Bill's respect for the man grew.

Then M'Bulu clapped twice loudly, startling Bill. The room was suddenly filled with white noise. M'Bulu leaned in closely to Bill.

"Now we can speak openly," M'Bulu said to Bill, just loudly enough for Bill to hear him over the noise. "Your Switch network is vital to South Africa, because it will make South Africa the next superpower, and will put us on equal footing with the United States, China, and Russia." M'Bulu paused for a moment to let Bill digest that statement, then continued. "Your State Department ignored the obvious challenges with having an American citizen participating in installing a piece of computer hardware in a Russian black site for a South African project specifically because of the importance of this project, and the stability that such an alliance can bring to our continent, and frankly, because they were ordered to ignore it by your CIA. There is officially no treaty, but there is a plan."

Bill was stunned, and was trying very hard to make sense of everything that had just been said, trying to understand the enormous global and historical impact of what he had just been told.

M'Bulu's watch beeped once, and M'Bulu sat back. A couple seconds later, the white noise shut off. Bill just remained still, processing the information. After a few more minutes, M'Bulu broke the silence.

"Doctor, we will need you to stay in Pretoria when you are here working on the project," M'Bulu changed the subject. "We have residences that we maintain for visiting dignitaries, and one has been assigned to you. Shall we go see it now?"

Bill was happy for the distraction.

"Yes," Bill responded. "I'd appreciate that."

M'Bulu stood and headed towards the office door, and Bill followed him. He heard M'Bulu speaking to an aide in Afrikaans.

Bill realized that he better learn the language.

CHAPTER 33: NO BASIS IN REALITY

The car slowed at the security gate to the housing area. The driver rolled down his window and spoke to the guard. Bill couldn't understand what was said, but after a short pause, the heavy gate rolled open, and their car was waved through.

As they were pulling into a parking space, M'Bulu handed Bill a security badge with his photo and some other language on it, and a lanyard.

"Wear this at all times at the office and here," M'Bulu instructed Bill, who immediately put the loop over his head and let the pass hang. Bill noticed it was heavy, and decided there must be some embedded tech of some kind in the badge; he'd check later.

The driver opened the car door, and M'Bulu and Bill got out and walked to the front door of a very nice, if small, cottage. M'Bulu instructed Bill to wave his pass over the panel on the door, and Bill did and heard the lock disengage. M'Bulu opened the door and motioned Bill inside.

The unit was very nice on the inside. A quick tour showed one large bedroom, two restrooms, a laundry facility, a desk with two monitors and another compatible docking station for his laptop, a flat television on the wall, two sofas and recliners, and a well-stocked kitchenette and refrigerator.

"There is a main dining hall for all of the dignitaries, so you don't need to cook, but you may if you choose to. The cooks are world-class, and can make almost anything you request. We will head there now so you can see the other amenities of our little neighborhood."

The two men walked a short walk to a long building. The "neighborhood", as M'Bulu had called it, was immaculate. Bill could tell that the building in front of them was the dining hall based on the smells coming from it.

I'm going to get so fat, Bill said to himself.

They entered the dining hall, and Bill saw that there were a few people sitting at tables, either alone or in groups, eating or drinking various things. He couldn't tell what the dishes were.

M'Bulu walked towards a table where two men were seated.

"Ah, good," M'Bulu called out. "You're both here already! How was your flight?"

The two men turned to face them, and Bill froze. The look of shock on Keith's and Heinrich's faces matched Bill's. M'Bulu walked to the table and sat in one of the open chairs, and motioned for Bill to sit with them. Bill did so.

"Doctors," M'Bulu began, "I am very happy to have you all here on this project. It is now time for us to have no more secrets so that this project can proceed unimpeded." Heinrich started to object, but M'Bulu just waved him off.

"Let us start with you first," M'Bulu said to Heinrich. "Doctor Torssen, if you would please give Doctor Fibulee here a full explanation of the Quantum Switch programme."

The silence around the table was palpable. M'Bulu just continued to stare at Heinrich. Bill noticed that the looks of shock on Keith's face and terror on Heinrich's had very deep meanings, but he didn't know why M'Bulu had used a different name for Heinrich, so he remained silent.

"I…" Heinrich began to protest weakly.

"Please Doctor," M'Bulu interrupted, "do not attempt to maintain the ruse. Both my Ministry and our Russian counterparts are fully aware that you are Doctor Erik Torssen, the original designer of the Switches and their core concept. Let us all work together going forward in full honesty. Now please, bring Doctor Fibulee up to speed on the Quantum Switch project."

Keith finally spoke.

"You... you're Erik Torssen?" Keith was stunned by this news. "So many things make sense now. Why did you lie to me?"

Erik/Heinrich didn't speak.

Bill wished he had popcorn. Should he ask the chefs for popcorn? He decided against it.

"Doctor vanGreig," M'Bulu broke the silence. "Doctor Torssen missed, completely by accident, being assassinated by Finland Financial. He bought a new identity and background, and with his experience, was easily able to assume the identity that we all know as Doctor Heinrich de Boer. Outside of this project, for his safety and ours, he is still Doctor Heinrich de Boer, but for our work on this project, please know that you are actually working with *the* Doctor Erik Torssen."

M'Bulu let the table be silent for a few minutes in order to let the other three men process all of this new information.

"If it helps," Bill offered in order to break the tension, "I feel pretty comfortable with the idea of quantum physics... I watched '*Star Gate*'. The film and all of the episodes of all of the series."

Erik dropped his head in disgust. Keith laughed very hard, as did Bill, at the ridiculous statement. M'Bulu smiled.

"Obviously, that science fiction crap has no basis in reality," Erik said through clenched teeth, still looking at the floor.

"If I may, Doctor," Bill responded, "neither does quantum physics."

"He has a point," Keith stated, laughing harder now.

And with that, Erik also began to laugh, and finally looked up.

"You do have a point, Bill," Erik conceded with a smile. Bill was still surprised to see Erik / Heinrich smile, but he was glad for it.

"Now then," M'Bulu took control of the conversation, "I believe we can move forward. Doctor Torssen, if you would please explain to Doctor Fibulee, the concept of the Switches up to now, and the quantum project underway."

"Please call me Bill," Bill interjected quickly.

Bill spent the next few hours listening to the technical explanations of the Switch concept, how it was originally built, how it had been enhanced, and now how design and experimentation to move the encryption functionality to a quantum processing system was underway. Bill had a very difficult time following the quantum parts, until he decided that it truly was science fiction, and was able to suspend disbelief in order to get through some of the more fantastical parts of the explanation. Keith occasionally jumped in to help dumb down a few of the very technical parts, and Bill was grateful for it.

Finally, Erik concluded his explanation.

Bill sat for a moment and took it all in, processing all that he had heard.

Finally, he spoke.

"Huh." Bill stated flatly.

Keith looked shocked.

"Heinrich just… I mean Erik, just rocked your understanding of the entire world of computer science and even how the universe and physics work," Keith asked, exasperated, "and all you have to say is 'huh'?"

"You know," Bill began, "I like to think that I am an intelligent person. I like to think that I am relatively good at designing and building complex processes. Hell, I've designed and built very complex processes. But this stuff… I am a Neandertal. I don't even think I've discovered fire yet…" Bill trailed off.

"Don't beat yourself up, mate," Keith answered. "This quantum stuff is almost all beyond me too. Like Erik told me in a previous life, 'don't try to understand it right now, just accept it so we can move on'."

Erik smiled. It was true. He really was the only person on this project that understood quantum physics. Amir did pretty well too, but he let his anger get the better of him. *That's a difficult loss*, Erik thought to himself.

M'Bulu spoke up again.

"Well, I need to get Bill back to Joburg so he can get some sleep and pack up and move in the morning. Good night, Doctors. We will see you at the office tomorrow."

Keith and Erik said their goodbyes, and M'Bulu and Bill walked back to the parking lot. The driver opened their car door as they arrived, and closed it behind them after they were seated.

"M'Bulu," Bill said after a moment. "I really do need to go home next week. I hope that plan has not changed."

"Our plans have not changed," M'Bulu reassured Bill. "The car will drop me off at the Ministry, then will take you back to Johannesburg. Please make arrangements to be at your office in Pretoria at the Ministry by 10:00 tomorrow morning. We'll work for a few hours, and then we will go back to the Quarters and get you settled."

"Works for me," Bill agreed.

Bill leaned his head back and processed what he heard that night, and made some mental notes about the other projects to discuss with M'Bulu in the morning.

The trip back to Johannesburg was uneventful, and Bill slept much more peacefully that night.

CHAPTER 34: EXOTIC FUNCTIONS

Bill had remembered to set a wake-up time for 5:30 a.m., and he felt pretty good when the alarm went off. He showered and dressed, then asked the room for breakfast while he packed. He was going to miss the interactive room, he decided. His breakfast arrived just as he finished packing, and the porter let him know that a car would be here for him at 8:30. Bill thanked the man and tipped him well, then devoured his breakfast.

Right on schedule, there was a knock on the door at 8:30. Bill had his suitcase and computer bag by the door, so he met the driver, and they proceeded to the car.

The drive to Pretoria was uneventful, and they arrived at the Ministry building at 9:45. The driver told Bill that he would guard his luggage until they went to the dignitary quarters at lunch time. Bill thanked him and headed towards the main entrance.

His badge seemed to give him more privileges than he had the day before, because doors were held open for him, elevators were reserved for him, and people generally let him get to his office without a hassle. He even got to bypass the security checkpoint, which saved him a solid ten minutes.

Bill was sitting at his desk, computer and monitors active, at 10:00 when M'Bulu walked in.

"*Goeie morey, Baas,*" Bill tried in Afrikaans.

M'Bulu looked surprised for a quick second, then burst into laughter.

Bill had no idea what was so funny, but assumed his pronunciation was wrong.

When M'Bulu could finally speak again, he explained.

"Bill, I am sorry to laugh. You must understand this: during Apartheid, it was expected that blacks would call whites 'baas', which is the Afrikaans word for 'boss', as you correctly assumed. But I grew up in a culture here where no white man ever called a black man 'baas'. I am very sorry for laughing at your ignorance, but the irony was just too much. I do, however, appreciate the attempt at respect."

Bill was horrified.

"Minister," Bill began formally, "I truly meant no disrespect. I am so sorry.

M'Bulu waved it off.

"Bill, you are learning a bit of our language, good for you," M'Bulu said with a chuckle. "I take no offense at the cultural slip. You could not have possibly known."

"Not really," Bill admitted. "I was just playing with an online translator. But I hope I pronounced it right."

"You didn't," M'Bulu responded, then burst into his familiar laughter. "But with all the time that you will be spending in our fair and mysterious land, I'm certain you will be fluent in no time, with the language and the culture."

Bill nodded agreement, and actually looked forward to that.

"Let's get down to it then," Bill got to work, hoping he didn't still appear too embarrassed. "There are several issues and tasks we need to discuss and coordinate, so let's jump right in." M'Bulu sat at the table with Bill, and the men began discussion of various issues.

Regarding the Switch project, Bill wanted to know why he was the project manager, when he had no experience with any of the technologies being used.

"You have the ability to lead without demanding that people follow you," M'Bulu explained. "People follow you because they believe that you will act in the best interest of both the team, the project, and the client. That is a very difficult balance to find, but you appear to exist in the center of that balance. I suspect it is why your three former employees will accept your very good job offers that you make to them when you are back in the States. And, you have earned my trust. So, I trust you to lead my projects. Is that enough of a reason?"

"Yes, and thank you." Bill answered.

M'Bulu and Bill spent the next three hours going over other projects and issues and agreeing on plans going forward or agreeing to table the issues for now. By the end of the conversation, the details were arranged for the NSC resources and management, and M'Bulu took the lead on explaining to the GlobalForce Chairman why these new projects were in the best interest of GlobalForce and why it was in the best interests of GlobalForce to promote Bill to President of the company (so that Bill had signing authority for contracts), Bill's location work schedule (three weeks per calendar quarter to be worked in Pretoria), and other minor housekeeping agreements.

"Well, now that we have those items sorted," M'Bulu said with a satisfied smile, "gather your things, and let us go meet your team for lunch and some more in-depth discussion on the Switch project."

"Sounds good to me," Bill said, and packed up his laptop as M'Bulu headed to the other office where Keith and Heinrich sat. He heard them all talking, and as Bill exited his office into the waiting area, Keith and Heinrich met him there.

On the car ride, the three doctors chatted mostly non-technically about the Switch Q project. M'Bulu asked how the new switches with the new quantum tech would be named, since they were not using numbers anymore. Keith suggested they rename the quantum concept part of the project, and then just call the boxes "Switch Qn" with the numbers starting from 4. They all agreed to that.

"Hey, I have an idea for the name for the quantum part of the tech," Bill joked.

The other three men looked at him expectantly.

"'Chevron Seven'!"

Bill laughed as he said it.

Heinrich swore in Norwegian, then quickly caught himself and switched back to English.

"We are not naming the quantum tech after that shitty show!"

Keith was laughing too hard to respond, but Bill covered.

"I'm kidding, Heinrich," Bill covered. "I may not understand the quantum workings, but I also know that most of the tech and concepts they wrote about in that show were completely fictional, except to ancient astronaut theorists."

"It just seems like you are not taking this seriously at all," Heinrich growled at Bill.

"I thought Norwegians were supposed to have a good sense of humor." Bill stated, staring at Heinrich.

Heinrich just stared back, not letting himself be intimidated.

"How about this," Bill offered after a moment, breaking the tension. "This quantum tech of yours, Heinrick... Erik? What should I call you?"

"Heinrich," M'Bulu clarified. "We cannot permit Finland FInancial or anyone else outside of this project to know of his existence, even with a slip of the tongue."

"Got it," Bill acknowledged.

The car arrived at the parking spot, and the driver opened the door, and the men climbed out of the car. M'Bulu headed to the dining hall, and the three doctors went to their cottages to drop off their suitcases, and then headed back to the dining hall to continue the conversation.

Once they were seated with their meals, Bill continued with Heinrich.

"This quantum tech of yours, Heinrich, is my understanding correct that, because of their quantum state, the processes do not actually take place within the four dimensions that we understand as our 'reality'?"

"This is correct," Heinrich answered, calming down now that he saw that Bill did take this seriously.

"And while this may be an oversimplification of the tech," Bill continued, "could it be also considered a client / server relationship in a similar way to the old-timey console / mainframe relationships originally operated?"

"In a very oversimplified manner, yes," Heinrich acknowledged after giving it some thought.

"And," Bill stepped into the esoteric now, "I thought I read or heard some legend that came out of CERN that with the Large Hadron Collider, the scientists on those projects had accidentally opened a crack to at least one other dimension in order to allow some eccentric particles through, only to have the particles destroy themselves right after getting here, because they can't exist in our dimensions?"

"*Exotic* particles," Heinrich corrected. "But yes. Either way, the problem with the theory that I hear you developing, is that no one at CERN will admit that other dimensions are possible."

Bill was happy for the encouragement from Heinrich finally, so he continued.

"Come on, Heinrich," Bill chided. "Just because they won't admit it, doesn't mean it isn't possible, right?"

A slow half-grin made its way across Heinrich's face. Bill continued.

"Minister Mabusa suggested that we not have secrets from each other on this project, Doctor *Torssen*," Bill was intentionally formal and direct, "and as the project manager on this project, I need absolute honesty from you, Heinrich. From you as well, Keith."

Keith just nodded.

"Okay, Bill," Heinrich straightened up. "*Ja*, the other dimensions are accessible, on a limited basis. You already know that the ANC is working with the Russian, Chinese, and American governments to fund this research at CERN. The research continues. We have some of the encryption figured out, but there are still unsolved processes. We are working to find a way to move all of that processing into the quantum realm, preferably offloading to virtual machines in the quantum space."

"Much in the same way that I offload a complex query to the database server and just have it return the result set, instead of having it run on my local machine?" Bill hoped his analogy was correct.

"Yes," Heinrich was surprised that Bill actually had it right. "Just like that."

"So, again, this may be oversimplifying," Bill continued ahead, "but does this mean that your quantum... uh... *cloud*, I guess, for lack of a better word, is the next 'cloud computing'?"

Heinrich thought for a moment.

"Yes, I suppose it is," he finally answered.

"So," Bill brought it together. "Q Cloud Processing."

"Or," Keith finally spoke up. "Q'Loud Processing."

They all sat for a moment, considering the new process name.

"That would help us keep the concept hidden," M'Bulu spoke finally. "If anyone ever overheard you talking about this concept, they would just think you were saying 'cloud', and dismiss it."

"Q'Loud it is, then," Keith stated.

"I still like 'Chevron Seven'..." Bill joked.

"You just want to be able to say 'chevron seven encoded' every time we compile new source code," Heinrich laughed.

"Oh man," Bill answered with mock seriousness, "I really do."

Then Bill changed to a serious tone for a moment.

"But please answer me this: you say that the engineers at CERN 'opened a tear into another dimension' and those *exotic* particles came through, but that's not how the Large Hadron Collider works, right? It is just supposed to smash things with other things and review the results, right?"

Keith and Heinrich exchanged glances, then Keith spoke up.

"Officially, your belief is correct," Keith answered. "But the reality is far more complex."

Bill looked at the table for a moment, processing this new information.

"I see," he replied.

"Doctors," M'Bulu took the opportunity to talk. "Please coordinate a secure way of having your teams interact, both for your quantum project, and for Bill's NSC project. I have your weekend to plan. Please meet at the parking lot at 9:00 in the morning, and pack clothes for one overnight stay, and whatever you would wear to the beach. You'll be vacationing in Western Cape this weekend."

M'Bulu stood and left the three men to their discussions.

Keith and Heinrich were very excited to hear that. Bill didn't know what to expect, but thought it sounded fun. Keith, Bill, and Heinrich spent the rest of the afternoon deciding on VPN providers and where to terminate the various VPN's, then had dinner and headed to their cottages.

Bill felt just the tiniest disappointment at having to turn off his own lights, but did so anyway.

CHAPTER 35: UNUSUAL BEHAVIOUR

The private jet trip from Johannesburg to Cape Town lasted just over two hours. Bill specifically did not sleep. He was enjoying the luxury of the aircraft. The LearJet 40 was equipped with eight very comfortable reclining seats, the food was as good as any that he had been served while in South Africa, and the sky outside was clear and gave him an unobstructed view for hundreds of miles on either side of the aircraft.

A limousine, with police escort, met their plane at the airport in Cape Town, and they began the two hour journey to Arniston to a private estate there.

"Doctor vanGreig," M'Bulu broke the relaxed silence of the car ride. "I am concerned about your former team member, Doctor bin Salman. Why is he no longer with you?"

Keith considered the question for a moment, then answered directly.

"As you know, Minister," Keith kept this formal, matching M'Bulu's tone, "Amir was very disappointed that he was not part of the team that turned on Switch 3. As you also know, I was surprised at his anger over it; I would not have been surprised that he was a bit upset, but the full rage he displayed did not make sense."

"And now," M'Bulu continued, "Doctor bin Salman is missing."

"Yes, Minister, that is correct." Keith answered honestly. "This has all been unusual behavior from him."

"The Russians have informed us that Doctor bin Salman cleared out his residence, and that he has been spotted in Pretoria, conducting surveillance on the Russian Embassy," M'Bulu shared with the group.

Keith and Heinrich were both clearly surprised by that news.

"That doesn't make any sense, Minister," Keith answered, thinking it through. "Does he think he can break in and unplug it or something? He doesn't even know where it is physically located. We don't even know the actual location."

"At this time, we do not know his motivation." M'Bulu lied. Everyone in the back of the limousine knew M'Bulu was lying, but no one addressed it.

The rest of the drive remained silent, but now, not as relaxed as before.

CHAPTER 36: WALKING SHARKS

Bill was overwhelmed by the entire experience of the private residence that had been rented for the weekend for his team. The estate was sprawling, with lush citrus trees and grass, the private beach with white sand, and the water of the ocean a deep blue. Every minor detail of the facility was designed for luxury. Bill decided that if he could live here, on this estate, he would move to South Africa.

Bill spent Saturday afternoon and most of the evening sitting on a large veranda overlooking the beach, watching the countless waves make white frosty tips on a remarkably blue ocean, and then crash on the whitest beach he had ever seen. He alternated between sipping fresh-squeezed orange juice and lemonade all afternoon. Heinrich had gone off hiking somewhere, Keith had gone up the beach to do some surfing, and Bill didn't know where M'Bulu was, but figured he was probably somewhere doing whatever a Minister of Home Affairs does on vacation.

Even though the sun set behind him, watching the colors make their way out of the ocean and up into the sky and the stars blink on was a remarkable experience. He had never really taken the time to appreciate a sunset looking east, and this one was spectacular.

Eventually, he noticed the aroma of something amazing cooking, and made his way to the kitchen. The chefs were preparing some foods that Bill didn't recognize, but he looked forward to an amazing meal. About the time the chef let them know that dinner was served, Heinrich, M'Bulu, and Keith all emerged from various parts of the house, and they feasted. Bill decided that he was going to stay up all night and lay on the beach to watch for the sunrise over this unfamiliar ocean, in hopes of seeing yet another new experience.

After dinner, Bill headed back out to the lounge chair on the beach, accompanied by Keith. They talked about the projects a little bit, then the talk turned to the sunrises and sunsets over the Indian Ocean.

"This is the view from my house too, man," Keith said. "I live right on the beach at home. I see that sunrise and sunset every day. That's why I was so pissed about having to go to Pretoria for this project."

"I can understand that," Bill replied. "Any danger to me sleeping out here? Walking sharks or lions or anything?"

Keith laughed.

"No, man, the walking sharks are in Australia," Keith said after a bit of thought and a chuckle, "but the crabs might find you, or a hyena. If you tell the staff that you want to sleep out here, I'm sure they could rig you a hammock. But bring a blanket, because those winds off the ocean will chill you a bit."

"How is a hammock going to protect me from a hyena?" Bill asked.

Keith burst out laughing.

"There are no hyenas here, mate!" Keith answered. "You have to stop being so gullible. We're not in a game preserve. Sleep well!"

Keith left Bill to his thoughts. Bill stood up from the lounge chair and walked to the nearest staff member and asked if a hammock was possible. They had one set up for him within a few minutes. Bill climbed in and wrapped up in the light blanket to listen to the ocean.

It seemed like only a few minutes that his eyes were closed until he heard the gulls hollering overhead. He opened one eye to see that the eastern horizon was already starting to lighten. Bill realized that he had just experienced one of the most restful nights he had enjoyed in a very long time. He stretched, rubbed his eyes, and adjusted his position in the hammock so he could see the horizon easier, then watched until the sun was fully above the ocean. He was impressed. Bill stretched again, and this time noticed that one of the staff members was standing a few feet away.

"Good morning," Bill said to the man.

"Good morning, sir," the man replied. "May I bring you anything?"

"Orange juice please," Bill answered, then added "and I will be back in a moment."

The staff member headed toward the kitchen, and Bill headed to the restroom. When he returned, he saw a large glass of freshly squeezed orange juice waiting on the small table next to the lounge chair. Bill spent the rest of the day in the lounge chair, standing only long enough to occasionally apply sunscreen.

As the saying goes, all good things must come to an end, and the weekend excursion was no exception. Bill did not regret the end of the weekend, because his brain was starting to nag him with all of the tasks still needing to be defined and tied down, but he would miss this place. The four men climbed into the limousine, and settled in for their two hour ride back to the airport in Cape Town.

About twenty minutes into the ride, M'Bulu's phone rang, and he answered it quietly. He spoke in a friendly tone with the person on the other end of the line, then held out the phone to Bill.

"It's for you," M'Bulu said to Bill.

Bill was surprised, but took the phone.

"Hello?"

"Hey Bill," a voice on the other end of the call said. "This is Kevin Blanchard. I'm the Board Chairman of GlobalForce."

"Oh, uh, hi, Kevin," Bill stammered. He realized at that moment that he didn't actually know any of the Board names until right now.

"You've had a hell of a first week," Kevin laughed.

"Mr. Blanchard," Bill responded, "I could never, in a million years, have ever dreamed up a week and a half like I've had in the last ten days."

"I know, it was a lot," Kevin acknowledged. "So, I want to bring you up to speed on things here. M'Bulu and I have talked every day, so I am in the loop on the NSC project that he has you working on." Bill noticed the obvious exclusion of the Q'Loud project. Kevin continued. "The Minister has set expectations with me that you will be spending four weeks per quarter working in Pretoria."

"*Three* weeks," Bill corrected.

M'Bulu laughed from across the car. He obviously knew what Kevin had just said to Bill.

"I know," Kevin laughed. "Neither of us thought you would let that slide. Anyway, M'Bulu also said that you would probably want some specific talent in Phoenix for the NSC project, as well as managing the development group in Johannesburg. We'll work that out when you get back. At the Minister's request, you have been promoted to the title of President of GlobalForce by the Board. Congratulations."

"Uh, thanks?" Bill answered.

"You're welcome," Kevin continued. "You are authorized by the Board of Directors to sign any contracts on behalf of GlobalForce for any projects that you believe are in the best interest of GlobalForce. Like, the NSC project, for example."

"Kevin, listen," Bill wanted to get some control of the situation again. "I appreciate all the faith everyone has in me on all of this, but the scope of some of these projects is pretty vast."

"I'm just hearing dollar signs," Kevin interrupted Bill.

Ugh.

"Got it, boss," Bill acknowledged Kevin's unspoken directive.

"One other thing," Kevin spoke quickly, "regarding Jerry, he has obviously been removed by the Board. We don't know the disposition of the issue with the FBI, but GlobalForce has been cleared, so we are business as usual now. The Board has decided to leave his position unfilled at this point, so you will be answering directly to the Board of Directors here, and to Minister Mabusa in South Africa. Any issues with that?"

"No sir," Bill accepted his new position.

"Great!" Kevin answered happily. "I'll have Connie schedule a lunch with you and the Board for a week from tomorrow. Safe travels!"

Kevin disconnected the call.

Bill's mood on the flight back to Johannesburg was bad; he mused to himself that the vast darkness below him matched his mood. The plane was still really comfortable though.

CHAPTER 37: HEALTH INSURANCE

Monday morning dawned as usual. In Pretoria, "as usual" meant that as soon as the sky started to lighten, one idiot bird with an awful honking sound would start squawking in a tree, and wake up the rest of the tree, and they would all start squawking, which would wake up another tree, and this noise would go on for over an hour. Keith called them "hadeda birds". They were awful. Bill hadn't heard them at the resort in Johannesburg, but Keith explained that it was only because that resort catered to high-net-worth clients, and that they had employees whose only job it was to keep the birds off the property. In Pretoria at the visiting dignitary quarters, they had no such luxury. Bill begrudgingly got up and got ready for work, grabbing a quick bowl of cereal before heading to his new office.

Bill was sitting at his desk making notes about the various projects when M'Bulu arrived.

"*Goeie dag*," Bill greeted M'Bulu.

"Good morning, Bill." M'Bulu laughed as he responded. "I see that we will need to find you a language tutor."

"Still bad, huh?" Bill asked, not really disappointed.

"*Ja*," M'Bulu replied. "But I appreciate the effort. What is on your agenda for today?"

M'Bulu sat while he and Bill went over Bill's list, the first item of business was to get the VPNs set up and all of his team using them. Next, Bill wanted to get offer letters for his database team and get them ready to step on at GlobalForce when he got back to Phoenix. There were a few other issues for discussion, and they were all discussed.

"One thing I would also like you to do," M'Bulu stated to Bill. "I don't believe that Francis La Pierre should be included on the National Secure Citizen project. And, I'm not sure I would like him to remain on the chip card project anymore, either. Doctor vanGreig has detailed some difficulties that he and the other team members in Johannesburg have had in trying to work with Francis. He's your employee, so I can't ask you to terminate him, but I will ask that you remove Francis from any of the South African projects."

"Understood, Minister," Bill took the hint. "I will make the necessary adjustments to our resource assignments."

Well, that solved that. Francis was not going to be a good fit in Bill's other teams, and while he may have been a satisfactory fit in the chip card team in Arizona, he was not a good fit anywhere else on any of the projects of the organization or its clients. He made a note to discuss that with Kevin.

———————

Bill spent the rest of the day working with Keith and Heinrich getting the VPN provider set up and the pipes connected to all three of their laptops, including two different ones on Bill's laptop, one to use with the NSC team, and a more secure one to use with Keith and Heinrich on the Q'Loud project.

That evening, Bill, Keith, and Heinrich had dinner together at the dining hall. Heinrich's personality changes since being outed as Erik Torssen, and the ensuing discussions about quantum processing and encryption, were pleasant, and Bill was glad to have him on the team. The three men talked and joked easily, and Bill was glad for the change.

"Well, mates," Bill was still trying to get comfortable with the dialect differences, "I believe I'll go watch a movie and get some sleep."

"They're called 'films' here," Heinrich corrected him. "What are you going to watch?"

"'Stargate'." Bill answered with a straight face.

Heinrich and Keith both laughed loudly.

"You can't watch that here, man," Heinrich chided Bill. "It's not available on any of the streaming services."

"Maybe not *here*," Bill already had this solved. "But, you just configured a VPN pipe on my laptop that gives me the ability to have an American IP address, so I can get into my PlusFlix account from here, and access that content. You two want to join me and heckle the science, while I bask in the American national treasure that is James Spader's acting?"

"Definitely." Heinrich answered.

The three men headed to Bill's cottage, and Bill fired up his laptop, easily logged into his streaming account, and started the film on the large monitor on the wall. Heinrich started heckling from the opening note of the opening credits. Bill decided this would be a unique experience, watching the film with an "expert" on all things quantum.

At about 9:30 p.m., a message beeped in on Bill's phone.

HEY

It was from Eileen. That was odd.

HEYB ACK/ HOW GOSDX THE GESTYATOIN?>

Good lord, his typing on this tiny keyboard was awful. The response was a couple minutes in coming.

ABOUT 2 WEEKS FURTHER THAN THE LAST TIME WE TALKED. WHO IS CONNIE PRATT?

"What the hell?" Bill said to himself. Why would Connie be reaching out to Eileen?

SHES TH HR MNAGAER AT GLOBFOIRCE, WYH?

Bill wondered if M'Bulu already had Connie reaching out to his old team. He calculated the time in Arizona, figuring it should be around 12:30 p.m. Monday afternoon. Connie must have acted swiftly. Bill would have to talk with M'Bulu about not jumping the gun like that.

SHE SAID SHE WAS CALLING ON YOUR BEHALF
REGARDING A JOB OFFER FOR ME. I TOLD YOU I'M NOT
GOING BACK TO WORK WHY WOULD SHE CALL ME?

Bill wondered if she had a price.

HWO FURM AER YUOU ON THYAT?

Bill lamented that he sounded like an idiot on text messages.

I'LL LISTEN TO YOUR OFFER, BUT I DON'T THINK
YOU CAN MEET MY DEMANDS.

Bill was happy to see that she was willing to listen.

WHOCH AREE?

Eileen took a full ten minutes to answer him. Apparently she hadn't
considered that he might meet any demands, so she must not have had
them ready.

BUY ME LUNCH TOMORROW AND WE'LL GO OVER THEM.

Got her.

I WONTY BE BACKL UNTOL MONDSAY> HOW ABOIT
THEN, ?

Quick reply this time.

WHERE ARE YOU?

PREWTORIUA

Another minutes-long delay.

YOUR SPELLING IS REALLY BAD ON THAT ONE, I
CAN'T FIGURE OUT WHAT YOU MEANT… PEORIA?

Ugh. Bill typed slower this time to make sure he spelled it correctly.

PRETORIA

Minutes later,

IN GEORGIA?

Bill chuckled to himself.

NOPER,. SOUTHJ AFRICXA

This should be fun, Bill mused.

WTAF ARE YOU DOING IN SOUTH AFRICA?

HEY LANMGUAGE! YOUI KISS YOURT BABY WITGH THAT MOUTH?

NOT YET. WHY ARE YOU IN SOUTH AFRICA?

LONGH STORY ILL TELLK YPOU AT KUNCVH ON MONDSAY

SOUNDS GOOD. I'LL TELL THAT CONNIE LADY THAT I'LL ANSWER HER AFTER YOU AND I TALK. WATCH OUT FOR LIONS. AND LEARN TO TYPE.

Bill sent one last intentionally bad message, just hitting random letters.

IUWENGILUNWERDI!

Let her figure that one out, Bill laughed to himself.

Bill stepped into the other room to call Connie, letting Keith and Heinrich continue their abuse of Bill's favorite film uninterrupted.

Connie answered on the second ring.

"*Goeie dag*, Bill," Connie said in perfect Afrikaans.

"What...?" Bill sputtered. "How do you know Afrikaans?"

Connie laughed.

"I had a good call with Minister Mabusa earlier today," Connie clarified. "He said you're going to want to hire your team from LookAtMe, and asked me to start reaching out to make sure they are available. Also he said to ask you about Francis. What about Francis?"

"Regarding Francis," Bill started with the easy one. "He's terminated. Have Kevin and a lawyer sit in when you terminate him. Severance is an equal match to any accrued vacation time he may have, that should make him happy. But I want a scary NDA signed with him first, and maybe throw in some 'national security' lies to make it sound worse."

"Can do," Connie sounded eager to get that done too. "What else?"

"Okay, so Eileen, Mark, and Kyle... Eileen will be difficult, because she told me she is going to take a few years off to raise her kid, back when I laid them all off at LookAtMe. We may have to make some accommodations, let's discuss those when I get back. Marky and Kyle should be easy, but we'll need to beat what they are making at Verve."

"Do you know how much they are making?" Connie asked.

"Yeah, I saw their offer letters, it's good money," Bill answered.

"Well, Minister Mabusa said that they are 'vital' to your project," Connie clarified. "So I'm sure we'll be able to charge that project sufficiently to cover the cost of them. I didn't know Eileen had a kid; how old is it?"

"About negative five months," Bill laughed. "She'll have her kid in about five months, and if we are going to keep her on my team, we'll need to make accommodations."

"No problem," Connie put Bill at ease. "I'll get out the ADA handbook and brush up on the pregnant, delivery, and post-natal rules before you get back. Anything else?"

"One question, how good is our health insurance?" Bill tried to act like it wasn't an important question.

"It's pretty good," Connie answered. "Funny you should ask, we are making an update to the policy this week. We'll be covering pregnancies and delivery as not pre-existing conditions."

Bless you, Connie. Bill thought to himself.

"Huh. Weird." Bill answered. "What a coincidence. Anyway, hold off on contacting Mark and Kyle until I get a chance to talk to them next week please," Bill wanted to try to talk with them first. "And have fun with Francis. I kinda wanted to do that, but I want him gone as soon as possible. Talk later, thanks Connie."

"You got it, be safe." Connie disconnected.

Bill rejoined Heinrich and Keith. Bill noted that Heinrich really hated this movie... film. But then Heinrich went too far and criticized Spader's acting. Bill reacted swiftly.

"Hey!" Bill shouted. "Don't you blaspheme in here."

CHAPTER 38: STILL WRAPPED

Amir's frustration just increased every day that he continued his surveillance of the Russian Embassy in Pretoria. He had tried to get a job at the embassy, but he was quickly dismissed at the guard shack with a brusque "not hiring". He watched carefully to get the names of the janitorial service and delivery vehicles that entered and left the gates multiple times throughout the day and night, and applied for jobs at all of those companies, only to be told by all of them that they were not hiring at that time.

Amir took walks and drives past the embassy each day to make himself less visible through repetition, but the guards seemed to ignore him completely. He had been in this business long enough to know that the more they appeared to ignore him, the more closely they were actually observing him.

When Amir had arrived in Pretoria the previous week, he found that there was already a cell operating there, and he was quickly integrated. He had not been forgiven for not running the script when Switch 3 had been activated, and none of his defenses seemed to be heard.

His leaders grew more impatient with Amir's failure, and soon the decision to plan a raid on the embassy was floated. Their cell would certainly suffer heavy losses of life, but that was not an issue, as all would be praised as martyrs. All they needed was to defend Amir for two minutes with the Switch 3, and the "package would be unwrapped".

Constant surveillance of the embassy would be launched, and detailed schedules of the activities would be compiled. Hidden cameras and microphones would be snuck onto the supplier vehicles. Eventually, with Allah's blessings, they would mount that attack. Then, if he survived the raid, he would find Keith and Heinrich, butcher them, and then take down the whole building in Johannesburg. They would all perish, and it would be glorious.

CHAPTER 39: NEW SCHEDULE

The conference call was a big one. Not because there were a lot of people on the call, but because of who the people were: the heads of the Russian General Intelligence Directorate, the American National Security Agency, the South African National Intelligence Agency, the Chinese Ministry of State Security, and a very uncomfortable Dr. Lars Schrengen, who was the head of Classified Projects at CERN in Geneva.

"Doctor Schrengen," the Chinese minister pressed. "It is imperative that more time be allocated to the Switch encryption project. All of the agency heads on this call have basically the same intelligence information, and it all indicates that attack attempts against the Switch network are increasing in frequency and complexity."

"I understand, Minister," Lars tried to speak some sense to the leaders on the call. "But we have already suspended many other projects in order to make more time for yours. Other project heads are growing suspicious."

"Doctor," the American joined in. "The four nations represented on this call have contributed ten times more to your little ray gun than all of the other projects combined. I believe we have earned at least a little more time with the collider than the other projects."

"*Da, ochen mnoga,*" added the Russian minister.

"Ministers, your project is already taking more than twenty five percent of the operating time," Lars protested.

"Then I suggest you make it fifty percent," the South African minister stated. "This project is far more vital than any other you have running. Your other projects are essentially trying to ascertain what happens when you smash two rocks together. The answer is 'sparks', and you've already proven that over and over again." The other ministers on the call nodded in agreement. "Our project uses verified, reproducible results of the collider to do consistent work that will secure the planet for the next one hundred years at least. Surely planetary safety and security for all of the peoples of the world is more important than smashing rocks together."

Lars considered what had been said. He wasn't sure how to allocate the amount of time these four powerhouses were demanding.

"Ultimately, Doctor," the Chinese minister continued. "If you are unable to make the changes and allocations for which we have asked, then your successor will. Please send out the revised project schedule by the end of the day today. Thank you, Doctor. Gentlemen."

The Chinese minister disconnected his connection, and the American director followed quickly.

"M'Bulu, I will call you directly in a few moments to discuss our other projects," the Russian minister stated.

"Understood, Sergey, talk with you then."

Both men disconnected, leaving Lars sitting alone in his office.

Lars closed the conference window on his computer screen and opened a copy of the current project schedule, changed the effective date to the following day, and began erasing more of the blocks, and putting the Switch project into the newly empty schedule spaces. Lars knew full well the amount of complaining that he would hear for the next three months over this new schedule, and he also knew there was nothing he could do about it.

Once the schedule update was complete, Lars saved it as a PDF, loaded his email, populated the Project Contacts group into the "To:" line of the email, attached the new schedule, and clicked Send. Then he shut down his computer, gathered his keys, and left the building.

On the drive home, the gravity of what he had done today weighed upon him until he was overwhelmed. This project was a disaster, and more time for the project meant more time for that unknown tunnel to be open. These men just do not understand the science and danger of what they are asking, Lars thought. Hell, no one does And, the Collider was never designed for this. Lars pulled to the side of the road, finally unable to drive or even breathe. He put the car into park, and got out to stand on the other side of his car and catch his breath. Great heaving sobs overtook him for a few moments as the enormity of his guilt crushed him.

After a few minutes, he took a deep breath, cleaned off his face, walked back to the car, and opened the door. He paused, thinking about the future. He looked up to see the sun setting, and the clouds in their reds and oranges and purples. It was a good sunset, Lars thought.

For just a moment, he felt peace.

And with that thought, and a smile on his face, Dr. Lars Schrengen closed his car door and stepped into the road just as the speeding lorry reached his position.

CHAPTER 40: ARNISTON

Keith and Bill were sitting at the table in Bill's office going over the project histories and timelines for the Q'Loud and chip card projects. Keith and Heinrich would not be participating in the NSC project, because they needed the Q'Loud to remain under the radar, and the NSC project needed to be the shining jewel of the Ministry of Home Affairs. They were wrapping up the last of their items when a clearly-rattled Heinrich slowly walked into Bill's office, having come from his weekly Tuesday morning conference call with the team at CERN.

"You alright then, mate?" Keith asked him, suddenly concerned.

Heinrich just walked over and sat at the table, and was silent for a moment.

"Lars Schrengen died last night." Heinrich finally said in a quiet voice.

"*Wat de fok?*" Keith responded immediately. "How?"

"They say that his car had broken down, and he apparently got it working again, and was about to get back into his car, but tripped and fell in front of a lorry." Heinrich repeated the news he had received on the call.

All three men were silent for a moment, then Bill broke the silence.

"I don't mean to ruin the moment here, but who was Lars Shrog... uh... who was Lars?" Bill felt like an ass for not remembering the man's name now.

Heinrich remained silent, but Keith explained.

"Doctor Lars Schrengen," Keith began slowly, "is… *was*, the department head for the black operations projects at CERN. Officially, he was the head of the team that managed the scheduling for all of the reactor allocation time at CERN, but his real job was to mask the classified operations with real ones."

Bill tried to process the scope of this news, and felt a twinge of guilt at finding himself factoring this news into his project scope.

"How many classified projects are running at CERN?" Bill asked, trying to get a better handle on the scope.

"Realistically, maybe ten people on the planet can answer that question," Keith answered. "Well, nine now. But we don't know."

"Forty seven classified projects," M'Bulu answered from the doorway. They hadn't noticed M'Bulu come in, and M'Bulu hadn't wanted to interrupt them. He walked in and sat with them at the table, setting down a sheet of paper. Heinrich just continued to look at the floor.

"Forty seven?" Keith asked, surprised. "How is that possible? There are only …" Keith calculated quickly in his head, "one hundred sixty eight hours in a week, and we consistently use more than forty of those hours. How is there any time for the education and scientific projects if there are forty seven, forty eight with ours, projects operating on that reactor?"

"This is why I am here," M'Bulu began. "Yesterday, several of the classified projects were suspended by their various governments, and more time on the Collider opened up. Our allocated time per week has been increased to 80 hours. Congratulations, Heinrich, you'll now have the time you asked for."

"This is not what I wanted," Heinrich said quietly, still looking at the floor. "Lars was a constant impediment to my project, but he was a decent person. I didn't want him to die over it."

M'Bulu looked surprised.

"He didn't die for this project, doctor," M'Bulu responded softly. "He had already changed the scheduling before this terrible event. And while he could have evenly allocated the time among the remaining projects, he did not, Heinrich. He allocated over ninety percent of the newly available time to your project."

Heinrich seemed surprised by that news. M'Bulu continued.

"How many times have you explained to Lars how important this project is, and how it will benefit all of humanity for a century at least? How many times did he say he was sorry, but that there was no more time to give to your project, regardless of its importance to the future? This new schedule, Heinrich," M'Bulu paused and tapped on the sheet of paper with the new schedule on it before sliding it across the table to rest in front of Heinrich. "This new schedule tells me that he heard you, and he agreed with you. Lars heard you, Heinrich. This proves it."

M'Bulu was certain that the words he spoke had been interpreted as he intended. It was unfortunate that Dr. Schrengen had jumped in front of that lorry, no one expected him to be suicidal over the directive they had given him. M'Bulu had seen the traffic camera footage showing the real story: Schrengen clearly jumped in front of that lorry, and there was nothing wrong with his car. Schrengen simply had shown that he was not capable of managing classified projects, but he also was unwilling to divulge any of those secrets. He took the honorable and clean way out of his predicament.

M'Bulu appreciated the cleanliness of the act, though the aftermath at the scene was anything but clean. The footage had been destroyed shortly after M'Bulu and the other directors had viewed it. M'Bulu was glad Schrengen had carried out their orders before making his final decision.

There would be a search for his replacement, but it would all be for show; the replacement was already in place, previously serving as Schrengen's second in command, and the replacement was loyal to what M'Bulu's team was calling the "Q'Loud" project, and there would be no further impediments to their progress.

"Take a few moments to collect your thoughts, then I need to meet with you all in my office." M'Bulu stood to leave. He patted Heinrich on the shoulder as he walked past.

"I argued with him for at least an hour every week," Heinrich finally spoke. "He was a constant problem to me. But he was a decent guy. I had no idea he was so depressed."

"I agree," Keith responded. "Well, let's go see what else M'Bulu wanted to talk about with us."

M'Bulu was talking on his phone at his desk when Bill, Keith, and Heinrich knocked on his office door. He waved them in and motioned to the conference table. They all sat and waited for M'Bulu to complete his call. When he was finished with the call, M'Bulu joined them at the table.

"First, do you know Doctor Karla Vanderzhen?" M'Bulu asked Keith and Heinrich.

"Yes," Keith answered. Heinrich nodded. "She is the Assistant Director of Resource Allocation at CERN."

"That is correct," M'Bulu stated. "She has been made the Temporary Director of Resource Allocation until a new director of that department can be found."

"If they are smart," Heinrich stated, "they will make her the permanent director. She is smart, and she backed me on my arguments with Lars."

"That is good to know, thank you, Heinrich. I will pass that along," M'Bulu answered, knowing that Dr. Vanderzhen would be the permanent director in a few weeks' time, after the show of searching for a replacement was completed. Dr. Vanderzhen also knew she would be the permanent replacement, as she was a staunch supporter of the Q'Loud project, and well-liked by the four administrators on the scheduling call the previous day.

"On to other items," M'Bulu began. "There is an issue of which I need to make you all aware."

M'Bulu spent the next two hours informing the team of newly discovered cyber attack attempts on the Switch network. While none of the attacks had been successful so far, the frequency and intricacy of the attacks were increasing every day. Their patterns led analysts to believe that these were not random attacks by amateur hackers, but were instead organized, targeted, and robust.

Bill was alarmed, but Keith looked unconcerned as he pondered that news.

Well," Keith thought out loud. "They can't get at the switches, because they can't access the IP range for the switches anyway. And the physical boxes in Helsinki and Phoenix are under twenty four hour armed guard, and the one here, no one knows where it is anyway."

"Wait, why can't hackers get at the IP range?" Bill asked.

"Because, *Erik* here," Keith answered, using Heinrich's real name for a moment, "designed the tech for the switches to have the first octet of their IP range set to 256."

"Nuh uh," Bill answered, half not believing Keith, and half impressed. "That's not a legal range, how can you do that?"

"Magic!" Heinrich answered, finally smiling again, and following it with a laugh. "The switches exist outside of reality, as far as the internet is concerned, and can only be accessed through the balancer in St. Petersburg. And *that* is the only box on the planet that can hear and talk through the veil of reality between 255 and 256."

"That's remarkable," Bill answered.

"Yes, it is," Keith responded.

"And the next level of Heinrich's magic will be the quantum processing which was explained to you previously," M'Bulu kept them on this track of conversation.

"I'm actually more impressed that you were able to fake a range address outside of the defined range," Bill said to Heinrich after a moment of silence. "That *is* magic."

"But let me bring this back around," Bill wanted to stay on this track as well. "You said they can't be accessed on the internet, and that the three physical boxes are under guard. What happens if someone does gain physical access to the boxes?"

"They could power down the box, but nothing else," Keith answered.

"But what if it stayed on, what could they do to it?" Bill pressed further. He knew there was more to this.

"There's nothing they can do to it," Keith answered calmly. "You saw Heinrich use the serial connection to console in, but there are literally two people on the planet that know what to do with it *if* they can gain access to the console connection. And that part of the internal software is turned off."

"Three people," Heinrich corrected.

"Well, yes, *three* people," Keith acknowledged.

"Hang on, I need a couple of explanations," Bill was missing some information. "First, who are the three people that know what to do with the Switch boxes if they get access?"

"Heinrich, Amir, and myself," Keith answered.

"And Amir is still missing." Bill stated. "Or has that changed?"

Bill, Keith, and Heinrich all looked at M'Bulu.

"Doctor bin Salman's whereabouts are still not known," M'Bulu lied. He thought it best to not let this team know that Amir and several compatriots had spent the last week reconnoitering the Russian Embassy across town in Pretoria.

"Okay," Bill continued. "And let's say that Amir did gain access to the Switch 3, and was able to console into the physical hardware. Why is that still not a problem?"

"There is a safeguard built into the software of the Switches," Keith explained. "The console subroutine that is used to run a few test commands is active when the operating system is installed on the hardware, but once turned off, it can not be turned back on. Literally, a new operating system must be installed on the Switch hardware in order to use the console subroutine again. You can't even use the same hard drive to install the new operating system, because there is a safeguard against that."

"So, at worst," Bill pieced it all together, "all an attacker can do is turn off the box? And at worst, all that would do is slow processing across the network for a few milliseconds while the balancer redistributed the traffic to the other two Switches? Is that correct?"

"Yes." Heinrich answered flatly.

"You're sure?" Bill verified.

"Yes." Heinrich answered again, flatly.

"And even if your guy Amir is able to mount an attack on the facility in Helsinki or Phoenix and gain physical access to the hardware, he still can't cause any damage?"

"Yes." Same answer from Heinrich.

"Then what are we worried about here?" Bill asked. "Other than the fact that I sit two meters and a fire wall away from that Switch 2 when I'm home?"

"Bill, let us be realistic here," M'Bulu stated in a serious tone. "It is not a fire wall, it is a regular wall. But don't worry, my friend, you will be long dead before they finally make it to the physical device.

With that, M'Bulu began to laugh hard. Keith did as well.

"Oh, I feel much better now," Bill replied, full of his best sarcasm.

"But in all seriousness, I believe you have misunderstood Heinrich's project." M'Bulu stated. "The processing work that we want to move to the quantum dimensions is not just the encryption, we want to move the switches themselves into the quantum realm."

Heinrich nodded.

Bill tried to process that for a moment. *Nope, no logic there*, Bill decided.

"So, what," Bill tried to use concepts he knew to paint this picture, "are you just going to run network cables through the event horizon to the Switch boxes that you somehow squish into the other side of that rip in the fabric of our universe or something?"

"Not exactly," Heinrich stated. "But close. The Switches on the other side will be virtual. And we'll use essentially a wireless connection to them."

Bill thought for a moment, then just started laughing.

"You can't keep that rip open, though, right?" Bill finally asked. "You can't use the LHC twenty four hours per day, seven days per week to connect to your quantum virtual machines."

"Well, about that," Heinrich answered, then looked to M'Bulu.

Bill stopped laughing.

"What?" Bill and Keith both asked at the same time.

M'Bulu thought for a moment, then nodded to Heinrich.

"We are building a modified Large Hadron Collider to power our network," Heinrich finally answered.

"You are not," Bill answered flatly.

"We are," M'Bulu chimed in. "It is much smaller, and is custom designed for the exact operation that is required for your project, but yes, we are building one."

"Where?" Keith asked.

Again, Heinrich looked to M'Bulu, who nodded again.

"Arniston." Heinrich answered. "Our trip down there was for me to check on progress. That's why I was gone hiking both days. I was checking progress on the site preparation."

Keith and Bill were stunned. Heinrich said nothing else while he let the news fully sink in.

After a few moments, Keith jumped up in a fury, and began shouting at Heinrich.

"This is the last fucking time, man!" Keith screamed at Heinrich. "This is the last time you hide things from me! No more! You tell me right now, man! Is there anything else you have not told me?"

Heinrich was looking at the floor now. M'Bulu waved off the security team that had come running when they heard Keith start yelling.

"No." Heinrich said quietly.

Keith stormed out of the room, grabbed his laptop from his desk, and left the building, taking his car back to his quarters. He spoke to no one else that day.

"Well," M'Bulu broke the tension. "I believe we should all call it a day."

Bill and Heinrich both stood up and left M'Bulu's office. They both gathered their laptops and shared a car back to their quarters. Bill grabbed a meal from the dining hall, but ate it in his cottage. He was still processing all of the news of the day when he fell asleep on the sofa.

CHAPTER 41: NO FAILOVER

Bill hadn't set a wake-up alarm, but that didn't matter, because the stupid birds began their honking well before be had to get up. It was fine though, he hadn't slept well, thinking about a miniaturized version of the LHC spinning around and staying on all the time with a virtual server or three handling data processing in there.

No one, not even Heinrich... Erik... whatever he wanted to call himself... not even that madman knew what would happen if they kept a tear in the very fabric of the universe open all the time, in violation of physics as we know them. And worse, no one, not even Heinrich, knew how to build computers or virtual machines in that dimension.

And even worse than that, there was no failover backup to the mini-LHC. If something went wrong with that, there wasn't one in Helsinki or Arizona to pick up the slack; the global transaction processing would just stop. Another horrible thought entered Bill's mind as he brushed his teeth: were there mini-LHCs also being covertly built in Helsinki and Arizona?

He would have to ask today.

CHAPTER 42: THE YANK IS RIGHT

Just like every other day, the hadedas sang Keith awake. *That Yank is right, they are annoying,* Keith thought to himself with a chuckle. But his mood turned sour again almost immediately as the memory of the news about the Arniston LHC returned to his attention.

"I'm going to have to stop you, mate," Keith said to the room, but directed to Heinrich. "You can't know what is going to come through if you leave that tear open, and you don't know what other information might come across those connections. This can not continue."

CHAPTER 43: MEMORIES

Heinrich missed his cottage in Akkarfjord, though he was sure Hans had stunk up the place irreparably. It was a simpler time. He wondered if Hans was even still alive, and if he was, how he was doing.

His cottage had the benefit of not having the bedamned birds outside his window every day at the crack of dawn.

Ah well, today he and Keith would have to come to terms with the fact that Heinrich had been doing a lot of extra work behind the scenes on the Switch project, and Keith would have to accept that the vast jump in progress that the Arniston Tiny Hadron Collider (Heinrich hated that name, because he hated marijuana) would provide them, and the planet.

If the Collider at CERN was safe, certainly a Collider one tenth of the size was one tenth of the risk. And the LHC was in operation twenty four hours per day every day, except during maintenance and upgrades, and there had been no beasties that had come through any of those dimensions during any of those tests.

Keith would have to get over it.

And by the time THC1 was due for any upgrades, he was certain they would have THC2 online, once they chose the location.

CHAPTER 44: HATE THE ANAGRAM

Bill and Heinrich met the driver at the parking lot at the normal time. Keith was not there; the driver stated that Keith had taken a separate car to the office fifteen minutes prior.

"Well," Heinrich stated, "this should be an interesting day."

"Agreed," Bill responded, "but let's wait to talk this through until we are in the office."

Heinrich just responded by nodding.

On the car ride in, they talked about the hadeda birds, and how the two men would revel in their extinction should it happen.

Once at the Ministry, Heinrich and Bill made their way to their offices, and then Heinrich came back to Bill's office. Bill motioned to the conference table, and sat with Heinrich. Bill leaned in to speak quietly to Heinrich, then paused, sat back, and clapped twice. Loud white noise immediately filled the room. Heinrich looked surprised. Bill just grinned, then leaned in anyway.

"I need you to tell me if there is a secondary small collider being built, and if so, where," Bill said just loud enough to be heard.

Heinrich thought for a moment, then answered.

"Not yet," he answered truthfully, "but there are plans for it once the first Tiny Hadron Collider is functional."

Bill looked at Heinrich for a moment, then started to laugh.

"'THC'?" Bill asked.

"I hate the anagram, but that's what stuck," Heinrich answered over the noise.

"Well, I need you to tell me how this won't destroy the planet and the universe as we know it some time," Bill was talking calmly, without any accusatory tone in his voice; he needed Heinrich to be honest with him. "There isn't time for that conversation before I go home, but when I get back, you and I are going to take a couple hour long car ride, and I need you to give me the full scope."

The word "scope" was very loud, as the white noise shut off just before Bill said it. Heinrich looked surprised, but then just nodded.

"You got it, boss," he responded at a normal tone.

"Thank you, Heinrich." Bill appreciated the respect. Time would tell if he was honest. "And now, we have Keith to calm down. I wonder where he is."

"He is in my office," M'Bulu said from Bill's office door. "Please join us."

Bill and Heinrich both startled, because neither of them had heard M'Bulu sneak up on them.

"How long have you been standing there?" Bill asked.

"Since about ten seconds before the white noise generator shut off," M'Bulu responded.

Bill and Heinrich stood and headed to M'Bulu's office. M'Bulu held Bill back for a moment.

"There is a little light at my desk that goes on when people use that noise generator," M'Bulu said very quietly to Bill. "And the cycle is two minutes before it turns off."

M'Bulu then turned and headed to his office. Bill just followed.

CHAPTER 45: CAN NOT UNRING THE BELL

Keith was sitting at the conference table in M'Bulu's office when the three men entered the room. Keith had his notepad open on the table in front of him. The page was blank. Keith did not look up.

"How's it then, mate?" Heinrich asked Keith.

Keith didn't answer, and still didn't look up.

"Right, then let's get to it, shall we?" M'Bulu stated, and went and sat at the table.

He then looked at Heinrich and Bill, who went and sat as well.

"The issue before us today," M'Bulu started, "is that Keith is upset that he was not informed of the design and construction of a smaller, dedicated, specialized Collider for use with the Quantum upgrades to the Switch network. Is that correct, Keith?"

"*Ja.*" Keith gave a quiet, curt answer.

"*Ja*, and Bill, do you have concerns as well?" M'Bulu asked Bill.

"I have a few, and the reasons are disparate," Bill began. "First, when you introduced Heinrich's alter ego to us last week, you said 'no more secrets between us', but you and Heinrich maintained that secret. If we are to have 'no more secrets between us', Minister, then the act of deception last week was unacceptable."

"Your point is fair, Doctor," M'Bulu responded to Bill. "What is your next concern?"

"There are a great many voices on the planet that we mostly dismiss as Luddite nuts for being against the operation, or even existence, of CERN. They warn us that the scientists at CERN could accidentally create a miniature black hole that would destroy our solar system and disrupt the galaxy around us. Some even say that it has already happened, but we just don't know it because we are on the event horizon and time itself is somehow disrupted. I can ignore their warnings, because… well, because I choose to, for lack of a better reason. I choose to ignore them because I think quantum stuff is cool."

Heinrich rolled his eyes. Keith continued to look at his notepad. M'Bulu continued to look at Bill.

"But, listen," Bill continued. "I don't know enough about quantum anything or the operation of the collider to be able to know what I should and should not fear…"

Keith slammed his hand down on the table.

"No one fucking knows!" Keith raged. "That's the problem! No one, not even you, *Erik*, knows what will happen in there! We don't really know what happens in Geneva, but at least the results are reproducible and consistent. But those experiments are not left on around the clock. The collider is turned on for a slice of time, results are gathered, and it is turned off and recalibrated for another experiment. It isn't left on long enough for something to find us. But you, you want to dial into one specific dimension, tear it open, and leave it open. And then you want to send consistent always-on high intensity microwave signals into it, and set up those virtual machines in there, and expect that there is nothing bad that can happen. *You! Don't! Know!* And you are completely ignoring the potential dangers."

Heinrich opened his mouth to respond, but Keith cut him off.

"And!" Keith roared. "When, not if, *when*, this virtual network fails, you will crash the Switch network, and all global transaction processing will fail in that moment, and you will have successfully doomed us all back to medieval times. That will be your legacy. The great Erik Torssen will not have ensured the safety and security of the people of the world for the next one hundred years, you will have doomed us to a thousand years of Dark Ages again."

Keith finally took a breath and looked at Heinrich, then Bill, then M'Bulu.

"And *you*!" Keith now turned his rage to M'Bulu. "These two *bliksems* are immigrants, but you and I, this is our land, our nation. And if you let him build that dedicated Collider, our nation will be the first to be destroyed. And, you continued to lie to me. Are you really even the Minister of Home Affairs, or is this all a front, too?"

"I am the Minister," M'Bulu answered, "but it is also a front."

Keith was stunned by that answer; he hadn't expected that at all.

"I will not tell you the rest of my responsibilities," M'Bulu continued, "because you would prefer to not know. I will spare you those details, but I will at least tell you that there is more to my job."

Keith considered the answer for a moment, then sat. After another moment, he spoke again, once again looking at the blank paper.

"You are going to kill us all, Erik," Keith said quietly. "The name Torssen will go down in history with Teppes, Khan, Mau, Stalin, Hitler. *If* anyone survives."

Keith trailed off. The room was quiet for a few minutes.

"You just don't get it, do you?" Heinrich finally asked quietly to Keith. "This has no risk. Our dedicated colliders will keep the dimension open without risk. They won't continually be spun up and shut down and reset, they will be able to run only one calibration, and will be able to run continuously to let the components settle down and run at top efficiency. The risk of using our own collider is significantly less than using the one in Geneva. Why can you not grasp that?"

Keith considered his response to Heinrich, then stood.

"Minister," Keith finally began, addressing M'Bulu instead of Heinrich, "I hereby resign from this project. I will happily remain on the chip card project, but I can not continue on this Switch project."

"Your resignation is acknowledged," M'Bulu responded calmly, "and declined."

"What? You... you can't decline my resignation," Keith responded indignantly.

M'Bulu laughed loudly.

"Please, Doctor vanGreig, now you sound as naive as your Yank leader here," M'Bulu said, jesting.

"Hey!" Bill protested.

M'Bulu continued, more seriously.

"Where would you go? Hm? What would you do?" M'Bulu stood, and assumed every bit of his authority as Minister of the Department of Home Affairs. "Would you run home to your beach in Durban, happily surfing in the morning, writing smart card encryption all day, then dinner and sleep, only to repeat it the next day? Ignoring your irrational fears about interdimensional quantum processing?"

M'Bulu stared at Keith for a solid minute before continuing.

"No, Doctor vanGreig, you can not unring that bell," M'Bulu continued. "You know now. Moreover, you are *complicit* now. If you try to leak the information, you will be just as discredited as the Luddites protesting in Geneva. You would lose all of the professional acclaim which you have spent a lifetime building. You would be ruined. And for what? An irrational fear of hadron colliders of any size?"

M'Bulu gave Keith another minute to let it sink in.

"Your resignation is rejected," M'Bulu finally stated.

After another moment of thought, Keith finally spoke.

"I still resign," he started. "I can not continue to help you destroy the planet, and I know you won't trust me to work on any of your other projects. No, I resign. I expect that by the time I return home, you will have caused every piece of tech in my home to be gone or wiped. I think I will go see my son in Paris, and then travel the world while I still can."

M'Bulu nodded.

"Your Nondisclosure Agreement remains in full effect," M'Bulu answered. "We will be very sorry to lose you, you have been a tremendous asset, and a wonderful person to work with. You will be taken under guard from here to the dignitary quarters to retrieve your personal belongings. Obviously, you will not be permitted to retain any technology items, as you have correctly guessed. From there, you will be flown on a private jet and driven to your home, where you will be dropped off. Be well, my friend."

M'Bulu turned toward the door of his office, and waved the two soldiers in.

"You will treat Doctor vanGreig with respect and care," M'Bulu commanded them. "He is not to be harmed, and is to be treated as an honored dignitary. Understood?"

Both soldiers saluted M'Bulu, and turned to face Keith.

Keith stood and stepped towards the soldiers, then stopped and turned to Heinrich.

"Don't take this wrong, mate," Keith said calmly, "but I hope you fail. Just not in a devastating way. You take care of yourself."

"No offense taken," Heinrich replied. "You stay safe too, my friend. You know where my cabin is if you want to go look at my fjord. It's yours to use."

Keith then turned his attention to Bill.

"Well, you're a long way from home, Doctor Fibulee," Keith said to Bill. "I'm sorry this journey has taken such strange turns. I wish you the best, mate."

"Thank you, Keith," Bill answered. "I appreciate all that you have taught me. *Veilig ry.*"

Keith laughed.

"When did you learn that one?" Keith asked, impressed at Bill's proper word usage and pronunciation.

"Just now, when it looked like you were leaving," Bill responded. "I wanted to say something meaningful, and 'see ya' seemed droll. Be safe."

Bill shook Keith's hand, and Keith turned to face M'Bulu again.

"Minister, it has been an honor," Keith stated to M'Bulu.

"The honor has been mine, Doctor vanGreig," M'Bulu answered. "As Bill so eloquently said, safe travels."

Keith then turned to the door and walked out, followed by his escort.

Bill turned back to look at M'Bulu and Heinrich.

Heinrich was clearly devastated, and M'Bulu also looked unhappy. He let them stew in their thoughts for a moment, then broke the silence.

"Well, this is a setback."

"You have a Norwegian gift for understatement," Heinrich responded.

"Thanks?" Bill answered.

The three men spent the rest of the afternoon completing their timelines and communication schedules, then had a catered dinner in M'Bulu's office to celebrate Bill's trip home the following day.

"In the morning," M'Bulu explained Bill's schedule to him, "your blue light brigade will arrive at 9:00. You will be chauffeured to the Executive Terminal at O. R. Tambo."

"I will not," Bill interrupted, incredulous.

"Yes you will," M'Bulu continued. "You will be met by a security team there who will drive you directly to your British Airways plane, and you'll be taken on board through the VIP door. Your flight will leave on time."

"What about Customs?" Bill asked, trying to get his bearings.

"Thank you for reminding me," M'Bulu answered. "May I see your passport, please?"

Bill dug his passport out of his computer bag and handed it to M'Bulu. M'Bulu took it and walked to his desk, opened a drawer, rummaged around and pulled out a stamp, inked it, and stamped the page in the back of Bill's passport. Then he returned the stamp to his drawer and closed it. He returned the passport to Bill, and sat down again.

"There you are," M'Bulu said comfortably. "All legal now. Did you have anything to declare?"

M'Bulu laughed at his own joke, as did Heinrich.

"I declare this to all be insane," Bill joked.

They all had a good laugh, and then they ended the night.

Bill and Heinrich shared a car back to the dignitary quarters.

"Have you ever had *akevitt*?" Heinrich asked Bill in the car.

Bill's blank expression answered Heinrich's question.

"Ah, you'll love it," Heinrich answered. "Come do a shot with me before you leave. We need to celebrate this new partnership."

Bill agreed. Once back at Heinrich's cottage, Heinrich poured out two shots of questionable-looking liquid, and handed one glass to Bill.

"*Skål*, my friend," Heinrich said, toasting Bill, and downing the drink in one swallow, coughing slightly afterwards.

"Uh, skole, I guess," Bill answered. He then sniffed the drink, and downed it in one gulp as Heinrich had done, immediately regretting his action. It took him a full minute to be able to breathe correctly again.

Heinrich laughed the entire time.

"Holy crap, what is that?" Bill asked when he was finally able to mostly breathe again.

"I told you, it is '*akevitt*'," Heinrich answered. "The drink of my ancestors. Before every long journey, they would have a great feast and get drunk on mead, but you have to fly for a long time, so we are drinking *akevitt* instead. A mead hangover is not humanly possible on a 747 for nine hours.

Heinrich poured another shot for them both and handed Bill's to him. Bill was feeling a very pleasant warm sensation spreading throughout his body.

"*Skål!*" Bill hollered, and downed the second drink.

"*Skål!*" Heinrich roared through his laughter and downed his drink. "No more for you tonight, since this is your first time drinking it, and you have to travel tomorrow morning. You'll thank me when you're on the plane and do not feel terrible. Travel safely, my new friend. Now, get out."

"*Skål!*" Bill hollered again, even though he didn't have a drink. "I appreciate it. I look forward to my next visit here. And I will talk with you on our calls. Be well, and please don't make a black hole and kill us all."

Both men laughed hard, and Bill headed back to his cottage.

CHAPTER 46: HOMEWARD

Bill slept well that night, and the hadeda birds woke him before sunrise again, right on schedule. He checked the clock to see what time it actually was.

4:52 a.m.

"You gotta be kidding me," Bill said to himself.

Bill got up and realized he didn't feel great. And, he realized he was really thirsty.

"Note to self: no *akevitt* before traveling," Bill muttered, heading to the kitchen for water.

Bill grabbed a bottle of water from the refrigerator, and gulped it. His stomach protested a little, but soon settled down. Bill brushed his teeth, showered, and headed to the dining hall, hoping it was open this early in the morning. It was, he was grateful. He asked the chef to make him something to heal what remained of his hangover and that would keep him from being hungry on the long flight. The chef smiled and got right to work. Bill went and sat at a table and began checking his emails, and a few moments later, the chef himself brought out the plates.

"There you are, sir," the chef spoke enthusiastically. "My father's own recipe, I hope you enjoy it."

It all smelled amazing, and Bill didn't ask what was in it, he just accepted it gratefully.

"Thank you very much, this smells amazing!" Bill answered happily. "This may become my pre-travel meal every time I'm down here."

The chef thanked Bill again and headed back to the kitchen. Bill ate the food with gusto, and was soon feeling much better.

As promised, promptly at 9:00, the security escort knocked on Bill's door.

The car ride to the airport in Johannesburg airport was uneventful. In Johannesburg, he and the security team were driven to the gate where the British Airways 747 was parked. Various workers were performing various tasks on the plane, and no one seemed to pay any attention to the limousine that had just driven under the starboard wing and up to the door on the building. Bill's guards stepped out, but asked Bill to wait until they cleared the area first. When they were satisfied that all was safe, they escorted Bill into the building, where he was met by a very friendly Customs agent who checked M'Bulu's stamp in Bill's passport and then wished him a safe journey.

"May I ask a question?" Bill inquired of the agent.

"Certainly," the agent replied.

"Why did the security detail have to 'clear the area' before they let me get out of the car?" Bill asked. "Is there a threat of attack even this close to the plane?"

"The ground crew are all safe, that is why they continued working," the agent began, "but you never know about snipers."

Bill was stunned and just stood for a moment. Then the agent and the security team all began laughing loudly.

"I'm just joking, sir," the agent said finally. "There are no snipers, but with certain government contractors, we use additional security tactics, and their actions are part of that. This was normal procedure for a key contractor such as yourself. I apologize for the joke."

Bill immediately felt better, and joined in the laughter at his own expense.

His security detail escorted him to his section in First Class, and Bill immediately protested.

"I'm not sitting in First Class," Bill stated to the security detail.

A flight attendant whose name badge said "Leslie" immediately walked over to see if she could resolve the issue.

"Is there something I can do to assist?" She asked Bill.

"I hope so," Bill responded. "I had a seat in Business Class reserved, but they led me up here. I appreciate the luxury up here, I really do, but I really would prefer to sit in Business Class."

The flight attendant looked puzzled for a moment.

"You don't want to sit in First Class? May I ask why?"

"This last two weeks in South Africa has been filled with unusual experiences and surprises, and I just need some familiarity," Bill explained. "I was very comfortable and happy in Business Class on the way here, your teammates in that flight were amazing, and I love this airline. I would like to have my trip home bring me back to a little normalcy. So, if it's not going to inconvenience someone else, may I please be moved to Business Class?"

The flight attendant smiled a little smile and nodded.

"Give me a moment," she stated. "I know just the solution."

After a few moments, the flight attendant returned with a very old lady.

"Doctor Fibulee," Leslie began with a wink to Bill, "here is Mrs. Statz, as you requested."

Bill was confused, but knew from the wink Leslie gave him to just play along.

"Oh, bless you!" Mrs. Statz bubbled. "This is an amazing birthday present! I've never flown First Class, and this is just so wonderful!" She gave Bill a hug.

"Well, you're certainly welcome, Mrs. Statz," Bill played along. "When I heard that there was someone on board celebrating their…" Bill got stuck, because he didn't know her age.

"Ninetieth," Leslie helped.

"Yes, their ninetieth birthday, well, I just knew that I needed to do something," Bill finished the lie. "I hope you have a wonderful birthday and that this helped."

Bill and his detail headed downstairs to Mrs. Statz's original seat, and Bill settled in.

"Well, gentlemen," Bill said to his security guards, "how far do you travel with me?"

"This is as far as we go," one of them answered. "There will be a security detail for you while you change planes in London, and your regular security detail will meet you when you arrive in Phoenix. This will be your routine now. When you arrive back here next time, we will meet your plane and escort you through Customs again and travel with you back to Pretoria."

"Okay then," Bill took in the news. "You guys be safe, and I will look forward to seeing you next time I'm here."

Bill shook their hands, and they left the aircraft.

Within an hour, the 747 was in the air and on its way north. Bill settled in for the flight and slept.

The layover in London was uneventful, and he was greeted at his next plane by a flight attendant named Melody as he walked on board.

"Doctor Fibulee," she began, "Leslie informed me that you prefer Business, so we have made the arrangements for you already. I can escort you to your seat now if you wish."

"Yes, thank you." Bill noted again how much he enjoyed flying on this airline.

Once he was settled in, Bill's London security detail left the plane, and shortly he was flying again. He wasn't really tired, because he had slept a lot on the previous flight, so he just watched the land disappear below him and give way to the North Atlantic Ocean towards Iceland. Bill wondered to himself what Iceland looked like from 40,000 feet, and looked forward to seeing it, but didn't wake up again until he was flying over the northern Hudson Bay.

CHAPTER 47: JET LAG

Bill felt surprisingly refreshed, waking up in his own bed on his first morning back home. And there were no bedamned honking birds outside his window. He enjoyed making his own breakfast, and having to turn off all the lights with a switch, instead of voice commands. *Those were nice features though*, Bill thought to himself.

It was still different now. Bill had two guards and a car service. He thought to ask one of the guards (who had introduced himself as Marcus) if he was going to be using his own car in the near future. Marcus had replied that he probably would not be, so Bill made a mental note to sell his car.

Bill did nothing on Saturday; didn't check emails, didn't review his project plans, nothing. He did decide to send text messages to both Kyle and Marky to set up lunch for Tuesday; he wanted his team at least hired this week.

The jet lag hit Bill surprisingly hard, but he also thought it might have a lot to do with the fact that it had been exactly 13 days since he got on the plane to go to Johannesburg. Reality as he knew it had changed so dramatically, and this was the first real chance he had to just mentally shut down and take stock of his new normal.

He slept most of Sunday, and caught up on his shows while he was awake.

CHAPTER 48: SUMMONING CTHUHLU

It seemed odd to have to set an alarm, since the last few days before the flight home, he had the hadeda birds to wake him up. Bill mused to himself how maybe they are an acquired taste, like labor pains. Then he brushed the thought aside... the birds were awful and he did not miss them.

It felt very odd to be sitting in the back of a town car with two guards driving him to work, but he knew to get accustomed to it, because this would be his new routine.

Connie and Kandi were happy to see Bill, and surprisingly so were the remaining programmers, even though they had only spent about 20 minutes with Bill before he left for South Africa. Bill made his way to his office and settled into his comfortable chair. Connie gave him about a half hour to get his bearings, then walked in with a list of items for him to discuss.

Lunch with Eileen was at 11:30 a.m., Connie had her new-hire paperwork ready in case Bill was successful, there was the meeting with the Board at 2:00 p.m., she mentioned that Kevin was not happy about getting bumped, and a conference call with M'Bulu and Kevin at 4:00 p.m.

Once they wrapped up, Bill logged into his laptop and into the Q'Loud VPN. He opened the project messaging client, and noticed that Heinrich was online. Bill typed a quick message.

GOOD... MORNING? HOW CLOSE ARE YOU TO FIGURING OUT HOW TO SUMMON CTHULHU?

Bill saw that Heinrich started typing a response right away.

HA! NO MATE, BUT I FIGURED OUT HOW TO OPEN THE
BIFROST. HAVING A PINT WITH THOR AND HIS MATES.

Bill laughed at that.

FUNNY. ANYTHING EXCITING HAPPEN TODAY THAT
REQUIRES A CALL?

Heinrich took a moment to respond.

I MADE A BIT OF PROGRESS ON THE ENCRYPTION
CONTROL BIT. WILL SEND YOU A SECURE MESSAGE WITH
DETAILS. NOTHING MUCH ELSE TO REPORT. M'B IS
LETTING ME WORK FROM THE DQ WHILE UR IN AZ.

Bill wasn't surprised that Heinrich was working from his cottage in the
dignitary quarters; the food was better, and the work environment was
more comfortable.

NO WORRIES. SEND ME THAT MSG IN YOUR MORNING.
I'M CURIOUS.

Bill hoped Heinrich made enough progress to have something
promising to report. M'Bulu was a patient man, but there had to be limits,
and Bill hoped he didn't reach them.

YEP. CHEERS.

SKOLE!

Bill knew Heinrich wouldn't let that misspelling go, but he didn't have
that little "circle a" thing on his keyboard.

SKÅL?

YES THAT.

Bill signed off the VPN and began putting together his notes for Eileen,
and then wrote up a summary for the Board meeting in the afternoon.

CHAPTER 49: PERSEVERANCE

Amir persevered.

Throughout his life, he had persevered.

This was no different.

It had been more than a week since he had arrived in Pretoria. Every day, he continued to watch the Russian Embassy, documenting each vehicle and person that went in or left, noting their times and as much detail about the appearance of each person as much as he could.

That night, as he and his brothers were having dinner, another member of his cell, Hassan, ran in excitedly, exclaiming about something they found that day. He ran to Amir and dropped several sheets of paper on the table next to Amir.

"What do you see, brother?" Hassan asked quickly.

Amir looked over the pages. They appeared to be a raw dump of an internet traffic log file. Amir stated as much.

"You are correct," Hassan said, then quickly clarified. "But these are raw internet traffic logs from inside Finland Global!"

Amir's eyes went wide, and he looked back to the papers.

"All praise to Allah!" Amir yelled. "How did we get these?"

Hassan explained that part of the Caliphate's ongoing attacks against the non-believers across the world were regular phishing attacks against all of the banks worldwide, as well as corporations, governments, and other targets of interest.

Occasionally, one got through.

In this case, the attack worked against a low-level help desk person at Finland Global, and once in, their hackers were able to access the traffic logs through their network. They hadn't made any attacks while inside the network, instead they gathered information and presented their findings, and awaited further instructions.

"Please tell them to continue to gather these logs," Amir said in a whisper and he dug through the information. "This is our way in. If we can find packets from the main routers in their network, maybe we can find a way to throttle them back. If we can throttle Finland Global, we may be able to destabilize the switches."

Amir felt a new wave of hope and anticipation as he read deeper and deeper into the raw technical gibberish.

CHAPTER 50: EXPANSION

Bill's lunch with Eileen was productive, but she wasn't interested in coming to work at GlobalForce. Even with the benefits package that they had put together, and the accommodations for pre- and post-birth, she still didn't want to.

"You are killing me," Bill finally gave up. "Like, literally, I am going to die right here, and you are going to have to pay the check."

"Nah, I'll just tell them you have bad jet lag from a long trip, and then take your wallet out of your pocket and leave." Eileen was cutting Bill no slack.

"Cold." Bill responded. They both laughed.

"Seriously though, tell me what it's going to take," Bill tried one last time.

"Okay, fine. I want to move to New Zealand." Eileen responded, giving a response that Bill would never have guessed.

"Come on," Bill answered. "That's a ridiculous condition. And I doubt I can get approval to cover your move expenses as part of your sign-on."

"Not now, duh," Eileen countered. "I mean in a couple years."

"Actually, that's probably not out of the question then," Bill thought it through. "But why New Zealand?"

"It's the healthiest place on the planet, and I want her to have a healthy life." Eileen had apparently thought this through.

"Wait, *her*?" Bill realized the word. "You're having a girl?"

"I am," Eileen smiled big.

"That's awesome, congratulations!" Bill said too loudly, drawing glances from nearby diners. "We can decorate your office accordingly." Bill had to try.

Eileen just looked at Bill and smirked for a long time.

"You put in writing," Eileen finally blinked, "that in two years, the company will bonus me $50,000 and cover my relocation to New Zealand."

Bill returned the long, silent smirk.

"You mean, your transfer to the new New Zealand satellite office," Bill corrected, laying the groundwork.

"Yeah, that," Eileen responded.

"You know that's going to be difficult," Bill finally answered.

"Let me know today, and I can start in the morning." Eileen responded. "Shall we say, 10:00?"

"I'm meeting with the Board in a little bit," Bill replied. "I'll pitch it and text you later this afternoon."

Bill and Eileen finished their lunch while making fun of the management team at their former job.

"That's a ridiculous request," Kevin responded.

"It's a little unusual," Bill countered, "but think about it for a minute, if we are still in business in two years, and we will be, because that contract with South Africa is for a minimum of three years, and we will likely have picked up other contracts in the southern hemisphere by then, so it won't hurt us to have an office there. Hell, it wouldn't hurt for us to have a satellite office in Pretoria either."

"No."

"Kevin, you're not even thinking it through," Bill argued.

"No."

"You know I can sell it to M'Bulu," Bill countered, testing his boundaries.

"Bill," Kevin began a measured response, "you've been with GlobalForce for just over two weeks. I realize this has been a very unusual time for you, the Board, and the company, and I realize that in that time, you've had some significant career growth."

Bill nodded.

"But I want you to understand me very clearly here," Kevin leaned in a little closer to Bill. "The position you hold within this company is at the request of a client. Your technical and leadership skills are mostly known to the Board, but they are almost all based on a year of Jerry over-selling you. Do *not* push too much harder, because this very thin branch that you are way out on can snap very easily."

Bill considered Kevin's words. He wasn't wrong about how Jerry must have oversold him before he stepped on. But he also would like to think that the way he had handled the two weeks in South Africa may have actually shown that he did have the skills for this position. Bill was about to respond as such, but then Kevin's phone rang.

Kevin looked at his phone, it was M'Bulu.

"That's odd," Kevin commented. "We are not due to call him for another hour and a half."

Kevin answered the call, spoke for a moment, then laid the phone on the table and pressed the speaker button.

"Go ahead, Minister," Kevin said to the phone. "You are on speaker."

"Very good, thank you," M'Bulu started. "Hello Bill, how are you enjoying being home?"

"I enjoy it very much, M'Bulu," Bill responded in the most informal way he could.

Kevin scowled.

M'Bulu laughed.

"Don't get too accustomed to it, mate," M'Bulu said with a chuckle, "we enjoy having you down here too much for you to be comfortable there."

Bill laughed in response, Kevin continued to scowl.

"The reason for my early call," M'Bulu began, getting down to business, "is because I would like you and the Board, Kevin, to consider something before our call later today. I would like you to consider a satellite office in Pretoria. I know you have your joint venture partner in Joburg, but with the amount of work you currently have with this Ministry, and the additional work which I am sure I can find for you, I believe it would be in the best interest of both the people of South Africa and GlobalForce for you to have a presence here. Bill may continue to use the dignitary quarters which have been assigned to him, but an office presence here would be appreciated."

Kevin looked stunned.

Bill dropped his head and just looked at the table.

"Actually, Minister," Kevin stammered, "Bill had brought a similar idea to me a few minutes ago. I have not had a chance to bring it to the Board yet. But I am concerned about the cost."

"That is a fair concern," M'Bulu responded. "I am sure we can enhance the contracts we have and bring a few more than can help defray those costs. Please talk with your Board of Directors and let me know the decision when we talk later today. Have a good afternoon, gentlemen."

M'Bulu disconnected the line.

Bill continued to look at the table.

"You went around me," Kevin finally said, clearly angry.

"No, I had no conversation with M'Bulu in any form today or over the weekend," Bill responded honestly. "This is the first time I have spoken with him at all since I left Pretoria."

"Then how the hell did he know?" Kevin demanded.

Bill glanced at his phone, but said nothing about it.

"I don't know," Bill lied. "I'll leave you alone so you can talk with the rest of the Board and have M'Bulu's answer at 4:00."

Bill stood to leave.

"Why don't you call him 'Minister'?" Kevin asked.

"I do when it's appropriate," Bill answered, and returned to his office.

Bill knew he had overstepped with Kevin. He felt bad treating Kevin the way he had treated James back at LookAtMe. James had deserved it, but Kevin didn't. Bill decided that he needed to go apologize to Kevin before the Board meeting started. He intentionally turned off his phone and left it on his desk as he walked back toward the conference room where the Board members were already assembling.

The room sounded quiet, so Bill figured that no one else had arrived yet, and just walked in. He then froze as he saw the fully assembled Board of Directors already in their seats and about to begin. They all looked at him expectantly, even Kevin.

"Uh, I am really sorry," Bill stammered. "I didn't realize you had already started. I'll come back."

"No, Bill, please stay," Kevin responded in an even tone, with no hint of anger at Bill, but Bill noticed that Kevin's eyes did not agree with his tone. "You're actually our first agenda item, so have a seat."

Bill turned to go sit in the back corner of the room, but Kevin called to him and motioned to a seat at the table right next to Kevin.

Oh, this is not going to go well, Bill thought to himself.

Kevin made a motion to bring the meeting to order, one of the other members seconded the motion, and the meeting began.

After voting on some other procedural item, Kevin introduced Bill.

"Everyone, at long last, I'd like to introduce Doctor William Fibulee," Kevin began. "He's had an interesting first two weeks with the company, just as we have all had an interesting two weeks. Bill, why don't you give us your perspective on the events since you stepped on, especially fill us in on the projects and events in South Africa."

Bill spent the next twenty minutes telling the Board about his trip, the National Secure Citizen project, and some additional consulting that Minister Mabusa has asked the company to perform. He fielded questions from the Board about certain details of the NSC project, but avoided mentioning the Switches. One of the Board members finally asked about the Switch 3. Bill hesitated, because he didn't know how much he could tell the Board members.

"Doctor Fibulee is hesitating because some of the project is classified," Kevin covered for him. One of the other Board members objected to Bill and Kevin holding back details of one of the important projects from the full Board.

Kevin considered the objection for a moment, then gave a response that Bill thought was brilliant.

"Let me ask you this," Kevin began. "When the US Government gave pieces of the Roswell UFO to Boeing so they could reverse engineer it and make a jet propulsion engine, did the CEO of Boeing at the time share the details of the classified project with the Board of Directors? When they gave pieces of the internal circuits to Motorola and Xerox to reverse engineer into transistors and integrated circuits, did anyone tell the Board of Motorola or Xerox about those details? Do any of the modern-day companies that have classified projects with any government reveal the classified details to their Boards? The answer is no. And for you to expect Bill to give the Board all of those details is unreasonable."

There was a burst of arguments from all around the table, which Kevin let go for a few seconds, then pounded the table.

"We can't just have the new guy doing whatever he wants without oversight!" Yelled another Board member.

"He *has* oversight," Kevin responded. "He has shared all of the details of all of the projects with me, and Minister Mabusa has given me the same details. So Doctor Fibulee is not just doing whatever he wants, he is operating with oversight, and with my blessings. He has brought all of his requests and suggestions for significant business decisions to me before acting on them, and since you have all voted to have me oversee this company from the perspective of CEO, I would think that you all have the belief in me to not permit a renegade employee."

Now Bill felt worse. He absolutely was a renegade, and he had not shared any of the details of the Q'Loud project with Kevin. And he felt like crap for it.

Another Board member spoke up, directing some venom at Kevin.

"How can you sit there with a straight face and claim there are no renegade employees? How do you explain Jerry?"

Now Kevin was mad.

"If you remember right," Kevin was speaking very precisely, "I voted *against* hiring Millgrew, because his terms were unreasonable. There were only two of you that agreed with me. So, *do not* blame any of the issues with Jerry on me. And, the activities that caused his departure from GlobalForce had nothing to do with anything he was doing at GlobalForce. Bill and Minister Mabusa have communicated volumes more information to me regarding the projects than Jerry ever did. So, let's be intellectually honest, shall we?"

The Board member opened his mouth to respond, then thought better of it and stopped. Bill decided to try to break the tension.

"I can give an update on the unclassified parts of the Switch project, if that's okay."

"That seems like a good compromise," Kevin answered. "Go ahead."

Bill explained that the Switch 3 had been installed in a secure facility somewhere in or near Johannesburg on the second or third day of his trip, and that the South African engineers working on it proclaimed that it was functioning as expected. A Board member asked why he said "somewhere near Johannesburg", and Bill explained that the vehicle in which they rode to the facility was without windows, and Bill didn't actually know where it was installed, nor did the South African engineers. Another director asked if Minister Mabusa knew where it was installed, and Bill answered that he was sure the minister did.

"Before we let Bill get back to work, there is one other item we need to discuss," Kevin stated. "Minister Mabusa called me a few minutes before this meeting and asked us to open a satellite office in Pretoria. I have already raised the objection that it would be prohibitively expensive to do so, and the minister explained that there would certainly be more contracts and projects for GlobalForce if we had a presence in Pretoria. So, I promised to bring up the concept at this meeting and that I would relay our decision on our call later this afternoon."

Now Bill felt worse for trying to strong-arm Kevin. He realized that no one had said anything for several seconds, and he looked up and around the room at the Board members. Their faces had a wide array of expressions at the concept.

Kevin finally started the discussion, and it lasted for about fifteen minutes. When the vote finally came, the decision was not unanimous, but the decision was no. Kevin looked at Bill to give Bill a chance to respond. Bill took the chance.

"Directors, if I may," Bill started. "I would ask that you reconsider your decision, and here's why, the National Secure Citizen project is a minimum of two years, and realistically will take three to four years to complete. It's a massive project. There is also some consulting work that we can do on the encryption improvement that they are working on for the Switch network. I am confident that we can charge off the office rental and expenses to any of those projects. So, I would ask that you reconsider your vote, and instead, put terms on it that Minister Mabusa must agree to before we launch that office, and that part of those terms include reimbursement for the expenses of setting up an office in Pretoria."

The various members of the Board all began talking to each other and over each other, and Bill remained silent. Kevin's phone beeped as a message arrived. Kevin read it briefly, looked surprised, glanced at Bill, then brought the meeting back to order.

"If I can get Minister Mabusa to agree to those terms, then I don't see an issue," Kevin stated, almost in a sarcastic tone.

Bill thought it was odd.

"Doctor Fibulee," a member who had remained silent until now spoke up, "if this motion is approved, it means you'll be spending a lot of time in the air and in South Africa. How do you feel about that? And, I am curious as to how you would vote if you were on this Board."

"Well," Bill answered thoughtfully, "The flight certainly is long, but if they keep booking me on British Airways in business class, the flight is acceptable. The minister had already discussed with Kevin and me having me down there two weeks out of every quarter, and we had agreed in principle to that. I certainly don't mind the food, it's exceptional. I guess if I were to do a Ben Franklin close on myself, I'm pretty sure there are more items in the 'pro' column than in the 'con' column. So, to answer your question, while I may live to regret this, I would vote in the affirmative."

"Thank you for your candor," the member responded to Bill.

Another member called for a new vote, the motion was seconded, and a new vote was taken. The result was still not unanimous, including Kevin's vote of "nay", but Bill figured Kevin's negative vote was purely ceremonial. The motion passed, and GlobalForce would open a satellite office in Pretoria.

Kevin excused Bill from the rest of the meeting, and Bill headed back to his office to wait for the call with Kevin and M'Bulu.

Bill and Kevin sat at Kevin's desk, with Kevin's phone on speaker. M'Bulu picked up on the second ring.

"Good evening, Minister," Kevin greeted MBulu.

"How's it, M'Bulu?" Bill also greeted M'Bulu.

"I am good, Bill, thank you." M'Bulu answered. "And good afternoon, Chairman."

Bill saw Kevin bristle a bit.

"Minister," Kevin began, "I want to address something before we jump into the call."

"Certainly, Chairman." M'Bulu answered. "Please do."

"Thank you," Kevin began. "I am uncomfortable with the level of familiarity between you and my employee. I feel like you and Doctor Fibulee have discussions and commit this company to plans before he has the authorization of the Board. I'm glad that you have a comfort level with him, because I believe that makes it easier for our organizations to work well together, but I need both of you to respect the organizational boundaries going forward."

"I see," M'Bulu began. "Chairman, when you and I spoke several days ago, and I asked you to please consider promoting Doctor Fibulee to the office of President of Global Operations for your company, you said you would make that happen. I know that you told Doctor Fibulee that he had the authority to enter into contracts on behalf of GlobalForce. It seems to me that having a good rapport with your clients can only be beneficial to the continued success of those projects. But, if you are uncomfortable with your representative maintaining a good working relationship, and even friendship, with members of your client organization, I can direct the other projects elsewhere. Please let me know how you would like to proceed."

Kevin didn't immediately respond, so Bill spoke up.

"Minister, Chairman, if I may?" Bill decided to match the formality. "I can understand Chairman Blanchard's concerns that his newest employee and newest company officer appears to be going rogue and flying all over the world and being chummy with the clients and wanting to open satellite offices. Were I in his position, I would have the same concerns. So, Chairman, I apologize for overstepping, and I hope you understand just how seriously I take this immense trust you and the Board have placed in me, and I hope that you understand that I will not abuse that trust or authority. Minister, I also appreciate all the trust that you have placed in me over the last two weeks, and I also take that very seriously. I will promise to both of you that I will do my best to meet expectations from both of you, and I also promise you both that at some point, I am going to push back on both of you in certain situations. You both have high expectations for me and for my team, and I will take those responsibilities very seriously."

Kevin and M'Bulu both recited platitudes, and they all sounded hollow to Bill.

"With all that having been said," Bill continued, "the new Pretoria

GlobalForce office will be opened on my next trip down there. I will be hiring my team for the NSC project, and they will work in the Arizona office, and will not work on the Switch project. In two years, I will transfer one of the NSC developers to the Pretoria office, though if she has immigration issues with her child, then she will probably relocate to New Zealand and work virtually from there. I know New Zealand is twelve hours ahead of Pretoria, and fifteen hours by air from Joburg, but we either have a satellite office almost equidistant from Phoenix and Pretoria, or we don't have Eileen."

M'Bulu remained silent, but Kevin began to protest.

"Kevin," Bill interrupted him. "I need certain team members, and Eileen is key. And having satellite offices in three segments of the planet under very different governments and political environments can't hurt. Plus, I will be charging that expense to the client anyway."

"And the client will authorize those expenses," M'Bulu interjected.

"I am going to run these projects the way I know how to run them, or I will not run them at all," Bill tested his boundaries again. He waited a moment to hear if either Kevin or M'Bulu were going to say anything.

When they didn't, Bill pressed it.

"Agreed?"

"Agreed." M'Bulu responded.

"I guess we don't have a choice, agreed." Kevin answered, begrudging Bill more authority than he had planned to.

"You do have a choice, Kevin," Bill countered. "You can always terminate me. And I know you can always terminate me. Arizona is a 'Right To Work' state, you can terminate me for no reason at all. So, please don't feel held hostage; you're my boss, and I won't forget that."

Kevin seemed to accept that.

"Moving on," Bill wanted to get the call back on track. "What did you two want to discuss on this call, and do I need to be here for this discussion?"

"Yes, I want you in here for this call." Kevin answered. "Minister, the Board voted to open the satellite office in Pretoria, as Bill mentioned. I do have a concern about it being empty ten weeks out of every quarter."

"I am pleased to hear that your Board of Directors has made that decision, Kevin," M'Bulu answered, trying to reduce the tension. "I had a thought about the office, if possible, I would like to sublet part of your office from you. We have a contractor that works for us that needs a place to work. The Ministry office we have him using is actually someone else's office, and right now, the contractor is working from home, and the security of that arrangement concerns me. If you would be willing to let us have part of that office, we would do the build-out and provide the security to the office."

Kevin considered it for a moment.

"I think that would be great, M'Bulu," Kevin answered, joining in the less formal tone. "When Bill is there next, he is authorized to lease an office, and we'll authorize him to set up the sublease with your ministry."

"I am very happy to hear that," M'Bulu schmoozed. "And now, Kevin, I would like to discuss a few other matters with you that do not require Bill's attention."

"Hey, I can take a hint," Bill stood. "Gentlemen, have a good afternoon, M'Bulu it was good to hear from you, as I am sure it was good for you to hear us."

Bill added that last part to make sure M'Bulu knew that Bill knew that the office was bugged, and that M'Bulu was listening to them. Kevin didn't catch the message.

CHAPTER 51: ONE DOWN

IN 2 YESRS ULL BE TXFRD TO HTE PRETORIA OFFOCE BUT WILL WORJ REMOTWLT FROM UR PLQCE IN NEW ZXELADN

As usual, Bill cringed at the spelling in the text message, but assumed Eileen would understand. It took her a few minutes to respond. Bill looked for his email from Heinrich while waiting.

AND MY BONUS?

ITKL BE IN UR COMTRAC5... WILL BR A PERGORMABCE BONUS ND I WIL; EZPECT U TO MEETY TEH REQRMNTS

Hopefully she took the hint. Bill waited for her response.

SEE YOU IN THE MORNING

Bill let out a little whoop.

I KNOQ

One down, Bill thought to himself.

Bill sent a message to Kyle to verify lunch the following day, and to Mark to try to set up lunch. Then he packed up his laptop and let his security detail know he was ready to head home.

Before leaving, Bill stopped by Connie's office to let her know the updated terms to put into Eileen's employment contract. Connie raised an eyebrow at the relocation and bonus, but told Bill that the papers would be ready in the morning. Bill thanked Connie and left. He could still hear Kevin and M'Bulu talking on the phone in Kevin's office. He looked forward to hearing both interpretations of that call in the morning as well.

On the drive home, he read the secure message from Heinrich. While the control bit wasn't quite working yet, Heinrich had a new idea involving something called a "God Particle" that the CERN guys had already located. Apparently this God Particle was stable, and at least one other experiment had successfully attached other atoms to it.

Heinrich went on for another three paragraphs, and Bill understood none of it. He decided that he would have a secure chat with Heinrich in the morning.

CHAPTER 52: PREVIOUS ITERATIONS

Bill woke to find a text message waiting for him from Mark.

HEY MAN, I HEAR UR TRYING TO GET THE BAND BACK
TOGETHER

Indeed, I am, Bill thought to himself.

I AMN. WANY TO GRT LUBCH ANF LET MW MAKE AM
OFFERT?

Mark took a while to respond, which was fine. Bill made himself breakfast and settled in to re-read the message from Heinrich and see if he could understand more of it now that he had a fresh brain.

Even with an energy drink and a healthy breakfast of peanut butter and jelly on toasted sourdough, the last three paragraphs of Heinrich's email were still beyond comprehension.

DUDE GET A NEW PHONE. THEY MAKE THEM WITH
VOICE TYPING NOW. YES WE CAN HAVE LUNCH, BUT I
LIKE MY CURRENT JOB.

Well, crap, Bill thought to himself.

WEDNWSDAT AT 1145 WORL FOR U?

Bill still had to try, Eileen's answer was originally no, too.

YUP. WHERE?

TEH NUNNRT. SER U THEB

The Nunnery was Mark's favorite burger joint, so maybe that would soften him up.

Returning to Heinrich's email and his inability to grasp it, he pulled up Heinrich on the video chat.

"Hey, how's it, Bill?" Heinrich greeted Bill after a few seconds, adjusting his headset as he answered.

"Good, Heinrich. Feel like explaining this God-element concept to me in a manner that I can understand?"
Heinrich chuckled.

"Yeah, I figured that one would be a challenging read," Heinrich responded. "I didn't try to dumb it down at all on that message, figured there was no point, because you'd be calling me about it anyway."

"And you were right," Bill answered. "So, let me suspend all disbelief and assume everything you are telling me is science fiction. Now explain it to me. I'll stop you and ask questions if you get too far ahead of me."

"Fair enough," Heinrich began his explanation. "First, imagine two bosons that have no mass, except in a vacuum."

"What's a 'boson'?" Bill interrupted.

"This is going to be a long call," Heinrich responded. "For the purposes of this discussion, think of them as two different tennis balls, but they have no mass, and no electrical charge."

"Got it, please continue."

"In a vacuum," Heinrich continued, "these bosons have mass, and can't move. When not in a vacuum, they have no mass and can travel inconceivably vast distances faster than light."

"Up is down, left is right," Bill summarized.

"For the purposes of this conversation, yes," Heinrich granted. "But there is a particle that was discovered a couple years ago called the 'Higgs Boson' that can theoretically control them in either state. And several teams have been running experiments on the Higgs Boson to test its control over the W and Z bosons."

"You lost me again there, bud," Bill interrupted again. "What are those?"

"Those are your tennis balls," Heinrich clarified.

"Then why didn't you say 'tennis balls'?" Bill asked.

Heinrich sighed.

"Fine," Heinrich resumed, now using his "talking to a child" voice. "The tennis balls with no mass that I gave you earlier have either a W or a Z on them. Better?"

Bill nodded.

Heinrich continued.

"So, I need to use a group of the tennis bosons to do my encryptions and calculations in my quantum dimension computer. I also need them to do my data transfer. If I am to use them to construct the quantum dimension computer, I need them to have mass, so they have to be in a vacuum, but if I'm using them to transfer data, then I need them to have no mass, so no vacuum. This may sound arrogant, but I have figured those two concepts out using the results of our tests at the Collider in Geneva, but I still have not figured out the method of controlling them. Literally I need to have the data start out not in a vacuum so it can travel across the universe in no time, think of that as my data network, then when they are ready to be computed, I need them to retain the information they are carrying, but convert to having mass and jump into a vacuum environment, do the calculations, then convert back to non-vacuum and non-mass states, and return the information across the impossibly vast space. And I need all of that to happen instantaneously, literally in an unmeasurably small amount of time."

Heinrich took a breath to let Bill process what he had just explained.

"Huh." Bill responded, knowing that Heinrich would hate that response the most. "So…"

"I swear to Odin," Heinrich interrupted, "if you make a 'Stargate' joke right now, I will blow up the planet."

Bill laughed hard.

"No, no 'Stargate' jokes," Bill promised. "But let me ask a few questions, as if I actually understood you."

"Go ahead," Heinrich encouraged.

"If I remember my Theory Of Relativity correctly, and I don't", Bill began, having difficulty even assembling a coherent question, "those data-carrying borons are intended to travel way faster than light, but that's a physical impossibility, because the closer they get to the speed of light, the more stationary they become, right?"

"That's actually pretty close," Heinrich was impressed. "A couple clarifications, though. First, they are called 'bosons'. Second, your Relativity understanding is correct, but doesn't apply to quantum elements, and we have found that the Relativity limits don't necessarily apply in some of the dimensions we have sampled. Actually, the limits imposed by Relativity as we know it appear to be the exception, and don't exist in most of the dimensions we have tested so far."

"Like a space-warp field in a certain star-travelling show I used to watch when I was younger?" Bill asked.

"Yes," Heinrich was happy with the progress Bill was making. "In that show, they get around the faster-than-light limitations by forming a bubble around the ship that is in a different dimension from our universe, and that dimension doesn't have the same speed restrictions that our space has. Then when they get where they want to be, they slow down to sub-light speeds and collapse the bubble, and drive around on more conventional propulsion."

"Yep, I knew that," Bill answered. "But that *is* science fiction. You're trying to tell me that you have to use those concepts to make the Q'Loud work, right?"

"Something similar," Heinrich continued, "but in our case, we have mapped the dimensions that we need for the two boson states. I just am having difficulties controlling them consistently as they change states and traverse dimensions. I made a little progress on that over the weekend."

"I am probably going to regret asking this question," Bill asked anyway, "but what are the difficulties?"

"Glad you asked!" Heinrich knew this was going to get too esoteric for Bill, but he went ahead with the explanation anyway. "The W and Z bosons have no charge, which means we can't assign them a binary value. Follow me so far?"

"Yes actually, please continue," Bill answered, happy that he followed that much of the explanation.

"Good, then strap in, this is where it gets murky for laymen," Heinrich warned. "In a few of the dimensions we have mapped, the W and Z bosons, even though they have no charge, can *transport* a charge without actually becoming charged. So, in those dimensions, we can get the data through, even though it's only one bit per boson."

"So, if you have unlimited speed," Bill tried to follow, "you could theoretically shoot enough of these tennis balls laden with one bit each across the universe to transmit the entire knowledge of humanity in a time frame so short that we could not measure it, right? In that dimension?"

"That's actually precisely correct," Heinrich was impressed, so he continued. "Now, in my chosen other dimension for processing, there is no heat, at least in the way that we perceive it. And it's something we are calling a 'perfect vacuum', because it provides a space that has absolutely nothing in it. No dark matter, no light, no atoms, no bosons, not even vacuum as we know it, just absolutely nothing. But if we shoot a glob of bosons or even atoms into it, they just clump together in whatever form they land in as they touch each other. We couldn't get them to form into anything coherent at first. So we had to figure out a method to spray the bosons into that dimension in a way that would form a framework onto which we can spray the atom to build a processor."

"Okay, you lost me again," Bill tried to follow, but this was just beyond comprehension, even in a science fiction setting. "How can you possibly build a computer atom by atom?"

"We use helium atoms," Heinrich stated as if it was common knowledge. "More specifically, we use one helium atom as a processor. So we squirt in the boson framework, fire a helium atom onto the framework, and then run the data through the framework, get our answer, retrieve the new boson data set, and translate that data set to the Switch balancer."

"Of course, helium, how could I have not known that?" Bill answered sarcastically. "So, what's the catch?"

"The catch," Heinrich was prepared for this question, "is traversing five dimensions with the data sets. We thought we had it figured out, but then we started getting unrelated answers coming back from the processor dimension, so we are working on encapsulating the packet more effectively as it travels through all five dimensions."

"Wait, what?" Bill wasn't sure he had heard Heinrich correctly. "How can we get an unrelated answer if we are opening a new pocket in a dimension, building the processor from scratch each time, and then destroying that pocket each time? There is nothing else to answer except that individual transaction. How can an answer be unrelated? And I thought you said there was perfectly nothing in it."

Well…" Heinrich began.

"What did you do?" Bill interrupted Heinrich.

He expected to hear that they had actually destroyed the universe and that this reality was just a puff of relativistic smoke from the remnants of their shared demise.

"Sooo, in order to traverse the five dimensions," Heinrich began, "we figured out that we can use gravitons to kind of shepherd the bosons across the dimensions."

Heinrich waited for the question.

"Well, of course you would use gravitons," Bill answered. "But pretend I don't know what those are, and why they were used."

"Gravitons are radiation created only by black holes," Heinrich continued his explanation. "The thing about gravitons is that they exist outside of time and space. There are scientists who think they have found ghosts of black holes from previous iterations of the universe, because there are large pockets of gravitons in various locations of our universe without a nearby black hole to generate them."

"Get the hell out of here," Bill interrupted. "*Previous iterations*' of the universe? Like previous universes from before the Big Bang?"

"Multiple iterations, yes."

He let Bill process that concept for a moment, then continued.

"Fortunately, the gravitons have the same properties in the other dimensions that we are using as in ours, so they are a perfect inert carrier for us. But the problem we had is that, while the gravitons were able to easily traverse the dimensions and carry the bosons with them, we didn't always get *our* gravitons back, and those foreign gravitons didn't have our bosons on them."

"Wait!" Now Bill was truly freaked out. "Who's gravitons did you get back?! And for that matter, who's bosons did you get back?!"

"You're misunderstanding me," Heinrich tried to calm Bill. "The gravitons we got back didn't have bosons at all, they were just random gravitons. We didn't actually get any communications from someone."

"If you had," Bill felt better now, "the first question I would have wanted you to ask is if your little experiment is what ended their universe."

Heinrich laughed.

"I already asked that, they said no," Heinrich joked.

"Good," Bill laughed at the answer. "Then we can proceed. Anyway, so now, you just need a way to keep your graviton - boson - helium network packets together, right?"

"Right," Heinrich was happy that Bill had followed the explanation this far. "So, we are experimenting with the Higgs Boson now to keep the packet together."

"Is that the Z or the W boson?" Bill asked, trying to tie this all together.

"It's neither actually," Heinrich explained. "The Higgs Boson is being called the 'God particle', because it can control the Z and W bosons and their two sister bosons, which I won't try to explain, because they don't calculate into this project. I tested a full packet over the weekend with a Higgs, and the error that returned was that the data bosons were out of sequence upon arrival at the processor. But the packet successfully traversed the dimensions for the first time, and contained only the items that we sent."

"I'm not clear on something though," Bill needed to find more dots to connect. "That dimension is empty, you said. So how are you getting other gravitons coming back? If there is nothing there, then there can't be gravitons either, right?"

"That's true," Heinrich answered, "but we put gravitons in there, and remember that gravitons exist outside of time and space, so we think we started getting some of our earlier empty gravitons back. By encapsulating the packets now, we shouldn't be getting any of the graviton debris."

"So you *did* break the universe?" Bill asked.

"No, gravitons can't be created or destroyed, just moved around," Heinrich danced. "We moved them into that dimension, and they will remain there until moved by someone else in one of the iterations of the universe after us."

"I'm not cool with that," Bill grumbled. "We have no idea what that may do to the processors. And basically, you took a pristine beach and threw your picnic trash on it. Don't do that anymore. And if you find a way to clean it up, please do. Anyway, congrats on the test results."

"Acknowledged, boss," Heinrich accepted the admonishment.

Bill could see that Heinrich was really excited about this test result, but he still felt uneasy about what they were doing, because this was one test of one transaction. There were over forty billion transactions running through the Switch network per day right now, and if they had to do more and more of these transactions per day, literally crossing five dimensions on the round trip, it just felt to Bill like forty billion or more chances per day to have something bad happen; something that they could not even conceive of, but would change, or possibly destroy, literally everything.

"One more question, Heinrich," Bill concluded, "you keep talking about five dimensions, but I have only counted three in our conversation. What are the other two?"

"We are only using three," Heinrich clarified, "but we are traversing five. Start in ours, that's one, goes to the next dimension to load up the values onto the W and Z bosons, that's two, then cross into the processor dimension, that's three, then back through the dimension with the new values on the bosons, that's four, then back to ours so we can send the answer through the Q'Loud, that's five."

"Got it." Bill let it sit. "Keep me informed on the progress. Meanwhile, I need to get to work."

"Yep, will do, boss," Heinrich responded, and disconnected the call.

Bill closed his laptop and got ready for work.

CHAPTER 53: ECCENTRIC

Bill arrived at the office just before 9:00. He saw a folder on his desk labelled "Chamberlain, Eileen". He checked the inside and found two copies of the employment contract with the terms he had requested, along with the usual HR paperwork.

As he was logging into his laptop and putting away the case, Kevin walked into Bill's office and sat down at the conference table.

"These really are comfortable chairs," Kevin commented. "Anyway, I wanted to bring you up to speed on my conversation with Minister Mabusa yesterday afternoon."

Bill wanted to be able to have a safe conversation, so he took control before Kevin said anything else.

"Good, I'd like to hear about it," Bill began. "I was going to walk over and get a drink next door, want to go with me?"

Bill stood, left his phone on his desk, and headed towards the door before Kevin could protest.

Kevin just followed Bill out the door, slightly irritated.

"What the hell was that?" Kevin asked as they walked.

"Because I assumed you were going to discuss some classified information from one of the projects," Bill exaggerated, "and we were not in a secure room. I needed a Dr. Pepper, and by being out here, we can talk

190

and I can get my drink."

"Fine, but you're really acting … eccentric." Kevin growled.

That made Bill laugh.

"Kevin, three weeks ago, I was sitting in an office, happily annoying my managers and bringing a steady flow of revenue into a company to make the shareholders happy. Then sixteen days ago, I got on a plane to fly to the other side of the world and start working on a project that literally controls all of the financial transaction authorizations in the world, and then got asked to lead development on probably the most privacy-killing project in the history of the world. So, I hope you will forgive me for occasionally forgetting my manners or my position within the company, because I'm still really off balance."

Kevin thought for a few moments.

"You're right." Kevin finally answered. "We really did throw you into an unusual situation with no warning, and this whole thing has snowballed more than any of us could have ever expected. So, yes, you're forgiven. Please keep me in the loop, and if I feel like I'm missing information, I'll ask you."

"Thank you," Bill truly was grateful for Kevin's understanding. "And thank you for backing me with the Board yesterday."

"You're welcome," Kevin replied. "Now, tell me why they hid the Switch 3 location from you, and I want to know if they are building another Switch."

"Fair enough," Bill had to tread very carefully. "They hid the Switch 3 because they are concerned about security for it. It's the most advanced of the three boxes, and they wanted to keep it as secure as possible. As far as I know, only a couple people and the ministry know where it is actually installed. I don't actually think the people that work in that server farm know what the box is. And to answer your second question, yes, they are designing more Switches."

"And are we participating in the design and deployment of those new Switches?" Kevin knew there was more going on that he had not been told, and he wanted an answer.

Bill stopped walking and turned to face Kevin.

"Kevin…" Bill started to lie, then paused to reconsider his words before he continued. "You know what? Yes. Yes, we are participating in the design, development, and deployment of newer, faster Switches. Our new contract on that project currently has us assisting in the improvement of the encryption, and has me as the project manager, because I know the least about the encryption process. But M'Bulu trusts me to lead it."

"Why did Keith vanGreig quit?" Kevin asked, surprising Bill. "Yes, I know he quit, but the reason for his sudden departure from the project was given as 'he decided to retire'. I know that's bullshit. Tell me why he really quit."

"Okay," Bill took a deep breath and decided to say as much as he could. "The level of encryption that is being designed is a quantum leap farther than anything that any government on the planet currently has. Keith threw an absolute shit fit in M'Bulu's office when Heinrich explained the details to us, and said that such technology can easily be misused, and could easily endanger humanity. When M'Bulu chose to continue the project anyway, Keith resigned. He said he was going to Paris to spend time with his son."

Bill knew that only he and Heinrich and M'Bulu could know about the Q'Loud right now, so he excluded that information from his explanation to Kevin.

"Well, that fits with what Keith told me when he called me," Kevin seemed happy with the explanation.

The two finished their walk in silence. Bill was horrified that Keith had contacted Kevin to tell him that he had quit, because Keith and Kevin shouldn't have known each other. M'Bulu needed to know about this. But Bill was also happy to hear that Keith had not spilled the most classified information.

When they got back from the store, Bill sat down at his desk and asked Kevin to close the office door. Kevin did, then sat down.

"Kevin," Bill began, knowing that he was in range of the bug now, "I really want to know what Keith told you."

Kevin recounted that Keith had contacted him because Jerry was no longer with the company, and as one of the key members of the project,

Keith felt like he needed to tell the head of the joint venture partner that he was no longer involved. Keith said that "Mabusa", not bothering to use his title anymore, had hidden some of the key elements of the project from both him and Bill, and that Keith could no longer work under those conditions. When Kevin pressed him about the key elements, Keith discussed the dangers of the new encryption model, saying that it was at such a level that it could be used to control the population, and possibly even destroy society.

Bill considered what Kevin had just told him.

"Well," Bill finally responded, "I disagree with Keith's explanation and assessment of the technology. I don't think it will be used to control the population. I think the encryption will give us the ability to further secure our information. I am uncomfortable that Keith thought he should reach out to you, because he worked for Johan, not GlobalForce or Jerry, so it was inappropriate. Anyway, I'm disappointed in him. I liked Keith, and I considered him a friend, but this was an unacceptable breach of protocol."

"I am disappointed that you didn't tell me," Kevin stated.

"Honestly, Kevin, I had a lot of other things on my mind, and I didn't think it was important," Bill answered honestly. "I figured that if Johan or M'Bulu thought it was important enough, they would tell you. And with that in mind, you should also know that one of the other developers on Keith's team walked off the job when he didn't get to go with us to install Switch 3."

Bill figured that would calm Kevin down.

"Why didn't you tell me about that before now?" Kevin pressed.

"Because, again, he wasn't our employee," Bill was starting to get irritated. "Keith and the other guy, I think his name was Amir, were not our employees. I didn't even know the other guy. I had met him maybe twice, and I don't think I actually ever spoke to him. If you want me to report to you about every person that comes on or off of any of the projects we are involved with, then I will let you know, but that seems like a bunch of unnecessary information."

"Howzabout you let me decide what is and is not unnecessary information?" Kevin snapped back angrily.

"Yes, sir, I will keep you informed of any personnel changes on any of the projects for which we are contracted," Bill responded formally.

"Thank you. Anything else?" Kevin started to calm down.

"You're aware that Eileen Chamberlain starts this morning, right?" Bill checked Kevin's memory.

"Yes, I am aware," Kevin answered. "I also know you have two more of your previous team that you want to bring on board, and Minister Mabusa has approved their expenses on the project. So, congrats on your team."

"Thanks," Bill responded, trying to not sound too excited to have his team back.

"Okay, I'll let you get to work," Kevin stood to leave Bill's office. "Please continue to communicate with me."

"Will do, boss," Bill answered as Kevin left his office.

I wonder how long until M'Bulu calls him. Bill wondered to himself.

Bill saw that it was almost time for Eileen to arrive, so he grabbed her file and headed out of his office to the reception desk. Bill was glad that Kandi had stayed on.

"Hey Kandi," Bill said as he approached the desk, "Eileen Chamberlain will be arriving in a few minutes. She's my new programmer. Can you bring her back to office twelve when she gets here?"

"No problem, Bill," Kandi answered in her usual bubbly style.

"Thanks," Bill said as he turned and headed back to office number twelve, which would be Eileen's office. He sat at her small conference table and reviewed her file while he waited.

Bill heard Kevin's phone ring down the hallway, and heard Kevin greet M'Bulu. After a moment, he heard Kevin's door close.

That didn't take long, Bill thought to himself.

Bill continued to read through the employment agreement, and found that it was just as he had asked for it to be. He was glad Connie had not given him a hard time about it. After a few minutes, he heard the door chime at the other end of the hallway, and heard Kandi and Eileen talk for a moment, and then heard their voices coming towards the office. Kandi shepherded Eileen into the office, then headed back to the front desk.

"You're late," Bill said, pointing to the clock which read 10:01.

"Whatever," Eileen responded.

"I'm glad you took the offer," Bill relaxed. "I think you're really going to like this project."

"We'll see," Eileen answered before setting her things on the desk. Then she sat down at the table with Bill. "Do you have my contract?"

"Indeed I do." Bill opened the file and slid the contract to Eileen.

Eileen turned the papers and began reading. She made a show of taking her time to read the four page employment agreement, then finally signed and dated the last page, and slid it to Bill for his signature. Bill signed it and slid her other employment docs to her for her to fill out later.

"Nope, I want a copy of that first," Eileen stated.

Bill pulled out another copy of the contract from the folder and slid it to her to sign, which she did and gave it back to Bill for his signature.

"It's as if you don't trust me," Bill acted hurt.

"I do trust you," Eileen responded. "But this is a really good contract, and I want it to be legally enforceable."

"Fair enough." Bill accepted her answer. "I have a lunch with Kyle in a bit to try to buy his soul, too. Because we are negotiating his employment, I can't have you at that lunch, but if he accepts, he'll be here soon enough. Let me take you to meet Connie from HR and Kevin the Chairman of the Board, then I'm going to head out. Your laptop is on your desk, it's new out of the box, so you can spend your afternoon getting that configured. Wifi password is in the top left drawer of your desk."

"Cool."

They walked to Connie's office, and Bill made the introductions. After that, they walked to Kevin's office, where the door was open again. Bill introduced Eileen to Kevin, and then escorted her back to her office.

"My office is the next one down the hall if you need me," Bill said as he dropped Eileen off back at her office.

"No problem," Eileen responded, then went to work on her laptop.

Bill went back to his office and busied himself with email until it was time to leave for lunch with Kyle.

Just before 11:00, Bill saw Connie, Kandi, and Eileen walk past his door, chatting and laughing.

"Hey!" Bill hollered at them.

Connie stuck her head into his office.

"Yes?" She asked.

"What's going on?" Bill knew something was up.

"We are going to lunch with Eileen to hear all of the stories about you from your previous job." Connie answered happily, then disappeared back to the lobby.

"None of it is true!" Bill yelled after them.

Crap, it'll all be true. Bill thought to himself. *Oh well.*

Bill grabbed his keys and wallet out of his desk and grabbed his phone and headed out to work his recruiting magic on Kyle.

"Hey man!" Kyle was happy to see Bill.

"Hey back!" Bill was grateful that Kyle was here so he could keep building his team.

They got a table and began catching up.

"So, you were in South Africa?" Kyle jumped right in. "That's wild.

You've only been gone two weeks, and already you're a world traveler."

"Dude, 'wild' doesn't begin to describe the last two weeks of my life," Bill said, laughing. "You wouldn't believe half of it if I told you, but let me tell you about the project that really made me sell my soul."

Bill explained to Kyle the scope and breadth of the South African National Secure Citizen card project. Kyle was as horrified and interested as Bill had been. They discussed the project in great detail over the meal, and as the plates were being cleared away, Kyle asked the big question.

"So, what's the catch?"

"There is no catch," Bill replied.

"There has to be a catch," Kyle countered.

"Nope, there is no catch." Bill explained further. "I have to spend two to three weeks per quarter in Pretoria, and there are a bunch of developers on the project that work for a joint venture partner down in Johannesburg, but I'm the project manager on the whole thing. You and Eileen will work from the office here, and you will be the senior developers on it. South Africa has a big problem with talent exports, and they apparently have no senior database developers down there. The two developers here are good smart chip programmers, but not database developers. So, you and Eileen are my rock stars. I'm having lunch tomorrow with Marky to try to get him on board too."

"How did you end up with this gig to begin with?" Kyle asked Bill

"Jerry," Bill answered. "Apparently, he had been talking me up as the project manager for this thing for a while, but couldn't pull me out of LookAtMe because of a conflict of interest. When they killed our work there, it gave me a reason to leave, and now yada yada yada, we get to work for South Africa."

"Just like that, huh?" Kyle laughed.

"Yeah, just like that," Bill responded with faux seriousness. "Don't overthink it. Seriously though, as much of a challenge as this project has been, Jerry did me a favor. I love this project as much as I hate it, and I wouldn't have it without him."

"Well, this sounds fun." Kyle appeared to be on board. "But, you're not going to get Marky. When he and I stepped on at Verve, we were immediately placed at the lead of the project, and we are royalty over there. I'll accept the very generous offer you're going to make me, but he likes the attention. I doubt you're going to get him."

"Well," Bill accepted Kyle's assessment. "I still gotta try."

"Hells yeah you do," Kyle agreed. "So tell me about my very generous offer."

Bill explained the offer to Kyle, which was essentially the same as the one Eileen had signed, just without the maternity accommodations, half of the bonus, and without the relocation.

"Damn dude," Kyle liked the offer. "Yeah, I'll take it. I'll give two weeks' notice tomorrow, but I'd like the offer today if possible. Can I start early if they walk me out?"

"Let's head back to my office now, and I'll do up your contract," Bill suggested. "And yes, you can start as soon as you're out of there."

"Cool." Kyle responded.

Bill sent a message to Connie to let her know he was inbound with Kyle to do up his contract, and to let her know the terms.

———————————

Bill gave Kyle the address, and they both drove back to the office. Bill escorted Kyle up to the office, introduced him to Kandi, walked him quickly past Eileen's office, and down to Connie. After the introductions were made to Connie, Bill took him back to Eileen's office to let them catch up while Connie finished up the employment contract. Eileen was very happy that Kyle was stepping on, and the two of them chatted happily while Bill excused himself to go sit with Connie.

"Interesting terms," Connie said quietly to Bill as he stepped back into her office.

"I know," Bill didn't push it.

"You know that this would not fly anywhere else, right?" Connie admonished Bill.

"Yes, I am very aware of that," Bill agreed, "but M'Bulu was very insistent that this NSC project be active and making progress and to beta within two years, and for that to happen, I need my team, especially if I am going to be splitting my time between that and the Switch project. And since I need my team, and the NSC project is important to him, I can do what I need to do in order to get my team."

"Okay," Connie replied ironically.

Connie typed a couple more items, then turned to her printer and retrieved two copies of the employment agreement for Kyle from the paper tray and handed them to Bill.

"Go in peace," Connie joked.

"And also with you," Bill responded in kind, and left Connie's office, headed to Eileen's office.

"Have you two caught up?" Bill asked them both. Both agreed that they had. "Good, I need to borrow Kyle for a moment."

Kyle excused himself from the conversation and followed Bill to an empty office, where they both sat at a small conference table. Bill slid both copies of the employment agreement across the table to Kyle.

"As promised." Bill explained. "Please read it, and sign the bottom of both copies. One will be yours, the other mine. The start date is two weeks from tomorrow, but I will start you sooner if you show up unemployed on my doorstep before that."
Kyle read the agreement, signed both copies, and turned them to Bill for his signatures.

"Welcome aboard." Bill said happily.

"Glad to be here!" Kyle responded with a grin.

"This will be your office," Bill explained further. "We'll have a laptop for you when you step on. It'll be new from the box for you to configure, but we will be using a VPN for all company projects. Also, get comfortable with the armed security guards. They are compliments of the South African government, because this project is a secure project, so they hired guards for us all."

"That's all cool," Kyle answered. "I'll be fine with them. Looking forward to starting."

"Awesome." Bill finished up. "Okay, go give Eileen a hug, and get out of my office. Let me know when you're starting."

"Cool," Kyle stood up. "Catch me later."

"Will do." Bill walked back to his office and prepared for his call with M'Bulu.

Bill closed his door, then loaded up the Q'Loud VPN on his laptop and plugged in his headset. Then he logged into the video chat service and waited for M'Bulu to beep him.

The chat client pinged about five minutes later. Bill clicked the Answer button.

"Good evening, Minister Mabusa," Bill greeted M'Bulu formally.

"Good afternoon, Doctor Fibulee," M'Bulu greeted Bill with the same formality. "Now that we have been formal, how is your day so far, Bill?"

"It has been good so far, thank you," Bill began. "My database resource Eileen Chamberlain started this morning, and my second team member Kyle Dobson just signed his contract with us a few minutes ago. I have lunch with my third team member tomorrow, but I am being told by both him and Kyle that he will likely not step on. I'll take my best shot anyway."

"If you can not convince him, how damaging is that to the project?" M'Bulu asked.

"Well, Marky and Kyle and Eileen and I wrote some serious magic together at LookAtMe," Bill bragged a little. "But it was a team effort. The project will already be hampered because I won't be a developer on the project, so we'd be down to three people if Marky does join us. If not, then we are down to two. So, basically, we would operate at about half the speed that we did at LookAtMe."

"If he doesn't join you, can the project be completed in two years?" M'Bulu pressed further.

"No." Bill stated with a sigh. "I mean, even if he doesstep on, two years is a stretch. Either way, I'd like to modify the contract to make it three years to beta, especially if I can't get him."

"We can discuss that," M'Bulu granted. "Would more money help convince him?"

"Money is always a motivator," Bill agreed, "but Marky likes being the center of attention. In our group at the previous gig, it worked in our dynamic, but that won't happen here, and at Verve, apparently he is worshipped. So, yes, money might help, but the amount of money it would take is not proportional to the other team members, and truth be told, Marky was the weakest programmer of the team. My inclination is to offer him the same as Eileen and Kyle, but with a much smaller bonus, and if he won't accept the offer, we leave him be."

"Very well," M'Bulu offered, "I will leave it to you, Please update me on that after your lunch tomorrow. If we need to extend the contract, we can certainly discuss that. But I may need you in Pretoria more to justify it."

"Of course you would," Bill laughed.

"As to your discussion with Kevin today, do you have concerns that he will interfere in any of these projects?" M'Bulu asked, turning the conversation awkward for Bill.

"Minister," Bill began, intentionally making this part formal. "Kevin Blanchard is my direct boss. I need to respect that. You obviously know the conversations that are had in the Board meetings, and in Kevin's office as much as in my office, but while I do try to make sure our client is happy with our work and progress, I ultimately need to follow the directive of my boss. With that having been said, I would be disappointed if he curtailed my team's ability to make solid progress on the projects for the client, and I would be upset if we lost projects because of his or the Board's decisions. I would hope that the management team and Board of Directors of the company would continue to make decisions that further the ability of the technical team to enhance shareholder value by allowing me to do my job."

"I appreciate your candor, Doctor," M'Bulu maintained the formality. "We share that hope. Let us continue to work together as effectively as we have so far, and if your management team does take counterproductive steps, then we can address them at such a time."

"Agreed, Minister," Bill finished up. "Let us not suffer future pain now."

"Well said," M'Bulu agreed. "How goes the Q'Loud project?"

"I had a good conversation with Heinrich this morning about that. He made a good breakthrough over the weekend. There are still many obstacles to overcome, but he seemed very positive about the progress." Bill hesitated for a moment. "I do have a couple of concerns, though, M'Bulu."

"Please explain them," M'Bulu encouraged.

"Part of the transaction process that Heinrich has tested and is building causes radiation pollution in a dimension that has none," Bill explained, trying to keep it as nontechnical as possible. "While I am not thrilled about that pollution, it appears that he has to develop a process to keep that pollution from interfering with the active transactions. This may cause us significant problems in the future, and I would like to resolve this issue now, rather than at some point after a catastrophic failure in the future."

"I see," M'Bulu considered Bill's concern. "If you can convince Heinrich to change paths enough to resolve this before your next trip, then that would be best. I will only join the argument if I have to. But if nothing else, we can have that discussion when you are here next time."

"Agreed," Bill wrapped up the call. "Thanks for the conversation. Be well."

"And you also, Bill." M'Bulu terminated the call.

Bill logged off the VPN and tossed his headset on the desk, and wondered who would be replacing Kevin.

CHAPTER 54: PROGRESS AND REGRESSION

Wednesday morning was mercifully uneventful, and Bill was glad for it. He spent the morning catching up on email and various reports before heading out for his lunch meeting.

Lunch with Marky went well, right up until Bill tried to convince him to leave Verve Software and join his team at GlobalForce. Mark loved the idea of the South African project, but really enjoyed the job at Verve. It wasn't that he didn't appreciate the really good offer Bill slid across the table, he just liked being a god at Verve. In the two weeks since Verve had brought Bill's system inhouse, they had brought on five new clients, all of which were larger than LookAtMe, and the challenge and magic was something that Marky didn't want to give up.

"So," Bill finally gave up, "there's nothing to convince you?"

"Sorry man," Mark replied. "It'd be great to work with you and Eileen again, but I really like it at Verve."

"Well, I'm sorry to not have you on the team here," Bill acquiesced. "But, I am glad you landed well after LookAtMe."

"Thanks," Mark responded. "I really do appreciate you getting me that gig. And, I haven't spent any of my severance yet, so that'll be a nice vacation when I take it."

Bill gave a half-chuckle at that.

Mark and Bill finished their lunch, caught up a bit more, then headed their separate directions.

Back at the office, Bill walked into his office to find Eileen sitting at his desk.

"That's my spot," Bill said in a deadpan voice.

"Where's Marky?" Eileen asked, ignoring him.

Bill sat down across from her.

"He's not coming," Bill answered her, the humor gone from his voice.

Eileen showed surprise on her face, then pondered a moment and nodded her head once before speaking.

"Bill, I want you to understand something," Eileen began. "You and I both know he was the weakest person on our team. Even though I have less years of experience, I am still a better developer than him. You have Kyle and you have me. And we both pretty much still code the same way we did before. So, don't sweat this. Just get us a little more time to complete the project, and we'll be fine."

Bill knew she was right.

"Yeah, you're right." Bill answered after a moment.

"I know," Eileen answered with no hesitation.

Bill chuckled at her response. At that moment, Bill heard the front door chime, and heard Kandi try to greet someone who just brushed past her.

"Dude, what the hell?!" Kyle stormed into Bill's office, surprising both Bill and Eileen.

"You tell me." Bill responded, still a bit startled.

"I just got walked out," Kyle answered, still annoyed. "I was just sitting there working, and my boss and someone from HR showed up and told me my services were no longer required, and that since I had not been there for ninety days, I was not entitled to any severance. Just walked me out. And

Mark was walking in as they walked me out. He wouldn't even look at me. I think he got me fired."

"Lame!" Eileen jumped into the conversation.

"Well, that fits with how lunch went with him," Bill answered. "Told me how much he loves it there, how much he loves the work there, how he likes being a god, stuff like that."

"Whatever." Kyle set it aside. "Looks like I need a job, so can I start now?"

"Yep, come on," Bill answered, and walked Kyle down to Connie's office to change his start date. "Once you're finished with Connie, you can hang out with Eileen, in her office, and let her bring you up to speed. I'll have your laptop here tomorrow morning. I'd spend the afternoon with you, but I have a call on another project in South Africa in a few minutes."

"No problem," Kyle answered, walking into Connie's office with Bill.

Bill explained the circumstance changes to Connie, who took it in stride and started changing Kyle's paperwork to show today as his start date.

Bill headed back to his office to catch up with Heinrich. That graviton pollution thing had really been bothering him since his conversation about it the previous morning.

GPT A MUMITE

While Bill waited for Heinrich to respond to his SMS message, and closed his office door, put on his headset, and logged into the Q'Loud VPN.

JUST GOT BACK FROM THE PUB

Oh great, Bill thought to himself.

SOBTR ENPUGJ TP TAKK?

If he's sober enough to understand what I just wrote, he's sober enough to talk. Bill really did need to get a phone with a larger keyboard.

A moment later, the video chat on the VPN pinged Bill to announce that Henrich was calling.

Bill accepted the call.

"How is it that I can type on my phone better with a few pints in me than you can sober?" Heinrich laughed in greeting.

"Whatever," Bill answered. "Someday I will get a new phone."

Heinrich laughed again.

"We all look forward to that day," Heinrich teased.

"I bet you do," Bill joked back. His phone then chimed the arrival of a new SMS message.

WE WILL HAVE A NEW PHONE WAITING FOR YOU NEXT
TIME YOU ARE HERE

That stunned Bill for a moment, it was from M'Bulu.

Bill set his phone back down, appreciative that M'Bulu was letting him know that his call was being monitored, but still not pleased about being monitored to begin with.

"You alright there, mate," Heinrich asked, now looking concerned at Bill's sudden change.

"Yes, sorry, just several things going on at once," Bill lied. "Okay, let's get down to the reason I wanted to talk with you. This whole concept of the particle pollution we are causing in that otherwise empty dimension is bothering me a lot."

"I thought you might come back to that," Heinrich responded calmly. "I could tell it bothered you yesterday morning when I told you about it."

"It did," Bill continued, "but I needed to think about it before I discussed it more in depth with you. There are two main reasons why it's bothering me, first that we literally are corrupting a pristine area seemingly without any hint of guilt over it, and second that our results were corrupted for a while by our own pollution. And instead of figuring out a way to clean up the pollution we left, and figuring out a way to not pollute with future packets, pack out our trash as it were, we just found a way to protect ourselves from our ever-growing pile of garbage. I'm not okay with that."

"Well, that's oversimplifying it a bit, mate..." Heinrich began to respond.

Bill cut him off before he could continue.

"How is that oversimplifying?" Bill felt his temper starting to come up. "We had an environment in which there was nothing. Literally nothing, correct?"

"Yes, but..."

Bill cut him off again.

"And we began introducing non-native particles into that environment, and then left them there when we were finished with them. Correct?"

"Also correct," Heinrich responded without trying to continue, knowing there would be more questions from Bill.

"And," Bill continued, "our early results were corrupted by that pollution. Correct?"

Heinrich just nodded, knowing where this would lead.

"And now," Bill wrapped up his arguments, "we are encapsulating our data elements with graviton particles, which we are also just leaving in that dimension. Correct?"

Heinrich nodded.

"So, explain to me where I am missing the point that this is not both morally reprehensible and scientifically dangerous," Bill concluded, and waited for Heinrich to give him a good answer.

Heinrich considered his response for a moment. Bill was pissing him off.

"Let me address the scientific question first," Heinrich finally answered, choosing his words carefully and keeping a tight control on his own anger. "There is no danger to leaving the particles in that dimension. We have our data encapsulated, so that won't be affected. We assume that dimension is at least as large as our dimension, so there's virtually no danger of having interaction between expired packets and new ones, and even if they do interact, it won't matter because of the packet encapsulation. And there is no chance, at least within the next trillion years, of that dimension filling up with the particles to the point that we can't create more packets there, so it's not our problem."

Bill was not impressed with the response.

"Heinrich," Bill needed to make Heinrich understand the scope of his impact. "Have you ever seen an old mine?"

That question surprised Heinrich.

"No, why?"

"I've toured a few old gold and copper mines in Colorado and Arizona," Bill explained. "Literally, there are dozens of square miles of mountains of debris where there used to be valleys or plains. All the debris they dug out of each mine to get to the minerals is just piled up. They were very efficient at hollowing out the natural mountains, and moving the guts of those natural mountains to a mile away or so, all in the name of progress. And they didn't give it another thought, because at the time, they figured they had a lot of space and wouldn't run out of it, so they just left the debris and didn't give it another thought. That's almost exactly what you're doing, but in this case, you're bringing materials into that dimension that would not otherwise ever get to that dimension naturally, and justifying it in the name of scientific gain."

"Well, that's not quite the same thing," Heinrich countered. "There's no chance of this being a problem, because…"

"Because there's no one to *report* it," Bill interrupted again.

"Why would anyone report it?" Heinrich was surprised by that response from Bill.

"That's just it, Heinrich," Bill clarified. "There are literally four people on this planet that know what you're actually doing. You, me, Keith, and M'Bulu. None of us is going to report it, but that doesn't make it less wrong."

"I hadn't thought about that," Heinrich answered. "But why would anyone report it?"

"My point is this," Bill was frustrated again. "There are only four humans in this dimension that know what you're doing. None of the four of us are going to report this to anyone, not that there is anyone we could report it to anyway. And that brings me back to the moral question: what gives us the right to shit all over a pristine dimension?"

"Bill, it's empty," Heinrich really wanted Bill to understand this. "There is no entity being damaged, either in this dimension or that one. And we have to assume that the other dimension is at least as large as is ours, so even at a hundred times more packets per day than the Switch network is processing right now, it will have an immeasurably small impact on that dimension, so no one is damaged."

"What if you're wrong?" Bill asked flatly.

That question also caught Heinrich off guard.

"I don't understand the question."

"What if you're wrong about the size of the dimension," Bill began to shred Heinrich's position. "What if it's the equivalent of a ten centimeter cube? I know you can calculate how quickly it would fill up if it was that size, and I am willing to bet that the answer is a fairly short number of days. What if there actually is some form of life in that dimension, but we just can't detect it, and that just makes you think it's empty, and that life form is damaged, or retaliates? Or what if your packets *do* start stepping on each other or interfering with each other?"

Bill paused for a moment to let Heinrich consider all those questions, then hit him with one last one.

"And, what if you're wrong and the dimension is really very small, like one cubic millimeter, and it becomes so packed with your particles that it hits critical mass, and you try to load in just one more tiny wafer-thin packet, and that puts it over. What happens to the LHC, the Q'Loud, the planet, the traversed dimensions, and even the very fabric of the universe? And don't try to tell me I'm being overdramatic about this, because you literally are doing interdimensional travel with these particles, so a failure like that would surely cascade, and would in all likelihood do so catastrophically."

Bill went silent, waiting as long as necessary for Heinrich to respond.

"You're right," Heinrich finally answered after several long seconds of thought.

The answer was not at all what Bill expected, and the surprise showed on his face, but he did not otherwise respond.

"Let me think on it," Heinrich continued, rubbing his face. "It's late, and the pints want me to sleep. I'll start figuring out a way to handle the packet cleanup."

"I appreciate that, Heinrich," Bill answered, happy with the progress. "Sleep well, and we will talk tomorrow."

"Yup, cheers."

Heinrich disconnected the call, closed his laptop, stood and walked towards the bedroom, shutting off the lights as he went.

If I destroy the universe, no one will know anyway, Heinrich mumbled to himself as he faded into sleep.

M'Bulu didn't seem as concerned as Bill, and that was also really bothering Bill.

"How large is the chance really that he will destroy all of creation?" M'Bulu asked.

"That's just it, M'Bulu," Bill was exasperated at this point. "We don't have any way of knowing. If I may suggest a compromise on this, maybe we can move forward without anyone being too upset."

"What are you thinking?" M'Bulu permitted the discussion, which Bill thought was a good sign.

"Temporarily suspend development work on the encryption part of the project until we perfect a way to remove all of the artifacts of each packet as part of the traversing process." Bill waited for the immediate rejection.

"How long do you think that would take?" M'Bulu answered, not giving the answer Bill expected.

"I honestly don't know," Bill responded honestly. "But a small delay now could save us a significantly more costly breakdown in the future."

"Please explain," M'Bulu gave Bill his chance to make his point.

"Let's say it causes a six to twelve month delay now, while we are designing that clean-up process," Bill began, hoping his argument would be good enough. "It means that we launch the Q'Loud processing six to twelve months later than we hoped, but there is no downside to that delay... no extra cost, other than the payroll for the additional development time."

Bill paused to read M'Bulu's reaction, saw none, and continued.

"But let's say we just leave it as is, move forward with perfecting the existing process, and launch the upgrade. Part of launching the upgrade is transferring all of the processing traffic away from the three existing Switches, and into the Q'Loud quantum platform. Then at some point in the future, because we step in our own mess in that dimension, something breaks, and we can't get responses back for a couple months until we fix it. The three existing Switches are offline, and it takes a week to get them turned back on. During that week, the planetary financial system stops. Even after we get the three retired Switches back online, the damage from the shutdown will take months to resolve. Worse, the damage to the reputation of the entire Finland Global transaction network that we have developed will be irreparably damaged, and they may lose their monopoly. But I believe that all of this can be avoided by not leaving behind debris."

M'Bulu considered Bill's scenario for a moment.

"I'll make you a counter proposal," He offered to Bill. "The next time you are here, we three will sit down and find a good compromise. Until then, Heinrich can continue with his current development, but we will address this in person. Agreed?"

Bill couldn't think of any reason why the development of a cleanup process couldn't wait until he was back in Pretoria in a couple months, so he agreed.

"Good." M'Bulu wrapped up the call. "Anything else to discuss today?"

"When I talk with Heinrich next time, I'll let him know the plan. Other than that, I think that covers it." Bill was placated. "Thank you for considering my concerns."

"Of course, Bill, have a good evening."

"You too, M'Bulu." Bill disconnected the call and sat back in his chair, forgetting to take off the headset first, only realizing it as the cord yanked them off his head.

He got up and opened his office door.

"Hey Kandi," Bill stuck his head out of his door. "Can you please add a wireless USB headset to our office supply order?"

"Sure, Bill!" Kandi answered happily.

Bill was drained. He did a lap of the hallway telling everyone he was going home, then joined his security detail for the drive.

He was mentally exhausted from the week, so he shut off his phone before he got home. Once inside, Bill warmed up some leftovers, ate them in silence, and went to bed.

CHAPTER 55: THE WRONG WEAPONS

Amir was bemused by the inability of his brothers to see the bigger picture. The meeting had devolved into planning a way to coordinate an attack on all three Switches at the same time, once they were all located. While such a coordinated attack may cause temporary disruption to the world financial markets, it wouldn't be any more successful in permanently raising the Caliphate than the event in 2001.

Amir listened for a few more minutes, then climbed up on the table.

"You are all idiots!" Amir yelled as loud as he could. That got the attention of the room, especially since most of the people in the room outranked him.

All eyes turned to Amir, and most were not happy with him.

"These attacks you speak of can not permanently cripple them and bring them to their knees!" Amir yelled louder than he intended to.

He moderated his speech.

"When Sheik bin Laden struck at the heart of the Americans, the attack only slowed them for a few months, but they came back stronger."

Amir had their attention now.

"Throughout history, those with the greatest power had the greatest armies. And to have those armies, they had to have great wealth. We have been using violence to sting them, but we have made no real progress in defeating them. This is because we are using the wrong weapons. We have no real wealth with which to combat them effectively."

Amir paused to look around the room.

It was silent. He continued.

"Capitalism, as much as we hate it, is what rules our world. Rather than using the guns and bullets and grenades that we have stolen from the Invaders, let us use their currency against them. Let us confiscate all of their money, bring down the financial markets across the world, and then build and supply our own armies. We have followers and cells in every village and city across the world. If we could give them weapons, food, electricity, vehicles, and they were the only ones to have these things, they would be the very powerful leaders of each village or city. And then we finally raise the global Caliphate with no opposition."

Amir was finished. There were a few murmurs as the other men in the room began to consider the possibility.

"There is no way to steal all of their money!" A voice from the back of the room yelled.

"There is." Amir countered.

This was his chance. He continued.

"My brothers, we are closing in on the location of the Switch here in Pretoria. Rather than destroying it, we need only to reactivate a command in the device, and I can access it from here. Then I can start transferring money from accounts all across the world into our own accounts. Slowly at first so as to not let our actions be tracked, but as our treasure grows, we can be more aggressive with the diversion of funds."

"What's to stop them from taking the money back once they find it?" Someone else in the crowd asked.

"We need to take over a bank. It doesn't have to be a large one, but we need to have our brothers as the officers and directors of that bank. Then we open accounts at that bank, and the funds transfers go to our bank accounts there. The banking laws of the nation where the bank is located need to be in our favor, so either the Carribean or Mauritius. The Caribbean is too close to the United States, so I think Mauritius is the best location.

The sooner we can take control of a bank, the better, because the answer to the location of Switch 3 has to be in the logs which I keep receiving, and as soon as we find it and I patch it, we can start transferring funds."

There was more murmuring around the room, and finally the cell leader climbed onto the table next to Amir.

"Brothers, this is worth consideration. Let us begin our planning. I will talk with my advisors about the bank."

The shouts continued.

Amir permitted himself a shred of hope of this plan working.

CHAPTER 56: NEW NEWS

Bill had not slept well. It's not that he was as concerned anymore with Heinrich ending this iteration of the universe, as much as that concepts of previous iterations of the universe, and a single insane human scientist being able to end the current one, were almost incomprehensible, Bill was comfortable that he and Heinrich and M'Bulu could come to an agreement about how to proceed forward in a safer manner. After giving it more conscious thought, Bill concluded that his restlessness stemmed from a lack of organization around his projects. That was easy enough to resolve, and Bill decided he'd spend the day at the office with his door closed and phone off, and would at least get the projects into their own task lists. There was too much slop in the specifications for Bill to actually develop timelines and milestones, and that bothered him too, but getting the task lists organized for the projects would at least give him a foundation to work from for the rest of the project planning.

Bill felt better after thinking that through, and headed for the kitchen to see what leftovers awaited him. As he was digging through the refrigerator, he grabbed the TV remote from the counter and pressed the power button. He heard the news come on, but didn't really hear the conversation. It was the sound of reporters and anchors talking over each other that drew Bill's attention from the various containers in front of him to the television screen in the living room.

There on the screen of his local station was a live feed from a news crew in a helicopter flying near a vast smoking crater. Bill closed the door and grabbed the remote and turned up the sound. The chyron at the bottom of the screen read "Massive Explosion At Mining Facility Near Arniston Western Cape". A chill went down Bill's spine. The reporters kept talking

216

about this mining complex, but Bill knew the truth from seeing the video. The "mining complex" that was being shown from a distance was not a crater, but rather a massive circle, precisely ten kilometers in diameter. The entire ring was smoking and in flames, and there were occasional small explosions still rocking areas of the complex.

Bill knew immediately what had happened, even though he had never seen it for himself.

The South African mini-collider had exploded.

Bill grabbed his phone to check in with M'Bulu and Heinrich. The screen was dark. Bill then realized that he had forgotten to plug his phone into the charger the previous night, and it was now dead. He immediately plugged it in and it began charging. Then he grabbed his laptop and headset and turned the laptop on to get onto the Q'Loud VPN.

At that moment, there came a loud knocking at his door. Bill hurried to the door and opened it to find his security guards. They were on high alert.

"Doctor, we come in," the guard named Vasily stated emphatically.

"Yes, come in!" Bill invited them in, and the other guard, Lüd, closed the door and locked it. Lüd began checking the rooms, and Vasily stood near Bill, talking quietly into his headset.

"You contact minister now," Vasily stated after a moment.

"Yup, I'm logging in now," Bill answered. "Do you know what the hell happened?"

"*Da*," Vasily answered in his deadpan thick Russian accent. "Big explosion. You contact Minister now."

"I'm on it."

No shit, big explosion, Bill said to himself as he connected the VPN and put his headset on.

The chat client pinged as soon as the VPN connected, and Bill clicked the answer button.

"Minister," Bill began without bothering with the usual pleasantries.

"What the hell happened?"

"Hello Bill," M'Bulu began right away. "We were concerned when we could not reach you, so I had the security team send a message through."

"Yeah, sorry about that," Bill felt really stupid. "Of all nights to forget to plug in my phone. My security team is here, and they seem to be on high alert. Are the other security teams in town also on high alert?"

"Yes they are, and your office will have extra security today," M'Bulu answered. "And I trust this day will keep you from ever forgetting to charge your phone."

"Count on it," Bill answered. "Now, what actually happened? I know that big burning ring I'm seeing on the feed through to my news station from the SABC is not a mining complex."

"You are correct," M'Bulu confirmed. "As you no doubt suspect, that was the Arniston mini-collider that we were building. Initial reports that I have received from my troops on the ground there indicate that there were coordinated attacks on several access ports and three different control rooms about two hours ago. The collider was running a test cycle, so it was charged at the time of the initial detonations. That is why you are seeing that the entire ring has exploded."

Bill was stunned by so many of the things M'Bulu had told him. First, that it was attacked to begin with, because it was supposed to be a secret as to what it actually was. Second, that the coordinated attacks were from both outside at key ports and *inside* the facility at three different control rooms. How had the attackers made it past the screening process to be able to be in key internal areas, and smuggle in explosives? Third, *it was running a test cycle?* Neither M'Bulu nor Heinrich had told him it was operational, even if only for testing. That was a problem.

"Minister," Bill had to choose his words very carefully. "Did you know that the mini-collider was operational, and that a test was scheduled today?"

"Yes." M'Bulu's answer was direct.

"Did Heinrich know that the mini-collider was operational, and that a test was scheduled today?"

Bill really wanted to know how out of the loop he was.

"No."

Well, that's good at least, Bill thought to himself. Then another thought hit him.

"Is Heinrich okay?"

"Yes, his security team is with him, and he will be under extra protection at his flat tonight, and he will be working from his flat for the foreseeable future, in order to consolidate his security teams." M'Bulu calmed Bill's fears about that.

Then another thought hit Bill.

"M'Bulu, any chance we know where Keith is?" Bill had a bad feeling about this.

"Bill, what I am about to tell you is very classified, so please keep that in mind as I tell you this," M'Bulu started, then Bill heard M'Bulu clap his hands twice, and the white noise come on in M'Bulu's office. "Since Doctor vanGreig left, he has been under constant surveillance, both by us and by known opposition cells. He has had no interaction with those cells, nor with our team. He seems to be doing exactly what he said he would do, and is spending time enjoying Paris with his son. But he is a very high-interest asset, both to us and to those who would damage our projects. At the time of the attack, Doctor vanGreig was in a pub, watching 'soccer', as you call it, with his son, eating a Reuben sandwich and drinking a local ale. There was no interaction between Doctor vanGreig and anyone of interest that we could detect in the days leading up to the attack, and no increased attention from the other surveillance teams either. So, he appears to be uninvolved. At this moment, he is still watching the match, and is unaware of the attack, although the other surveillance teams appear to have increased attention on him, probably in anticipation of our security teams contacting him."

M'Bulu stopped speaking, because the white noise turned off.

"I see," Bill took it all in. "Well, I am happy that everything seems to be under control with him."

"Doctor, at this point, I think you should get to your office while we await further news," M'Bulu suggested. "Your team will undoubtedly be frightened, and a strong leader with a calm voice would be very beneficial."

"Agreed," Bill began. "When will the strong leader with the calm voice be arriving?"

Bill intended it as a joke, but he felt more calm than his team probably did at this moment. M'Bulu waited a moment before he answered.

"Do you know the phrase 'uneasy lies the head that wears a crown'?" M'Bulu asked Bill, with no hint of joking in his voice.

"Yes, I read Shakespeare in high school," Bill didn't feel any better. "But I'm hardly the king in this situation, M'Bulu. I'm sure it weighs more heavily on you right now than on me."

"That is true, Bill," M'Bulu countered. "But like it or not, in Arizona, you wear the crown for this project."

Bill considered M'Bulu's words for a moment.

"I am so writing a bonus for me into our contract renegotiations," Bill responded, eliciting a chuckle from M'Bulu.

"Fair enough, my friend," M'Bulu answered. "Let us deal with today's atrocities first, then discuss the new contract Monday."

That surprised Bill.

"I was joking about the renegotiations, actually," Bill answered.

"I know that you were, but there will undoubtedly need to be changes now," M'Bulu responded. "Once we get an idea of the scope of the damage and the changes that we will need to make to the projects because of the loss of the assets, there will be many changes. For now, please go to your office and calm your team."

"Understood, Minister," Bill acquiesced. "Be safe, my friend. Talk with you later."

Bill disconnected the call and closed his laptop, and just sat for a moment, gathering his thoughts. Then he looked to the television screen to watch the continuing damage in real time. There were still small explosions occurring at a few various points around the ring. After a few moments, Bill realized that the small explosions were *only* occurring at those few points, and surmised that those must be the access ports. There were also three large fires burning, one at the center of the circle, and the other two a few hundred feet away from the main ring on opposite sides of the ring. Bill figured those were the control rooms.

Good luck explaining this to the news, Minister, Bill said to himself, then let Vasily know that he was going to grab a shower, and then they could head out to the office. Vasily acknowledged with his usual grunt and nod.

The office conference room was in pandemonium, and Bill could hear it as soon as he walked through the door. There were extra guards at the main door and surrounding the building, all trying to look like it was normal for them to be there. Kandi wasn't at the front desk, but there was a sign on the front door saying that the office was closed for "team building exercises". Bill rolled his eyes at that.

Bill stopped by his office and dropped his laptop bag onto his chair before heading down to the conference room. Bill rounded the corner into the room, and was immediately beset by everyone shouting questions at him at the same time.

"Hey!" Bill tried to bring the room under control.

Kevin immediately asked the first question while everyone else was thinking about theirs.

"Why are you not answering your phone?" Kevin yelled at Bill.

Shit, Bill thought to himself, then pulled his phone out of his pocket and turned it on. After it booted up, the new message notification began playing in a long staccato stream as he was notified of over forty unread messages.

"Sorry," Bill shouted down the room again. "This will be the last time I forget to charge my phone overnight. I'm guessing you would all like to know what is going on, and I have answers, so let me get through them, and then you can ask the unanswered ones."

The room quieted down, and Bill began his explanation.

"I already spoke with Minister Mabusa," Bill started his run-down of the approved story. "For those of you who don't know, the Minister is head of the South African equivalent of our Department of Homeland Security. Within ten minutes of the main explosion this morning, the Minister was in communications with authorities on the ground in Cape Town. Initial reports that he has are the same as what you have undoubtedly heard on the news this morning: a large mining facility outside Cape Town had a catastrophic event and exploded."

Bill paused to give the room a moment to process what he had just told them. He felt awful lying to his people, but if the worst happened, it was best that they not know. *Hell, if the worst happens, it's better that I not know*, Bill thought to himself. As he was about to continue, Bill caught Kevin's eye; Kevin clearly did not believe Bill. That would be another conversation for later in the day.

"Then why," Eileen started the interrogation, "did all of our security teams go on heightened alert this morning before I was even able to see this on the news?"

"Well," Bill began improvising, hoping his answer would sound reasonable. "Because that Switch in our server room is vitally important to the financial transaction validation network across the world. If one of them goes down in an uncontrolled or unplanned outage, it causes ripples across the balancer and the other two Switches. So, whenever anything like the South African Mine Disaster happens anywhere in the world, we can expect to see our security teams be a little more protective of us until the all-clear is given."

Eileen's facial expression made it clear she didn't believe him either.

"So, it's just another Wednesday around here," Kandi piped up.

Most of the rest of the room laughed at that. Kyle looked like he calmed down slightly at the joke, and the rest of the room relaxed significantly. Only Eileen, Connie, and Kevin seemed like they were not buying Bill's explanation.

"Well, Friday, but yeah," Bill played along. "Anyway, the Minister and Kevin and I will remain in close communication today and all weekend, and I'll be happy to give everyone an update on Monday morning after my call with the Minister."

"So, is the surreal amount of security I experienced this morning going to continue all weekend?" Kyle got in on the interrogation.

"Vasily?" Bill yelled towards the open conference room door.

"*Da?*" Bill heard from the other end of the hallway.

"Is the enhanced security for our people going to continue throughout the weekend?" Bill shouted back.

"*Da.*"

"*Spasibo!*" Bill yelled back to Vasily.

"*Pozhaluysta.*" Vasily responded again. Bill hadn't expected that, and it caught him off guard for a moment. Bill continued.

"Well, there you have it," Bill said to Kyle.

"You'll get used to them," Kandi reassured Kyle. "They're kind of nice to have around, especially if you want to go out for a burrito in a bad neighborhood late at night."

The room laughed at that, except for Connie, Kevin, and Eileen.

"Okay," Bill wrapped up the meeting, "in the interest of security and as a team building exercise, lunch today will be catered, so please everyone coordinate what you want and we'll get that ordered. Kandi, if you would please work your magic with the caterers, I would appreciate it."

"Of course, Bill!" Kandi answered happily.

"That's it, then." Bill concluded. "Kevin, got a minute?"

Kevin answered by standing up and walking out the door.

Eileen stopped next to Bill on her way out of the conference room.

"When you are finished with your meeting," Eileen whispered, "I would appreciate a quick conversation."

"Yup, you're next on my list." Bill whispered back. "Meanwhile, if you could keep Kyle calmed down, I would appreciate it."

Eileen responded by glaring at Bill for a moment, then also leaving the conference room.

Bill headed into Kevin's office and closed the door behind himself. He didn't dare break protocol by sitting before being invited to do so.

"If you lie to me," Kevin began before looking up from his desk, "this will be your last hour at this company. Clear?"
Kevin looked at Bill now.

"Yes, sir," Bill responded formally. "Crystal."

"Thank you," Kevin replied. "Sit."

Bill did.

"Is that disaster down there really a mining facility?"

Bill didn't answer.

"Got it," Kevin continued. "What is it?"

Bill remained silent.

Come on, M'Bulu, call him! Bill screamed internally, feeling the walls close in.

"Not going to answer me?" Kevin was restraining his anger admirably.

"Chairman Blanchard," Bill had to be really careful. "As you know, there are some classified aspects of our project with our South African client, and as we have previously discussed, I am unable to share certain details with you on those projects. I hope you can understand the very delicate position I am in right now with your line of questioning. You asked me not to lie to you, and I have not. But I am unable to answer your questions at this time."

Kevin was quiet for a moment, then sat back in his chair and cleared his throat.

"Doctor Fibulee," Kevin began, "your services with GlobalForce are no longer required. Please clear out any personal items from your office and leave immediately. Your final paycheck will be mailed to you later today."

Oh, Kevin, Bill thought to himself, with pity in his heart. *You just fired yourself.*

Bill waited a moment to see if M'Bulu would call while Bill was still sitting.

No such call came.

"Understood." Bill stood and extended his hand. "It's been good working with you, Kevin, and wish you luck in your future endeavors. I'm sorry we had to part on these terms."

Kevin stood and shook Bill's hand.

"Agreed," Kevin responded. "Under different circumstances, I think we would have made a good leadership team."

With that, Bill turned and left Kevin's office. He left the door open. As he was heading down the hall to Eileen's office, he heard Kevin's phone ring.

"Good morning, Minister," Kevin answered the call. Bill didn't bother to listen to the rest of the call, because he had a pretty good idea how it was going to go. He walked into Eileen's office to find Eileen sitting at her desk, Kyle across from her.

She looked mad, and he looked scared.

"Let's take a walk," Bill suggested.

"To where?" Kyle asked.

"Just across the street to get a soda," Bill said in a commanding voice, enunciating each word.

Eileen and Kyle picked up the unspoken message and stood up to join Bill. They walked out of Eileen's office towards the front door.

"Vasily, we require soda," Bill said to his guard.

Vasily spoke briefly into his headset, and within a few seconds, four more guards appeared from various positions in the office to join Vasily and Lüd.

"Okay, guys, this is a little ridiculous. We are just walking to literally right there to get sodas." Bill was exasperated and pointed to the convenience store a hundred feet away from their office. "We do not require a presidential motorcade."

"No motorcade, just security detail," Vasily responded, deadpan.

"Six burly Russian dudes carrying weapons and using headsets escorting two little programmers and a magnificent project manager is going to raise some eyebrows at the Gas N Burp," Bill responded. "Any way to maybe not be ridiculous while still providing coverage?"

Kyle and Eileen scoffed at the "magnificent project manager" phrase, but Vasily had no sense of humor, so he merely started quietly speaking Russian into his headset again. After a moment he nodded.

"*Da, sdelay eto.*" Vasily said to his headset. Then he turned to Bill. "Snipers will cover you, we wait just outside door. If trouble, then we join you. And Lüd is German."

"Ha, snipers…" Kyle laughed, then he looked at Eileen and Bill and realized it wasn't a joke. "Holy shit! Snipers?"

"*Da.* Snipers. Help to keep away riff-raff." Vasily answered Kyle, then he laughed loudly, along with the other five guards.

Bill was impressed to finally see that Vasily did have a sense of humor, albeit a dark one.

"Vasily, *ty komik,*" Bill said in Russian. That was now the extent of his knowledge of the Russian language, but the shocked look on Vasily's face let Bill know that Vasily would now always be wary of him. It was nice.

"We go now," Bill said in his best Russian accent, and headed out the door, with Kyle and Eileen in tow.

Vasily and the security team waited by the office door as promised as Bill and his team walked to the store.

"Dude, is there really a sniper with his rifle pointed at my head right now?" Kyle was petrified.

"No," Bill responded calmly. "But if I remember my sniper vernacular, the 'spotter' is watching the whole area for any sign of trouble. The bullet won't hit you. This is the safest you've ever been in your life."

Kyle didn't seem any calmer after that, but he did stop trying to look over his shoulder.

"Want to tell me why we suddenly have jumpy security guards around us this morning after a mining disaster on the other side of the world?" Eileen jumped right in.

"Okay, yes," Bill began, giving as much information as he could without getting all three of them in trouble with M'Bulu.

"You know how the Switch 2 in our server room is one of three Switches controlling all of the authorizations for almost all of the financial transactions in the world?"

"No," Eileen answered. "You had not shared that information with me."

"Okay, when we get back, I'll give you both a tour of the server room," Bill offered. "Anyway, there are three of these Switches across the world that control authorizations for most of the aforementioned financial transactions for the planet, and there is a centrally located load balancer connected to all three of them. We were working on an upgrade to the Switch network, and needed an ultra-secure location for that research. We had a piece of a lab in that facility in Arniston. It was easier to hide it there. The reason for all our enhanced security today is because when that mine exploded, our lab was likely destroyed along with the rest of the complex. Until the authorities in South Africa determine the cause of the blast and the status of the lab, they are protecting the existing three Switches and the load balancer more carefully. And as part of that extra protection, they are also protecting the facilities and key personnel of those facilities."

"Aw, we're key personnel?" Eileen responded with fake excitement.

"Actually, you two are known to the South African government, because I told them I wanted my team for the NSC project," Bill clarified. "So yeah, you're key personnel."

The three stopped discussing any details as they entered the store, and after they paid, they headed back.

"Weird, I don't see snipers," Kyle commented as they were walking back.

"You see that wind vane on the southeast corner of the roof of the building?" Bill answered Kyle. "That's a periscope. They're behind the facade up there."

Kyle turned a little pale at that, but kept walking.

"Idiot, that's not true," Eileen taunted Kyle.

"Dude, you have to stop messing with me," Kyle breathed a sigh of relief. "I thought you were serious."

Bill just shrugged.

When they arrived back at the office, Vasily opened the door for them, then spoke quickly into his headset, glancing sideways at Bill.

Bill thanked Vasily, and walked in the door to see Kevin standing in the lobby, trying very hard to hide his fury.

"May I speak with you for a moment?" Kevin said through gritted teeth.

"Sure, Chairman," Bill figured it was important right now to show Kevin respect in front of the team. "Your office or mine?"

"Mine please," Kevin responded. He was not calming down.

Bill headed back to Kevin's office, with Kevin one step behind him.

Bill walked into Kevin's office, and stood waiting for Kevin. Kevin closed the door behind him, then went and sat at the little table in his office, and motioned for Bill to take a seat.

"While you were out," Kevin began slowly, enunciating each word, "Minister Mabusa called me. He explained to me that there are certain pieces of information that you are not permitted to share because of the level of classification on them."

Bill was impressed at the self-control that Kevin was exhibiting, so he tried to remain quiet and let Kevin say what he needed to say.

"With that in mind," Kevin continued, "your services are still required, and I rescind my previous dismissal of you."

"I appreciate that, Chairman," Bill said as humbly as he could muster.

Bill waited for Kevin to say something else, but Kevin just continued to stare at Bill.

"Chairman," Bill began.

"Stop it, just call me Kevin."

"Fair enough," Bill continued. "Kevin, you asked me to not lie to you earlier, and I was following that request. But you are entitled to an explanation. So, if I may give you an incomplete answer to your question from this morning, I do have some answers for you."

"I'd appreciate that, and I won't push you on the incomplete parts," Kevin seemed happy with the compromise.

"Okay," Bill began carefully. "As you may expect, when an explosion that large happens at any facility around the world, every security force on the planet goes on alert until they figure out what happened. As you saw, our security teams went on heightened alert, and that was normal. The rest of the story is that we apparently had a secure lab there where they were doing some design work on some upgrades for the Switch network. We don't know the status of the lab, nor the people working there, but because Switch project assets were most likely affected, we are on heightened alert until we have those answers."

Bill stopped. He was stretching the truth awfully thin with that explanation, just like he had with his developers, and he didn't want to go too far.

Kevin sat and considered what Bill had told him.

Bill remained silent.

Kevin finally spoke.

"You and the minister got your stories straight this morning before you came in."

"No, sir." Bill answered honestly. "From the time I found out about the attack until I was here this morning was literally less than an hour, and I spoke to Minister Mabusa for less than five minutes. And that conversation was all knowledge transfer to me about the very little information that the minister actually had."

Kevin continued to look at Bill, trying to find any hint of falsehood.

"What you just told me is essentially the same thing he told me," Kevin finally answered. "Except that he told me the location of the lab was in the center of the facility."

"Well, that is information he had not told me yet, so that's interesting," Bill said with some surprise in his voice.

"In any case," Kevin continued, "it looks like my employment here is contingent on cooperating with you, so I have no choice."

"Kevin," Bill responded carefully, "it would be easier for me and the rest of the company if you continued to do your job as CEO and board chair, and for me to do my job as whatever the hell title you said I have. I don't want to be a rogue operator like Jerry was. This organization will function better if there are checks and balances on the members of the senior executive team, and in order for that to happen, you and I both need to do our jobs, even if they clash."

Bill said that last part as much for M'Bulu to hear as to strengthen his working relationship with Kevin.

It's a deal," Kevin said happily.

He then stood and extended his hand. Bill stood and shook it.

They had an accord.

"I'll let the minister know that I'm unfired," Bill said jokingly.

"Pretty sure he already knows," Kevin answered with a wink.

If you only knew, Bill thought.

Bill left Kevin's office and headed back down the hall to Eileen's office so he could start the quick tour he had promised earlier.

"Hey!" Connie hollered from her office as Bill passed by.

Bill spun around and stuck his head into Connie's office.

"Yes?"

"Get in here and tell me what's happening," Connie commanded.

Bill stepped into Connie's office and closed the door behind himself, then sat in a chair in front of Connie's desk.

"I will tell you as much as I can," Bill began.

"Or you could tell me everything," Connie countered.

"How about if I tell you as much as I told Kevin?"

"Fine." Connie wasn't happy, but she let it go.

Bill gave Connie essentially the same explanation that he gave Kevin.

When Bill was finished with his explanation, Connie sat quietly for a moment before speaking.

"Is that the official story that M'Bulu has authorized you to tell those of us without clearance to know the truth?" Connie asked.

"Yes." Bill didn't bother to try to dance.

"As you were," Connie responded, dismissing Bill.

Bill left Connie's office without trying to smooth feathers, knowing it wouldn't have helped.

––––––––––––

Bill took Eileen and Kyle into the server room and began explaining what the various servers in the equipment racks were, and then stopped finally in front of the very boring-looking 9U black box in the middle of one of the end racks.

"This unassuming little device here," Bill began, pointing at the unit, "is known as 'Switch 2'. It was the second of the three Switches in the transaction network. There is one in Geneva, this one, and one somewhere within a seventy-mile diameter of Johannesburg. They are all connected to a load balancer in St. Petersburg. Almost every financial transaction in the world, whether money transfer, real estate transfer, precious minerals transfers, all of them are validated through this network."

Bill gave them a moment to let that sink in.

"How many transactions per day go through this network?" Kyle finally asked.

"Last I heard, about forty billion per hour, no joke." Bill answered. Kyle and Eileen both looked shocked. "The load balancer in general routes the North and South American transactions through this box, all of the European transactions through the box in Geneva, and the Middle Eastern, Asian, African, and Australian transactions through the one in South Africa. It may shift them around a bit depending on loads, but generally, that's what happens."

"So," Kyle continued, "what if one breaks?"

"Well, planned outages happen regularly for maintenance," Bill continued. "But the company that owns the network knows when the slowest times are in the areas for each Switch, so they can plan them. Since I've been on board, there have been no unplanned outages, but if there was one, they'd see a spike in the balancer, which would be distributed to the remaining two Switches."

"What if the balancer goes down?" Eileen asked.

"Then you better have some tangible assets you can use for trade," Bill answered after thinking about it, "because there will be no debit cards until it's back online."

"That does not give me comfort," Eileen responded.

"Well, me neither," Bill countered. "But if the balancer goes offline, being able to pay for your waffles on a Saturday morning will likely be the least of your worries."

Eileen did not seem placated, but Bill moved on with the tour and then led them back to Eileen's office to go over the NSC project. Eileen and Kyle were both as staggered by the scope and violation of personal privacy that Bill originally was, but were also as excited about the project as Bill originally was.

After the meeting, Bill looked at the clock and figured he better catch up with Heinrich, so he headed back to his office, closed the door, put on his headset, logged into the Q'Loud VPN, clicked open the chat client, and started a call with Heinrich.

"Hey mate," Heinrich answered after the second ring.

"How's it, Heinrich?" Bill responded nonchalantly. "Any excitement since last time we talked?"

"No, not much," Heinrich played along.

"Anyway," Bill brought reality back, "you're safe?"

"I am, *takk*," Heinrich replied.

"Sorry there, Heinrich, I don't know that word," Bill answered, confused by the word he hadn't heard before.

"Oh, uh, that's Norwegian for 'thanks'," Heinrich caught himself. "I guess that explosion this morning has me off balance more than I thought. Sorry about that."

"No worries," Bill waved off the mistake. "We are all more rattled than we want to admit. Tell me what you know that I have not already heard from M'Bulu."

Heinrich relayed that it had been a coordinated simultaneous attack from inside the three control rooms and at each of the access ports, which Bill already knew. The Ministry had not told Heinrich who had tried to take credit for the attack, so he was still waiting to hear that. Based on what Heinrich knew from the inspections of the site that he had done, and from the images on the news, there would be nothing salvageable from the site, which would put them behind schedule considerably on the quantum work.

Bill processed what he had heard, then asked a more targeted question.

"Heinrich, how long ago did you know that facility was ready for live testing?"

"Today." Heinrich's one-word response did not successfully hide the rage he was attempting to control.

"Understood." Bill responded after a moment. "Sounds like we need to have a difficult conversation with the Minister."

"That is an understatement, mate," Heinrich was still doing a decent job of holding back his anger, and Bill appreciated it.

"I'll set up a time for the three of us to talk, meanwhile keep your head down," Bill wrapped up the call. "Also, please don't put any of this in email when we are discussing the 'mining facility'. Until we know the real story and have our defenses shored up, let's keep the written communications to a minimum on it."

"Agreed," Heinrich seemed pleased that Bill was taking this as seriously as he was. "Thanks, Bill."

"Talk soon, get some sleep, and maybe stay out of the pubs for now." Bill wanted Heinrich to be under close guard until this was controlled.

"Count on it," Heinrich agreed. "Cheers."

Bill disconnected the call, took off his headset and tossed it on his desk, and closed his laptop.

He couldn't even blame any of this ridiculousness on Jerry anymore; this was all his own fault for agreeing to work on the Switch quantum projects.

I knew I should have bought that donut franchise instead of becoming a programmer, Bill mused to himself.

Through his closed door, Bill heard the front door open and Kandi cheerfully greet the caterers. He went to join in the "team building lunch", and tried to take his mind off of the world events, if only for an hour.

CHAPTER 57: GREATER GOOD

Amir was furious.

"Why would we attack a *mine*?!" Amir screamed at the assembled leadership group. "Do you realize just how much security has increased because of this stupid attack? I am finally able to start tracking the traffic, and maybe even find physical locations, but now there is three times as much security at every location we have been watching. This attack served no purpose but to interfere with the operation *here*!"

"My brother," one of the leaders said in response to Amir, "you would do well to remember your place. You do not lead these cells. We do. We can not tell every member of every cell all of our plans."

"*You* should at least communicate with each other as leaders!" Amir shouted back. "*You* as leaders should have known that the attack would interfere with our far more valuable operation here in Pretoria than to blow up a mine!"

"It was not a mine," another leader said quietly.

"What?" The answer caught Amir off guard. "What was it?"

"It was a fully operational scale model of the Large Hadron Collider," the man answered.

Amir was stunned into silence, and he sat down. What was going on in Arniston? Amir wondered to himself.

The other leader continued.

"The South African government was building a smaller version of the Large Hadron Collider. We got word two days ago that they were going to do a full power test on it today. We don't know what their reasoning was for building it, but it was being funded by the military and the Department of Home Affairs. We had to act swiftly to make this statement, so we had a short call between the leaders, and acted. I am sorry that it may have negatively affected the work you are doing momentarily, but today was a great victory for Allah, and surely He will see fit to also guide you to great success with your work."

Amir considered the words and the implications of what he had heard.

The fact that Home Affairs was involved along with the military made it clear to Amir that nothing good would have come from it.

He was able to accept that while his work would be delayed, the strike was for the greater good.

CHAPTER 58: BAGELS

Bill's phone pinged, letting him know he had a new text message. Bill contemplated not answering it yet and going back to sleep, but with the events of the previous day, he figured it might be important. He reached for his phone and saw that it was 4:15 a.m. Then he brought up the message.

VPN CHAT NOW PLEASE

It was from Heinrich. He seemed upset, since he was only polite when he was upset and trying to not sound upset. Bill responded.

GTIVEW ME A MINUYE

Bill had long since given up on cringing from the bad spelling in his messages.

Bill walked to his laptop and started it up, then headed to the bathroom while the laptop got itself ready. Bill went back and sat at his desk, logged into the operating system, then thought for a moment.

"Vasily?" Bill shouted.

"*Da?*" Bill heard the reply from somewhere in the house.

How is it that Vasily never sounds tired? Bill wondered to himself.

"Feel like bagels?" Bill shouted back.

"*Da.*"

"If I give you cash, can we send Lüd for bagels while I take this call?"

"*Da.*" Came the response a moment later.

Bill put on his headset and logged into the Q'Loud, then into the chat client. Heinrich pinged him as soon as Bill was connected.

"Good morning, Heinrich," Bill said groggily. "What's up?"

Lüd came into the room, and Bill pointed at his wallet in the key box. Lüd went to it and took out $20, showed to it Bill, then he headed back outside.

"They are shutting us down," Heinrich said, the panic and anger clear in his voice.

"That can't be right," Bill answered, figuring Heinrich had overheard something incorrectly.

"I just heard," Heinrich responded. "They are terminating all of our projects at the LHC. I just heard it from Karla Vanderzhen."

"Let me talk with M'Bulu and find out the real story," Bill tried to calm Heinrich. "You know M'Bulu would not let that happen."

As Bill said that, the chat client pinged, showing that M'Bulu wanted to join their conversation.

"Hang on a second, Heinrich," Bill interrupted. "M'Bulu is calling me, let me bring him in."

Bill clicked the button on the screen to bring M'Bulu into the call.

"Hi, M'Bulu," Bill greeted his new caller. "I have Heinrich on the line with us, too. We were just talking about you, this is really good timing."

As if this was an actual coincidence, Bill thought to himself.

"Hello Bill and Heinrich," M'Bulu played along so as not to acknowledge the eavesdropping. "I'm glad you're both on, because I have some news for you that I want to go over before you two start hearing rumors."

"That's fine," Heinrich chimed in, "and then I'd like to go over a couple things on the project with all three of us on this call."

"Agreed, "M'Bulu began. Then Bill heard M'Bulu clap twice, and the white noise come on in the background in his office. "As I'm sure you both know, the mini-collider in Arniston was destroyed. I have received additional information that the extremists that attacked the facility were quite thorough, and unfortunately quite knowledgeable, and nothing about the facility is salvageable. After conferring with the partners on your quantum project, it has been decided to dedicate the LHC in Geneva to the Q'Loud project."

M'Bulu paused to let his news be processed by his two engineers. They undoubtedly had heard incorrect information, and he wanted to let them re-evaluate what they had heard with his new information.

"With this in mind," M'Bulu paused for a moment, because the white noise had shut off, so he clapped twice again and waited for it to start again before he continued. "With this in mind, it has been decided to take the LHC offline and upgrade it to be able to produce the kinds of results that Heinrich will need it to produce for the foreseeable future. At some point, we will build a new mini-collider somewhere safer, probably in remote areas of Russia, and transfer the quantum functionality for the Switch network there, but for now, Bill and Heinrich, yours will be the only project running on the Large Hadron Collider, under the guise of processing some amazing new information that was collected from the origin on the universe."

Bill remained silent.

The white noise shut off. M'Bulu did not restart it.

"That is amazing!" Bill could hear the pure joy in Heinrich's voice. "Minister, I don't have the words to express my gratitude!"

"Don't be too pleased," M'Bulu responded with a slight chuckle. "This new work will consume almost all of your time, Heinrich. And Bill, when you are rewriting your contract, please make sure that you are here for at least two consecutive weeks every two months."

"Understood, Minister." Bill had a thousand questions, but they could all wait.

"How soon can I get the rest of the time on the Machine?" Heinrich was ready to go immediately.

"Well, that will take a bit of time," M'Bulu wanted to set a realistic expectation. "The device will need to be taken offline in order to build in the upgrades. Heinrich, what I need you to get started on, and deliver as soon as possible, are the new specifications for the device to support your processes. Anyway, I wanted to let you both know the real story before you got some incorrect news, like we were shutting down the project or something else equally ridiculous. All of the other projects are being suspended, and it will appear that yours is also being suspended, but that is only for appearances while the upgrade is completed under the guise of routine maintenance, and then we'll get to work."

"Whaaat?" Bill said with a bit of humor in his voice. "We would never believe that you would let the project be shut down, would we, Heinrich?"

"Uh," Heinrich stammered, "no, no we would never think that, heh heh" Heinrich trailed off.

"Well, I am glad we have had this conversation," M'Bulu wrapped up the call. "Heinrich, how soon can you have the specifications to me to pass along to the engineering team?"

"Monday morning GMT," Heinrich answered, excited. "I'll start work on it immediately."

"Don't rush, this needs to be correct," M'Bulu laughed slightly at Heinrich's exuberance. "Take your time and get it right. Be thorough. If it takes you a week or two weeks, that is fine."

"And I'll have a talk with your security team to make sure you are eating," Bill chimed in. "You mad scientists are all the same, you forget to eat and drink."

"Probably a good idea," Heinrich acknowledged.

"Very good," M'Bulu answered. "Heinrich, check in with Bill with periodic updates. I look forward to hearing your progress. Bill, if you could remain on the call, I have a few items to go over with you."

"Thank you, Minister," Heinrich stated happily and disconnected the call.

"You realize, M'Bulu," Bill began after he checked the chat client to ensure that Heinrich had logged off, "Heinrich just went from the saddest person on the planet to the happiest in those five minutes."

M'Bulu laughed.

"Yes, I'm sure he did," M'Bulu answered. "Now you and I must discuss a few things. First, as I mentioned, I'll need you down here more than we had originally discussed, so please include that in the new contract. Second, the National Secure Citizen project has suddenly become much more important because of the attack, so we need to step up work on it. Any chance of having your team move to Joburg?"

"Almost no chance of that, Minister," Bill answered after thinking it through for a minute. "As I said previously, Eileen wants to move to New Zealand, but that's almost as far from you as she is here. And she won't be willing to move to South Africa at all."

M'Bulu thought for a moment.

"Twelve hours ahead is easier to work with than nine hours behind," he finally stated, thinking out loud. "Let me consider that and other solutions and we can talk more about that later."

"Okay," Bill agreed. "So, I will start writing up bullet points for the new contract over the weekend and discuss them with you Monday, then I can have the new contract on Tuesday."

"Good," M'Bulu seemed happy for now. "I will talk with you on Monday. Have a good weekend, Bill."

"You as well, my friend," Bill disconnected the call and closed his laptop just as Lüd entered carrying bagels.

"Did Vasily already get one?" Bill asked Lüd.

"*Ja, zwei,*" Lüd answered.

Bill had no idea what Lüd said, but caught the "ya", so he assumed the answer was yes. Bill wondered why they would have a German guard working for a Russian supervisor guard. Then Bill bit the bagel and realized he didn't care.

CHAPTER 59: ARROGANT OR STUPID

Amir checked his theory for probably the twentieth time. And for the twentieth time, the raw data supported him.

He finally found the first crack in the Finland Global Financial Switch network.

Amir asked one of his assistants to run and tell his leader, and ask him to bring as many of the best technology men as were in their cell.

For the next three hours, Amir continued to check the data on other sheets of paper, muttering to himself and circling sets of numbers and drawing arrows.

Eventually, Amir's cell leader entered the room with two other cell leaders and several of the computer hacking team.

"Well, little brother, what is it you have found?" The leader asked Amir.

"I have found a mistake, and I have found the Switch 3 that was installed in South Africa," Amir responded, barely above a whisper.

"And why does this matter?" The leader responded.

"Now that we can track it," Amir continued his quiet explanation, "we can eventually locate it, and we can get into the hardware, and I can activate the back door."

"Explain to me again how this will work," Amir's leader still did not understand any of the technology.

"With the back door open," Amir explained again, "I can inject transactions into the network that will allow us to transfer currency to us, into our accounts in Mauritius. Once we have emptied all of the electronic currency from across the planet into our accounts, we purchase the world from itself, and the Caliphate will be complete."

"I do not understand how you will do that, but first you must find the device," the leader continued. "These are ten of our best computer experts. Teach them what to look for, and work with them to find your device. Then we will plan how to get you to it. Meanwhile, I am returning to Cape Town for a few days to search for brothers that did not join the Prophet yet."

"I would be happy to explain it to you, if you would like to know," Amir offered.

"Can you explain it in a non-technical way?" His leader asked.

"Yes."

"Then please do."

"Think of it like this," Amir began. "Consider water canals for farming. Far upstream, there may be only ten diversions from the main river, and then those ten taps are split off more and more depending on the size and needs of the farms downstream."

Amir paused to make sure his leader was understanding so far. The man nodded, so Amir continued.

"In the case of the financial network which we seek to access, they have been very careful to only allow the water to flow from one source, in this case Finland Global Financial, and then they run one pipe to the Switch 1 in Geneva, and another to the Switch 2 in Arizona. They should also have run a pipe to the Switch 3 in South Africa, but the Russians made a mistake. They connected the Switch 3 to a South African network, instead of their own pipe, and because of that, we can track that specific device to a physical location in South Africa."

Amir paused again to wait for questions.

"So," the leader began, "because the Russians were arrogant or stupid and just connected the box in South Africa, they have exposed the entire world to divine justice?"

"Yes, brother," Amir said in quiet tones, struggling mightily to hold back his enthusiasm. "That tiny mistake, of literally one keystroke, will have this massive global impact."

"Find that box," the leader answered. "I will discuss with the other leaders."

The leader turned and left.

"My brothers," Amir began the technical explanation to his team of hackers, "the Russians made a critical mistake when connecting the Switch 3 into their network. Let me explain. Switch 1 and Switch 2 are both connected to the Finnish IP range in the 2.255.250.nnn range, as they should be since they are within the Finland Global network, protected behind the balancer in St. Petersburg, which is in the Russian subnet range of 2.19.205.nnn. We would expect the Switch 3 to have one of the remaining IP addresses in the Finnish range, and be able to see it connecting through the Russian subnet, but it isn't. There is another subnet showing traffic to and from the balancer in Russia... it is in the range of 2.19.255.nnn. That is a South African subnet range. The Russian engineer that mapped the IP address, either by accident or intentionally, wrote 255 instead of 205 in the third octet. That Switch 3 is in South Africa, and is outside the Russian network and firewall. We should now be able to track those packets to a physical location, and then we can plan our entrance."

The room erupted to shouts of joy. Amir let the joyous outbursts continue for a few moments until he calmed the room and set them to working.

CHAPTER 60: PLANS WITHIN PLANS

Bill was in a surprisingly good mood, considering all that had happened in the previous week, and all the new work before him now. He was happy for Heinrich, but was concerned about Heinrich's health now, as he was sure that Heinrich would forget to eat and sleep.

Bill had a thought as he sat eating his breakfast of leftover enchiladas from the previous night.

"*Vasily Ivanovich*," Bill called to Vasily, barely able to contain his laughter at the thought of catching Vasily off guard again.

Vasily's head popped out from around the corner in the hallway by the front door, a very surprised expression on his face.

"*Da?*"

Bill could no longer contain his laughter, but Vasily did not share his mirth.

"Oh my gosh, I just wanted to see if that would work!" Bill continued to laugh. "I read in a Tom Clancy novel or something that Russians will sometimes call each other 'Ivanovich' or 'Alexandrovich', even though it's not their middle name. I don't understand why, but now I know."

"Is not for you to know," Vasily answered in a very serious tone, "and is not quite accurate."

That caused Bill to laugh harder.

"I think you know more about *Russkaya kul'tura* than you reveal," Vasily stated, deadpan.

Now Bill couldn't breathe through his laughter. The thought crossed his mind that he may actually have a stroke, and that irony only made the laughter stronger. He took a moment to recover his composure, while Vasily waited, bemused.

"*Prosti menya*," Bill finally had control of himself. "Anyway, do you have the ability to speak directly with Heinrich's security team?"

"*Da.*"

"Good," Bill continued. "Can you please check in with them to make sure Heinrich is eating, drinking water, and sleeping?"

"Is odd request," Vasily responded.

"*Da*, is odd request," Bill tried to match Vasily's speech patterns, then returned to normal. "But Heinrich is more a scientist than a human, and he will forget to eat, drink, sleep, use the restroom, bathe, and sometimes even breathe if someone does not remind him. Geniuses and artists sometimes value their science or art more than self-preservation. So, *muy drug*, will you please ask your counterpart in Pretoria to check on Heinrich, and to remind him often to eat, drink, sleep, and go to the restroom?"

"Da, right away," Vasily answered.

"*Spacibo*," Bill thanked Vasily in his language.

Vasily paused for a moment, looking at Bill, then narrowed his eyes.

"*Vy Russkiy.*" Vasily said in a hushed but accusatory tone.

Bill said nothing, just stared back at Vasily and narrowed his own eyes.

Vasily waited a moment, then walked back to his post, talking into his headset.

Bill was pretty sure that Vasily just called him a Russian, but didn't know for certain, and decided to check the online translator later to see if he was right. He laughed a bit again, then went back to his enchiladas, trying to enjoy them as much as possible while home, because there was such a lack of good authentic Mexican restaurants in Pretoria and Johannesburg.

Back at the office, Bill headed out of his office, notebook in hand, and down the hallway towards the conference room.

"Programmers! Mount up!" Bill hollered as he neared the end of the hallway.

He sat at the table and waited for his team to join him.

After a moment, Eileen and Kyle walked into the room with their notebooks in hand, and took seats at the table.

After another moment of waiting for Taylor and Sienna to show up, and them not showing up, Eileen finally had to ask.

"I have to ask, did you ever tell them that that film is one of your favorite movies?"

Bill realized that it had never come up.

"Hang on," Bill stood up and walked to the other two programmers' offices and asked them to join him in the conference room.

Once everyone was seated in the conference room, Bill addressed the first item of confusion.

"Sorry about the confusion," Bill began to Taylor and Sienna. "I forgot that all of us have not worked together as a team for the last several years. Whenever one of us was calling a meeting of this team, we'd just yell that, and we'd all head into our meeting."

"Well, that explains that," Taylor said with a slight chuckle. "I just thought all that time on airplanes had made you insane."

Bill dropped all expression from his face and just stared at Taylor for a moment, waiting until Taylor showed physical signs of discomfort.

"Dude, not cool," Kyle laughed. Then to Taylor he said "Bill is a master of the 'resting disappointed face', so whenever you see him doing it, there's nothing going on and he is harmless."

"You are the strangest supervisor I have ever had," Taylor said to Bill.

"You have no idea," Eileen said to Taylor.

Everyone laughed. Then Bill noticed that Sienna was not laughing and was still looking down at her notebook.

"Sienna, what's up?" Bill asked, concerned.

Sienna said nothing for a moment, then took a deep breath and finally looked up.

"This has all been too much," Sienna began. "In the last three weeks, we got a new supervisor, who we met for like one day and then was gone again for over a week, we got raided by the fucking FBI and then Jerry disappeared, we have armed guards following us around both at work and at home, we have two new people who really I know nothing about, no offense to you two, Kyle and Eileen, the world has gone insane about that mine blowing up on the other side of the world, and now you're turning out to be just as crazy as everyone else around here! I can't do this anymore!"

Sienna stood up, gathering her notebook and pens.

"I quit."

With that, Sienna turned and walked out of the conference room. Bill heard Connie intercept Sienna and route her into the HR office, and then the door close.

"And then there were three..." Taylor said to himself.

"Well that was awkward," Bill addressed the discomfort in the room in order to stop it. "Taylor, is there anything you'd like to say? Without quitting, hopefully?"

"Well," Taylor began, "I know Sienna has been unhappy here for a long time, long before you started, and she doesn't speak for me."

Bill nodded acknowledgement.

"I appreciate that."

"I like my job," Taylor continued. "But the thing that always bothered me, a little less so now, was that I always felt disconnected from the project, because Francis was always the one talking to the team in Johannesburg, so everything I heard about what we were working on, or how our modules were being used or tested, always came through Francis' arrogant little filter. I really always wanted to work with those guys directly, because on the rare or accidental occasion when I got to interact with them, I enjoyed it."

"So, what's the difference between then and now?" Bill asked.

"Well, I have a team here that seems more engaged now," Taylor answered, acknowledging Eileen and Kyle. "You two seem like you're good to work with, and Bill, you seem like a good boss…"

Eileen and Kyle both rolled their eyes at the comment about Bill, and Bill gave them a mock threatening glare.

"But," Taylor continued, "now I'm the only smart chip programmer here. You two are both database engineers. Francis is long gone. Sienna doesn't appear to be coming back, so now, out of eighty smart chip programmers, I'm the only one not in Johannesburg."

Bill considered Taylor's words for a moment, stood and walked over to the door and closed it, then returned to his seat.

"So, team," Bill began carefully. "Who here would like to relocate to somewhere else in the world for this project? Show of hands, please."

Eileen immediately raised her hand, surprising everyone else, except for Bill.

"Eileen wants to move to the new satellite office that we are going to open in New Zealand in a couple years," Bill said, addressing the surprise on the faces of the other two. Kyle looked even more surprised at hearing that. "Taylor, do you have family here?"

"Just a brother in California," Taylor answered. "Why?"

"Kyle," Bill addressed his long-time team member, "you've always talked about wanting to get out and see the world. Is that still the case?"

"Well, yeah," Kyle answered. "But where are you going with this?"

Bill sat back and looked at the ceiling for a moment, formulating his next words carefully. He started to speak, but then stopped, clapped his hands twice, startling the other three people in the room, and then when nothing happened, he continued.

"What I am about to tell you is classified," Bill began, then glanced at his phone, knowing M'Bulu would be listening. "I mean, Kevin and Connie know this, but you three have not heard this yet."

Bill paused for dramatic effect.

"That mining disaster in southwestern South Africa was an attack, not an accident. Whatever it was they were mining pissed off a group of activists from around the world, and they blew it up. Because of that, the urgency of the NSC project just got ratcheted way up, and I am getting pressure to move my highly skilled team to Johannesburg. I have been resisting that, because I didn't figure any of you would want to move to Johannesburg."

"I'll go!" Kyle and Taylor blurted out, almost in unison.

That caught Bill by surprise.

"Wow, really?" Bill asked. "I thought I was going to have to work at it."

"No, man, seriously," Kyle spoke up first. "I'd love to move down there. And my girlfriend definitely wants to live abroad, too. We've talked about how cool it would be to live in South Africa since I started here."

"Yeah, that'd be a dream for me, too," Taylor jumped in. "I've done a lot of research on the area, and I've seen the office on the video conferences, and the interactions I've had with people down there have been cool. I'll go."

Bill saw Eileen covertly wipe her eyes, he wasn't sure why.

Well," Bill began, "this could work out very positively then. My entire chip card programmer team would all be in one place, which makes me feel better about securing that code, and I'd have one strong database engineer there, which would make them happy. Kyle and Eileen can still work together, but she can be here or in New Zealand, and when the minister wants to see a database face, we can show him Kyle's face, such as it is."

The room laughed at that, even Eileen.

"So, all of this will vastly change my conversation with Minister Mabusa this afternoon," Bill brought the meeting to a close. "How soon do you two want to move?"

"Everything I own will fit in a big suitcase," Taylor answered. "I can go this week, I just need to deal with my apartment lease and sell my car."

"The company will handle your lease," Bill answered, "and just take your car to one of those places that pays cash for decent cars and get it over with. If there's a big loss for you, I'll expense the difference. It won't be this week, but after my call this afternoon, I'll have more accurate answers. One other thing, I'm going to send an email to the smart chip team to let them know that you're my liaison, and that they should be interacting with you directly. And that you're the new lead. I'll let you tell them that you've decided to join them there."

"Wow, cool, thanks!" Taylor was happy.

"Kyle, the NSC project will be run from the GlobalForce satellite office in Pretoria," Bill addressed the next steps for Kyle. "That office doesn't exist yet, but I've already been tasked with setting it up next time I'm down there. So, you won't be moving until after my next trip, but you can help me choose the new location, so you'll be going with me. Expect that trip probably next week, with your move to be shortly thereafter. Anything the company needs to handle for you?"

Kyle looked both surprised and happy at the news.

"Um, yeah," Kyle gathered his thoughts. "I also need to deal with my lease, and I need to sell my car and Anita will probably want to sell her car. And she has to give notice at her job."

"I'm sure the minister will have something she can do at the Home Affairs office, so I'll ask for a work visa for her as well, if she wants to work there." Bill saw this all changing quickly. "Same with the lease and cars as I told Taylor, just bring me receipts and documentation if you need me to reimburse you. Now go call your girlfriend and tell her the news. Hopefully she will be as excited as you think she will be. Okay, class dismissed. Eileen, hang back please."

Kyle and Taylor both jumped up and headed out of the conference room, talking excitedly. Bill got up and closed the door behind them and returned to his chair.

"I guess Sienna should have held off on her little pity party for a minute, huh?" Eileen said, trying to sound happier than she was showing in her expression.

Bill just looked at Eileen and gave her a moment to say what was bothering her, then took the lead when she remained silent.

"Tell me," Bill nudged.

"I can't believe that brat is just going to leave!" Eileen finally answered, her voice unsteady and a little louder than she intended.

"You were going to leave," Bill answered softly.

"That is not the same thing!" Eileen was genuinely upset. "He's breaking up the team, and you're letting him. Hell, you're helping him!"

"It kinda is the same thing," Bill began. "You were going to move to New Zealand in a couple years. So, the team would have been broken up at that time. And really, when Marky decided to not join us, the team was already breaking up. And if I am to put a finer point on it, when you three left LookAtMe, you broke up the team when you decided to go have a baby."

"I didn't *decide* to go have a baby," Eileen was really mad now, and Bill realized he had chosen his words poorly. "I *decided* to be a stay-at-home mom."

"And how was that going?" Bill asked softly. He knew he was on very dangerous ground now, but he really wanted to know what she was thinking.

"It was fucking awful," Eileen broke. "I was bored out of my head by noon the first day. I was going to come work here even if you only met half of my demands."

"You really shouldn't give away your negotiating secrets like that," Bill chuckled. "But I knew you would need something to do besides being her mom. And that's why we built in the considerations for your time after she is born. I want you to be as much of a mom to her as you want to be, and I want you working on my team."

"Yeah, well, your team just fell apart," Eileen answered.

"*No it didn't*, Eileen." Now Bill was getting irritated. "*Our* team is still intact. Kyle is still on our team, Taylor is more on our team as of five minutes ago than he ever was, and *you* are still on my team. Just the geography has changed. And, I got to keep the two strongest members of my database team."

Eileen considered that for a moment. Bill waited to let her speak first.

"I want to go now," Eileen finally said.

"Okay," Bill answered. "Let's go grab lunch."

"That's not what I mean," Eileen corrected him. "I want to move to New Zealand now."

Bill was caught completely off guard.

"What? Why now?"

Eileen remained silent for a moment, then nodded her head once, and took a deep breath before answering.

"Gary has been cheating on me, for a long time," Eileen began. "Like since before I got pregnant. And I've been lying to myself to try to not believe it. So, I need an advance on my pay to hire a lawyer and get the divorce going, and I want to move as soon as it's finalized. And I want my mom to go with me to help with the baby. Can we do all that?"

Bill thought it through.

"Hell, probably," Bill finally said. "Normally I'd say no, but nothing about this project has been normal. I'll be able to give you an answer to that after my call with the minister this afternoon."

Bill heard his phone ping with a message, but now was not the time to touch his phone.

"Thank you," Eileen said, wiping the tears off her face.

"You're welcome," Bill answered softly. Then he changed to a commanding tone. "And stop it. There are no tears in database engineering."

"I'm freaking pregnant, idiot!" Eileen snapped back in a mock-angry tone. "These aren't even mine, they're some emotional, moody chick's tears."

"Fair enough," Bill played along. "Lunch?"

"Hell yes, we are starving" Eileen answered and stood up, her facade solidly back in place.

Bill followed her out of the room.

As they were walking to their offices to drop off their stuff, Connie hollered to Bill.

"Bill, a moment before you leave, please!"

We need to get an intercom, Bill thought to himself.

"Be right there," Bill answered. Eileen shrugged and sat at her desk to wait.

"'Sup?" Bill asked as he rounded the corner into Connie's office.

"Sienna is gone," Connie began. "Kevin authorized only paying her any unused accrued vacation time, since she gave no notice. She wanted a severance package, and Kevin actually laughed at her. She got more pissed. Anyway, we cut her a check for the twenty-six hours of unused leave, took her keys, let her get her backpack out of her office, which Vasily searched, and which pissed her off more, and she left."

"Well, I'm sorry to lose her," Bill responded. "Taylor felt like she was a decent programmer, but I don't need that negativity on this team. We are all under a remarkable amount of stress, and her extra sensitivity was going to bring us down. Maybe she will get a gig wherever Francis is working."

"Maybe," Connie acknowledged.

"Okay, I am off to lunch," Bill ended the conversation.

"Vaya con Odin," Connie answered.

"Will do," Bill said as he left her office.

As Bill walked down the hallway to his office, he saw Vasily at the other end, standing with Eileen, waiting for him.

"Vasily, any chance we can just go get lunch without an armed escort?" Bill asked him.

Vasily just looked at Bill with his standard expressionless face.

"Of course not," Bill answered himself. "What was I thinking?"

Bill thought he saw a hint of a smirk on Vasily's face, but let it go.

"Where are Kyle and Taylor?" Bill asked Eileen, who just shrugged.

"Oh, they left right after they got out of the meeting," Kandi answered Bill. "They were really excited about something, and said they were going to get lunch and then run errands."

Eileen looked at Bill with just a hint of a smile.

"Looks like our team is still intact," she said.

"Looks like it," Bill answered, then headed towards the front door, with Vasily leading the way.

"How in the hell can you possibly justify these expenses to whomever you have to justify expenses to?" Bill asked, exasperated.

"Bill," M'Bulu chuckled, "what was the expression that angered you so on your first trip here?"

"Yeah, I get it," Bill didn't want to have to repeat the phrase, because he was pretty sure it would still anger him.

"Good," M'Bulu moved on. "Please forward the information to me for Ms. Chamberlain's advocate firm there, and we will make arrangements to engage that firm on her behalf. Meanwhile, I will reach out to my counterpart in New Zealand to arrange for your satellite office formation and Ms. Chamberlain's immigration and work papers, and also the necessary documentation for her mother and child. Additionally, I will need to know the full information for Kyle's partner so I can arrange for her documentation."

"I'm speechless, M'Bulu," Bill answered after a moment.

"I hope that now you understand my level of urgency, and the importance of these two projects to my government," M'Bulu answered. "You have shown me that you are key to the success of both, and that your people are key to your success. And while you did not choose Heinrich, you have found a way to lead him well, too. I see success in our future."

"As do I, Minister," Bill answered. "I'll get on this contract amendment and try to have it to you by the end of my day tomorrow. Again, M'Bulu, thank you."

"And my thanks to you and your team, Bill," M'Bulu answered, then disconnected the call.

Well, that went well, Bill thought to himself.

"You've gotta be shitting me," Kevin was stunned at the summary Bill had just given him regarding the call with M'Bulu.

"I know, it's a little stunning," Bill answered.

"So, we won't have any of our techs in this office anymore?" Kevin was trying to understand the scope and aftermath of all these new decisions.

"Well... no," Bill didn't bother to try to dance around the answer.

"Then what's the point of even having this office?" Kevin seemed to be panicking a little.

"Well, we have Switch 2 here," Bill was trying to help Kevin through the concern. "That's important. And, if we are to have a satellite office in Pretoria, and I guess now one somewhere in New Zealand too, either way, we need to have a head office, and the South Africans are pretty keen on having their technology partner headquartered in the United States. So, call it a figurehead here."

"You're sitting in the next board meeting with me to help explain why this entire office is still relevant," Kevin grumbled after a moment of thought.

"Can do," Bill hoped he didn't sound like a smart-ass to Kevin. Kevin seemed to not take offense.

"Well," Kevin concluded their meeting, "go tell your people the next steps. And maybe stop by Connie's office first to let her know that three of our employees will be offshore shortly."

Bill headed out to spread the word, and did stop by to explain the news to Connie as requested. Connie explained that there would be additional fees because of the currency exchanges and international direct deposits for the three employees, but it was all possible. Bill was happy to hear that. He headed to the conference room to update the team.

"Programmers! Mount up!" Bill hollered from the conference room, testing Taylor's memory. After a couple minutes, Eileen, Kyle, and Taylor all walked into the conference room and took seats.

"I wanted to bring you all up to speed after my conversation with Minister Mabusa," Bill began. "In short, all transfers have been approved."

The team interrupted him to cheer and high-five each other.

"Hang on, you heathens," Bill calmed them down. "I need to set realistic expectations with you. Taylor, you're going as soon as you're ready. Kyle, you'll be travelling with me next week to help me find and set up the office. While we are in Pretoria, you'll be staying in the Visiting Dignitary compound they have down there. It's higher security, which will be important to this project, but it's really nice living. They house me there when I'm in Pretoria. You have been invited by the minister to bring along Anita on this trip so they can help her find a gig as well. Then you can travel to Johannesburg to look for a 'flat'."

Kyle and Taylor were really happy to hear the news.

"Eileen," Bill addressed her individually, "your situation is different, but it has been approved. I'll discuss the details with you later one-on-one in your office."

"That works," Eileen answered happily.

"So, Taylor," Bill wrapped up the meeting. "Get your code checked in, get your office cleaned out, get your car sold, and get your lease for me. Kyle, I'll get with you later today after I talk with Eileen about her plans. Class dismissed."

——————————

Bill finished his planning meetings with his departing team members. He felt both happy and sad for them. He would miss Kyle and Eileen, and Taylor a little bit now, too.

As Bill was envisioning a completely different new future for his technical team, Kevin stuck his head into Bill's office.

"Got a minute?" Kevin asked.

"Sure," Bill answered.

Kevin closed the door and sat down.

"I am concerned about the new contract that we are going to sign with the South African government tomorrow," Kevin stated.

"Why?" Bill was surprised to hear that. "You heard M'Bulu say that they were going to cover all those new expenses."

"I am concerned because we literally have one client now," Kevin explained. "What happens when these projects are wrapped up?"

"Then I will retire," Bill answered jovially. "And I would suggest you do the same."

"I'm not joking," Kevin responded, somewhat irritated.

"Neither am I, Kevin," Bill countered, changing to his serious voice. "I get your concern about having all of our work centered on just one client, but we will be wealthy from these contracts, but I'll be too busy to enjoy it until it wraps up. So, I'm going to put the money in the bank, and when these projects are wrapped, I'm going to retire and go spend insane amounts of money in my favorite resorts."

"It really is that simple for you, isn't it?" Kevin asked.

"Yes Kevin, it really is," Bill answered. "This project is already paying us really well, and is going to pay us even better starting tomorrow. Work hard now, and look forward to a good retirement."

"Okay then."

Kevin stood up and left Bill's office.

That was weird, Bill thought to himself.

CHAPTER 61: CONTRACTUAL

The contract was revised and blessed by the American lawyers. Kevin read it through one more time, nursing his coffee as he read. Occasionally he shook his head slightly, and Bill figured those were the places where there was some ridiculous fee that would never have been accepted if the client was not a government entity with no real oversight.

"I almost feel dirty signing this," Kevin finally said after finishing reading.

"I know, Kevin," Bill agreed. "There are some expenditures that are wildly unusual, but this is what the client wants."

"'Unusual' is an understatement," Kevin said with an ironic chuckle, then he picked up his pen and signed and dated the contract, then did the same to the second copy. Once they were signed, he slid them across the desk to Bill.

"Send them off to the minister," Kevin finished signing, and put his pens away.

"Will do," Bill answered. "He's using a diplomatic courier for this, so I'll let him know that we have the docs ready."

Bill's phone pinged the receipt of a new SMS message.

MY COURIER WILL BE THERE IN 15 MINUTES, SECURITY TEAM IS AWARE

"Well, look at that," Bill said, then read the message to Kevin.

"Sometimes I feel like we are bugged," Kevin said with a hint of humor in his voice.

"Yeah, heh heh, it does seem so sometimes, huh?" Bill really felt bad keeping the secret from Kevin, but Kevin knew Bill had secrets, and had previously given permission for Bill to have them, so Bill set aside the guilty feelings.

Bill stood and left Kevin to his emails, and headed to the front desk with the contracts. He spoke with Vasily, who did indeed already know the courier was coming. Bill asked Vasily to give the folder with the contracts to the courier directly, and to escort that person to their car to ensure nothing happened to the documents. Bill almost felt foolish making the request over 28 pieces of paper, but the value of those pieces of paper to GlobalForce was vast, and Bill wanted the documents protected until they were in the courier's car.

Vasily assured Bill that all would be handled as Bill asked.

Bill headed back to his office to await the inevitable call from M'Bulu and catch up on emails. He also needed to have a call with Heinrich to see how things were progressing there.

After lunch, Bill thought to himself, and jumped into his emails.

CHAPTER 62: ERIK'S TOY

"You asked to see me?" Amir's cell leader asked, growing impatient that Amir had not acknowledged his presence next to Amir for several moments.

"Oh, yes brother," Amir said, slightly startled. "Good news! We have verified for a certainty that the Switch 3 *is* in South Africa, and is connected to the Russian Embassy, but doesn't appear to be *in* the Russian embassy."

"That does not sound like good news," the leader answered.

"It is," Amir responded happily. "Now, we can change our surveillance efforts. Rather than watching the embassy, we need to instead monitor where all of the people and vehicles that enter the embassy may go. We should put trackers on all of them. And if we can get microphones into the vehicles, then we may hear the information we need."

Amir's leader pondered the news for a moment.

"It will be done," he finally said, and turned to give instructions.

Amir returned to his keyboard.

I will find your toy, Erik Torssen, Amir spoke the threat in a whisper. *And when I do, with Allah's assistance and grace, I will use your magic box to win this war.*

CHAPTER 63: WASTED TRIP

Heinrich looked terrible. Bill was now very concerned.

"You look awful, Heinrich," Bill said to Heinrich as soon as the picture loaded up on their chat.

"I feel fine," Heinrich responded with a chuckle. "The LHC is going to be so far advanced from where it is now once we finish the upgrades on it!"

Heinrich was obviously in his element, but Bill still worried about his health.

"Yeah, that's great," Bill remained on point. "Are you eating and sleeping and bathing?"

Heinrich laughed.

"Yes, mate, I am," Heinrich calmed Bill's concerns. "These damn Russians keep reminding me to do all of those things. They even turn off all my internet access to force me to sleep. And the minister scheduled food to be brought to me from the dining hall three times each day. And my guards threatened to put an IV in my arm if I don't get enough fluids. So I am fine."

Bill would have to thank Vasily for that.

"I am happy to hear that," Bill answered.

Heinrich chuckled at that.

Bill continued.

"Tell me about your proposed upgrades to the LHC. And use terms I can understand."

"Oh, this thing is going to be a titan, man," Heinrich was clearly excited about what the future would bring.

"Be careful with that word, my friend," Bill responded with mock seriousness. "The last time some marvel of modern technology referenced that word, it was brought down by an ice cube."

Heinrich laughed hard at that.

"So noted," Heinrich replied. "I'll make sure I put in a lot of room for safeguards to make sure this thing doesn't get away from us."

"Appreciated," Bill acknowledged. "Anyway, how close are you to being finished with the design upgrade documentation?"

"It's getting there," Heinrich said after a moment of thought. "What day is today?"

"Tuesday."

"Tue-...," Heinrich clearly did not know that time was passing outside his bubble. "Okay, well anyway, I should have the proposal ready to go over with you and the minister by Monday."

"That works, I will schedule a meeting with the minister for that day," Bill wrapped up the call. "Stay sane, and remember to breathe."

"Will do," Heinrich answered with a chuckle. "Cheers."

"Cheers," Bill disconnected the call.

Bill's phone beeped, and he picked it up and read the message.

YOU WILL BE FLYING ON SUNDAY MONDAY. JUST PLAN TO MEET IN MY OFFICE ON TUESDAY TO GO OVER THE UPGRADE PLAN.

Bill doubted he would ever become accustomed to the surveillance under which he now lived his entire life.

I wonder what will happen if I get a girlfriend? Bill thought to himself, then answered himself. *Serves them right if they listen in on that mess.*

Bill chuckled to himself, then answered M'Bulu.

RTOGERT THJAT

Bill then sent a quick email to Heinrich and M'Bulu to let them know that the LHC upgrade proposal would be a meeting at the ministry on Tuesday. They could put it on their own calendars.

The meeting did not go as planned, and Bill was not happy about having to fly halfway across the world only to find out from M'Bulu that the budget and project plan were grossly understated and completely insufficient.

"M'Bulu," Bill finally was able to speak after the long argument between M'Bulu and Heinrich, "you could have told me all of this from my comfortable nest in Phoenix. There was no reason for me to fly here to hear that we have a lot more work to do before you approve this budget."

"On the contrary, Doctor Fibilee," M'Bulu changed to formal, so Bill paid close attention, and he noticed that Heinrich had calmed down too, and was also paying attention. "I wanted to make sure that you and Doctor de Boer fully understand the gravity of this project plan and budget."

M'Bulu clapped twice, and the white noise turned on.

"You will not have another chance at upgrading the Machine for several years," M'Bulu continued, leaning in so Bill and Heinrich could hear him. "These will be the only changes you can make to structure and systems before the second Machine is built and operational. It is imperative that you include everything in this budget and plan that will carry the Machine through for that entire time."

M'Bulu sat back and let Bill and Heinrich think about what he had said. A few seconds later, the white noise shut off.

"Well," Bill finally said, "it looks like we have a lot more work to do. Heinrich, let's head back to your place and figure out our plan for restarting work on this plan before I head home tomorrow."

"Yup."

After pleasantries, Bill and Heinrich returned to Heinrich's flat and enjoyed some lemon lime sports drink while starting over on their project plan before his flight home the next day.

CHAPTER 64: OFFICIALLY CERTIFIED

Bill heard the front door chime, and a new voice chat with Kandi. Then he heard Vasily's and Kandi's footsteps approaching his office. Kandi introduced the new person as the "South African Travel Liaison". Bill motioned her to sit, which she did, and then Vasily stepped into the office and closed the door. Bill thought that was odd.

"I'm sorry, I missed your name," Bill felt dumb for not paying attention after hearing the woman's title.

"Mikysa Farnsworth," she responded.

"Ms. Farnsworth," Bill began, "how may I be of assistance?"

"I am actually here to assist you with your travel plans for next week," she began. "The Minister has asked that the embassy here facilitate all of the travel arrangements and accompanying documentation for you and your team going forward."

"I appreciate that," Bill responded, then looked at Vasily.

"Vasily, why are you in here?"

"For coordination of travel plans," Vasily answered in his usual dry way.

Bill was confused.

"If I may, Doctor," Ms. Farnsworth stepped in, noting Bill's confused look. "The government of South Africa has placed your team on our list of

VIPs now, due to the importance and security of your projects. As such, your security teams will travel with you going forward. Your security team leader here needs to know what the plans are so he can coordinate his personnel."

Now Bill was stunned.

"First things first," Ms. Farnsworth continued in Bill's silence, "You, Mr. Smalley, and Ms. Stapelton will be travelling to Pretoria, with the arrival time to be approximately noon local time on Monday."

She stopped speaking and looked to Bill for acknowledgement.

"Listen, I apologize," Bill was exasperated. "You really have me at a disadvantage here. You are much more prepared for this conversion than I am, because I just got reminded not five minutes before you arrived that I am traveling next week. First, which travel agency are you with?"

Ms. Farnsworth smiled disarmly.

"No, my apologies, Doctor Fibulee," she clarified. "I work in the South African embassy. I arrange travel for diplomats and dignitaries and other various VIPs when they are to travel on embassy vehicles. You and your personnel and security teams will be flying on a South African government-chartered aircraft."

She paused to give Bill a chance to process what she had just said, then continued after a moment.

"You will fly from Phoenix to Miami, where you will re-fuel, then will fly direct to Pretoria, landing at Waterkloof Air Force Base. From there, you will be taken by car to your previously-assigned quarters. Quarters at the Visiting Dignitary Housing have been assigned for Mr. Dobson, and for Mr. Smalley and Ms. Stapelton temporarily until they locate an acceptable residences in Johannesburg, and I have their work permits here."

Ms. Farnsworth removed some documents from her folder and set them on Bill's desk before continuing.

"The minister will have your permanent work documentation waiting for you when you meet with him on Tuesday, and permanent resident documentation will be arranged by the ministry for Dobson, Smalley, and Stapelton once they are in-country. Do you have any questions?"

Bill just looked at her for a minute before answering.

"Dozens," Bill stated flatly.

He was pretty sure he heard Vasily laugh, but when he looked, Vasily's face was unchanged.

Bill continued.

"I'm sorry, Ms. Farnsworth, this is just very new to me," Bill fumbled. "First question: who are Smalley and Stapleton?"

"Taylor Smalley is on your team, and Anita Stapleton is his domestic partner," Ms. Farnsworth answered without a hint of derision.

"I'm an idiot," Bill answered.

This time, Bill was sure he heard Vasily laugh, and when he looked, he detected the slightest hint of a smirk on Vasily's face.

"Not at all, sir," Ms. Farnsworth answered right away. "It's very common when first arranging these kinds of trips to feel slightly off balance. That is why I'm here, to help you through it all. In the future, this will become easier for you."

"I appreciate your assistance more than you can imagine, Ms. Farnsworth," Bill recovered. "So, what are our actual travel plans?"

"The minister asked that I suggest that you pack light for your time in Pretoria, because he suggested that you should just acquire a wardrobe in Pretoria in order to ease your travel. Bring your passport as always. Mr. Dobson, Mr. Smalley, and Ms. Stapleton all indicated that they were able to pack what they needed to bring into one large suitcase each, so they should bring that and their passports. The car will pick you up between 8:00 and 8:30 on Sunday morning, and will take you to the executive terminal, where you'll be met by the flight crew, and you are scheduled to be airborne by 10:00 Sunday morning."

"How do I get home?" Bill wanted to know that answer, because this was all going very quickly.

"You return on an embassy charter two Sundays after you arrive," Ms.

Farnsworth answered without hesitation.

"Well, okay then," Bill took it all in.

"Since this is your first trip like this," Ms. Farnsworth concluded, "I will meet you at the executive terminal when your car arrives to take you through the diplomatic procedures. Since you are traveling on a diplomatic flight and coming out of a diplomatic automobile, you do not go through Customs or your TSA checkpoints. That usually causes raised eyebrows, but that is how it works."

"No Customs?" Bill joked. "I'll be sure to pack cocaine and firearms."

"Is not joking matter," Vasily spoke up suddenly, admonishing Bill for the first time since they knew each other.

Ms. Farnsworth shook her head.

"You still don't want to joke about things like that, doctor," Ms. Farnsworth clarified. "International transportation of illicit substances into South Africa is punishable by death. And they are not humane about it in the ways that your nation is."

"My bad," Bill stood down. "Then if there is nothing else, I will see you at the executive terminal on Sunday morning, Ms. Farnsworth."

Ms. Farnsworth closed her folder and smiled and stood, extending her hand. Bill stood and shook her hand.

"Very good, doctor," Ms. Farnsworth answered. "I will see you then."

Vasily opened the door and Ms. Farnsworth walked out. Vasily paused and looked back at Bill for a moment, shaking his head, then also left.

Yup, I'm an idiot, Bill thought to himself.

"Programmers! Mount up!" Bill hollered on his way to the conference room, paperwork in hand for Taylor and Kyle.

The team all took seats at the table. Bill slid the various packets across the table.

"Congratulations, you are now officially certified to live and work in South Africa," Bill said to Kyle and Taylor.

Eileen conspicuously cleared her throat.

"You get nothing," Bill joked. "Seriously though, your documents will take a bit longer while we work through the other items for you here."

"I figured," Eileen agreed, "but you could have at least slid a blank piece of paper or something for me so I don't feel left out."

The team laughed.

"Okay, let's discuss plans," Bill turned the meeting serious. "Kyle and Taylor, we all will be picked up early Sunday morning by South African diplomatic cars to be taken to the airport for our flight to South Africa. We'll arrive basically late Monday afternoon, and we'll get settled. Kyle, you and I have a meeting at the ministry on Tuesday, and they'll get you settled into an office. Taylor, you and Anita will be driven down to Joburg on Tuesday so you can meet your team, and meet the representative that will help you find living space that is acceptable to the government for your safety. Then we'll all meet back in Pretoria for dinner."

Kyle and Taylor looked stunned.

Bill continued.

"Eileen, I'll be there for a couple weeks, so just keep working on your stuff here. You can work from home or in the office, your choice."

"I'll probably do afternoons at home," Eileen answered. "That way I can keep getting my mom moved in and Gary moved out."

"Wait, what?!" Kyle was shocked. "Gary is moving out?"

"I guess I forgot to tell you in all the excitement," Eileen answered him. "I'll tell you about it later, but yeah, I am moving on without him."

Kyle didn't answer, but just looked stunned.

"Okay, class dismissed," Bill wrapped up the meeting. "Kyle and Taylor, get your code checked in, go see Connie about any paperwork updates, and get packing. For the rest of the week, your job is to get prepped for relocation to South Africa. And yes, take your laptops. I will see you on Sunday morning at the airport. Eileen, business as usual, you already know your tasks."

"Yup," Eileen agreed.

The team filed out of the room. Bill followed them a few steps behind, a little overcome with nostalgia.

CHAPTER 65: THE FIRST DROP

Amir scrolled through the list of transactions in the account, and checked the balance again.

"Five hundred thirty billion Euros," Amir whispered to himself.

In the six months since the other operating team had located and successfully infiltrated the location of Switch 3, and reopened the back door to Amir, the operation was still only running infrequent and relatively small thefts in order to continue to avoid detection. Amir had insisted that they keep the amounts relatively small, and that no two transactions pulled from the same bank, same victim, or same nation, in a row. Amir insisted that the rogue transactions must remain untraceable for as long as possible, and not having a pattern to the transactions was important.

Amir had also watched with humor and satisfaction as the disputes for the transactions rolled through the system, and with each rejection of a dispute, Amir's plan was justified a bit more with the leadership. At some point, the complaints were going to reach the management team at Finland Global, and at that time, more scrutiny of the Switch network was sure to follow, but for now, the infallibility of the Switch network was unquestioned. And Amir rejoiced in the arrogance of Finland Global.

"Five hundred thirty billion Euros is just the first drop, *Erik*," Amir said quietly to no one in the room. "We will take it all, and you will be the villain."

CHAPTER 66: TWENTY-TWO MONTHS

In the eighteen months since moving his team to South Africa, Bill had spent less and less time in Arizona, and hadn't been back to America in over two months. As he sat in the commissary eating his breakfast and preparing for the start of the week meeting with his team, it struck Bill that he was enjoying the work, and didn't miss being "home". Pretoria now felt as much like home as Phoenix ever had. He grinned for a moment at that irony, then went back to his notes.

Bill's new phone pinged in a new message. He checked it to see a message containing only a photo from Eileen. It was a picture of Matilda sitting on a sheep, Eileen holding her in place. Matilda had the biggest smile on her face. Bill mused that Eileen looked happier than he could ever remember her looking. New Zealand fits her well, Bill said to himself.

South Africa fit his other two primary team members well too, and the productivity on the chip card programs had been a remarkable success. As much as Bill had initially personally been against the NSC project, while his concerns still existed, he tried to make himself feel better by ignoring the destruction of personal privacy that the project, his project, was causing within the nation. The project was in maintenance now, with only occasional major version releases, so it didn't take up much of his time. Kyle and Taylor were both working on the project now, and were both in Johannesburg full time, as M'Bulu had eventually added a RFID chip to the National ID card, and folded the National ID card project into the NSC project. Taylor gave Kyle regular updates, and Bill relied on Kyle as the project lead.

That gave Bill the opportunity to ignore his screaming conscience and instead focus on the Switch Q project. Not that the Switch Q project gave him any less mental heartburn, it was just different from the NSC project.

Bill's phone pinged again.

YOUR MESSAGE SAYING HOW ADORABLE SHE IS FAILED TO REACH ME

Bill realized he had been lost in his thoughts, and forgot to respond.

MY BAD, SHE IS ADORABLE

Bill was still surprised when his messages were free of abhorrent typos, even though the automatic correction feature would sometimes put in words that were not what he intended. Bill figured that was a lesser evil than his bad spelling.

I KNOW

Bill remarked on the confidence change in Eileen since her relocation to the southern island nation fifteen months ago. She seemed healthier, happier, far more confident. He was happy that the projects had offered this opportunity for her.

ARE YOU GOING TO BE READY FOR THE STATUS CALL IN AN HOUR?

Bill knew the question was unnecessary, but he hadn't verbally sparred with her in quite a while.

ARE YOU?

"There she is," Bill said to himself and set the phone back down on the table.

He finished his breakfast and notes, and headed back to his cottage.

———————

Just as Bill was wrapping up the video conference with his NSC team, he heard a knock at his front door, followed by Vasily greeting Heinrich, who helped himself to a bottle of water from Bill's refrigerator, and then sat down at the table with Bill.

Bill closed his laptop as he finished the call.

"Good morning, Heinrich," Bill began. "You ready for the final presentation this afternoon?"

"Ja," Heinrich answered in his usual short, arrogant way, with just a hint of a grin.

"Good," Bill answered in kind. "Run me through the science fiction that we are going to want funded."

Bill was glad he was sitting down when Heinrich opened with the nine hundred sixty billion Euro budget. When Bill tried to object, Heinrich ignored him and plodded on through the justifications. Most of the expenditures were for upgrades and enhancements to various components of the Large Hadron Collider, including many safety upgrades, several of which Bill had to demand.

The timeline was approximately twenty-eight months. Bill had no idea if that was realistic or not, but after their meeting with M'Bulu later in the afternoon, Bill would regroup with Heinrich and they'd work on any changes that might be suggested. Bill was glad that he had been able to convince M'Bulu to let them do the main presentation for the upgrades to The Committee, as M'Bulu had referred to them, via a video call, rather than having to travel to Geneva.

Bill was sure that eventually they would have to make the journey before funding was approved, but for today, he'd be home by dinner time.

———

"Your budget is acceptable," M'Bulu finally stated, causing Bill to almost fall out of his chair, "but the timeline is not acceptable."

"Is there a timeline you had in mind?" Heinrich asked, not bothering to wait for Bill to ask the same question.

"Yes," M'Bulu answered flatly. "Fully functional within eighteen months."

"That's fu-" Heinrich began, clearly suddenly outraged.

"Minister," Bill interrupted Heinrich quickly in order to regain some stability in the conversation. "Obviously, in order to shorten the timeline as significantly as you have asked, the budget will go up, but we still may not be able to reduce it that far. There are many elements of the project that have dependencies that may not be able to be completed concurrently. Please give us a few days to rework the timeline and budget, and let us get back to you once we have new information."

"Granted," M'Bulu answered happily. "I will push back the presentation with The Committee until a week from tomorrow, so you and Heinrich do not feel rushed and can be very thorough in your reworking of the budget and timeline."

Bill caught the code phrase from M'Bulu. Several months prior, Bill had presented a budget for an enhancement on the other project to M'Bulu, and M'Bulu had laughed and said it was too low. When Bill had remarked that he was surprised to have heard that, M'Bulu had told him that if he ever felt that Bill needed to turn up a budget for some reason, he would just use the phrase "be thorough", and Bill would know to charge more.

"Understood, Minister," Bill answered, acknowledging both the new timeline and the new budget directive.

M'Bulu bowed his head slightly with a hint of a grin and disconnected the call.

"It's not possible, even with more money," Heinrich growled.

Bill looked at him for a moment.

"You sure?" Bill finally asked.

"Yes." Another typical flat, and arrogant, response from Heinrich.

"Doctor *Torssen*," Bill finally stated, snapping Heinrich's attention to full power with the use of his real surname, "I believe this is the first time I've heard you be wrong without realizing it."

Heinrich's face actually registered surprise, rather than anger.

Bill continued.

"I may not be a quota physics-ologist like you, but I do know project timeline bullshit when I hear it."

Bill saw the slightest crack in Heinrich's facade of confidence, so he continued.

"I know that if I went through every dependency in your timeline, I would find at least three that could be accomplished concurrently to something else."

Another crack in the facade.

"And if I can find at least three of them, that means that I can easily take six months off your timeline, and cut it down to twenty two months. That means I only need to find one more mistake in your dependencies to get us down to eighteen months."

Heinrich finally broke.

"There is no way to get it down to eighteen months," Heinrich's loud words sounded more defensive than angry, which surprised Bill. "I'll spend time going through it, but you don't understand the science of these pieces. All we need is one uninformed project manager to force through a stupid change, and the world could end."

Nice jab, Bill thought.

"Well, go home and take a look," Bill answered. "Can you make all the safety testing concurrent and move all of it to the end of the project?"

"N... no," Heinrich answered quickly.

"You hesitated," Bill pointed it out. "Wouldn't be doin' my job if I didn't ask why."

"Just something in my gut tells me that it would be a bad idea," Heinrich responded after a moment of thought. "I don't know why yet, but I think it's a bad idea."

"Well, go prove me wrong," Bill finished up the meeting. "Let's have breakfast on Wednesday and talk about your preliminary findings."

"Got it, boss," Heinrich agreed. "See you then. By the way, what is a 'quota physics-ologist'?"

"It's what you are," Bill responded with a straight face.

"Do you mean 'quantum physicist'?" Heinrich asked, trying to meet the same level of humor.

"Whatever," Bill answered, still in character. "You science-ists and your made-up words... get out."

Heinrich half grinned and turned towards the door.

Vasily showed Heinrich out, and Bill was left alone with his thoughts. It didn't sit well with him that Heinrich was uncomfortable about something with the modifications to the tech or timeline, but was unable to define the discomfort.

"It's too low," Bill stated flatly around a mouthful of Pretoria-style Denver omelet at their Wednesday morning meeting.

"What is that American expression?" Heinrich was way too prepared for Bill's objection. "'Hypocrite much?' *Ja*, that's the one."

"How do you mean?" Bill knew he was being set up, but played along, because he was pretty sure where this was going.

"You were gob smacked when I was at almost a trillion Euros," Heinrich began, "but now you're telling me that this new number is too low?"

"Yes," Bill answered, attempting to match the same style that Heinrich used too often.

"The new budget is almost fifty percent higher," Heinrich argued.

"Maybe," Bill countered, "but are you down to eighteen months?"

"No, but I am down to twenty-two," Heinrich answered, concern growing in his voice.

"Then the budget is still too low," Bill answered, knowing Heinrich would be exasperated by the response.

"How can you believe that?" Heinrich was exasperated. "You were the one who was so upset about the original budget, and now you're still saying it's too low?"

"Heinrich," Bill began, trying to calm Heinrich down and get him on the same page, "what was the minister's only objection?"

"The timeline," Heinrich answered easily.

"Right. And what did the minister say about the budget?"

Heinrich thought for a moment before responding.

"I don't think he said anything about it," Heinrich finally stated.

"He said 'be very thorough in your reworking of the budget and timeline'," Bill reminded Heinrich, attempting to match M'Bulu's accent as he quoted him.

"Okay, yes, I remember that," Heinrich responded with a chuckle.

"Good," Bill continued. "And again, what was his only objection?"

"He objected to the timeline," Heinrich repeated.

"Right. And regardless of this budget," Bill finished his point, "the only condition the minister gave us was that the project must be completed in eighteen months."

"Bill," Heinrich was clearly frustrated, "I'm telling you I can not get the project down to eighteen months. The best I can do is twenty-two."

"Did you shuffle the safety tests to the end like I suggested?" Bill asked, not expecting it to have been done.

"Yes, some," Heinrich acknowledged. "But we can not move them all. Some need to be run before we can attach other mechanical parts. This is as short as I can make it, regardless of budget."

Bill considered Heinrich's words while he enjoyed another bite of his omelet.

"Okay, my friend," Bill concluded. "Finish up your breakfast, and spend the rest of the time tightening up the timeline. And make absolutely sure the budget will support the project and any surprises."

"If you say so," Heinrich answered nonchalantly. "Then two trillion Euros it is."

"No, it isn't," Bill responded flatly.

CHAPTER 67: THERE ARE NO CABLES

"I am telling you," Bjorn was in full rage now. "There is no possible way that the network is authorizing unauthorized transactions! It is physically not capable."

"We understand that you believe your words, *Gospodin* Rødtskjegg," the Russian official spoke from the video conference. "But we have now identified almost four hundred billion Euros of transactions that were authorized by the Switch network that have been disputed by the owners of the originating accounts. We expect this number to go higher as more of the disputes are researched. And all of these transactions, regardless of their origin, have been deposited into one of ten different accounts at one bank in Mauritius. How do you explain this?"

Bjorn had no answer, but he was sure it was not from a flaw in the Switch network nor in the devices themselves.

"Ministers," Bjorn tried a different tack. "It is physically impossible for a bad actor to inject fraudulent transactions into the network. The only way to inject transactions into the network is through a cable plugged into the back of the physical devices, and those ports are under direct twenty-four-hour surveillance. None of them have a cable plugged into that port."

"Are you sure?" The Chinese minister asked.

"Yes!" Bjorn picked up his laptop and walked to the screen showing the video feed from the three cameras pointed at the backs of the Switches around the world, and pointed the camera from his laptop at the screen.

"There!" Bjorn let his anger show. "THERE. ARE. NO. CABLES. PLUGGED. INTO. THOSE. SLOTS."

Bjorn returned to his desk and set his laptop back down, adjusting the top back to his preferred angle.

"Mr. Rødtskjegg," Minister Mabusa took the questioning in a different direction. "How do you account for the fact that in every one of these transactions that have been found to be fraudulent, there is no originating record from the financial institution?"

Bjorn was stunned, and didn't respond right away. The minister took the opportunity to continue.

"And in every one of those cases, some process within Finland Global Financial's network apparently generated some sort of originating record, and fed it into the validation stream."

Minister Mabusa's direct examination, though calm, was withering, and after a moment, he continued.

"If, as you say, there is no possible vulnerability in the Switch network, then what other system within Finland Global's operation may be the compromised node?"

Bjorn still could not respond, as he had no idea how any of this was possible.

"Ministers," Bjorn finally responded, his anger replaced with worry and humility. "I will raise this issue to the highest levels of network security within the organization, and we will locate any compromised machines or processes and resolve this issue."

"See that you do," the American participant stated harshly, and disconnected.

The other participants disconnected just as abruptly, but without comment, leaving Bjorn alone in his office to contemplate the impossible.

"I told them we would need Erik eventually," Bjorn finally said to himself. "Too bad they put him on that plane. Now we have no way to truly fix this."

Bjorn opened a new email, and began typing the description of the issue. He included all of the top officers of the company, his boss, and head of Network Operations in his distribution list.

If this got away from them, Bjorn swore to himself that he would not be the one taking the fall.

CHAPTER 68: ACTIONABLE DATA

Bill and M'Bulu sat at the small conference table in M'Bulu's office. A staff member entered the room with a box, and approached the table.

"Your lunch, Minister," the aide stated.

"Ah, thank you, Keila," M'Bulu responded.

M'Bulu's aide set plates in front of M'Bulu and Bill, and then handed them each wrapped sandwiches. Bill thanked the aide, and then unwrapped the sandwich.

"Turkey breast with provolone and dill pickle slices, 'easy mayo', as you call it, on sourdough, I believe is your favorite?" M'Bulu answered Bill's unasked question.

"I see the NSC project is returning actionable data," Bill answered. "And correct, thank you."

M'Bulu laughed.

"We had Clausen dill pickles and sourdough starter brought into the commissary at the Dignitary compound for you," M'Bulu continued. "I had to approve the requisition."

Bill appreciated the fresh-baked bread.

"M'Bulu," Bill said after enjoying the first bite, "I don't even care that you're watching what I eat. This is great, thank you. I didn't realize that this had been brought in special for me."

"You are welcome, my friend," M'Bulu answered with a laugh. "Now let us discuss the status of the budget and timeline for the quantum Switch processing."

Bill took another bite of his sandwich and swallowed it before answering.

"Sure. It's at one trillion two hundred billion Euros right now, and will take twenty-two months."

Bill took another bite to let M'Bulu consider his response.

"You may increase the budget to one point five trillion, but it must be completed in eighteen months," M'Bulu stated after a moment of thought.

"Minister," Bill set down his sandwich and switched to formal for a moment, "it doesn't matter how far we increase the budget, we can't make it faster. Nine women can not make a baby in one month."

"Ah, but they can if you start with nine very pregnant women," M'Bulu answered cryptically.

"I don't even know what that means," Bill countered.

"Pre-assemble everything at the same time," M'Bulu explained. "That way, you don't have to wait for the main build to be completed on the downstream parts."

"Then do the final tweaking on site," Bill said as much to himself as to MBulu, picking up on the thought process. "We were already planning to do that, but maybe we can do more pre-build, and increase the engineer headcount on the tweaking tasks. That might buy us a little more time. Can we change the completion time part of the contract to say 'eighteen to twenty-two months'?"

"I'm sure I can convince The Committee to agree to that," M'Bulu granted. "But Bill, they will still want it completed within eighteen months regardless. You and Doctor de Boer should plan to leave Sunday afternoon for the trip to Geneva. You will present on Tuesday morning."

"I thought we were going to do the initial presentation via video conference," Bill clarified.

"You were, but you are ready now, so we will leave Sunday," M'Bulu concluded the discussions.

"I will inform Heinrich," Bill answered, and finished his sandwich.

CHAPTER 69: MISTAKEN FOR SOMEONE ELSE

Bill awoke to sunlight streaming through his hotel window, and for a moment was aware of the absence of the racket from the hadedas that normally served as his alarm clock.

The flight up from Pretoria the previous afternoon had been uneventful, and the plane was very comfortable. Bill slept well. Dinner at the South African embassy in Geneva was every bit as good as the food he had come to enjoy in Pretoria.

Bill got out of bed and stretched, looking out the window. He immediately regretted not bringing his camera, as the view from his suite was spectacular. Bill wondered to himself if he had time to go get one here and go sightseeing. He decided he would check with M'Bulu at breakfast.

An hour later, Bill was sitting at the table in the restaurant with M'Bulu and Heinrich. M'Bulu was laying out their schedule for the day and evening, mostly diplomatic meet and greet type of meetings so M'Bulu could show off the top assets of the Switch project. There would be no time for camera shopping or sightseeing before the meeting. Neither Bill nor Heinrich were comfortable with these types of meetings, but they agreed to go along with it in advance of the big meeting the following day with The Committee.

Bill had a thought.

"Minister, have we considered that there may be an issue if Heinrich is mistaken for someone else?" Bill phrased the question carefully.

"Yes, actually," M'Bulu answered right away. "If anyone does make a comment or ask a dangerous question, we will laugh it off as ridiculous, and move on. It is imperative that none of us react with anything but humor."

"Fair enough," Heinrich answered. "I haven't been that guy in years."

The three men laughed and finished their breakfast, then set out for their day.

CHAPTER 70: STING THEM

"Brother!" One of Amir's technical team hurried into his office. "They have found our intrusion!"

"Abdel, calm down, and tell me all of the details," Amir needed to know all that they knew, and needed his assistant to be calm so he would miss nothing.

Abdel took a calming breath and began to explain what they knew. The back door that they had been using for months to monitor network traffic at Finland Global network suddenly stopped transmitting any log information for about an hour, and then started transmitting again, but quick analysis found that the log traffic was just repeated loops of old logs, and not valid. Clearly, the network team at Finland Global had found their low-level connection, and rather than closing it, made a clumsy attempt at trying to fool Amir's team.

Amir grinned, and laughed to himself.

"Abdel, do you have enough control to get back into that network control node and access the command path in it?" Amir had a thought.

"Yes, brother, I believe we do," Abdel answered.

"Good. Go in, erase the BIOS in the network distribution node and reboot it, then do the same to the computer that you're using to access their network. It won't bring them down, but it will sting them, and they will know we are not to be underestimated. They will not find us again." Amir wanted to strike a bit of a slap at the network team at Finland Global for thinking Amir was stupid enough to believe their fake data feed.

A slow smile crept across Abdel's face.

"Immediately, brother!" Abdel ran out of the room to finish the task.

"I'm coming for you, Erik," Amir said to himself.

CHAPTER 71: IN SESSION

The Committee was already in session when Bill and Heinrich were shepherded into the room.

The room was mostly dark, the faces of The Committee members were not really clear enough in the dim light, but Bill was sure he could identify M'Bulu as one of them. He was unable to make out the other seven faces. Bill and Heinrich were led to a heavy-looking ornate table in the middle of the room, well-lit from above, facing the desk behind which the members sat. There was a pitcher of water and two crystal glasses on a silver tray on the table between the microphones. Bill grabbed a glass and filled it right away, knowing he would probably need it during the meeting.

Once they had settled into their chairs and their microphones tested, a light lit M'Bulu's face. He adjusted his microphone and began speaking.

"Doctors Fibulee and de Boer, welcome." M'Bulu began. "We appreciate your willingness to come before The Committee today to discuss your plans for the upgrade of the Large Hadron Collider in the furtherance of the Quantum Switch program."

Bill and Heinrich mumbled their thanks into their microphones, and M'Bulu continued.

"As you know, there are several nations covertly involved in the Quantum Switch project." M'Bulu then introduced each representative at the desk and the nation they represented as each face was lit up. M'Bulu represented South Africa, West Africa, and Democratic Republic of Congo, which came as a surprise to Bill, because he knew nothing about the involvement of the other nations he represented. The other nations represented at the desk were China, Germany, Switzerland, Russia, Mauritius, and the United States.

There was one more to introduce.

"And finally," M'Bulu said with a dramatic pause, "Doctor Keith vanGreig, whom I believe you know."

"Keith!" Bill and Heinrich both yelled simultaneously.

"Hello, chums," Keith answered happily as his light came on. "Good to see you still breathing."

"You have some explaining to do," Heinrich said with a laugh.

"We'll grab a pint tonight after dinner, and I'll catch you up," Keith promised.

"Um, Doctor vanGreig," Bill began, intentionally being formal, "it's not that I'm not happy to see you, because I really am, but what are you doing on this board? I thought you decided to walk away?"

"Well," Keith decided to give a straight answer so they could move on. "Within a week after I left South Africa, I became aware of my tail. A few days after that, I became aware of another one. Then I realized that the second tail was following the first one. So, I reached out to Minister Mabusa and asked him to stop having me tailed. He was surprised, because neither of the tails were his, so he had both tails eliminated and provided security for me since then. After I got my anger out of my system, I agreed to consult on this project. I figured, if I can't stop you, I will instead sit on this board and be a nay-sayer."

"How about if you just come back on the team instead?" Bill asked.

"I am afraid that will not be possible," the Russian representative spoke up. "Doctor vanGreig will continue to serve as our liaison to the project."

Bill sat back, surprised at the admonishment.

M'Bulu resumed control of the meeting.

"Doctors, if you would please present your budget and project plan, we would be very appreciative. We will break in two hours for lunch, and then resume at 1:30 this afternoon, during which time, the members will ask questions. You have the floor."

Bill looked at Heinrich, who indicated that he wanted to go first, so Bill let him.

Heinrich presented his one point five trillion Euros budget and hit the high points of the various expenditures. He spent the first ninety minutes on these topics, and then the Chinese representative interrupted.

"I apologize for the interruption," the Chinese representative stated. "You have not told us the timeline yet, and I want to make certain that this is also addressed in your presentation."

Heinrich stammered a bit, so Bill took over.

"Minister Xa," Bill did his best impersonation of a diplomat. "We anticipate the project will be completed within eighteen months, with a four-month contingency."

There was no answer from any board members, so Bill nudged Heinrich to continue. As Heinrich picked up where he had been interrupted, Bill made eye contact with M'Bulu, who was smiling. Bill assumed that was a good thing.

Heinrich concluded his presentation right on time, and Minister Mabusa gavelled the lunch break. An aide escorted Bill and Heinrich out the door and to an exquisitely decorated dining room, which was under heavy guard. Bill was relieved to see Vasily and his team in the room. Bill waved to Vasily, who only responded with a wink.

M'Bulu and Keith joined Bill and Heinrich for lunch, and Keith caught them up on the minutiae of the many months since they had last spoken.

Bill then asked Keith if they should be concerned or happy that he was the liaison to The Committee.

Keith laughed.

"Mates," Keith began, "I hate this fucking project, yeah. But if you two can make it safe enough for me to like it, then I'll be your best friend."

"Fair enough!" Bill laughed. Heinrich nodded agreement, then laughed too.

They finished their lunch in loud, friendly conversation.

Just before 1:30, M'Bulu and Keith were escorted away by guards, and then shortly thereafter, Bill and Heinrich were escorted back to their table in the meeting room, guarded by Vasily and his team.

The afternoon session was grueling. Bill thought it interesting that there was not one question regarding the budget. Every single question was related to how to get the timeline under eighteen months.

Several times, Bill had to argue directly with a board member to tell them their request to reduce or remove a safety item from the project was short-sighted, wrong, and / or dangerous. Several times, members of The Committee tried to intimidate Bill, but after a quick glance at M'Bulu each time before responding, and seeing no hint that M'Bulu wanted Bill to back down, Bill stood his ground. When the members went after Heinrich, Bill stepped in and fielded the queries, keeping Heinrich's anger in check.

The only time Bill let Heinrich respond for a moment before stepping back in was when the representative from Switzerland commented that it's unfortunate that Doctor Torssen could not be involved, because the member was certain that Doctor Torssen would be able to meet all the guidelines.

"Minister," Heinrich began, "I knew Doctor Torssen well, and I know that he was not enough of a fool to agree with your assessments. Neither am I. Do not pretend to know what Doctor Torssen would have agreed with, because you have no idea, and you dirty his memory with your lies."

Bill pulled him back after that, and fielded the rest of the inquiries and comments from The Committee for the rest of the day while Heinrich simmered, but remained quiet.

As they were nearing the end of the day, Keith finally asked a question.

"Doctors, would you be willing to let me see the full technical specifications of the project, and let me discuss possible changes that may help speed the process just a bit?"

Bill began to answer, but then Heinrich spoke up.

"Doctor vanGreig," Heinrich began, then paused for dramatic effect, "we would be happy to."

Bill realized that he had been holding his breath, and breathed out.

"Doctor vanGreig," the American representative spoke up. "Would it be possible for you to travel to South Africa to go over the project plan with Doctor Fibulee and Doctor de Boer, and report back to us on the progress?"

"I would be happy to coordinate with Minister Mabusa on such a plan," Keith answered.

"That would be acceptable," M'Bulu answered. "If there is no other business, I declare this meeting adjourned."
M'Bulu banged the gavel, and the lights on the board members all went dark.

Vasily and his team entered the room and stood around Bill and Heinrich until the members of The Committee had filed out, and then escorted Bill and Heinrich to a conference room.

Vasily and the head of Heinrich's team remained in the room while the other security team members waited outside. After a moment, there was a knock, and Vasily opened the door, letting M'Bulu and Keith into the room. Vasily and the other guard then stepped out.

"How's it, lads!" Keith greeted Bill and Heinrich.

"Good!" Bill said, then to M'Bulu, "What's with all the extra security?"

"There has been a credible threat made against the network," M'Bulu answered. "We are going from here to the airport now, rather than staying tonight. Your luggage is already on the plane. I will explain in more detail when we are in the air."

Bill was suddenly very aware of his mortality, and stayed close to Vasily until they were on the plane.

CHAPTER 72: NEW MODULE

M'Bulu hung up the phone and looked at Bill.

"You wanna tell me why we have fighter jets off both sides of our aircraft?" Bill was trying to stifle the panic in his voice, but only had moderate success.

"It is merely precautionary at this point," M'Bulu began. "But we will have fighter escorts until we are back in Pretoria, and then you will all remain under heavy guard at the dignitary quarters until the scope of the threat has been established."

"M'Bulu," Bill stated a little louder than he intended, "what threat?"

M'Bulu explained that the network administrators at Finland Global had identified an intrusion into their network. The intrusion didn't seem to do any damage, and was just reading raw traffic logs from one of the network switching nodes, and sending it to a masked IP address that changed every hour. Because of the constant change, they were not able to identify the location of the intruder. After realizing that they would not be able to use the IP addresses to track the intruder, they decided to block the intrusion, and just feed them old recycled logs, to throw them off.

Keith stifled a laugh.

"That's stupid," Heinrich interjected with a snort.

"Heinrich!" Bill snapped at Heinrich, but M'Bulu waved Bill off.

"Actually, Doctor de Boer is correct," M'Bulu answered. "Within an hour of the fake logs being sent, the intruder broke through the block that had been installed, wiped the BIOS of the network node and restarted it, then wiped the operating system of the infected machine, and restarted it. The damage to the infrastructure in the bank was substantial."

"Is the Switch network okay?" Keith spoke up.

"They had the traffic for the Switch network running through three redundant nodes," M'Bulu checked his notes to make sure he was still explaining it correctly. "So while there was a minor blip while the traffic stabilized, the Switch network remains operational."

"Well, I'm glad to hear that it's unaffected," Bill was relieved.

"I said it was 'operational'," M'Bulu corrected Bill. "I did not say 'unaffected'."

Bill felt the hair on the back of his neck stand up. A quick glance around the cabin showed that he was not the only one very worried now. He looked at Vasily, who only raised an eyebrow.

"Please explain, Minister," Bill wanted an answer.

"The reason Finland Global even found the intrusion was because they were looking for a larger problem," M'Bulu began. "Over the last several months, there have been almost five hundred billion Euros of transactions approved by the Switch network that have been reported as fraudulent."

"That's not possible," Keith interrupted, then looked to Heinrich for support.

Heinrich nodded in agreement.

"That is what we have been telling the entities who have initiated disputes on the transactions," M'Bulu continued his explanation. "But the truth is this: in every case, in *every* case, when we have traced the entire transaction through the system, there is no originating action from a bank. The transaction shows up in the system, is approved, and the funds are converted to Euros and deposited into one of ten different accounts at one bank in Mauritius."

"That's suspect," Keith interjected. "How do we know Minister Karter is not involved in this and feeding information back to the attackers?"

"We do not know that," M'Bulu agreed. "As of tonight, he is gone."

"Who is Minister Karter?" Bill asked.

"He was the representative of Mauritius," Keith answered.

"Glad to hear that he is no longer on The Committee," Bill answered. "But there's still the matter of these ghost transactions. Keith, is there *any* way to inject transactions into the Switch network or boxes without it going through that 256 IP magic thing?"

"No," Heinrich answered. Keith nodded in agreement. "You have to be physically connected to the port on the back of the box. Remember when we turned on that Switch 3 in Pretoria? Remember when I unplugged that cable from the back and handed it and the laptop to the guard there? That's the only way in."

"It was not in Pretoria," M'Bulu spoke up.

"Minister, please," Keith answered. "This is not the time for spy games. I grew up in that neighborhood."

M'Bulu began to answer, then stopped and went silent again.

"Okay," Bill continued. "Tell me the process for installing the boxes again, even the parts before I was involved."

"Right," Heinrich began. "We build all the boxes from identical plans. We install the software from the one master copy, which I have with me at all times." Heinrich patted his laptop case before continuing. "We hook it up to a test network, and run a series of test transactions through it to make sure it is responding appropriately to all of the possible transaction types that can be submitted. Once it's ready to go, we take it to the installation location, hook it up to the network and mains, power it up, plug in a laptop with the console application, log into the Switch, run three more test transactions, and if they give the appropriate responses, we disconnect, and that's it."

"Actually, that's wrong," Keith jumped in.

"How?" Heinrich asked.

"Just before disconnecting the console cable, you permanently disable the console interface port," Keith corrected.

"Right, sorry about that," Heinrich acknowledged. "I disable the console interface on the Switch, and then I disconnect, and that's it."

"And it's the same every time?" Bill asked.

"Yes." Heinrich gave his signature Torssen-style answer.

"But it's not," Bill countered.

"What do you mean?" Heinrich showed a bit of irritation at Bill's response.

"When I was with you on my very first trip to Joburg," Bill began, "you told me at the office that Switch 3 was 'better' than the first two. You said it had a faster processor and more memory. What other upgrades did you make to it?"

"None." Heinrich stated flatly.

"You're sure?" Bill pressed.

"Yes, dammit," Heinrich was getting mad again, but Bill kept going.

"Same operating system software?" Bill continued down his mental checklist.

"Yes, same software," Heinrich continued being defensive. "I installed it myself on all three switches."

"Heinrich, stay with me here," Bill needed Heinrich to participate. "I'm not blaming you for any of this, I'm just thinking out loud. You say you 'permanently disable' the console port. How?"

"The last command we run before disconnecting removes the console port driver from the BIOS," Heinrich explained. "It is a dead connector after that."

"And no one could have tampered with the command you send to kill that port?" Bill kept going.

"No, that software is only on that laptop," Keith jumped in. "It's never out of the sight of either myself or Heinrich."

"Well, Amir did have it, but why would he…" Heinrich stopped mid-sentence and yanked his laptop out of his bag, powered it up, and logged on.

Heinrich typed furiously for a few seconds, then ran his finger across the screen while reading something, then gasped.

"Oh no."

"What?" Bill and Keith asked simultaneously.

"He commented out the code that kills the console port, and just put in a delay timer for two seconds, then sends back the success message," Heinrich explained in hushed tones. "That port is still live."

Bill interpreted the look that crossed Keith's face as one of horror.

"But it's a physical port, right?" Bill tried to find the silver lining.

"Yes," Heinrich acknowledged. "And they'd have to have access to it to be able to inject those transactions."

"And there is a very short list of people who grant physical access," Keith added.

"Minister," Bill directed the question to M'Bulu. "Was the Minister from Mauritius authorized to grant access to that room, more specifically to Switch 3?"

"All access is to be cleared through me," M'Bulu answered. "When we land, we will proceed to the installation site, and you will check the box. Meanwhile, I will have the access log since the time of your visit sent to me for review."

Heinrich and Keith spent the rest of the flight checking the rest of the console commands.

M'Bulu spent the rest of his flight on his phone.

Bill felt helpless, so he paced the cabin looking for something to do. He found a deck of cards.

"Vasily?" Bill asked his guard as he walked to the back of the plane where Vasily was sitting. "Do you know the card game 'War'?"

"*Da.*"

"Want to play?" Bill was desperate for a distraction.

"*Da*, I destroy you in War," Vasily answered with the second genuine smile Bill had ever seen from him.

"Nice try, Vasily," Bill shot back. "But I'm not German."

And that was the first real laugh Bill heard from Vasily.

M'Bulu, Heinrich, and Keith all stopped what they were doing to look at Vasily and then Bill.

Both men shrugged and went back to their card game.

Bill relaxed for the rest of the flight.

It was early Wednesday morning when their plane touched down at Waterkloof. A motorcade was waiting for them at the Executive Terminal, and they were quickly loaded into the cars and on their way to the facility.

Bill tried to remember the turns their vehicle took during his last trip to this facility. It felt like a lifetime ago to Bill. He watched the now-familiar landscape pass by the window.

In a short time, the motorcade approached a blockade on a side street. There were multiple fire, police, and utility trucks parked along and across the road. The other cars in the motorcade pulled to the side of the road, but the car in which Bill's group was riding was waved through, followed by the car containing Keith and Heinrich and their security.

"Was there an attack?" Bill asked, afraid to know the answer.

M'Bulu laughed quietly, then answered.

"No, they are just keeping up appearances for the roadblock. The official story is that there is a natural gas pipeline that was vandalized, so they are keeping the area secured until that is fixed."

Such a response seemed like overkill to Bill, but Vasily nodded his approval, so Bill didn't say anything more.

Their car approached a nondescript office building, turned into the rear car park, and approached a dock. As they slowed, the overhead door opened for them. Both cars pulled into the building, and the door closed behind them.

Bill immediately recognized the warehouse once inside.

Vasily and the other security members exited the cars and did a quick sweep, then returned to the cars and opened the doors. M'Bulu got out, followed by Bill. Keith and Heinrich approached them from the other car.

"Look familiar, mate?" Keith asked Bill with a smile.

"It sure does," Bill answered, trying to not sound terrified. "Shall we head to the closet?"

Keith laughed and gestured towards the office door. Vasily and the security teams escorted them to the small office door through which they had passed the last time, and once in the office, Vasily entered the small closet and disappeared for a moment. Then, as before, the closet slid aside, and the elevator door opened, with Vasily waiting for them.

The group stepped onto the elevator and began their journey to the server room far below ground. Something did not sit well with Bill.

"Why was there no one in the building when we arrived?" Bill asked.

M'Bulu just smiled.

"Vandals attack gas line," Vasily answered. "All employees evacuated."

"But they didn't actually attack the gas line," Bill answered. "Why would they be..."

Bill stopped as he realized that it was just for appearances. Vasily raised an eyebrow at Bill. Bill just looked at the floor.

Keith began whistling "Ride of the Valkyries". Everyone laughed, including the security guards.

As the doors opened, Keith stopped whistling. Before them was the cavernous room with uncounted rows of server racks. The hum of the cooling systems was not loud, but at the same time, almost overwhelming. A technician in a white lab coat and tight hair bun was waiting for them.

"*Goeie middag*, Dr. Vanderzhen," M'Bulu greeted the technician in Afrikaans.

Bill and Keith noticed that Heinrich was stunned. Keith shrugged.

"*Goeie middag*, Minister," she responded. "*En, goeie middag, dokters.* Right this way."

The technician turned and began escorting the team to the row which housed Switch 3.

Heinrich held Keith back a step.

"What in the nine realms is she doing here?" Heinrich asked in a whisper yell.

"She has a certain amount of pull with The Committee," Keith explained. "She wanted to be here when we check the Switch box."

"Nothing good can come from this," Heinrich hissed. "I respect her work on the LHC, but she should not be looking over our shoulders down here."

"Mate, she's been looking over your shoulder since Oslo," Keith's words stopped Heinrich in his tracks. "She distracted the guard that was on the way to collect you to get on *that plane*. She is the one that facilitated the perfection of your new personal documents to become Heinrich de Boer. She is the one that talked to the minister to get you hired on to my team. Karla knew you long before you knew her. Now be nice."

Keith turned and continued walking, leaving Heinrich standing with his thoughts for a moment. His security guard motioned for Heinrich to catch back up to the group, so Heinrich started walking fast until he was next to

Bill.

"Remember when that guy at the LHC died a while back, and I was upset, but then they put a new person in charge of scheduling projects?" Heinrich whispered to Bill.

Bill thought for a second, then nodded.

"That's her, mate," Heinrich continued, pointing at Karla.

"That seems odd," Bill whispered back.

"*Ja*, it is," Heinrich responded. "We'll talk about it later."

Bill nodded again, and the group continued to the specific server rack.

Both the front and rear doors of the rack were open, and Vasily escorted Heinrich and Bill to the rear. Bill saw that the two lights on the back of the Switch 3 were blinking very fast, indicating a lot of network traffic. He assumed that was a good thing. Heinrich pulled his laptop out of his bag, followed by a serial cable, which he plugged into his laptop, and then into the port on the Switch 3 box.

Heinrich powered up his laptop, and after a few seconds, began typing. Keith joined Bill in watching.

After a minute or so, Heinrich dropped his head.

"Fuck man," Heinrich stated quietly. "The port is still live. It's off, but it's live. The driver is still there."

Keith dropped his head too.

Through the gaps between the other boxes in the rack, Bill saw M'Bulu dial his phone and walk away from the group.

"So, other than the obvious," Bill finally asked, "what does that mean?"

"It means," Heinrich said with a long sigh, "that anyone with the right software could come to this rack and install software on it to falsify transactions, or anything else they wanted to do."

"I agree, that's bad," Bill acknowledged. "But the minister said that no

305

one gets to this box without his clearance."

"Let's hope that has been enforced," Keith added. "Meanwhile, you should download the BIOS and the current OS, and let's check it back at your flat."

"*Ja*," Heinrich answered. "Already doing it."

After Heinrich had finished downloading everything from the Switch 3, M'Bulu and Karla had a quick conversation about whether or not to leave it on, eventually deciding that the loss of functionality to the network was worse than any potential financial losses, so they decided to leave it on. Karla had a team going back over the video logs to attempt to see if anyone had accessed the back of the Switch 3 box, and she and M'Bulu decided that she would stay with the team while that was underway.

Back at Heinrich's flat at the dignitary quarters, there was a flurry of activity. Bill felt useless. Heinrich and Keith were glued to Heinrich's laptop, trying to find if the software in the Switch 3 had been altered or not, M'Bulu and Karla were on a call with The Committee, and Bill just sat, watching the news and trying to keep himself occupied.

"What... is *that*?" Heinrich exclaimed.

Keith leaned in closer to look at the laptop screen.

"Put this up on the big monitor, mate," Keith answered, and turned to look at the large monitor above the desk.

The editor window expanded across the monitor, and Keith stepped up close to it. Bill walked over and tried to understand what he was reading. It wasn't a programming language he knew, so he didn't understand the specifics, but as Keith pointed to certain sections and he and Heinrich discussed them, Bill knew it wasn't good news.

After a few minutes, M'Bulu and Karla walked over to join them, and waited while Keith and Heinrich finished their initial investigation. Finally, they both turned to face the rest of the team.

"Someone added this module to the software," Heinrich finally stated. "It permits a specific malformed originating bank code in the header to be processed successfully no matter what. Basically, this can be used to steal anything from anyone, as long as the attacker has the bank account number and bank number of the originating bank. And we can't stop it."

"Are you sure?" Karla asked.

"We will spend the rest of the day working on a patch," Heinrich answered, looking to Bill and Keith for support, "but it's not promising. We can let you know in the morning."

"We will let you get to it, then," M'Bulu answered. "Dinner will be brought in. Dr. Vanderzhen will be at my office meanwhile."

"Understood," Bill acknowledged.

"Mate, there isn't much you can do here," Keith said to Bill, looking away from the monitor for a moment. "You should head back and get some sleep. We'll wake you if there is any news before you get here in the morning."

Bill looked to M'Bulu, who nodded in agreement, and then to Vasily, who merely shrugged.

"Okay," Bill acquiesced. "But if *anything* happens, you wake me."

"*Ja baas*," Heinrich agreed, and went back to work.

"Vasily," Bill said, turning to his guard, "we go now."

"*Da.*"

Vasily spoke briefly into his headset, then escorted Bill out the door and over to his flat, followed by M'Bulu and Karla and their security team on the way to M'Bulu's office.

Bill did not sleep soundly that night, and when he did sleep, he had nightmares of weird quantum creatures attacking him, or worse, alternate universes where everything was steampunk.

CHAPTER 73: NO NEWS IS GOOD NEWS

Bill woke from yet another nightmare. Checking the clock and seeing that it was almost 5:00 am, he decided to get up and get going.

Bill pulled on a t-shirt and shorts and shuffled to the restroom, giving a weary wave to Vasily down the hall. Bill wondered to himself again how Vasily never looked tired.

Shuffling into the kitchen, Bill asked Vasily if he had any word from M'Bulu or Heinrich's security team, and received an all-quiet answer. *No news is good news, I guess,* Bill thought to himself.

After sucking down a large bowl of coco pops and a big glass of orange juice, Bill showered and prepared himself for a long day. On the walk to Heinrich's flat, Bill realized he hadn't heard the hadeda birds yet, and found some humor in the idea that for once, he could yell and wake all those bastards up, but then thought better of doing so while surrounded by armed guards before dawn in a secure facility that was on high alert.

Arriving at Heinrich's flat, Bill found Keith and Heinrich where he had left them the night before, still typing away and saying technical things to each other.

"Hello, boys!" Bill said cheerfully, trying to set the mood. "How goes the work?"

"Is it morning already?" Heinrich asked, surprised by the passage of time.

"Heinrich, this is what I was talking about," Bill joked. "You have to remember to eat and breathe and sleep."

"*Ja*, I think you were right," Heinrich grinned back.

"I guess you will be wanting a status report then," Keith asked Bill.

"Yes, please," Bill didn't bother to hide his impatience.

"I'll give a complete report with the minister and Karla get here," Keith began, "but the short answer is this: we can't stop them from running these fraudulent transactions through the Switches without them knowing that we are onto them. We don't know what kind of action they would take if we stop them anyway, and we don't want a repeat of that attack in Arniston to happen in Geneva."

"An explosion at the LHC would destroy most of Europe," Heinrich added.

"And, you know, the world economy," Bill added.

"Both correct," Keith continued. "Anyway, what we *can* do is log every bad transaction, and we can start tracking all of the transactions going out of the accounts where the fraudulent transactions deposit their funds."

"Right," Heinrich joined in again. "And then when we have the Q'Loud up and running, we can send all the armies of the world against those groups that were running the bad transactions."

"Right." Keith said with a smile and a nod. "And we can use the Q'Loud network to reverse the bad transactions and any payments made out of the bad guy's accounts."

Bill considered their plan for a few seconds before responding.

"I think you two need some sleep," Bill answered. "That is a terrible plan. They could steal tens of billions of methods of payment in that time."

"It's the only plan we have, and it has the benefit of being the only one that we wrote," Heinrich responded with only a slight hint of defensiveness. "We can install it today."

Keith nodded agreement.

"Well," Bill accepted the idea for the moment, "button up your code for install, and I'll argue against it when M'Bulu and Karla get here. And then we'll go install it anyway."

"Already doing it, mate," Heinrich answered.

"Good," Bill acknowledged. "Now what do you two lunatics want for breakfast?"

Bill phoned their breakfast order over to the cafeteria, and it was delivered a few minutes later. Heinrich and Keith finished building their installation set, and ate breakfast while the three men talked and waited for the arrival of the minister and Doctor Vanderzhen.

Back in the elevator on the way underground, Bill was still not happy that he was overruled by the entire group, even though he knew it was going to happen.

"I want it on the record that I am completely opposed to this plan," Bill stated emphatically after a few moments of silence. "Nothing good can come from this."

"Your objection is noted again, Doctor," Karla answered with a hint of irritation in her voice. "It was noted every time you raised the objection this morning. We are still going to proceed. By logging all of the transactions, we can reverse them later. But we can not let these bad actors know that we are aware of their actions and tracking them."

Bill rode the rest of the way to the vault in silence, but he did catch the sympathetic glance from Keith.

Fortunately, this time Bill did not have to take any actions for the modifications that were made to Switch 3, and he was glad for it. This trip, he would not be walking behind the rack, and instead just stood with Vasily in front, waiting for Heinrich to upload the changes.

After a few minutes, Keith and Heinrich emerged from behind the rack.

"It's done," Heinrich announced, purposely avoiding making eye contact with Bill.

Bill just shook his head and started walking back to the elevator, not bothering to wait for the rest of the team.

CHAPTER 74: ALMOST THREE SECONDS

"Yes brother, I am sure," one of Amir's team repeated. "Switch 3 went offline for almost three seconds."

"Run a transaction," Amir decided after a few moments of consideration. "Let us ensure that our package is still working. And, take it from the personal account of Bjorn Rødtskjegg. We will teach him to interfere with our plans."

Amir waited while the other man typed and looked at his screen.

"The transaction was successful, brother," the other man finally stated after several seconds. "And I verified that the funds are in our account now."

Amir was unsettled by the unscheduled downtime of Switch 3.

"Was the time for the completion of the transaction any different from before?" Amir wondered if something may have been added to his patch, and that the outage was from a reboot of the Switch 3.

"No, brother, no difference."

The outage still nagged at Amir.

"If that Switch drops again, here is a list of two more transactions I want you to run," Amir said, handing a piece of paper to his assistant.

CHAPTER 75: A MESSAGE TO HEINRICH

Back at Heinrich's flat, the team watched the large monitor as Heinrich brought up the log feed to see if any bad transactions had run through the network since their patch was activated.

One transaction showed up in the list. Heinrich clicked on it, and the details of the transaction appeared.

"This is interesting," M'Bulu said after reading the information. "They attacked Bjorn Rødtskjegg. They must have noticed the reboot downtime. It will be interesting if we can find out why they would attack Rødtskjegg for that. Also interesting to know that they know he is alive."

"Why's that?" Bill asked, not sure of the connections.

M'Bulu and Keith looked at Heinrich.

"Bjorn Rødtskjegg," Heinrich explained, "was supposedly also killed in the plane crash that killed me. As far as we knew, there were maybe ten people on the planet that knew he was still alive. Looks like the bad guys know he is still alive too."

"I have a thought," Keith said after a moment of thought. "Heinrich, can you please reboot Switch 2?"

"I can," Heinrich was confused by the request, "but why?"

"I want to test a theory," Keith answered.

Heinrich shrugged and typed a few commands.

While waiting for Heinrich to respond, a SMS beeped into Bill's phone.

[SYSTEM CRITICAL REPORT]: SWITCH 2 HAS POWERED DOWN

Then a couple seconds later, another appeared.

[SYSTEM CRITICAL REPORT]: SWITCH 2 HAS RECOVERED FROM AN UNPLANNED RESTART

"It should be back up now," Bill said after reading the messages.

Keith grinned.

"You still get the warnings?" Keith asked Bill.

"Yeah, I should probably reroute those to Heinrich," Bill answered.

After about five seconds, Heinrich looked up.

"Rebooted," Heinrich reported. "Balancer is stabilized across all three devices."

"Good, thank you," Keith acknowledged. "Now let's see if we see another retaliatory transaction."

The group watched the log list for a few minutes, and nothing new appeared.

"Now please reboot Switch 1," Keith asked.

Heinrich didn't question this time, and typed.

Heinrich's phone pinged twice, Bill assumed they were the warnings for Switch 1.

"Let me guess," Bill said with a grin, "something about a 'system critical message'?"

Heinrich just grinned in response without looking away from his monitor.

"Switch 1 is online, balancer is operating normally," he reported.

All eyes turned to the log list on the big monitor.

"Still not seeing any more bad transactions," Bill mumbled, then turned to Keith. "What's your point, Keith?"

"Humor me, mate," Keith continued. "Restart Switch 3 now."

Heinrich shrugged and restarted Switch 3.

A SMS message beeped into Heinrich's phone, then a few seconds later, another beeped in.

"Switch 3 is back and balanced," Heinrich reported unnecessarily.

The team watched the log panel and a new transaction popped up, followed by another one a minute or so later.

The victims of the two new bad transactions were Phil Michum and Oleg Rostova.

Everyone except Bill looked surprised.

"Well," M'Bulu stated before Keith could say anything. "That *is* interesting."

"It sure is," Keith answered, still staring at the screen.

Karla nodded her agreement, Heinrich just looked at the floor.

"Someone want to fill me in here?" Bill joined in, not bothering to hide his frustration at being out of the loop.

Keith and M'Bulu both looked at Heinrich again, who nodded and began his explanation.

"Phil Michum and Oleg Rostova," Heinrich started slowly, "were engineers that I worked with way back in Oslo at Norway National Bank, before I died."

Heinrich paused a moment to let that sink in with Bill before continuing.

"They, along with Bjorn Rødtskjegg and I, were supposed to be on that plane I mentioned before that crashed and supposedly killed the entire team. Bjorn, Phil, and Oleg popped up at Finland Global working on trying to get Switch 3 built before they outsourced the build of Switch 3 to Keith and I when we were at Simunye. Bjorn is the guy who sold me out to Finland Global and got my project stolen in Oslo. So, serves him right that they are attacking him, but I don't know why the baddies would be attacking Oleg and Phil."

"Let me see if I can piece all of this together," Bill said after a moment of thought. "Your old boss and coworkers that were supposed to have died with you but didn't are alive and well and apparently working for Finland Global, and the bad guys attacked all three of them after Switch 3 rebooted, but not after the other two boxes restarted. Is that correct?"

"That is correct, doctor," M'Bulu answered.

"Well that tells me that they think this Rotskeg guy is messing with them," Bill said after thinking about it again for a few minutes.

"'Rødtskjegg'," Keith corrected with a grin. "But there's much more to note from this. They know that Bjorn and his team are alive, and have extensive personal details on all three of them. Further, they think that Bjorn and his team are trying to track them, and have retaliated against Bjorn and his team in an attempt to warn Bjorn to not take any further action. And, they also have no vision into Switch 1 or Switch 2, only to Switch 3. This means they have physically been in contact with Switch 3 in the time since we installed it."

Bill, Keith, and Heinrich all looked to M'Bulu.

M'Bulu looked to Karla, who nodded, and then he spoke to the team.

"Fourteen weeks ago," M'Bulu began the rest of the story, "Doctor bin Salman and a known Chechen terror operative walked into the main office of the front company above the technology vault, and said the passphrase of the day to the receptionist. Because they had that passphrase, they were escorted to the vault. The Chechen spoke with a perfect Moscow royalty dialect, they bluffed their way past the guards, and Doctor bin Salman connected his laptop to the back of Switch 3."

Bill, Keith, and Heinrich were stunned by the news.

M'Bulu continued.

"They were in the building for less than five minutes," M'Bulu continued. "After their visit, they met up with another vehicle, and the Chechen's body was transferred to the other vehicle, which later disposed of the Chechen's body. We have been able to track all of this from the NSC data, once we knew the starting point at the facility. We also found some gaps in the NSC data gathering net, because we didn't see the Chechen come into South Africa, nor did we see where Doctor bin Salman began or terminated his trip. The bad transactions did not start until after the next regular maintenance reboot of Switch 3, so they knew that an unscheduled reboot would cause immediate action. They were patient and methodical."

Keith, Bill, and Heinrich were all silent as they considered the new information they had been given.

A new transaction popped up on the log list. The information for the transaction was not random. The bank name: Norway National Bank in Oslo. The account number was a closed one, which Heinrich hadn't used since being escorted out of Norway National years ago.

The account holder name: Erik Torssen.

The amount of the transaction: R0.00.

"That was a message to you, mate." Keith said to Heinrich.

Heinrich was stunned and did not speak.

"Seems to me," Bill chimed in, "they know who you are, and they know you're in South Africa because they used Rand as the currency. But why would they take zero Rand?"

"Because any amount other than zero would have set off red flags on an account closed so long ago," M'Bulu explained. "And you are correct, Keith, this was a message. Gentlemen, this is now a race against time to bring the Q'Loud project operational."

At that moment, both M'Bulu's and Karla's phones chimed. They both looked at their phones and then each other.

"Gentlemen, if you will excuse us," Karla said, and turned to leave the room, M'Bulu one step behind her.

Keith, Heinrich, and Bill continued to watch the bad transaction log. Simultaneously, four dispute records popped up, one for each of the bad transactions. The origins all showed Geneva, Switzerland, except for the one against Erik Torssen from Norway National Bank. That dispute originated in Oslo, filed by Norway National Bank. The other three were filed by the account holders.

Heinrich looked surprised.

"Those men are fools," Keith said, shaking his head.

"They just do not understand what is going on, do they?" Heinrich responded.

"Let me guess," Bill joined in. "They just confirmed to the bad guys that they are alive, and that those are their accounts, right?"

"Confirmed specifically to Amir and his team, but *ja*, they did," Keith answered. "And Norway National Bank responded as they should have when a long-closed account is charged, and which gave away nothing about Heinrich."

"And because neither Erik nor I responded to the attack," Heinrich continued with a wry smirk, "and Bjorn and his team all did, it's a good chance that Amir thinks Bjorn and his team are the ones investigating Amir's actions. That may work in our favor."

Keith nodded and continued to watch the monitor.

Bill had a sudden worrying thought.

"Keith," Bill needed clarification, "did Amir know anything about the National Secure Citizen Project?"

"No, why?" Keith wasn't sure where Bill was going with the thought.

"Then he doesn't know about the extent of our ability to track him," Bill continued. "I mean, he clearly is trying to avoid surveillance, but he didn't know just how much we were able to track him. I know I need to let Kyle know about the gaps we found so he can get those plugged, but we may be able to find their little lair yet."

As they were considering Bill's latest discussion, M'Bulu and Karla walked back into the room.

"Gentlemen, I know this is not going to be a popular decision," M'Bulu began, while Karla looked at the floor. "The timeline for the Q'Loud project has been changed to twelve months."

Heinrich started to respond angrily, but then stopped, and began scribbling on his notepad. After a moment he looked up.

"I need a night of sleep before I answer you," he finally responded.

"Nice restraint, Heinrich," Bill commented. Keith nodded.

"You have it," M'Bulu granted.

Karla began to object, but M'Bulu silenced her with a glare.

"We will give the doctors a night to get their thoughts organized, then we will discuss planning," M'Bulu stood his ground.

"Minister," Bill began formally, "is it possible for me to talk with Kyle in person tomorrow?"

"Yes, I can make that happen, "M'Bulu answered. "You will have lunch with him tomorrow at your flat."

"Appreciated," Bill was happy M'Bulu didn't ask any more questions about it, and that he didn't let Karla ask any either.

"Well, it is getting close to dinner time," M'Bulu ended the day. "We will rejoin you all here at 9:00 in the morning tomorrow for breakfast, and we will discuss details of the Q'Loud schedule change. Have a nice evening."

With that, M'Bulu turned to leave. Karla remained where she was standing.

M'Bulu stopped at the front door and turned back to her.

"Doctor Vanderzhen," M'Bulu stated, his glare withering upon her, "we have much to discuss. Please join me."

Karla knew it was not optional to decline the meeting, and reluctantly followed M'Bulu out the door.

Bill, Heinrich, and Keith watched them leave. Heinrich spoke up after the car had driven away.

"You know I couldn't complete this project in eighteen months," Heinrich stated calmly. "Twelve months is out of the question."

"I'm not sure we have a choice now, Heinrich," Bill stated sympathetically.

Keith just nodded.

"Get some sleep," Bill said, turning to leave. "I mean it, get some sleep. I will have them cut power to your flat if you don't."

"I will," Heinrich chuckled.

On the walk back to Bill's flat, Bill asked Vasily to ask Heinrich's security team leader to turn off the power to the flat if Heinrich wasn't asleep by 10:00. Vasily nodded and spoke briefly into his headset, then nodded acknowledgement to Bill.

Bill ended the day the way he had started it: a large bowl of coco pops, but no orange juice. He needed to sleep tonight, because he expected the next week or so was going to be a lot of long days.

The following morning, the hadedas woke Bill.

I did not miss you yesterday, Bill grumbled to them.

Bill got up and showered, and decided to wear comfortable clothes today, in anticipation of not seeing his bed again for at least eighteen hours.

When he got to Heinrich's flat, the car carrying M'Bulu and Karla was just arriving.

Bill walked in with them.

"Good morning, team," M'Bulu greeted the assembled braintrust. "Any new bad transactions overnight?"

The list was still up on the big monitor, and Bill saw several more lines. He recognized four of the names: Keith vanGreig, Karla Vanderzhen, Heinrich de Boer, and M'Bulu Mabusa.

"Well, that's ballsy," Bill commented.

"Indeed it is, doctor," M'Bulu answered, "but not unexpected. However, it is surprising that they acted so soon and at such a high level."

Bill looked over and saw that Karla was definitely seething.

"I recognize the other names, too," Keith spoke up. "They are the other members of The Committee, and a couple of other managers at the LHC."

"Correct," M'Bulu confirmed.

M'Bulu waited a moment for Bill to comprehend just how unafraid the terrorists were acting now.

"Doctor de Boer," M'Bulu finally broke the silence, "do you have a report for me?"

Heinrich sighed, then looked briefly at Bill before turning in his chair so as to not have to continue to make eye contact with his project lead.

"I do, minister," Heinrich began, "but Bill isn't going to like it."

"Tell me you didn't..." Bill began, trying to stop Heinrich from saying what he was afraid Heinrich was going to say.

"If we bundle all of the safety features at the beginning of construction as we discussed some time ago," Heinrich continued, interrupting Bill, "we can be ready to operate in twelve months."

Yup, he did it, Bill thought to himself.

"Excellent, thank you doctor," M'Bulu stated. "Please submit the equipment list and updated project plan on Monday."

"It may take me a little longer than Monday," Heinrich answered. "I need to finish the budget section."

"That won't be necessary, doctor," M'Bulu waved away that step of the project plan. "Just submit the equipment list and project specifications. We will begin right away."

"Understood," Heinrich acknowledged the unspoken infinite budget change.

"Hang on a second," Bill was stunned by the new disregard for safety on the project, and wanted to put a stop to the carelessness. "You *can not* just blow off the safety features, regardless of the price!"

M'Bulu spun and faced Bill, who noted that this was the first time he had seen actual rage in the eyes of the Minister of the Department of Home Affairs.

"*Doctor*," M'Bulu shouted, then calmed himself and continued, anger still thick in his voice, "your concerns are noted. We will go forward with Doctor de Boer's project plan. Do you have any further questions?"

Bill knew that was not a question, and answered appropriately, knowing there was only one acceptable answer.

"No, Minister Mabusa, I do not."

M'Bulu took a deep breath to calm himself. The rest of the room remained silent.

"Bill, I understand your concerns, I promise you that I do," M'Bulu said in a much softer voice to Bill. "The importance of the Q'Loud coming online without delay is increasing more and more each day, as you see from the transactions overnight. We must find a way to both address your concerns and achieve this new timeline. Please find that compromise."

Bill considered M'Bulu's words for a moment, then stood up straight and faced M'Bulu.

"Minister Mabusa," Bill began, as formally as he could, "I will do as you have asked to the best of my abilities. Please note that effective one business day after the Q'Loud system is operational, I resign."

M'Bulu stood up slowly, and walked to face Bill, standing very close to

Bill, all vestiges of the informal gone from his stance.

"Doctor Fibulee," M'Bulu said slowly, enunciating each word slowly, "your terms are acceptable."

Bill fought the urge to swallow hard, his emotionless facade not at all representing his inner turmoil, as he continued to stare down the Minister of the Department of Home Affairs of South Africa.

After a few interminable seconds, Bill thought he saw the slightest hint of a grin beginning to form on M'Bulu's face. Bill raised an eyebrow, and M'Bulu began to laugh and stepped back.

"You have brass ones, mate," M'Bulu said through his laughter.

"No," Bill said, going to sit down and taking a deep breath, "I don't".

M'Bulu laughed harder.

Everyone in the room, including Vasily, let out their breath. Only Karla did not look calmer.

"Dr. Vanderzhen," M'Bulu said after a moment, "Let us leave the doctors to work. Bill, you have a lunch in a couple hours, and I will see all three of you on Monday morning in my office at 10:00. Have a pleasant weekend, gentlemen."

M'Bulu left the flat without looking back. Karla stood looking at Keith, Heinrich, and Bill, as if waiting for one of them to say something.

Keith broke the silence.

"See you Monday, Karla," Keith said, dismissing her.

––––––––––––––

"You got old," Kyle said as he walked into Bill's flat, escorted by Vasily.

"The hell are you talking about?" Bill said in greeting.

"You're a lot more gray than the last time I saw you six months ago," Kyle chuckled.

"You just saw me on the video call a week ago. But yeah, I'm a little more gray," Bill acknowledged. "But I rock gray hair. My hair is glorious, I look amazing. Stop being jealous."

Kyle kept up the chop-busting.

"Yeah, keep telling yourself that, dude."

There was another knock at the door, and Vasily escorted in the meal cart from the cafeteria.

"You live well here," Kyle noted as Bill uncovered the food.

"They feed us well," Bill agreed. "They even brought in some of my favorites from home. The tamales here are killer. But I do miss potlucks."

Bill and Kyle dove into their food and Kyle caught Bill up on the last several months of news. Anita had finally found a job that she loved in Bryanston, and was having no regrets about the move to Johannesburg. Bill was happy to hear it, and his slight guilty feelings at causing the move finally left him.

Then they got down to business.

Bill explained the gaps that had been discovered, and that the video feeds at the edges of the gaps would be delivered to Kyle the following morning. Kyle agreed to keep Bill and Minister Mabusa updated.

After Kyle left, Bill wondered again as to whether or not he should have told Kyle just how critical the NSC project had become, since these attacks and their perpetrators were now being hunted using the NSC. *Ignorance is probably bliss in this case*, Bill thought to himself, then decided he was glad he hadn't told Kyle.

CHAPTER 76: DOUBLE-EDGED SWORD

Amir was satisfied with the decisions made in the meeting, and agreed that he and his team would step up the confiscations accordingly. He was still uncomfortable with the idea of targeting the leaders of global corporations and government officials of nations hostile to their cause, but the reasoning was sound; those people did have larger amounts that could be transferred to the Caliphate.

In Amir's opinion, they were doing battle with a very sharp double-edged sword. One edge was bringing hundreds of billions of euros into their accounts, and the distributions that had been made to their brothers and other allies of the Caliphate around the world were the most substantial that he could ever remember, already far in excess of the contributions from Sheik Gaddafi and Sheik bin Laden, may the blessings of the Prophet be upon them.

But he also knew that the other side of the sword would undoubtedly strike at their own funding source soon enough, and the funding would be cut off at the same time that a great new battle would be brought by the enemies of Allah. Amir had calculated approximately the amount of the global treasure that would have to be gathered and controlled before the glory of the Caliphate was inevitable, and they were not near that point yet, despite their success thus far.

Amir arrived back in his workroom, and handed off the list of the next transactions to be run. He noted that all of the disputes from the transactions they had run against The Committee and their minions had been filed as expected. Soon, Amir thought, they would need to start running transactions against the global companies that insured banks against these thefts in order to make them really hurt.

Amir closed his eyes for a moment, waiting for the report back from his assistant that the new batch of transactions had been completed.

I wonder if I will live to see the Caliphate, he wondered to himself. *Maybe.*

CHAPTER 77: NOT THE KING

Bill wandered into Heinrich's cottage a little after 10:30 the next morning.

Keith and Heinrich were at the kitchen table, books and papers spread across it, several balls of crumpled paper on the floor, both leaning over their laptops, typing furiously, occasionally scribbling something on a piece of paper or referring to a book. Bill sat down on the sofa and continued idly eating the bowl of coco pops he had brought with him.

After a few minutes, Keith spoke to Bill without looking away from his work.

"You going to help, mate?"

"Nope," Bill answered, taking a noisy bite of his cereal. "I know you two are over there figuring out how to shoot a black hole through the planet and kill this iteration of the universe, and I will not be an accomplice to it. That's why I'm eating this cereal instead of something healthy: because, why?"

"I believe the Yank expression is 'drama queen'," Heinrich said to Keith.

All three men chuckled.

"Seriously though," Bill spoke up, "what can I do to help? There is no budget for me to work on, we already know the timeline, I know you two are removing safety features to make the project fit in those twelve months,

327

so I'm not sure what I can do to help."

"What makes you think we are removing safety features?" Heinrich asked, looking up from his laptop.

"Those balls of paper on the floor," Bill answered.

"Those are not safety features," Heinrich raised his voice slightly, though still in jest. "They are budget sheets that we don't need anymore."

"Oh, well that's okay," Bill answered.

"Except for a couple that are safety features," Keith added.

"I knew it," Bill answered, taking another bite of cereal.

Keith and Heinrich continued working while Bill finished his cereal.

"Doctors," Bill stated after a few minutes, "Please put me to work. I can not just do nothing all weekend."

Heinrich and Keith looked at each other for a moment, then Heinrich shrugged and turned to Bill.

"All right, mate, I suppose you can be the helper," Heinrich offered.

"That's great!" Bill answered happily. "How can I help?"

"Keep an eye on that list of bad transactions and tell us if any new ones show up," Keith answered. "Last we knew, there were forty two so far since midnight."

"Ouch," Bill winced at the high number so far, then looked over to check the count.

"Uh, guys, the count is almost two hundred."

Keith and Heinrich spun in their chairs, then got up to go look closer at the list.

"I recognize several of those names," Keith noted, pointing to a few of them. "CEO, CEO, prime minister, president, general, CFO. They are really stepping up the attacks. And they are making very strategic choices."

"Seems like they are poking a hornet's nest," Bill commented.

"They are," Keith answered, "but they are choosing targets that have a significant interest in keeping the news quiet about being personally attacked. They are playing an increasingly dangerous game, but they are playing it well."

"Amir was a great chess player," Heinrich offered.

"He was," Keith agreed. "And he is playing it now."

Two more transactions popped onto the list. Bill noted that they were both American state governors.

"I wonder..." Keith said, most to himself, then turned to Heinrich. "Restart Switch 3 again, mate."

Heinrich didn't ask why this time.

Two chimes to Heinrich's phone, then Heinrich turned back to the list.

"It's back," he reported.

Less than thirty seconds later, three more transactions popped onto the list. The victims: Bjorn Rødtskjegg, Phil Michum, Oleg Rostova.

"That confirms that," Heinrich said to the room. "But I wonder why they didn't hit my old Erik account in Oslo this time?"

"Confirms what?" Bill asked.

"That they think Bjorn's team in Geneva is controlling Switch 3," Keith answered.

"I wonder if they know about my connection to Erik," Heinrich added.

"Well, we saw they hit your account last night," Keith answered, "along with the rest of this team, except for Bill. So they know you're working on the Switch project, but I don't know if they know you're Erik. Either way, they think we all work for Rødtskjegg, and not Bill."

"I would like to stay under their radar for as long as possible," Bill said.

"Definitely," Keith agreed. "Since we don't know how much they know, I think Heinrich and I should start sending the status reports, and excluding you in the written ones. You can just sit with us as we write them. And you should not attend the video conferences directly either, just sit with one of us. The longer we can keep them unaware of you, the better."

"No argument from me on that," Bill concurred easily. "Now put me to work."

"Well, you love your Gantt charts," Heinrich observed, "so start a blank one, because we have to make all this fit."

"Mmm, Gantt charts," Bill played along. "Vasily?"

"*Da?*"

"Can I go get my laptop, or do you have to send one of your team?"

Vasily's expressionless face told Bill the answer, but Bill disobeyed.

"Cool," Bill said, crossing to the door. "I wanted to grab a lemon lime sports drink anyway."

"Mate, you are the strangest person I think I have ever met," Keith commented. "You don't know the difference between sparkling and still water, but you'll give a description of a drink instead of using the name."

"First of all," Bill responded, stopping at the door, "I didn't know the Afrikaans word for 'sparkling water' at the time, and I don't like to be brand-specific when it comes to my lemon lime sports drinks."

Bill opened the door, and Vasily stepped in front of him to check the surroundings, letting Bill proceed once he had checked.

"He said 'sparkling water' in English!" Keith hollered after Bill.

"Your jibberish is incomprehensible," Bill yelled back as the door closed.

"Mad bastard," Keith commented to himself.

Heinrich chuckled and agreed, then both men went back to their work at the dining room table.

Bill returned a few moments later with his laptop and a green sports drink with the label removed. Heinrich and Keith laughed hard at that, then all three engineers got down to work.

After eating dinner, Bill, Keith, and Heinrich were all still very awake, and made the decision to work through until after dinner the following evening, and then stop by 8:00 pm so they could all get good rest before their presentation at the Ministry office on Monday morning.

Bright and early Monday morning, Bill chatted with M'Bulu while Keith and Heinrich got the presentation ready on Heinrich's laptop and connected it to the projector on the ceiling of M'Bulu's office.

"So, I really have misgivings about the overall safety of this whole plan, Minister," Bill again belabored the point, but M'Bulu was accustomed to it. "We really have compressed a lot of what would be disparate safety checks into a small number of groups. And it came out to just under thirteen months, but we'll find a way."

"I understand your concerns, Doctor," M'Bulu maintained the formality for the purposes of this part of the conversation, and to show Karla that *his* team was working on *his* project, and was not subject to her commands. "And I appreciate you making us all aware of the potential issues in advance."

"This has to be completed within twelve months," Karla stated, looking directly at Bill.

Bill took a beat before responding.

"Doctor Vanderzhen," M'Bulu stepped in to answer. "As Doctor Fibulee stated a moment ago, they will find a way. Your responsibility will be to ensure that the cover story for the 'maintenance overhaul downtime' will be believable, and enforced."

"I am aware of my responsibilities, Minister," Karla responded, not stepping back from her push to take the lead on the Q'Loud project.

"I know that you are," M'Bulu answered in a calm voice. In his head, he made the decision to send Karla back to Geneva that afternoon, and casually sent a message from his phone to the security team to have her bags packed for her and waiting with the plane after lunch.

"We are ready," Heinrich finally announced.

Bill sat down in front of Karla, turning his back to her without another word. M'Bulu grinned to himself at the intentional snub.

Heinrich and Keith went through the presentation, occasionally stopping to answer questions from M'Bulu and Karla.

When they had completed their portion of the presentation, Heinrich turned off the projector, and Bill stood and faced the group to go over his portion of the chat.

"As I said before the slide presentation," Bill began, "the Gantt chart shows thirteen months, but with strong attention to efficiency every day of the project, we believe we can reduce it to twelve months. The contractors and vendors are not going to be pleased with giving me daily updates on a months-long project, but we all have to adapt on a project with this level of importance. With those daily updates, I will adjust the chart daily as well, and we will see incremental changes that we expect to become a cumulative month of efficiencies."

Bill paused momentarily for questions. There being none, he continued.

"Aside from the colossal threat from a technology failure which I have raised ad nauseum, my biggest concern now is actually keeping a project this large and complex, with contractors and vendors from across the globe, a secret. We already have bad actors that are aware of it, and that are taking nefarious action against some of the key members of the project team."

"Doctors, thank you for your excellent and informative presentation," M'Bulu stated, wrapping up the meeting. "Let us meet for lunch at the cafeteria at the VDQ at 1:00 this afternoon. Doctor Vanderzhen and I have some additional topics to discuss before that."

Bill, Heinrich, and Keith bundled up their laptops and excused themselves, then headed back to Heinrich's flat to discuss areas of concern each of them had with fine points of one or another pieces of the project.

Once the team had left his office, M'Bulu motioned for his guards to leave and close the door. He then sat forward and clapped twice, starting the white noise generator. M'Bulu leaned in close to a startled Karla.

"Doctor Vanderzhen," M'Bulu began in a tone that left no question in Karla's mind about the seriousness of his words. "You will work *for* my Q'Loud team, not manage them. Doctor Fibulee is my team lead, and he will lead them under my supervision. If Doctor Fibulee gives you an order, you may assume the order came directly from me. You will not give his team members orders. I should not have had to have this conversation with you twice in two days. I will not have this conversation with you a third time. Am I clear?"

"Yes, Minister," Karla answered through gritted teeth.

"Good," M'Bulu sat back and clapped twice again, terminating the white noise generator before the end of its cycle. "Your car is waiting."

M'Bulu then stood and went and sat at his desk without another word to Karla, who stood and gathered her things. As she started towards the door, it opened, and her security team joined her and escorted her to her car.

Karla was surprised when they arrived at the airport, and were taken to the jet at the executive terminal. When she questioned her team, she was informed that the minister had instructed them to escort her back to her home in Geneva immediately. She saw two of her security team loading her luggage into the back of the plane.

Fuming, she boarded the plane, and was soon airborne.

––––––––––––

M'Bulu arrived at Heinrich's flat just before 1:00 pm. The four of them chatted informally about the morning's presentation, with M'Bulu asking some minor clarifying questions and offering some unofficial commentary.

When the food arrived, the four men went to the table to begin eating. Keith was the first to ask about Karla.

"I see that we only have four meals delivered. Will Karla be joining us later?"

"She will be joining you in Geneva when you all arrive there," M'Bulu said flatly, in a tone that let the others know there would be no more discussion of Karla.

During lunch, the conversation remained light and casual. After the meal was finished and the dishes returned to the cafeteria, M'Bulu changed the lunch gathering to a formal meeting.

"Doctors," M'Bulu began, "your time in South Africa has concluded. On Friday morning of this week, we will all be heading to Switzerland for the remainder of the Q'Loud project. Please pack and conclude any other business that you may have here before Friday morning."

M'Bulu waited a moment to let his team get over their shock.

"The twelve month timeline started last week," M'Bulu just kept the surprises coming. "Bill, please update your chart."

Bill knew there was no point in protesting, so he went and got his laptop, and made the change to the start date of the project.

"It is now twelve months, *three* weeks," Bill announced when it was finished.

M'Bulu just smiled at Bill.

"I know," Bill answered M'Bulu's unstated comment.

"Also Bill," M'Bulu continued, "please hand off management of the National Secure Citizen project to Kyle."

Now Bill was really stunned.

"Minister…" Bill trailed off, not sure which of the competing thoughts to discuss first. "You pushed me so hard to lead that project, even though I didn't want to. Why would you want me to hand it off now?"

"Does it require any attention from you anymore?" M'Bulu answered in a soft voice.

Bill was contemplating an accurate answer, but M'Bulu continued.

"Kyle has been your team lead on the project for over a year, correct?"

Bill nodded in the affirmative. M'Bulu moved to his next point.

"Are there any aspects of the project that Kyle does not know?"

Bill shook his head.

"Do you have any doubts of Kyle's ability to continue to lead the project without your occasional meddling?"

"No, Minister," Bill answered after a moment of thought.

"There you have it," M'Bulu concluded. "You chose your team well, you trained your team well, you led your team well, and now you have two exceptional leaders from your team on that project. Your work on the project is complete."

Bill felt a sense of both pride and loss, and did not have words for a few moments. Heinrich and Keith were respectful of his silence. Then Bill realized what M'Bulu had said about his team members.

"Wait, what did you mean '*two* exceptional leaders'?" Bill was perplexed.

"The government of New Zealand has reached out to us about branching the application and deploying their own version of NSC, but it will include a raft of environmental inputs as well," M'Bulu explained.

Bill smiled.

"I think Eileen will enjoy that," Bill beamed with pride in his team. "Thank you, Minister." Bill was truly grateful.

"Bill, you will attend your regular team meeting tomorrow afternoon in person in Johannesburg," M'Bulu was wasting no time. "But you will travel in the morning so that you can have separate meetings with Kyle, Johan, and Eileen. In your meetings with Kyle and Eileen, you'll transfer control of the projects to them, and in your meeting with Johan, you will sign the contract that Kevin Blanchard had drawn up to engage Simunye Holdings as the development shop for the NZNSC project that Eileen will lead."

"Why did I not know about any of this?" Bill asked, only slightly miffed at being out of the loop on the NSC project branch.

"I didn't want you to be distracted," M'Bulu answered innocently. "And Kevin was happy to have me reach out to him about something for a change."

Bill chuckled at that.

"I guess I should call him on the ride to Joburg tomorrow and catch up with him," Bill suggested.

"Yes, you should," M'Bulu agreed. "Doctors, I will see you Friday morning at 9:00 at the executive terminal. As for the bad transactions, if any more are charged against your accounts, we will automatically dispute them for you. Meanwhile, you should not have any personal expenses anyway, so if you do have a need for any spending money, just let me know and we will accommodate you. You will be staying in an ultra-high security facility at the LHC for the duration of the project, under heavy guard, so please make peace with having more guards around you at all times."

Bill looked to Vasily, who confirmed all was well with a wink.

"If there is nothing else," M'Bulu concluded and stood and headed to the door, leaving Keith, Heinrich, and Bill sitting quietly at the table.

After they heard M'Bulu's car leave, Heinrich finally spoke.

"You like Shakespeare, mates?"

Both Bill and Keith nodded.

"*Nok en gang til bruddet, kjære venner…*" Heinrich recited.

"You know I don't understand Afrikaans, Heinrich," Bill replied.

"It's not Afrikaans, mate," Keith answered for Heinrich. "It's Norwegian. He's quoting Henry V from Shakespeare. 'Once more unto the breach, dear friends…'."

"I only know a couple lines of that speech," Bill admitted, "but I'm pretty sure he's getting his troops ready for a difficult battle with that speech, right?"

Heinrich shook his head in feigned disgust.

336

"Basically, yes," Keith answered.

"Then, once more unto the breach, indeed," Bill said more to himself than to the others. "I'm going to go get my notes and charts for the NSC together and get to sleep early tonight. Join you two for dinner tomorrow?"

"*Ja*, sounds good mate," Heinrich answered. Keith nodded his head.

Bill stood and packed up his laptop and headed towards the door, then stopped as another thought stunned him. He turned to face Heinrich and Keith.

"Shit, I just realized, I'm the General in that speech, huh?"

"Well, the king, but yes," Heinrich answered sympathetically.

Bill looked at the floor for a moment, trying to come to grips with the new thought, then turned back towards the door, still looking at the floor but not moving.

"We go now, General," Vasily said after a moment, that hint of a grin on his stone face.

"*A ty*, Vasily?" Bill hoped the new Russian words from him would throw Vasily off just a little, but instead Vasily laughed.

I'm actually going to miss him when I retire next year, Bill thought to himself, and headed to the door.

Approaching the door, Bill spoke to himself as much as to the others in the room.

"I'm not the king, and I'm not a general."

Heinrich and Keith exchanged a look, but remained silent.

CHAPTER 78: BRANCH

Bill slept terribly, and was happy to hear the first hadeda of the day squawk the break of dawn. He got up and headed to the kitchen for orange juice. Vasily, of course, was already up and keeping watch.

"*Dobroye utro*, Vasiliy," Bill greeted Vasily, continuing to work on his Russian language skills.

Bill considered asking Vasily for travel tips through Russia for his world travel plans after he retired.

"Good morning, Doctor," Vasily responded in his thickly-accented perfect English. "Your Russian speaking is improving."

"*Spacibo*," Bill answered, and put his mind to making breakfast.

Once they were in the car on the way to Johannesburg, Bill put on his headset and dialed the GlobalForce office.

A familiar, very bubbly voice answered the phone after the second ring.

"GlobalForce Incorporated, this is Kandi, how may I direct your call?"

"Good afternoon, Kandi," Bill responded without saying anything else.

"Bill!" Kandi's voice was so loud it made Bill wince. "Oh my god, how are you?! I have not talked to you in forever!"

"I am good, Kandi, how are you?" Bill answered, genuinely hoping she was well.

"I am great! I have so much to tell you!" Kandi answered.

Bill really did want to catch up with her, but right now was not the time.

"Kandi, how about this," Bill offered, "right now, I need to talk with Kevin about some contract stuff, but if you call me tomorrow night after you're off work, I promise to catch up with you. That work?"

"Yes it will, I will call you then," Kandi promised. "Hang on a sec, I'll get you Kevin."

"You're amazing, thank you," Bill said.

He heard Kandi giggle before she put him on hold.

Kevin made Bill wait almost a full minute before picking up the phone.

"You've got a lot of nerve calling me," Kevin sounded really angry. Bill wasn't sure why.

"Hey, good afternoon, Kevin," Bill tried to sound positive. "What's... ah... what's happening in Arizona? Everyone good?"

Kevin didn't respond for a few seconds, then started to laugh.

"I'm just busting your chops," Kevin said through his chuckles. "Sounds like life in South Africa agrees with you. The minister keeps giving me great reviews every week of you and your team."

"You talk with him weekly, do you?" Bill was surprised to hear that.

"Well, yeah," Kevin countered, "someone has to keep me filled in."

"That's fair," Bill accepted the shot. "So, this New Zealand contract, let's talk about that."

"Alright," Kevin's voice changed as they got down to business. "The contract with New Zealand was already signed, late last week, actually."

Interesting timing, Bill thought to himself. Kevin continued.

"Your rock star down there will lead that project, and your rock star in Johannesburg will continue to lead the project for South Africa. They'll continue to work together in project manager capacities on their separate projects, but because the New Zealand one is a 'branch' of the South African project, not sure exactly what that means, they will continue to work together. And to try to maintain as much stability in both projects, it made the most sense to me, Minister Mabusa, and the minister's counterpart in New Zealand, Nigel Williamson, that we use Simunye Holdings as the development shop for the NZ branch."

"Wow, Kevin," Bill was surprised how much had been done in Bill's absence. "It sounds like you don't need me on either of the NSC variants."

"Ah, don't feel left out," Kevin waved away Bill's hurt feelings. "You built a great team, and now it's long past time for them to take off the training wheels. You go finish up your project. I hear you're retiring in a year. And, no, we don't need you on the NSC projects anymore."

"I guess you're right, Kevin," Bill finally responded. "M'Bulu said the same thing basically. I guess I need to take my trophy and move on. And yes, when the other project is finished, I'm retiring. You should too."

"Nah, I'm going to stay on," Kevin answered. "The two NSC projects will be ongoing for years. I figure I'll stay on at this cushy job until I'm sixty-five, and retire then."

"Well, you do you then," Bill answered. "So anyway, I'm on my way to Joburg now. I'll sign the contract with Johan on behalf of GlobalForce, then talk with my two team leads, and then address the whole group and bring them up to speed."

"Sounds good," Kevin acknowledged.

"Oh, wait," Bill had another thought, "you need to get board resolutions to give Kyle and Eileen authority to sign contracts for the company when needed. You know, since I won't be on the NSC projects anymore."

"Already done," Kevin answered. "I'll email them to you in a moment so you can share those with Kyle and Eileen when you meet with them."

"Appreciated," Bill answered.

There was an awkward silence, which Bill eventually broke.

"So, I guess I'll let you get back to that nothing you're doing," Bill joked.

"Yup, I guess so," Kevin answered. "Be safe in Geneva, my friend. Check in sometimes, and stop by and see us to turn in your notice when you retire. You have an insane amount of paid time off accrued."

Bill laughed at that.

"I'll take the lump sum payout when I retire next year," Bill answered. "Hey Kevin. Thanks for everything."

"Thank you too, Bill," Kevin replied. "Be safe."

"Yup," Bill ended the call, feeling very uncomfortable about the day ahead of him.

Bill met first with Johan and signed the contract for Simunye's work to begin on the New Zealand branch of the NSC project. Once that was done, Bill informed Johan that he was stepping off the NSC projects completely, and that Kyle would be the project manager on the South African project, answering to Minister Mabusa, and that Eileen would be the project manager on the New Zealand project, answering to Mister Williamson in New Zealand. Johan was only slightly surprised to hear the news, but was happy with the new assignments, as he and his teams already had good working relationships with both Kyle and Eileen.

Next, Bill requested and was given an office with a network connection so he could talk with Kyle in private, and then Eileen over a secure connection.

Bill headed to The Pit, as the developers called the room in which they all sat, and tried his old trick.

"Programmers, mount up," Bill said in a soft voice, not wanting to be disruptive if no one knew the catch phrase.

They didn't, and Bill got a few strange looks. Kyle jumped up and walked to Bill.

"Um, why did no one know our phrase?" Bill asked Kyle as they walked to Bill's temporary office.

"Man, we have enough trouble down here not being viewed as crazy Yank cowboys," Kyle laughed through his explanation. "Did you know that most people here think pretty much all of the land west of Washington, DC, is populated with Old West towns and saguaro cactuses?"

"Yeah well, we keep looking for the Zulu Wars, so we're probably even," Bill answered.

"Probably," Kyle laughed. "So what brings you down from your little palace in Pretoria?"

"News, my son," Bill answered.

Once they were in the office, Bill closed the door and sat behind the desk, and motioned for Kyle to sit.

"So, good news, and scary news," Bill began. "Which do you want first?"

"The good news," Kyle answered.

"Well, too bad, it's all scary," Bill began.

Kyle listened to Bill's explanation of the project changes, and to the news of the promotion Kyle was receiving today. Bill explained that Kyle would now be answering to Minister Mabusa as the client contact, and to Kevin Blanchard at GlobalForce as his direct manager. Raise and bonuses of course to reflect the additional responsibilities.

"Now here's the bad news," Bill changed to the next topic.

"Hang on, man, I'm still a little stunned," Kyle interrupted.

"Nope, no mercy," Bill continued. "You are no longer a programmer, you are a project manager. You tell others what to code, and they go code it. It's actually a very liberating feeling once you get accustomed to it."

"That will be painful," Kyle acknowledged. "How long did it take you to deal with it?"

"I'll let you know. Anyway, after our meeting with Eileen in a few minutes, we will be going out to that room," Bill said, pointing in the general direction of The Pit, "where I will inform the team of the change, and then I am off to Geneva for a year. And when that project is finished, I am retiring."

"Holy shit!" Kyle almost fell out of his chair. "You're not old enough to retire."

"Kyle, this entire South African experience has taken a lot out of me," Bill explained. "I need to clear my head for a while. Realistically, it'll just end up being a sabbatical, because I can't not work, but I need to grab my camera and see where the landscapes take me."

"I get it," Kyle acknowledged. "Well, thanks for the opportunity down here, man. We love it here. And I love the work."

"You definitely earned it," Bill said. "Now, for your first responsibility, I need you to make a branch of the code."

"Why?" Kyle thought it was an odd request.

"Because the New Zealand government licensed it from the South African government," Bill got ready to drop the next surprise on Kyle. "Eileen's team will be making the changes to their branch, and she and you will be coordinating on the mutual code."

"Say what?"

"Yeah, I forgot to tell you," Bill continued, "Eileen will be your peer, running the New Zealand project. Simunye Holdings was just contracted to develop the New Zealand source. I'll be telling her about all that in a few minutes."

A huge smile spread across Kyle's face.

"She is going to hate not being able to code anymore," Kyle laughed.

"Maybe," Bill acknowledged. "Now get out of here for fifteen minutes so I can tell her, then come back in so I can talk with you both together about a couple other notes."

"Yup, back in fifteen," Kyle said, and left the room.

"That's not your normal background," Eileen commented as soon as the call was connected. "Where are you?"

"I'm actually in Johannesburg," Bill answered. "Had some high-level contract stuff to do here, and some loose ends to tie up."

"Okay," Eileen acknowledged. "So, what's up?"

"I wanted to bring you up to speed on some enhancements to the NSC project that were announced today," Bill began. "I found out yesterday afternoon that Minister Mabusa and his peer in New Zealand have been discussing the NSC project. New Zealand wants it."

"Williamson?" Eileen asked.

"Yeah, I think that's his name," Bill was a little surprised that she knew his name.

"Well, that explains that," Eileen said as much to herself as to Bill.

"Explains what?"

"I got an email from one of his assistants that he wants to meet with me at the end of the week, and I didn't even know who he was before I researched it," Eileen explained.

"Well, you maybe want to write back and accept the meeting," Bill answered. "It'll be important after I tell you the rest of the story."

Bill explained the project branch and Eileen's new responsibilities, including that she was now the project manager on the NZNSC project, and would report directly to Mister Williamson on the project, and Kevin Blanchard on the GlobalForce items.

Eileen took a moment to respond.

"Why am I not reporting to you?"

"Because," Bill took a deep breath before telling her the rest. "Because I am stepping off the NSC projects to go work full time on the Switch project, and we are moving the entire project to Switzerland for the next twelve to thirteen months, and it will require my undivided attention. And then after it's finished, I'm retiring."

Eileen actually laughed.

"Bitch, please," Eileen scoffed at Bill. "You'll never retire. I mean you are old, but not old enough to retire."

Bill laughed sarcastically, but didn't respond. He knew there was more coming.

Eileen remained silent for another minute, looking slightly away from the camera.

"I'm mad at you," she finally said, still not looking at the camera.

"I know," Bill acknowledged.

Eileen remained in her thoughts for another minute.

"What are you going to do when you retire?" Eileen asked, continuing to look away.

"I'm going to buy a bunch of memory cards and a new lens or two for my camera, and follow it around the world," Bill answered, giving her time to fully embrace the enormity of the work and related news that Bill had just heaped upon her.

"You better follow it down here for a little while," Eileen said in a faux angry voice.

"You know I will," Bill continued to give her space.

Eileen finally looked back at the camera and began to address her new responsibilities.

"How much is my raise?"

"A lot," Bill was glad she decided to keep the project. "When you have your call with Kevin tomorrow, he'll go over all that with you, since I am no longer your boss."

Eileen was silent again for a moment, but this time did not look away.

"You know I just wanted to stay home and not work anymore, right?" Eileen was joking and Bill knew it.

"No you didn't."

"There is a lot more to say," Eileen concluded after another moment of thought, "but we'll save that for when you come visit."

"Agreed," Bill was glad to move the conversation along. "I have some stuff to go over with you and the new PM on the NSC project, so let me get him in here, and we'll cover those items."

Bill sent Kyle a SMS, and a few seconds later, Kyle re-entered the office and sat next to Bill so Eileen could see them both.

"Eileen, meet Kyle Dobson," Bill jokingly introduced them. "Kyle will be stepping on as the project manager for the South African NSC project. He will be answering to Minister Mabusa on the project, and to Kevin Blanchard at GlobalForce."

"Wow, look at you, getting promoted," Eileen joked with Kyle.

"Well, I heard you got the same promotion in Kiwi land," Kyle joked back.

"Yeah, I just found out," Eileen answered.

"So, let's get down to business," Bill was aware of the passage of the afternoon, and needed to make sure he didn't forget to transition anything, then sat forward and tapped at his keyboard for a moment before continuing.

"I have just sent to both of you copies of the GlobalForce Board of Directors Resolutions authorizing you two to sign contracts and stuff on behalf of GlobalForce in relation to your respective projects. So, you two, my little minions, will work together to branch the South African NSC code base, and Kyle, you will hand off the branch to Eileen and her team. Eileen, there are some environmental snooping features that Williamson wants to add for the New Zealand version, so work with him on those requirements. Also, Eileen, I already signed the contract with Simunye Holdings for them to provide the development talent for your new NZNSC project, and young Kyle here has agreed to give you half of his best programmers for your project."

"No I didn't," Kyle immediately objected.

"Well, my last official act is to order you and Eileen to pick teams from Simunye's talent pool," Bill clarified. "If you have a dispute, work it out. Both of these projects are equally important. You two are the new project managers on these two projects specifically because of the importance of them. You two have worked together long enough that I believe this will be a seamless transition."

Kyle and Eileen were both silent for a moment.

"You got it, boss," Kyle finally answered.

"Technically, he's not our boss anymore," Eileen corrected.

"Cold," Bill chided Eileen.

"Do either of you have any last questions for me before we move Eileen to the big monitor in the Pit and tell everyone else the news?" Bill asked his protegees.

"I can't believe you're just going to retire and dump these projects on us," Kyle said with an exasperated voice.

"You're both perfectly capable of taking on these projects," Bill answered. "I've never dumped a project on either of you that you couldn't handle. This is the natural progression of these projects. And with the NZNSC project being signed, I didn't have to decide between the two of you as to who I would put in charge of the South African project when I stepped off."

"Right, because Eileen wouldn't have worked nicely for me," Kyle joked.

"Nope, especially since I'd have been your boss," Eileen shot back.

"Oh, you two," Bill answered playfully, then stood up. "Shall we move this call to the Pit?"

"Wait, who would you have chosen?" Kyle added.

"Exactly," Bill responded and left the room.

"Dude!" Kyle hollered after him.

Eileen's call had been successfully transferred to the large monitor in the Pit, and Bill and Kyle stood next to it, all eyes on them.

Bill announced the new project and contract for Simunye Holdings, which brought a round of excited applause from the room. Bill then informed the room that he was stepping off, and announced the promotions of Kyle and Eileen, which brought another round of loud applause.

Bill explained that they would be selecting their teams from the existing talent pool before any hiring would take place, and that he would be leaving all of those decisions to Kyle and Eileen. There was a murmur through the room as the various technicians talked with each other about which team they wanted to be on.

Bill was glad for it. He expected both projects to be wildly successful, and he stated as much.

Then Bill opened the floor for questions, and after deferring to his two new project managers for all of the answers, they wrapped up the meeting, Bill spent an hour shaking hands with everyone, then made his way to the front door, and shook hands one more time with Johan and Kyle.

Kyle walked Bill out to the waiting car.

"I expect that you will keep in touch sometimes," Kyle was fighting for words.

"You know I will," Bill was feeling rough, too. "And both you and your counterpart in New Zealand can reach out to me with questions. I'm not going to disappear."

"I know," Kyle responded, then just looked at the ground.

Bill had one more thought.

"Hey, do me a favor," Bill wanted to somehow protect Kyle and Eileen from the bad transactions that were sure to eventually reach them, even though he couldn't actually tell them. "With each of your paychecks, start buying a lot of physical gold and silver. I can't tell you why, but just do it. And tell Eileen to do it too next time you talk to her."

"That's a weird last thing to say to me," Kyle laughed.

"That wasn't the last thing, you morbid freak," Bill joked, then turned serious again. "Just do it, okay?"

"Yeah man, I will," Kyle answered.

Bill extended his hand and Kyle shook it, then they embraced in a bro hug, and Bill got in the car.

Kyle watched the car drive away, then went back inside to the Pit, where Eileen was still talking on the monitor with a group of programmers.

"Hey!" Kyle yelled. "Stop poaching all the good talent!"

CHAPTER 79: CHESS THERAPY

Bill ate alone in his cottage that night, not feeling like talking to anyone. There wasn't much to pack, and he still had two more days to do it.

He didn't feel like going to do some work with Heinrich and Keith, either. Bill was sure they were deep in the middle of getting the project plan assembled and sent ahead to Geneva so vendors could be identified and other preliminary start-up work could be initiated in advance of them stepping on there the following week.

So, Bill sat in silence. The sun had not quite set yet, and he realized he had probably eaten dinner too early. And, it was too early for bed. And, he had nothing to do for the next two days, so he figured he better pace himself on getting all that nothing done.

Bill continued to sit in silence.

After a few minutes, Bill became aware of footsteps walking towards him. He turned towards the living room to see Vasily approaching him, with a box in his hand.

"We play chess," Vasily stated.

"What?" Bill was caught completely off guard.

"We play chess," Vasily repeated precisely.

"Vasily, I'm really tired," Bill answered. "And how do you know I play chess?"

"I know," Vasily non-answered.

"I don't really feel up for a game," Bill just wanted to feel bad for himself and not do anything else.

"Then you lose," Vasily sat and grabbed a pawn of each color from the box and put one in each hand, then closed his hands and extended them to Bill.

Bill just looked at Vasily.

After a moment, Vasily dipped his right hand, then turned it over and opened his hand, exposing the black pawn.

"I play white pieces," Vasily answered, and started setting up his pieces on the board.

When he was finished, he looked at Bill, who had still not moved. So Vasily began setting up the black pieces for Bill. When he was finished, he looked at Bill again.

Bill just stared back for a full minute, then gave up and sat forward and moved a pawn.

Vasily shook his head.

"*Da*, you lose," Vasily said with a chuckle and moved a knight.

Bill shook his head and made another move without thinking.

This time, Vasily did not react, but sat motionless for a moment, then looked up at Bill, with what appeared to be real anger on his face.

Bill was stunned.

"Okay, let's start over, I'll pay attention," Bill acquiesced, reaching for the pieces to reset.

"*Nyet!*" Vasily roared, completely shocking Bill, who sat back quickly.

"You think you are only one worried or upset!?" Vasily yelled at Bill, fully showing his rage. "I am worried! I am upset! This assignment is most dangerous of career! But I am not little bitch! You stop being little bitch now! *Pryamo seychas*! No more feel bad for yourself!"

As soon as he had finished yelling at Bill, Vasily picked up the board and poured the pieces back into the box, set the board in the box, put the cover on, clipped his weapon back onto his vest, and walked back to his post, leaving Bill in stunned silence.

Bill's first reaction was to get mad at Vasily. *Where does he get off calling me a bitch?* Bill thought to himself. *I didn't sign up for any of this, they came to me. They recruited me. I didn't want to move to South Africa and play with transdimensional crap.*

Bill sat in silence for a few more minutes.

I miss my desert.

A few more minutes of quiet contemplation later, Bill realized that he had signed up for all of this. He was forced to admit to himself that he liked the power, he liked the recognition. And he was sure he would like the money when he started spending it in a year when he retired. He may not like where all his work had led, but he had been a willing participant. *Hell, I drove this train for a lot of it.*

Bill sighed heavily, then leaned forward and set up the chess board.

"*Vasily Ivanovich*," Bill called to the front door.

Vasily didn't look around the corner.

"*Shto?*" Vasily did not use his usual respectful voice for the response.

Ouch, Bill thought to himself. *He really is mad.*

"Chess?"

Vasily looked around the corner at Bill, and then at the chess board. Then he walked around the corner towards the table, speaking briefly into his headset. Next, he unclipped his gun from his vest and sat down.

Bill went first, playing the same bad opening move as earlier, but this time looking defiantly at Vasily as he did it. Vasily actually permitted a chuckle to escape, and moved his knight in his same opening move from the previous game.

"*Da*, you lose."

Eventually, Bill did lose. Badly. And, fairly quickly. But he was happy to have his head on straight again, and comforted to know that his guard didn't think badly of him.

He wasn't sure why that mattered to him, but it did.

Once the game was over, Vasily clipped his weapon back onto his vest and went back to work.

Bill decided to catch a little news, and headed towards the television when his phone rang. It was Kandi. He had forgotten all about that call.

Kandi was happy to fill Bill in on all the new news. With her raise, she had been able to start sending her mom money every month, and her mom got a new apartment in a gated community in Henderson. Kandi had started back to school, and decided to study international business management. Bill laughed ironically at that, and gave her a fake warning to choose something else more stable. They talked about Eileen's daughter. Apparently, Kandi and Eileen stayed in touch and talked several times a week. That gave Bill a little pang of guilt. After basically listening for a little over an hour, Bill told Kandi that he was happy to hear all the great news in her life, and said he looked forward to catching up again next time he was in town, and told her to stay in touch. Kandi ended the call with her signature "byeeee!"

International business management, Bill thought to himself. *I have to get her to change her mind on that...*

Bill had a bowl of coco pops and went to bed.

CHAPTER 80: SHUT DOWN FOR MAINTENANCE

Bill woke to the song of the hadedas. He wondered to himself if he would actually miss them or not. *Probably not*, he thought to himself.

Bill got up and headed to the kitchen for some orange juice. That, bottled water, and milk were the only things he kept stocked in his fridge. He didn't feel like cereal this morning, and hoped he could head to the cafeteria this morning. He was craving what he had continued to call a "Pretoria Denver omelette". It was the same as a regular Denver omelette, but made in Pretoria. Bill thought the name was funny. He knew he was the only one, but Bill decided that funny was funny, regardless of the number of people who agreed.

He also hoped he would be permitted to actually eat it in the cafeteria, because the lock-down was really starting to irritate him. *For my own good, abundance of caution, blah blah blah*, Bill said to himself.

"Vasily!" Bill called out to his security team lead.

"*Da?*"

"Any chance I can eat at the cafeteria this morning?"

"*Nyet.*" The reply took a couple minutes to arrive, and Bill had actually begun to have hope, only to have it dashed.

"Fine," Bill answered, sounding only slightly less disappointed with the answer than he actually was.

Bill walked to the house phone and called his order into the cafeteria, then let Vasily know it was coming, and headed to the shower.

After a refreshing shower and a good meal, Bill decided to go check in on his little team of mad scientists. He arrived to find Keith and Heinrich sitting at Heinrich's dining room table finishing their breakfast, laptops nowhere to be seen.

Bill did notice that the bad transaction list count on the monitor showed over eleven thousand bad transactions.

"Morning, team," Bill greeted the other two as they continued to eat. "That count is staggering."

"And brazen, too," Keith answered. "They have been hitting the highest profile targets. They are smart. They know if they continue to hit people and companies that have something to hide, there's less of a chance of publicity getting the Switch network shut down."

"How much have they stolen so far?" Bill was almost afraid to ask, but did anyway.

"Last I looked," Heinrich answered nonchalantly, "just under four trillion euros."

Bill was stunned by the number, and didn't speak for a moment.

"How can they still be avoiding attention?" Bill finally asked. "Some news agency somewhere has to have found it by now."

"There have been a few reporters that have attempted to break the story," Keith admitted, "but there are powerful people that have convinced their editors to not run the story yet. Interestingly, no press organization or employee has been hit yet. Like I said, they are smart."

Bill sat and watched the count tick upwards at a rate of about one per minute while Heinrich and Keith finished their breakfast, then joined them at the table to discuss plans.

Keith and Heinrich filled Bill in on their progress from the previous day. The project plan had been forwarded early afternoon to the team in

Geneva, and there had been questions overnight and into the morning for clarification of various items. They gave Bill updates on a few items that he could amend in his Gantt chart, as incremental progress had been made on them, chipping away ever so slightly at the four-week overrun on the deadline.

"So, what's left?" Bill asked his team, not sure there was any reason for them to wait for two more days to travel.

"Nothing, man," Keith answered first. "I'm packed and ready to go."

"I'm ready too," Heinrich chimed in.

"Vasily?" Bill wanted to see if there was any prep work the security teams needed to accomplish first.

"*Da?*" Vasily stepped around the corner.

"Is there any reason why we can't travel to Geneva today or tomorrow, instead of waiting until Friday?" Bill asked.

"Wait, I check and tell you," Vasily's short answer came as he went back to confer with the three security teams present in the cottage, as well as with teams in the ministry and in Geneva.

About ten minutes later, Vasily joined them with his answer.

"Security in Geneva ready, minister approve. We fly in morning."

The team were all happy to hear the news. They agreed to have dinner in Bill's cottage that night to go over last minute items. Heinrich planned to spend the day packing up the remaining computer equipment, and Bill was going to pack and have a call with the minister.

Back in his cottage, Bill turned on his laptop and plugged in his headset. While waiting for it to finish booting, he sent a quick SMS to M'Bulu.

GOT A MINUTE?

M'Bulu's answer a minute later was for Bill's chat client to start ringing on his laptop. He clicked the Answer button, and M'Bulu's image appeared.

"Good morning, Bill," M'Bulu appeared to be in a good mood. "Are you and your team getting restless?"

"Good morning, Minister," Bill answered cheerfully, matching M'Bulu's mood. "Slightly. If we didn't travel before Friday, we were just planning to eat popcorn and watch the bad transaction count increase until then. Thanks for letting us go sooner."

"Ah, you should enjoy the quiet times while you can," M'Bulu chuckled. "Soon enough, you will miss them."

"Probably true," Bill acknowledged, then got down to business. "Keith and Heinrich have updated me on a few items that I can add progress to on my chart, which I will do momentarily. Is there any other news that you want to share with me before we travel tomorrow?"

"No, nothing of any interest," M'Bulu answered nonchalantly. "The teams all got very busy as soon as the plans arrived, you know of the progress, and all seems on track. I have a few meetings here tomorrow, so I will not be able to join you in Geneva until Friday, but until then, you will be in charge in Geneva. I can tell you that Doctor Vanderzhen will probably attempt to assert her power and try to make you take orders from her, but don't let her. You are in charge of that project when I am not there. Keith will be able to speak for The Committee to rein her in if she fights you too much."

"Appreciated," Bill answered. "I'll wield my power with great restraint."

M'Bulu chuckled.

"I know that you will, Bill," he answered. "And if things look like they are getting away from you, just rely on your security team and Keith. All of the security at the Collider is provided by us, and all of the other security teams answer to your Vasily. He and his teams are tasked with keeping you and your team safe, and to make sure nothing interferes with the project."

"Understood, Minister," Bill answered, this time the formality was genuine.

"Good," M'Bulu wrapped up the call. "I will see you for dinner on Friday night. You and your team will use my jet tomorrow, and I expect to use it myself on Friday, so please do not scratch it."

Bill laughed.

"I will do my best, M'Bulu, and thank you," Bill answered.

"One more thing, Bill," M'Bulu said, leaning forward, his voice serious. "To ensure that my plane is not scratched, you will have fighter jet escorts the entire way. Please do not be alarmed by this, we are just providing the escort out of an abundance of caution."

"Well, now I *am* nervous," Bill answered, slightly unnerved.

"You should become comfortable with this level of security until after the project is complete, Bill," M'Bulu explained. "There are literally no more important people on the planet at this moment than you and your team, even though you are anonymous. The actions that will take place around you and your team to maintain your security will be commensurate with that importance. They may feel extreme to you, but the actions will be necessary."

"Come on," Bill responded, only half believing M'Bulu's words. "That can't actually be true."

"It is true, Bill," M'Bulu replied in a softer voice. "As you Yanks say, 'you are no longer in Kansas City'. In truth, this is the world stage, and you are working under it to raise it to the new level that will be enjoyed by humanity well past your lifetime and mine."

"First of all," Bill said, rubbing his temples, "the expression is 'I don't think we are in Kansas anymore', and I wasn't in Kansas anyway. I was in Arizona. And second, I still have not, and probably will never, wrap my head around the full scope of just how much this project will affect the future and outlive both of us and our grandchildren. It's a lot."

"This is fair," M'Bulu nodded. "As long as the project stays on schedule, you may keep your head unwrapped."

"Gee, thanks," Bill answered sarcastically. "See you Friday night, my friend."

"Looking forward to it, my friend," M'Bulu responded, and disconnected the call.

Bill took off his headset and shut down his laptop.

"*Literally no more important people on the planet at this moment*," Bill said quietly to the empty room, doing his best impersonation of M'Bulu before switching back to his own voice. "Am not."

Bill saw Vasily looking at him from around the corner by the front door.

"Please don't tell him I just did that," Bill asked Vasily.

Vasily grinned and went back to work.

Bill busied himself getting packed before dinner.

It was a good day for flying. The sky was clear, and Bill didn't see any clouds below them. They were flying high enough that Bill thought he could see the curve of the planet. What he was sure that he could see were the four fully-loaded fighter jets flying with them.

Bill wished for a distraction, but there was none to be had. Heinrich was making notes in his journal, and Keith was asleep.

Maybe Vasily would enjoy a game of chess, Bill thought to himself, and walked to the back of the plane and asked.

"*Nyet*, Doctor," Vasily answered quietly, shaking his head. "Too busy with job today. Maybe Saturday."

"I understand," Bill responded, feeling a little stupid for forgetting the level of stress on Vasily right now. "I'll look forward to the game on Saturday."

Vasily gave Bill a quick, barely visible grin, then began speaking into his headset. Bill returned to his seat, and watched the fighter escort out the window.

The flight to Geneva was uneventful, and Bill noticed Heinrich breathe a deep sigh of relief as the jet came to a stop at the executive terminal.

"You okay?" Bill asked him.

"Yeah, mate," Heinrich answered. "Just kept having a nagging feeling about the last important flight I was supposed to be on, and was hoping for an uneventful flight this time."

"Don't you jinx us," Bill said with mock seriousness. "It's bad enough you're violating the rules of God and physics with this project."

Heinrich chuckled and headed for the front of the plane.

The drive in the motorcade to the secure facility that Bill would call "home" for the next twelve to thirteen months was uneventful, but Bill still felt a pang of Imposter Syndrome watching the phalanx of cars with armed guards in the other vehicles escorting them the whole way.

As they were arriving, Bill saw Vasily talking quietly into his headset, then nodded and looked at Bill.

"*Da*, I will inform," Vasily said into his microphone, then pulled it away from his face to address Bill. "Doctor, I am to inform you that Doctor Vanderzhen will see you in her office before you are escorted to your quarters."

"Well, the minister did warn me," Bill answered. "Okay, I guess we will go to her office first."

"*Nyet*, not whole team, only you," Vasily clarified.

"Wait a minute," Keith began to interrupt, but Bill cut him off.

"Keith, I'd like to keep you as a special tool that I only use in the most serious of situations," Bill said to Keith. "I would prefer to not hide behind you every time she raises her voice."

"Understood, mate," Keith acquiesced. "Just give the word, and I'll step in."

"Appreciated," Bill acknowledged, then turned back to Vasily. "Are there any surprises I should know about?"

Vasily didn't immediately answer, but looked to Keith.

"There are always surprises when dealing with Karla," Keith answered.

"Hang on a second." Now Bill was frustrated. "I thought you two liked her. Back when that other guy died tragically, you two both said you liked her."

"Well, yes," Heinrich spoke up. "We liked her as the scheduling director, but she is clearly now trying to flex her authority, because she believes this entire project falls under the scheduling department at the Collider."

"I would argue that it doesn't," Bill replied, showing a little confidence. "The Collider is shut down for maintenance. There is nothing to schedule. Technically, the Scheduling department should be on leave until the upgrades and testing have been completed and signed off, and only then should Doctor Vanderzhen and her Scheduling staff be back on site."

Keith began to smile, and then so did Heinrich. They both looked to Vasily, who showed a hint of a grin, and then began speaking into his headset.

After a moment, he stopped talking and continued looking at Bill. After a couple more minutes, Bill's impatience overwhelmed his ability to wait quietly.

"Well?" Bill finally asked.

"*Shto?*" Vasily responded, actually using an innocent tone.

"Anything new to report?"

"*Nyet.*"

"Then may we please go to our quarters?" Bill asked.

"*Da.*"

"Thank you," Bill answered, trying not to sound smug.

Heinrich and Keith did their best to hide their smiles too.

As they were walking to their new quarters, Bill's phone chimed in a message.

TOMORROW MORNING AT 10:00 LOCAL TIME, YOU WILL HAVE A MEETING WITH KARLA IN YOUR OFFICE TO DISCUSS YOUR AGENDA, PLEASE LET ME KNOW WHEN YOU HAVE TIME FOR A QUICK CALL BEFORE DINNER TONIGHT

Well, that's interesting, Bill thought to himself.

ACKNOWLEDGED

Bill looked forward to his call with M'Bulu after settling into his room.

CHAPTER 81: UNUSED PRIVACY SCREEN

Bill wasn't sure what to think when the aide led Bill and his team, and their security teams, down the long hallway past many important sounding doors, but then he saw the mahogany double doors with a plaque that read "ENHANCEMENT SCIENCE LEADERSHIP TEAM, Dr. William M. Fibulee, Director".

Bill stopped for a moment, stunned by the plaque.

"Hey, look at that! Cheers man!" Keith slapped Bill on the back in congratulations.

The aide continued to the doors and opened both, swinging them open to show a lavish, massive office. To the left was a conference table and eight chairs, with three large monitors on the wall directly behind the table. To the right were three very comfortable-looking sofas arranged to face each other with a coffee table between them all. Continuing past the sofas were two desks facing each other on opposite sides of the room. Each desk had two large monitors on them, and each had a large monitor on the wall behind them. Past those desks at the far end of the room was a large, ridiculously ornate desk with two monitors on one end, and a phone at the other end. Behind the desk was a wall made of floor to ceiling windows, and the light streaming through reflected off the ornate marble floor tiles.

Bill just stood and took in the spectacle. Keith and Heinrich walked past Bill and high-fived before heading to the two smaller desks and settling in. Bill noted that the walls were some type of dark wood, and he felt a fleeting pang of disappointment at the loss of the white board walls from his old office in Pretoria. The aide excused himself and left the room, closing the doors as he departed. Vasily began speaking with the other security team members, assigning positions.

After everyone appeared to be where they were supposed to be, Vasily stepped close to Bill and spoke quietly enough that only Bill heard him.

"Are you afraid of desk?"

That snapped Bill out of his paralysis. He looked at the desk, then to Vasily.

"Da, ny mnoga."

Vasily actually laughed, causing everyone in the room except Bill to look at him in surprise.

"I check for you." Vasily responded in his still-quiet voice, then walked to the desk and made a show of checking it for traps and bugs, then stood and announced loudly to the room that it was safe.

Out of options for avoiding taking his seat at the big desk, Bill sighed and walked to the front and touched the surface slightly, almost as if he was afraid it would shock him. Next, Bill walked to the back of the desk, and sat in the chair. He immediately recognized it as the same very comfortable chair he had in his office in Arizona. He mentally sent a thank-you to M'Bulu, put his arms on the desk and folded his hands, then lifted his head and addressed his team.

"Team, it is time for my meeting with Doctor Vanderzhen," Bill announced. "Since The Committee has apparently seen fit to house us all in the same office, I'll need you all to go find something to do while I meet with her."

Keith looked up from playing with his laptop and getting the monitors all connected.

"We don't need to leave, mate, just activate the privacy screen."

Bill stared back at Keith with a blank expression. Vasily leaned over from where he was still standing behind Bill and pulled a small panel from the front of the desk, then pressed a blue button. Bill jumped, because he had forgotten Vasily was still behind him, and then watched as an opaque white wall unfolded along a hidden track in the ceiling and floor, enclosing

Bill's section of the office. All of the sound from the other side was muffled out as the screen attached itself to the far wall. Bill looked to Vasily, impressed.

"Am I to assume that any meetings I have behind this screen will still include one or more members of my security team?" Bill asked Vasily.

"*Da.*"

Bill accepted the answer, then pressed the same button on the panel, and the screen retracted into its original invisible hiding spot.

"Okay, that is just cool," Bill said out loud, mostly to himself, but he noticed both Keith and Heinrich shoot him a glance and a grin.

Remembering his task, Bill cleared his throat.

"Vasily," Bill began. "Please invite Doctor Vanderzhen to join me here at her earliest convenience."

No sooner had he finished the request, an aide opened the door at the far end of the office and announced the arrival of Karla, who pushed past the aide and stomped her way towards Bill's desk.

"What gives you the right to keep me waiting," Karla demanded as she approached Bill's desk, then stood directly in front of him. "I told you I wanted to see you in my office yesterday afternoon right away. Instead, you ignore me until 9:30 this morning, and then keep me standing in the hallway for a half hour? Who do you think you are?!"

Bill saw Keith and Heinrich both turn their heads to watch Bill's response. Keith was ready to verbally shred her, but waited for Bill's reaction first.

"Doctor Vanderzhen," Bill said in his smoothest, calmest tone, "good morning. Please take a seat. We have several topics to cover."

Karla remained standing.

"I said in my message that I wanted to see you in *my* office," Karla said through gritted teeth.

Bill turned to Vasily.

"Vasily, did Doctor Vanderzhen ask to see me in her office?" Bill asked, maintaining the very calm tone.

"*Nyet*," Vasily answered. "Message said Doctor wanted to meet with you. No location stated. We assume this office."

Karla lost her patience.

"That was not the fucking message," she screamed at Vasily, who remained motionless and expressionless.

"Karla," Bill needed to calm her, because he didn't want this to escalate too much. "You're here now, I apologize that the message that was transmitted to my team was apparently garbled. So, let's talk now. Please, sit down."

Bill kept his tone calm, but emphasized the last two words so that she would know it was not a request.

Karla stood her ground for a moment, eyes blazing, then finally sat with a huff.

"Thank you," Bill tried to remain sounding peaceful. "Now, before we go into the items I have to cover with you, what did you want to discuss?"

"I wanted to give you the schedule for you and your team," Karla began. "I have already given the other teams their task lists and schedules, so you need to have yours."

Karla handed a file folder to Bill, and he accepted it and laid it on his desk without opening it.

"Thank you," Bill answered. "I will review it with my team today. What else did you want to discuss?"

Karla was caught off guard. She expected Bill to go through the schedules and tasks in the folder right away.

"Um, well, that was it," Karla sputtered.

"Great!" Bill kept up the enthusiasm. "I don't know if you spoke to Minister Mabusa last night, but his instructions to me were that I was to

366

meet with all of the department heads here in my office right after lunch. You are excused from that meeting, obviously, since you and your team are all on leave during the enhancements."

Karla's response took a few seconds.

"What do you mean, we are 'all on leave during the enhancements'?" Karla was back in full rage again.

"You and your team are in charge of scheduling and coordinating the projects," Bill explained. "Until the enhancements and upgrades are complete, there are no tasks for you and your team to complete, so you are on leave effective today."

Bill waited a moment for her to realize what he had just told her.

"I really appreciate all you've done for this program, Karla," Bill concluded. "I'll look forward to working with you when we restart the Collider. Vasily will see you out."

Karla still did not speak, but stood as Vasily approached her, turned without another word, and stomped out.

"Well," Keith said after the door closed. "That did not go as I expected. And you forgot to use the privacy screen"

Bill flinched slightly at the oversight.

"I have a question, lads," Heinrich said to them all. "I thought we were supposed to be nice to her. Is that no longer the case?"

"We may be again," Keith answered. "But right now, she wants to control more than The Committee is willing to grant her."

Heinrich just nodded his acknowledgement.

The meeting with the department heads was uneventful, and Bill let Keith and Heinrich do most of the talking, since pretty much the only words Bill understood were "Gantt Chart", and not much else. He let the Engineers speak the language of engineering. It seemed to Bill that it would be more effective this way, and then he'd ask Heinrich and Keith for a summary after the meeting.

After the department heads had left, Bill's team updated him on the progress of each of the teams, and they adjusted the tasks in the timeline accordingly. As of that moment, the teams were ahead of schedule. That made Bill happy, and would surely make M'Bulu happy when Bill talked to him the following day with a status update.

When the conversation was finished, Bill called the meeting to an end. Heinrich stopped him before he stood.

"Bill, I have a request," Heinrich stated.

"Tell me," Bill answered, hoping it was an easy one, because he was still feeling jet lagged.

"I'd like to spend my time down in the big room actually supervising the work."

Bill looked to Keith to see if Keith was going to object. Keith simply shrugged.

Since Bill could think of no good reason to keep Heinrich away from his beloved dark arts, he acquiesced.

"Go," Bill answered with a small smile. "Send me daily updates so I can keep the project schedule current, and I want to see you once a week up here, on Fridays at 11:00 in the morning."

"Thanks!" Heinrich answered happily and headed to his desk to get his laptop.

He quickly packed up and headed for the door, moving as fast as his security team would permit.

"And I want you to report any major events in person when they happen!" Bill yelled after Heinrich, who was already in the hallway. "And tell me immediately if Karla shows up!"

"*Ja*, boss," Bill heard Heinrich yell from down the hallway just before the office door closed.

"What did I just do?" Bill asked Keith.

"You just ensured that this project is going to be finished early," Keith answered with a grin, then stood to return to his desk.

"You're all mad scientists," Bill grumbled.

Keith laughed and typed a few keys, then turned to see the bad transaction list on the monitor behind his desk.

Bill walked over and looked at it, trying to get a feel for how bad the attacks had become. The counter incremented at a steady pace, now at about two per minute. Bill was happy that it had not increased in speed too much, but even at the current speed, it was a lot. The total had exceeded seven trillion Euros.

"M'Bulu is not going to be able to hide this much longer," Bill said mostly to himself.

"Nope," Keith answered anyway.

Bill returned to his desk, and made a few notes regarding topics he would cover with M'Bulu the following day at their meeting. Then Bill turned around in his chair and looked out the window, looking past the airport to Lac Léman, and the Alps just beyond. He let his mind wander, and tried again to make sense of the last two weeks. After a few minutes, Bill forgot about the work, and just visually inhaled the splendor of the mountain range. He decided that he would go do some real sightseeing with his camera there when this was all finished up.

A few minutes later, Keith spoke up.

"I have some catching up to do with The Committee, then I'm going to eat a snack and find some sleep. See you back here in the morning?"

"Yeah, I should grab food and sleep too," Bill answered without turning. "See you in the morning."

Bill heard Keith and his security detail leave. He looked at the mountains for a few more minutes, then turned in his chair and shut down his laptop.

"Vasily, I am weary," Bill said as he put his laptop into the case.

Vasily mumbled into his headset, then nodded towards the door.

Bill obliged, and headed towards the door, and was then escorted back to his room, where he found one of his favorite meals, Swedish meatballs, waiting for him.

"I'm so glad they serve Swedish food in Switzerland," Bill said aloud to himself as he dug in.

Soon after dinner, Bill felt the weight of his eyelids, and went to bed.

The morning dawned clear, and gave Bill a spectacular view of the Alps from the window wall in his room. Bill ordered breakfast and ate it in his room while he watched the sun march across the mountains and the shadows and crags change shape as the light moved across them.

"Yup, I'm going to spend time with the camera in those mountains after this is all over," Bill said out loud to himself.

As the morning wore on and Bill realized he had accomplished exactly nothing the entire morning, he started getting ready for his lunch meeting with M'Bulu to bring him up to speed on the project. He let Vasily know that he'd be ready to go to his office soon, then headed to the shower.

The meeting with M'Bulu went well, with no new surprises. Bill was thankful for that. The minister was pleased to hear that the project was exactly 0.87 hours ahead of schedule, noting that it was a good omen for the project, and expressed confidence that Bill and his team would actually be able to bring the project to completion under the 12-month deadline. After a short lull in the conversation, Bill decided it was time to clarify the Karla issue.

"Minister, what exactly is Karla's status with the project and the LHC?"

M'Bulu thought for a moment before answering.

"As you know, Doctor Vanderzhen has provided extremely valuable support for this project and certain team members since well before South Africa was involved in the project," M'Bulu began.

Bill nodded in acknowledgement, but did not interrupt the explanation.

"When she replaced the unfortunate Doctor Schrengen," M'Bulu continued, "she initially performed admirably in keeping the project on the track, as was directed by The Committee. Sadly, shortly after taking over the key position on the LHC's team, Karla began to demand more and take less direction, and began to act counter to the directives of The Committee. Because of this, she was... demoted, and it is hoped that when Doctor de Boer has completed the upgrades on the machine, Karla can rejoin the team."

Bill considered M'Bulu's words for a moment.

"I hope so too," Bill finally answered. "She really did help us a lot."

As the meeting concluded, M'Bulu let Bill know that he was returning to Pretoria that evening, and that he would look forward to Bill's weekly status reports.

Bill sat alone at his desk for a few minutes after the minister had departed, and just looked out the window, lost in his thoughts. He wondered what this project would actually accomplish when it was finished, then wondered if it actually would ever be finished. The technology really was beyond his ability to comprehend, and he was certain that the simplified explanations that Heinrich had given him were so elementary as to be ridiculous to those who may actually understand them.

"As if anyone understands the technology," Bill mumbled out loud to himself with a chuckle. Bill turned his chair back to his desk, closed his laptop, loaded it into his bag, and stood to leave.

"Vasily, any chance we can go hiking this afternoon?" Bill asked his head of security.

Vasily just looked at Bill with a blank stare for a moment, then gave the slightest hint of a smirk.

"Yeah, I figured I'd ask anyway," Bill sighed.

"*Ponimayu.*"

CHAPTER 82: FIVE MONTHS LATER

As Heinrich finished his updates, Bill knew he should be happy with the progress.

In the five months and a couple weeks since the project had been underway, Heinrich had been able to find "task efficiencies", as he called them, that had brought the endpoint for completion down from thirteen months to eleven months, nineteen days.

His assembled key team members all seemed pleased. But Karla, who had been reinstated to the team four weeks prior at the request of Minister Mabusa, noticed Bill's discomfort.

"You seem uncomfortable about something," Karla said to Bill.

Bill considered his words.

"It's just that we have, in the past five months or so, shaved forty three days off of this project," Bill explained. "I can not shake this feeling that a bunch of the safety measures and procedures we had in the original project design have been ignored or glossed over, and I worry for this planet."

"Mate," Heinrich began, "we have not glossed over any safety measure, I promise. After the low power test next week, you'll feel much differently."

"Let's hope," Bill acknowledged. "Okay, class dismissed."

CHAPTER 83: LOW POWER TEST

Bill awoke with a bit of a startle, as he wasn't sure he had heard thunder or dreamt it. His room was darker than it would normally be, but a quick glance at his clock told him it was almost time to get up. He turned his gaze to the window and saw that it was darker outside than usual, because there was a storm outside. A flash of lightning and a rumble of thunder a few seconds later confirmed the presence of the storm.

This can't be a good omen, Bill thought to himself.

Normally, Bill liked thunderstorms. The power of the storm, the resultant negative ions, the smell of fresh air after the rain, the thunder, all of it.

But not on this day.

He really wanted to have no unknown variables today during the test. A serious thunderstorm was definitely a group of unknown variables. Maybe they could reschedule the test. He decided to push for that. Technically, he could order it, but he'd listen to his senior staff before making the decision.

Bill called down for a Denver omelette and orange juice, then decided he needed some comfort food too, so he added a small bowl of coco pops to the order, then headed to the shower.

The conference room just off to the side of the main control room was full of shouting, and none of it was happy. Bill tried to calm the room

373

several times, but was having no success. Bill was getting angry; every single one of the mad scientists in this room was unwilling to consider that they were about to break the universe, and he felt like a lone voice in a very scary wilderness.

Bill looked up to see Vasily looking at him, apparently ready to take action. Bill just gave a single nod.

"*Tishina!*"

Bill wasn't sure what the word Vasily had roared meant, but it didn't matter, because the room went silent.

"Thank you, Vasily," Bill accepted the control of the room and continued in his sternest voice. "Now, if this room gets crazy like that one more time, I am suspending the testing until such time as I feel like it. Are there any questions?"

He made eye contact with each of the dozen or so scientists in the room, daring them to ask him a question. There were none, so Bill continued.

"I'm going to ask my question again, and this time, I would prefer that the room not decide to try to shout me down," Bill continued. "I am not asking this as a rhetorical question, I am honestly asking for the pros and cons of my query. So, in light of the stormy weather outside right now, why should we not delay the test? And don't give me some obvious answer like 'because the Machine is inside', I'm looking for the scientific reasons why it is safe to continue, and honest scientific reasons why it may be dangerous to continue. And if no one gives me any reasons why it is unsafe, then I'll know you're all lying to me, and I'll suspend this test."

Bill took a moment looking around the room. All of the scientists were angry, except Keith for some reason, who was trying hard not to smirk.

"Ready? Go," Bill prodded the room.

The scientists all looked around the room at each other, then all eventually looked to Heinrich, who actually looked the most angry. So, Bill singled him out.

"Doctor de Boer," Bill called on him, while walking to the white board, grabbing a marker, and drawing a line down the middle. "Can you please give me one reason why we should, and one reason why we should not, continue with this test?"

Bill turned his back to Heinrich and wrote "Pros" at the top of the left half of the board, and "Cons" at the top of the right half. Then he turned to face Heinrich and waited.

Heinrich just glared back at Bill, but said nothing.

Bill met Heinrich's stare for a moment, then turned and wrote "Dr. de Boer wants to" under the Pros list, and turned back to face Heinrich.

When Heinrich still said nothing, Bill turned and wrote "Dr. Fibilee doesn't want to" under the Cons list, and again turned back to face Heinrich.

"I can play this game all day," Bill finally said. "And the closer we get to 2:00, the happier I'll be, because this will project be delayed."

Finally, Keith spoke up.

"Doctors, Bill is not trying to stop this test," Keith explained, trying to play the diplomat. "He and his guard are the only two people in this room that do not have a working understanding of quantum physics. Under these circumstances, thunderstorms are as scary to him as they were originally to prehistoric neanderthals. The only difference here is that the neanderthals didn't have the ability to shut down scientific progress because they were afraid of a little lightning."

Bill started to agree, but then was pretty sure Keith just called him a neanderthal.

"Bill, you said that we can't use the excuse that the facility is underground," Heinrich finally spoke up, clearly trying very hard to maintain his temper. "But it really is that simple. This facility runs on internal power. There are no connections during this test to the outside world. We really are off the grid. The storm physically has no way to affect this test."

Several of the scientists around the room nodded in agreement with what Heinrich said. Bill noticed that Keith didn't, but he considered the scope of Heinrich's words for a moment before answering.

"I understand what you're saying, Heinrich," Bill answered, "and I truly do appreciate that we are talking this through now, but it really isn't that simple. It is true that the vast majority of this facility is deep underground, but there are a few connected buildings that are not. Even if we have significant electrical grounding on the surface buildings, there are still physical connections to the underground facility that are conductive."

Bill gave Heinrich and his acolytes a moment to consider his words before continuing, and was glad to see that they were at least thinking about what he said.

"And, while I'm at it," Bill continued, "even if we had sufficient air gaps between the surface parts of the facility and the underground parts, the other parts are in the ground... where the lightning grounds. What is to stop a large bolt from reaching deep enough to affect the machine while it's running?"

"Well, that's not really..." Heinrich started before Bill interrupted him.

"And, *this time*," Bill was on a roll, and wasn't going to let Heinrich interrupt until he laid out the entire scenario as he saw it, "the reactor is running for the first time with completely untested technology, opening tears into three other dimensions that we have only ever tested on a small scale, and never while a thunderstorm was raging overhead. So, you can not say, with any kind of scientific certainty or intellectual honesty, that the storm physically has no way to affect this test."

Heinrich opened his mouth to speak, but then stopped. Bill wrapped up his admonition of the scientific team.

"Now, if you are all willing to be intellectually honest with me, I will give you a fair hearing on this subject. If not, I have forty three days that I can push back this test before I have to start explaining why we are behind schedule."

Bill again made eye contact with each scientist in the room. This time, he saw hints of fear. Except for Keith, who Bill thought was trying not to laugh.

"So let's start over," Bill concluded. "Convince me that this test is safe with the storm overhead. I'm going to go for a walk for ten minutes to give you all a chance to figure out how to explain your positions to me with words I can understand."

Before the assembled team could say anything, Bill stood and walked to the door, Vasily leading the way. As he walked past the windows, he saw that Keith had stood and taken his position at the front of the room. Bill was grateful for it.

"Where do you want to go?" Vasily asked.

"Meh, wherever," Bill answered. "Let's just walk around for ten minutes. I'm just letting them worry. Keith will get them on track."

"You read Sun Tsu," Vasily answered.

"Who?" Bill asked with a smirk.

Vasily chuckled and shook his head, but continued walking in front of Bill and looking as menacing as usual to anyone in their path.

Bill was glad that Vasily appeared to play along. Bill was pretty sure Vasily was getting annoyed with the braintrust in the room too, so this break was good for both of them.

After ten minutes, Vasily had Bill back at the door to the conference room, and escorted him in. Bill walked to the front of the room, and was happy to see that there were several items written on the board in both columns, but upon reading them, realized that they were all in science words that he didn't understand.

"This is a good start," Bill said to the board, then turned to face the team. "Who wants to explain these to me?"

As Bill looked around the room, he noticed that all of the scientists had sheepish looks on their faces, except for Keith, who looked furious. Bill figured he should start with Keith.

"Doctor vanGreig, would you like to start?"

"No, mate, I'm just going to sum it up for you," Keith answered.

Yup, he's angry, Bill thought to himself.

"As it turns out, there *is* a low-percentage danger of the new technology on the machine running during a thunderstorm," Keith began.

Bill saw Heinrich drop his head to look at the floor, and Keith continued.

"The mini-collider that they had running in Cape Town experienced several *anomalous readings*, as *Doctor De Boer* explained," Keith was angry enough to use Heinrich's formal name, "whenever there was a storm outside during operation. What *Doctor De Boer* and his team down there failed to do was properly document that there was an actual pattern to the anomalous readings, because they failed to include the timing of lightning strikes in correlation to the anomalous readings from the reactor."

Bill was pretty sure Keith had just told him to abort the test, and now Bill was mad at Heinrich for hiding important information from him. Bill clarified, just to be sure.

"Doctor De Boer, this better be the best explanation of your career," Bill said through gritted teeth, "because this neanderthal just became afraid of lightning again, and I will kill this project."

Heinrich's head snapped up, his face a mix of panic and pleading.

"Make it good," Bill gave Heinrich one more chance.

"Bill, you can't kill the project... please!" Heinrich begged.

"No more bullshit, Heinrich, this is your last chance to not withhold critical information from me," Bill answered, not bothering to hide his anger. "So, in words I can understand, what is the anomalous reading, and why should I believe that it is not a fatal flaw in this entire project?"

"It's not a fatal flaw," Heinrich began. "In fact, there was no power spike or anything else that made us concerned. The anomaly was that when there was a lightning strike, if there was a virtual processor open at the exact same time as the strike, the processor would just dissolve, and we would have to re-run the whole process on that transaction. But because of how fast the entire process was, the loss in efficiency of the process was fractions of nanoseconds, and the servers on the other side of the quantum paradigm would not measure any loss of speed."

"Let me make sure I'm understanding this," Bill was having a hard time putting the pieces together. "The destroyed processors are not destroyed by an electrical spike, right? And the machine is completely undamaged by

378

electrical spikes, right?"

"Correct on both assumptions," Heinrich answered as he nodded.

"Okay, so what's causing the processors to dissolve?" Bill didn't understand that part.

More silence and sheepish looks from around the room, including from Heinrich, finally pushed Keith over the edge again.

"Antimatter," Keith stated angrily.

Bill laughed, then noticed no one else was enjoying the joke with him.

"Wait, seriously?" Bill asked, still unsure that the entire room wasn't having a massive joke at his expense.

"Seriously," Heinrich verified.

Bill was stunned, and went and sat at the table.

"I thought that was theoretical," Bill finally stated.

"Nope, sorry mate," Keith answered. "It's been produced and measured multiple times right here at this facility. It exists. And once we knew what we were actually looking for, we found it being produced in nature regularly."

Bill was glad he was sitting, because this was almost overwhelming.

"Assuming I have the capacity to comprehend any of this," Bill began, hoping he'd be able to follow along, "explain to me how there is a correlation between your processors dissolving and thunderstorms and antimatter. And, I am begging you, use terms I can understand."

"I will try," Heinrich began. "For the last few years, astronomists have regularly detected that in large thunderstorms, significant lightning strikes generate massive gamma ray bursts shooting up from the top of the storm clouds over the strikes and into space."

Heinrich paused to see if Bill was going to ask a question, but received a blank stare from Bill, so he continued.

"Through a process that I am not going to bother to try to explain to you, there are also antimatter bursts created during the gamma ray bursts. And since I am trying to make your head explode anyway, I'll also tell you that these gamma ray and antimatter bursts can, and regularly do, follow the magnetic lines of the planet in space, to the point that they can take out a satellite that couldn't even see the original storm because it was below the horizon, but because the satellite is aligned with a magnetic line upon which the burst is traveling, the satellite gets roasted anyway."

Heinrich stopped, and watched Bill for a moment. Bill still had no reaction or response.

"Did I break you?" Heinrich finally asked.

After a moment, Bill nodded his head slightly and finally answered.

"Yup, I think so. What all this tells me is that there is no way for this to be safe, and I need to have Vasily shoot everyone in this room, including myself, in the head, and then lay waste to this facility in order to save humanity. Does that about sum it up?"

"No, that is precisely not my point," Heinrich answered, trying not to sound like he was talking to a learning-challenged small child.

Bill was growing more and more disgusted with this entire project, and with himself for permitting himself to have ever joined it.

"Then get to the explanation of how these satellite-killing antimatter bursts are affecting your other-dimensional processors but not destroying us, the planet, and our universe as we know it."

"Bill, you're overthinking it," Heinrich tried to calm Bill down, but could see he wasn't getting far. "But here's the rest: as far as we can tell, there is no antimatter in the dimension where we build the virtual processors. When the antimatter is passing into space, the quantum twin of the antimatter is apparently flying the other way, and if one or more quantum antimatter elements make it into the stream and into the processor dimension, the antimatter element is destroyed because it cannot exist in that dimension, and that destruction takes the open processor instance with it. When that processor step is destroyed, no key response data is passed to the next step, and the process fails. In our existing process, we already trap for missing or invalid key response errors and reprocess the transactions anyway. It's really no big deal."

"Setting aside how bad all of that sounds," Bill was still against this whole project, "what happens when the processor pocket is destroyed?"

"What do you mean?" Heinrich was confused by the simplicity of the question.

"So, the anti-antimatter thing flies through everything and gets into that open interdimensional tear that you're using to build and run that virtual processor, and the whole thing does... what? Explodes? Ceases to exist? Just closes and leaves our debris in that other dimension? What happens to it? Remember a long time ago when we discussed cleaning up your packets after you create them and not just littering on a pristine beach?"

"Yes, I remember that," Heinrich replied. "When we had a packet failure and ran the transaction through the process again, there was no sign of the destroyed 'packet', as you're calling it, so it looks like the entire instance, along with the quantum antimatter pieces are completely destroyed."

"Now I'm calling bullshit," Bill responded right away. "I remember from my Science 101 class in school that matter does not just go away, it is converted to energy. So, where did the energy go? If it didn't come back through to us, and there's no sign of it in that dimension, then where is it? It can't not be anywhere. And what even is the corresponding destruction of antimatter into anti-... what? Anti-energy?"

"The truth is, we don't know," Heinrich answered.

"And there it is," Bill responded, happy to finally get the truth. He thought for a moment, choosing his next words carefully. "Heinrich, I can't quite shake this feeling that you and I had this exact same conversation in a previous iteration of the universe, and in that one I said 'ah well, it's only going to be tested at one percent, what can possibly go wrong?', and then a couple hours later, previous us ran the test, and then this iteration of the universe was suddenly formed in place of the last one. But, since previous me didn't send current me a message to tell current me to not let this test proceed, I'm going to allow the test this afternoon. But if there are any antimatter anomalies, I want to know about them, and this time, I want to know where that energy goes. Am I clear?"

Bill made eye contact with every scientist in the room again, and each nodded in the affirmative.

"Now get out," Bill ended the meeting, but did not move from his chair. "Keith, please stay. Vasily, I would like to speak to Keith alone, please."

Vasily nodded and cleared everyone else out of the room, then exited and positioned himself immediately in front of the door to bar anyone from entering until Bill permitted it.

"I believe your Yank expression is 'Rand for your thoughts'," Keith joked when the room was empty.

Bill chuckled.

"That's not even the right currency, but I get your point," Bill countered. Keith gave a short chuckle in response.

After a moment, Bill sighed and looked up to face Keith.

"Keith, you walked off this project once before because Heinrich was hiding important information from you," Bill stated.

Keith just nodded.

"You were obviously angry earlier, but you're still here," Bill continued. "What's different now than last time?"

Keith thought for a moment.

"First, I don't necessarily disagree with that solution involving your bodyguard," Keith said with a chuckle. Bill chuckled darkly too.

"But," Keith continued, "the bottom line here, mate, is that this project is going to get finished, whether or not you and I remain on the project. This project is well past the halfway point, and even though your Gantt Chart shows we still have a few more months to go, you and I know that the first beta test means that we are farther along than that. Your chart is a lie, too, man."

"That's fair," Bill acquiesced. "And you're probably also right that there is no stopping this thing."

"Right," Keith continued, "so let's stay on this project, and make sure these mad bastards don't kill us all, hey?"

Bill considered Keith's words.

"Yeah, you're right," Bill finally conceded. "You ever regret coming back?"

"What, and miss all this fun?" Keith answered with a lot of fake enthusiasm. "Nah, man, if the world is going to end, I at least want to see the show."

"Speaking of mad bastards..." Bill answered with fake horror.

Both of them laughed, then Bill walked to the door and asked Vasily to round up the group.

The storm above them was raging as 2:00 approached, and even though the control room was insulated partly by the ground and partly by the structure around them, the thunder still shook the facility. Bill wondered to himself if this was his embrace of the Acceptance phase of dying, or was just him trying to make himself feel better with dark humor. There was no right answer, so Bill put it out of his head. Standing in the back of the control room with Keith, Bill tried hard to shake the feeling that he was about to witness the end of, well, everything.

"Relax, mate," Keith said quietly, covering the microphone of his headset. "Think of it like this, if it was a clear day, we wouldn't have had a chance to test what happens with storms until we were at full power."

Bill just nodded once in acknowledgement.

The clock changed to 1:50.

It was time.

"Doctor de Boer," Bill announced over his headset, a little surprised at how loud it was throughout the room, "control is yours. Please begin the final checks."

Heinrich acknowledged, and began going through his checklist with the other team members. Bill just listened, not trying to understand the words they were saying, but occasionally catching one he did know.

The clock ticked over to 2:00. Bill found himself holding his breath.

Heinrich gave the order.

"Intensity control, bring us to zero point one percent power."

After a moment, a voice responded.

"We are at zero point one."

Heinrich began calling another checklist, and eventually brought the newly-updated LHC to one percent power.

Bill let out his breath. This was torture.

The test was over in less than five minutes. Bill realized that his entire body was tense, and willed himself to relax. He then realized that he had forgotten to pay attention to how many lightning strikes happened during the test.

After the collider and all its supporting systems were shut down or brought back to their idle status, Heinrich turned to Bill, smiling.

"Anticlimactic, hey?"

"I mean, yes," Bill answered, "but I want to see a whole bunch of answers."

"How about you buy me breakfast tomorrow?" Heinrich replied, still in a jovial mood. "Give me a chance to look over everything with my team and give you those answers."

"My office, say 9:00 in the morning?" Bill offered.

"Perfect," Heinrich chirped happily, then turned back to his console and began talking to his team through his headset.

Bill turned to Keith, who was also smiling.

"*Et tu*, Keith?" Bill asked, exasperated.

"Well, he is right, mate," Keith answered. "It was anticlimactic. And, we're not dead."

"Are you sure?" Bill asked, his mood still not improving.

Never," Keith answered with a laugh. "Come on, let's get you one of your lemon lime sports drinks. You'll feel better after that."

Bill and Keith turned and left the control room and headed back to Bill's office to drink a lemon lime sports drink and watch the bad transaction count increase.

––––––––––––

Bill rubbed his temples. He missed the days when he only had to consider four dimensions.

"I'm trying to understand this, Heinrich, I really am. But I just can not accept that the energy went nowhere."

Heinrich was growing increasingly frustrated that Bill was focusing on the six packets that were affected by the storm, instead of the rest that were not. They were a statistical anomaly, and not worth the concern, but Bill just kept at it.

"Let me try saying it a different way," Heinrich offered.

Bill nodded.

"During the test, there were seventeen lightning strikes, of which, six disintegrated a processor packet with anti-protons," Heinrich looked to Bill to see if he was following, Bill didn't stop him, so he continued. "So, out of the entire batch, 0.006% failed. That low of a percentage just does not matter."

"And I'm saying," Bill was still not convinced, "that your count is important, because if you extrapolate those numbers to full power, and are running a consistent stream of transactions through the collider, the number of packets that will be destroyed will be a vast number, even if it's only 0.006%. In that one percent power test you ran, you stopped at a hundred thousand transactions, right?"

"Yes, but…" Heinrich started.

Bill interrupted.

"But how many transactions could you have run in that test if you hadn't stopped it at a hundred thousand?"

Heinrich did a quick calculation in his head.

"For the seventeen seconds the collider was in a state to process transactions, roughly twenty quadrillion."

Bill opened his mouth to answer, but stopped because he was so shocked at the answer.

"Holy crap, it goes that fast?"

"Yeah, man," Heinrich answered. "I told you it's fast."

Now Bill tried to do some calculations in his head, but quickly gave up.

"That's… I don't even know how many transactions per day that you'll be able to run."

"I can give you the actual number if you want it," Heinrich responded, pulling out his graphing calculator.

"Howzabout instead you tell me how many destroyed processor packets will be killed in a four hour storm at a hundred percent operation instead?" Bill shot back at Heinrich.

Heinrich didn't take the bait.

"Okay, mate, you need to tell me why you are so hung up on the destroyed packets."

"I said it yesterday, Heinrich," Bill tried to maintain an even tone. "That energy from those destroyed packets had to go somewhere. It didn't come back through at you, so where did it go?"

"You're correct, it didn't come back through on us," Heinrich agreed. "And it didn't flip to either the predecessor packet or the following packet, so it stayed in the processor dimension. And since we destroy those packets anyway when we are done with them, again, it goes nowhere."

"That's the flaw in your logic right there," Bill felt like he might be making progress finally in this conversation. "In the normal packets, you destroy them, so those packets go nowhere. But in those normal packets, you're not leaving anything in that dimension, right? You open the packet, squirt in the dots that make the processor…"

"Bosons," Heinrich corrected.

"Bisons, whatever," Bill continued undeterred, "and then when you send the answer through to the next dimension, you destroy the packet in the processor dimension, right?"

"Yes."

"So, in the good packets," Bill wrapped up his argument, "there's no energy caused by the packet destruction because there's nothing in it. So we're not polluting that dimension with our little boson smashing energy blasts. But in that 0.006% during the storms, eventually that energy from the captured anti-protons, if nothing else, is going to build up in that other dimension, and it has to go somewhere. And as with every closet stuffed full of debris, eventually someone gets buried under an avalanche of debris when they open that door."

"No, that's actually not right," Heinrich answered, suddenly seeing the flaw in Bill's argument, and hesitant to clarify. "But I see the problem with your calculations."

"Good, then please explain what I missed," Bill responded.

"Remember that atom we squirt in there to build the processor on, as you so eloquently put it?" Heinrich further clarified. "That stays there. It doesn't come back. It's destroyed along with the packet."

The realization finally hit Bill.

"So wait, you're telling me that a hundred percent of the packets cause that energy dissipation when the packet is destroyed as part of normal operations?"

"Well… yes." Heinrich didn't bother to try to soften the answer.

Bill took a moment to consider his next actions, then stood.

"Doctor Erik Torssen, you are under arrest for crimes against humanity."

Heinrich laughed, but Bill maintained his scowl.

Heinrich stopped laughing after a few seconds when he realized Bill might not be kidding.

"You are joking, right?" Heinrich finally asked Bill.

Bill didn't respond, but continued to maintain his glare. Bill was so very happy with Vasily when he heard Vasily chamber a round in his weapon behind him for effect.

Heinrich turned very pale, and showed actual fear on his face. He looked once at Vasily's rifle, then back to Bill.

"Bill, mate," Heinrich was pleading now, "you're misunderstanding, there's no damage happening. There is nothing in that dimension to damage, and nothing is coming back through anyway. There are no crimes being committed. No one is damaged, no place is damaged. The operational losses of packets cause no damage, because unless one of five expected responses come back, the transaction is reprocessed anyway. *There! Is! No! Damage!*"

The last four words from Heinrich were in full panic. Bill remained stoic, and he was certain Vasily did not change his stance behind him. Bill was waiting for Heinrich to fully crack before he said anything else.

"*Bill!*"

There it is, Bill thought to himself.

"Do I have your attention now, Heinrich?"

"Yes!"

"Good," Bill sat back down and continued. "Now, I will give you one more chance to convince me that the energy loss from *all* of your packets is not damaging that other dimension. And make this explanation good, because the fate of the rest of this project depends on your explanation."

Bill turned to look at Vasily, both for effect and to see how intimidating

Vasily was acting. Upon seeing his stance, Bill was glad Vasily was on his side. Bill wasn't certain if Vasily was attempting to look as intimidating as he was, or really was prepared to execute Heinrich, but for the moment, the effect worked.

Bill turned back to look at Heinrich and raised an eyebrow just to top off the intimidation factor.

"Okay," Heinrich was fully pleading now, "just call off your soldier!"

Bill turned back to Vasily.

"Vasily," Bill stated calmly, "please stand down."

Vasily didn't move. Bill played along.

"Thank you."

Then Bill turned back to Heinrich.

"You have the floor, Heinrich."

"There is no damage to that dimension because we create the dimension each time!" Heinrich was still very much in a panic, and Bill was having a difficult time understanding him through the speed at which he was speaking. "It is an artificial dimension! When we close the packet, the dimension itself ceases to exist! The processor, the energy, the dimension, it all ceases to be! It's gone! It just no longer exists. Please, you have to understand this!"

Bill squinted his eyes as he considered what Heinrich had just said. It all sounded a little too convenient, as well as impossible. Heinrich misinterpreted Bill's expression as disbelief.

"Bill, I am speaking the truth!"

"Are you though?" Bill asked, his voice dripping with skepticism.

Heinrich's new expression made Bill feel bad for being this cruel, but only for a split second.

"*Yes!*"

Bill still was not actually convinced.

"Heinrich, here's my problem with your explanation," Bill laid it out for Heinrich. "I don't really understand any of this quantum stuff. In truth, no one does, not even you. At best, you're an ancient humanoid who is just now slightly less afraid of fire, and at best, I haven't even evolved fins yet. Quantum everything is so far beyond us that it's become a common crutch for bad science fiction writers. And yet, here you are, using the very technology that no one truly understands, and you're going one step further by creating an artificial quantum pocket and claiming that you are certain no damage is coming from your little abomination. How can you possibly know that there is no damage to the very fabric of the multiverse, if such a thing even exists?"

Heinrich shrugged and held up his hands.

"Educated guess?"

Bill dropped his head, then turned back to Vasily.

"Okay! Okay! I don't know!" Heinrich shouted his admission.

Bill turned back to Hienrich and regarded him for a full minute, during which time Heinrich became more and more uncomfortable and awkward.

"Okay, Heinrich, final last chance," Bill was finished with this conversation. And this project. And this self-serving mad scientist. "If you're wrong, and the 'artificial' dimensions are not actually destroyed, and it blows up on us, what will happen?"

Heinrich considered the scenario and his answer for a moment.

"Honestly, we probably won't know," he finally answered. "We will probably just cease to be. One millisecond of a flash, and then just... oblivion. The light from the flash probably won't have a chance to register in our brains before we all become nothing."

Bill considered the first answer from Heinrich that he believed was completely honest.

"Are you a religious man, Heinrich?" Bill asked him.

"As you know, I'm Norwegian, so, not particularly," Heinrich answered, slightly confused.

Bill laughed at the answer.

"Then you should be Lutheran," Bill quipped.

Now Heinrich laughed, and the therapy of the chuckle eased the tension in the room considerably.

"Anyway, I was raised Lutheran, and much to my mother's dismay, it didn't really stick," Bill continued. "But Heinrich, I do believe in a higher power, and if religion is right, and we have to answer for our sins to a higher deity, how do I explain myself to God, and how do you explain yourself to Odin, for snuffing out Creation? Not just all life on Earth, but potentially all of creation. What kind of afterlife is that going to bring us? What concentric circle of Hell do we get? I'm pretty sure Dante missed the 'destroyed all of creation everywhere' circle in his journal."

Heinrich considered Bill's words for a moment.

"I see your point," he finally conceded, looking down to the floor. After a moment, he raised his head again and looked directly at Bill. "I don't have a valid answer for you beyond what I've said. Everything that I know from all of my research and experimentation with this technology tells me that this process and its components are one hundred percent safe. If something goes wrong, it will be from human error."

"Which human?" Bill asked pointedly.

"What do you mean?" Heinrich was surprised by the question.

"Which human is most likely to make the error that kills us all with the new machine?"

"I still don't understand the question," Heinrich stammered.

"If a human is likely to make the mistake that blows it all up," Bill clarified slowly, "which human on your team is the most likely to make that mistake? This is not a rhetorical question."

Heinrich considered his answer for a moment, then dropped his head because he was ashamed of the answer.

"Karla Vanderzhen."

Bill was blown away by the answer. He had actually expected Heinrich to blame the potential mistake on himself, but to deflect it to Karla was completely unexpected.

"That's a hell of an accusation," Bill finally answered. "You want to explain yourself? She literally saved your life and made this whole monstrosity possible, even if she is disappointed with how the management team has worked out."

"That's just it, Bill," Heinrich explained. "I know what I owe Karla, and I feel like shit pointing at her, but she is the only one that is jealous of your success on this project. She thinks she should be in charge of the project, not some former database programmer from Arizona who has no ability to grasp the technology involved in this new magic. As far as she is concerned, you got her kicked off The Committee, and until that event, she was one of the seven people on the planet that had the most to gain from the project. Now, she's just another low-level physicist working at CERN. Yes, she saved me, but you pushed her out. That's how she sees it. I don't think she would sabotage the new tech with the intention to kill us all, just to replace you. But any sabotage while the machine is running will kill us all."

Bill turned to Vasily, who was already speaking into his headset, so he turned back to Heinrich.

"Anyone else I need to remove from this facility?"

"No, everyone else on the project is entirely focused on the project," Heinrich answered.

"And you're sure there is no way for your artificial packets to kill us?" Bill asked again.

"N... No," Heinrich answered.

"Why did you hesitate?" Bill replied.

"I already said, it's as safe as it can be," Heinrich responded, starting to let his panic show again.

"No," Bill corrected, "you said 'this process and its components are one hundred percent safe'. Which is it?"

Heinrich's shoulders fell.

"It's as safe as it can be," he conceded.

"Tell me the truth," Bill pressed, "what is the possibility that this could fail and kill us all?"

"Less than 0.006%?" Heinrich tried to joke, then looked terrified as Vasily immediately raised his weapon and pointed it at Heinrich's head.

"Hold!" Bill shouted and raised his hand, as if the action could possibly stop Vasily from executing Heinrich.

"Seriously, that's a real answer!" Heinrich pleaded.

Bill turned back to face Vasily.

"*Ne nado*," Bill whispered in Russian to get Vasily's attention, then switched to English. "Please don't. I believe him."

Vasily took a breath, then moved his eyes to Bill and back to Heinrich. After a few seconds, he lowered his weapon with an angry grunt, keeping his eyes on Heinrich.

"Spacibo," Bill whispered, then turned back to Heinrich.

"Doctor de Boer," Bill said after a moment, stressing Heinrich's alternate name, "you may continue your work. But Heinrich, no more surprises. Please?"

"Agreed," Heinrich responded with a deep breath. "I need to go change, then I'll get back to work."

Bill chuckled and sat back in his chair and watched Heinrich leave.

"What do you think, Vasily?"

"I think I should shoot him," Vasily responded.

"You're probably right," Bill answered.

CHAPTER 84: PHILANTHROPY

"Good morning, M'Bulu," Bill greeted M'Bulu as their weekly status call started.

"Good morning, Bill," M'Bulu's tone was jovial. "Before we get down to business, I want to let you know that I spoke with The Committee last night. They asked me to extend their appreciation to you for bringing this project to its completion eleven weeks early. Your bonus will reflect their appreciation."

"Well, thanks for the cash," Bill answered with a chuckle, "but if I had my way, we'd still have a couple years of safety tests before we go live next week."

M'Bulu laughed loudly.

"You have become predictable, my friend!" M'Bulu said through his laughter. "I told them you would say almost exactly that."

"Yeah, well," Bill grumbled in response, "I'm just glad I'll be on the other side of the planet when this thing blows up."

That drew even louder laughter from M'Bulu.

After getting control of his laughter, M'Bulu began going over his notes with Bill. The final test results had shown no anomalies, to which Bill had noted that there were no thunderstorms to cause anomalies. M'Bulu glossed over that point and continued. As the project launch would be twelve days hence, M'Bulu would be arriving mid-week next week, along with all of the members of The Committee, except for Keith, who was already in Geneva on Bill's team. M'Bulu wrapped up the meeting, and asked Bill if he had anything else to go over.

"Just one point, Minister," Bill answered, switching to formal. "I have not changed my mind regarding stepping off this project when it is launched. At that point, you will need an administrator to take over for me. Have you given any thoughts as to my replacement?"

M'Bulu took a moment before responding.

"We have, actually," he finally answered. "The Committee was unanimous in their first choice, but Doctor vanGreig was unwilling to accept the position. He will be stepping off as soon as the project launches as well."

Bill was surprised to hear that, as he thought Keith would stay on, despite the scientific disagreements with the team.

M'Bulu continued.

"We also considered Doctor de Boer, but we agree that he played fast with loose truth, to use your expression, and decided he would not be the right candidate."

"Um," Bill corrected, "the expression is 'played fast and loose with the truth', but I agree. I know this is all based on his idea, but I think he is so concerned with actually accomplishing the end that he can't see the dangers. So, have you selected my replacement, or are you still looking?"

"The Committee has selected Doctor Karla Vanderzhen as your replacement."

Bill was shocked by the answer, and waited a moment to see if M'Bulu would laugh and make it clear that his answer had been a joke. No laughter came.

Bill's response was less than articulate.

"Whuuut?"

"Think about it, Bill," M'Bulu had been ready for this discussion. "Karla always considered the Q'Loud project to be hers. When you were put in charge of the project, and then she was sent home, she lobbied, successfully, to at least be on the technical team. You had no objection to her at that time. Then when Heinrich expressed his concerns and she was removed from the project again, all she wanted was to be there to make sure the Machine and the facility were managed properly. Heinrich may have been right that she may have made changes that could have destroyed the facility, but she would not have done so maliciously. Her one true goal is to make sure that facility, and the Machine, are protected. She even calls the Machine 'hers'. Her heart is in the right place, and she wants this to all be successful."

Bill considered M'Bulu's argument.

"Good argument there, boss," Bill finally responded, then winced at the accidental use of the term. M'Bulu just grinned. Bill continued. "Want me to bring her in before the go-live and start transitioning the responsibilities to her, and help everyone see that it is a peaceful transition of power?"

"That is completely up to you," M'Bulu answered. "But that would at least make for good optics."

"Does Keith know?" Bill asked.

"He does," M'Bulu confirmed. "He abstained from the vote when The Committee decided. He said he would follow your lead on the decision, since he is leaving anyway."

"Well, I appreciate Keith's confidence," Bill responded. "If it's acceptable with you, I believe I will reach out to her and ask her to step on Monday morning. That will give us plenty of time to introduce her as the new leader before go-live. The day after we bring up the new technology, I'll hold a meeting with everyone and formally hand over the reins. She deserves that much from me."

"The Committee will appreciate your thoughtfulness," M'Bulu answered, bringing the call to an end. "I will see you Tuesday. Be safe."

"Be well, my friend," Bill said and disconnected the call.

Bill turned in his chair to see Vasily still standing behind him.

"Vasily," Bill asked, "what are you going to do after I resign? Become Karla's head of security?"

"*Nyet*," Vasily answered thoughtfully. "I retire. Travel world. Maybe write blogs."

Bill laughed at the joke, and Vasily joined him.

"Maybe our paths will cross again," Bill said wistfully.

"*Mozhet byt*," Vasily responded with a smile.

"Would you please ask Keith's team to ask him to join me at his earliest convenience?" Bill asked Vasily.

Vasily just nodded and spoke quietly into his headset.

Bill sat and looked out at the Alps while he waited for Keith to arrive.

After a few minutes, Bill heard a quiet knock at the door across the room from him, and Keith stuck his head in.

"Hey mate," Keith said quietly, still hiding behind the door, "you wanted to see me?"

"Yes, get in here and sit down," Bill answered, turning back to face the desk. "Why are you acting weird?"

"No reason, man," Keith lied, badly. "How was your call with the minister?"

"It was good," Bill replied, keeping his voice bored. "He's going to come out here next week, and will stay until after the go-live. I also reminded him that the following day, I am stepping off, so I'm sure there will be a meeting with The Committee that day."

"Yeah, I'm going to resign that day too," Keith responded, appearing to calm down. "I'll wait until right after you give your resignation, then I'll follow suit. Did the minister give you any information about the search for your replacement?"

Bill decided to have a little fun with Keith.

"No, he said the search continues, but nothing firm," Bill lied, doing a good job of keeping his face straight. "I will be interested to know who they choose. But I'm sure they'll choose well… it's not like they're going to choose Karla, ha ha."

"*Ja*, wouldn't that be something!" Keith answered a little too loudly and quickly.

Bill just sat and looked at Keith, letting the awkward silence do the work.

"But, would Karla actually be a bad choice?" Keith finally asked nervously.

"I don't know, Keith, would she?" Bill answered drily, still maintaining eye contact with Keith.

Keith finally broke and dropped his head.

"He told you, didn't he?"

"Of course he told me," Bill responded. "What I want to know is, why didn't *you* tell me? And then I want to know why you didn't want to tell me."

"The answer to your first question is easy," Keith answered. "It wasn't my place to tell you, it was M'Bulu's."

"Fair," Bill accepted the answer.

"And in answer to your second question," Keith continued, "I thought you would be a lot more worried about it, given her history."

"I will admit that it surprised me," Bill confessed, "but after his explanation, it made sense. And just so you know, I am having her start coming to work in this office starting Monday morning so the teams can all see that this will be a peaceful transition, and that Karla will have my full support as my replacement."

"That's mighty philanthopic of you, man," Keith responded, sounding slightly impressed.

"I never wished her any ill will," Bill continued, "I just didn't want her to add complexities to managing this monster. If she wants my gig, and The Committee trusts her, then she can have it. No skin off my teeth."

"Glad to hear it," Keith answered. "That will make for a good conversation at the next meeting."

"Good," Bill concluded that discussion. "Now, if you would please initiate a call with Doctor Vanderzhen, I'd like for the three of us to talk about her stepping on here on Monday morning. Then I'll need you to let The Committee know of my plan. The minister already knows."

Keith happily dialed Karla's number, and he, Karla, and Bill all talked for about an hour. Karla was very appreciative of Bill's intended treatment of her during the transition, and was very grateful to him for supporting her. Karla agreed to be in Bill's office the following Monday at 10:00 a.m., and Bill said he would have a desk ready for her, as well as a new badge and security team. They ended the call with pleasantries.

"Lunch?" Keith asked.

"*Ja, ek is baie honger!*" Bill responded, hoping he still remembered the phrase.

Keith laughed loudly.

"Mate, it is good that you're not in Pretoria anymore, your Afrikaans is still awful," Keith joked.

"I said it exactly the way you taught me to say it!" Bill protested. "How was that awful?"

Keith just laughed again and stood and walked towards the door, waiting for Bill and Vasily.

CHAPTER 85: FOUR DIRECTORS OF THE APOCALYPSE

Bill noticed that Vasily was on his headset a lot this morning. He decided that once he saw Vasily take a break, he'd ask what was up. He trusted that if there was something urgent, Vasily would tell him. Eventually, Vasily informed Bill that Karla's security detail was assigned, and that she was in the building. Vasily seemed to calm down after that.

Right on time at 10:00, there was a knock on his office door, and Karla was ushered in. She walked across the room with a very different demeanor than the last time they had met in this office, and Bill was happy for it.

"Doctor Fibulee," Karla said very gracefully, extending her hand, "I appreciate this opportunity more than I can say."

Bill shook her hand and motioned to a chair in front of his desk.

"Doctor Vanderzhen," Bill matched her level of professionalism, "I could think of no one else that I thought should be my successor. I was very happy when Minister Mabusa informed me of The Committee's choice. It brings me great peace to know that you agreed to take over the project when I step off."

Karla looked at him for a moment.

"You actually mean that, don't you, Bill?" Karla asked, dropping the political veneer from her tone, and changing to a sincere one.

"I really do, Karla," Bill again matched her tone, and answered her sincerely. "Let's go sit at the table, we have much to collaborate on."

They moved to the table, and Bill brought Karla up to speed on the project and its current minutiae. Lunch was brought in, and they worked through the meal. As the day ended, Bill asked Karla to join him again the following day to continue final plans for the go-live, and to discuss transition plans.

Tuesday was more of the same, and much progress was made. Bill decided to have Karla sit in on all his meetings with department heads the following day at their regularly scheduled times, in order to make sure Karla was completely in the loop on all of the notes from each department head, and in order to make sure each department head knew to give Karla the same respect they were giving Bill as his time with the project wound down. M'Bulu joined them in the early afternoon, and the three of them spent the rest of the day discussing M'Bulu's expectations of the project after the new technology was functioning. They all seemed to agree, and Karla was excited to take the helm of the newly upgraded Collider.

The meetings with the department heads all began pretty much the same way, with each department head showing surprise that Karla was in the meeting, and Bill explaining that Karla would be succeeding him as the project manager after the following week. Most of the department heads were happy to see her back, and Bill spent extra time propping up Karla to the ones that still carried a grudge or distrust.

For the two or three that remained negative, Minister Mabusa offered them the opportunity to step off as heads of their departments, and that seemed to resolve the issues.

Bill finished each meeting with a schedule update, letting each manager know that starting the following Monday, they would be doing daily status meetings instead of weekly, in anticipation of the event on Wednesday. All department heads agreed.

When the meetings were all finished, Bill, Karla, and M'Bulu remained sitting at the table going over a few remaining items. As that conversation wound down, Karla noticed Bill's dark demeanor.

"Are you regretting your decision to step off?" Karla finally asked Bill.

Bill gave a dry laugh before responding.

"Just the opposite, Karla," Bill explained. "I still believe this project will kill us all, but I am in a very small group that believes that. That being said, I signed on to this madness, and I will continue to execute my responsibilities to the best of my abilities until I resign. I will remain the Director of the Enhancement Science Leadership Team until I'm not."

Bill paused, considering his words and parsing the emotions that he was trying mightily to keep in check before he continued.

"Next Wednesday is weighing heavily on me. I know the skies will be clear, I know every engineer in that room will be operating at peak efficiency, and all may go well that day, but I still don't believe it's safe."

"It's as safe as it can be," Karla responded, trying to soothe Bill's concerns.

"That's just the point though, isn't it, Karla," Bill responded. "'As safe as it can be' doesn't mean 'safe' at all. All it means is 'least dangerous as we can figure out'. In my opinion, which I have stated dozens of times, this project was rushed by The Committee, which at the time included both of you, and I am still certain that the grasp of quantum physics and quantum engineering by those scientists in that room is barely rudimentary. And I don't like it. And I hope you all survive, but I honestly fear for humanity after we unleash these updates to your Machine next week."

"There really is no changing your mind about that, is there, mate?" M'Bulu asked Bill.

Bill shook his head slightly before he responded.

"I'm sorry, M'Bulu, no. I gave you my word that I would see this project to completion, and I will. But it doesn't change my belief."

"I appreciate your willingness to complete your task," M'Bulu answered.

Karla remained silent and looked at the table.

Bill broke the silence.

"Well, shall we have Keith meet us at the restaurant and have one last big meal together?"

M'Bulu smiled. Karla looked up at Bill, relief on her face.

"That sounds great," she said, letting go of her discomfort at the awkward nature of the discussion they had just completed.

Bill turned to Vasily.

"Vasily, will you join us for the meal?"

Vasily spoke quietly into his headset, then waited a moment before answering Bill.

"*Da*, I will join you for this meal, *spacibo*."

"I feel like we are the Four Directors of the Apocalypse here..." Bill mumbled.

M'Bulu chuckled,

Bill then sent Keith a SMS to join them in the restaurant, then stood and walked his notepad to his desk before he joined the other three people at the door for their walk to the cafeteria.

CHAPTER 86: ONE MORE SPECTACLE

Bill really did not sleep much during the night, and his stomach was upset this morning. He forced himself to eat, because today was not likely to give him many opportunities for a lunch break.

"I feel like I should quote Oppenheimer," Bill mumbled to himself, forgetting that his microphone was on, as he heard his voice boom the complaint across the room.

The room erupted in laughter, and Bill visibly winced at his lapse of good judgement. Fortunately, the room appeared to think he was making an intentional joke. A quick glance at M'Bulu told Bill that M'Bulu did not share the joke. Bill mouthed the word "sorry" to M'Bulu then turned his attention back to the large monitor in front of him.

Karla announced the ten minute mark before final checks over the PA system.

The room began to quiet down as the engineers and department heads took their places and adjusted their headsets.

At the appropriate time, Bill looked to Karla for the timing, and she nodded to him at exactly 9:00.

"Doctor Vanderzhen," Bill announced, beginning the process, "please begin go / no go."

Then Bill turned off his mic.

Karla nodded to Bill, then began working her way down the sizable checklist, announcing each item and waiting for the "go" or "no go" from the team member responsible for the call.

It took almost a half hour for the list to be completed. Bill kept hoping for a "no go" with every call, but none were to be had.

Karla looked at Bill before announcing that all systems were "go".

Bill took a deep breath and let it out slowly before keying his mic back on.

"Thank you, doctor," Bill acknowledged. "Doctor de Boer, you may bring The Machine up to stand-by status."

"Acknowledged."

Bill thought Heinrich sounded just a little too happy to get permission to start the power.

Heinrich called out various commands and queries, receiving answers over the PA system before moving on each time. After a few moments, the little block on Bill's monitor that was supposed to display the power level of the LHC changed from "no reading" to "0%".

"Control," Heinrich announced with an obvious smile in his voice, "power is nominal, all readings within expected parameters, the Machine is standing by."

Heinrich then turned to Bill and gave a quick wink. Bill scowled and pointed to Heinrich's screen. Heinrich turned back to his screen with a grin.

"Thank you, Ops," Bill acknowledged.

Bill gave a quick look to Keith, who returned the glance with a shrug. Next Bill looked to M'Bulu, who gave Bill a quick smile before nodding.

"Ops," Bill continued the process, "please bring the Machine to five percent power."

Heinrich acknowledged Bill, then began going through his list to bring the power level up.

Bill watched as the power level in the block on his screen edged up to "5.00%".

Again, Heinrich announced that all was operating within expected parameters.

"Ops, please run five seconds of test transactions, and report status," Bill cleared Heinrich to continue the process.

Bill watched his monitor to see the transaction count and watch the number of failed transactions. In the five second test, the system processed over a trillion transactions, of which six failed and had to be reprocessed.

Bill was still shocked at how fast the new technology could process the transactions.

"Control," Heinrich snapped Bill out of trying to calculate counts at full power. "Test transactions completed. All systems operating within expected parameters."

No going back now, Bill thought to himself.

"Ops, make your power level ten percent, and run five seconds of test transactions, then report again please."

Heinrich acknowledged, and Bill watched his monitor as the test progressed.

Another completed test, and another report of "all systems operating within expected parameters."

The room spent the next hour and a half incrementing by five percent until they reached a successful test at one hundred percent capacity on the Machine.

Bill continued to stare at his screen, specifically at the slowly flashing big, green "100.00%" in the top left quadrant. They had accomplished a safe start, and the number of bad transactions was so low that even Bill had to admit to himself that the number was negligible. The number of test transactions that was run through the system that morning had a lot of commas in it, and the number of bad transactions was twenty nine. Bill didn't like it, but he knew he didn't have a basis for a successful argument.

"Control?"

Bill realized that he had been lost in thought, and looked up when he heard Heinrich try to get his attention over the comms. Bill looked up and over to Heinrich, and realized that everyone in the room was staring at him.

Oh crap, how long was I zoned out? Bill thought to himself.

"Uh, sorry about that, Ops," Bill tried to cover his lapse. "I was just trying to calculate the percentage on those bad transactions, but that number is really good."

"Thanks, Control," Heinrich beamed.

Bill decided it was time to break the tension in the room.

"Welp, I guess that's a wrap," Bill began with fake levity. "Who's up for lunch? This thing will just run itself, right?"

The room erupted in laughter. Bill was glad for it.

"Seriously though," Bill brought a bit of control back to the room, "whoever doesn't need to be here to babysit this abomination, lunch is on me. Congratulations to every one of you. Well done."

With that, Bill stood, dropped his headset on the table, eliciting a loud pop over the PA system since he had forgotten to turn off the mic, and walked to the door, not bothering to look to see who was following him. He heard the room erupt in celebration behind him.

As Bill followed Vasily out the door and down the hallway towards the cafeteria, Vasily spoke briefly into his headset then turned his head towards Bill and started down a side hallway.

"We divert."

"Okay, why?" Bill was a little surprised by the abrupt detour.

"Minister ordered."

That sounded odd, and slightly alarming, to Bill.

Why would M'Bulu not want me to go to the cafeteria? Bill wondered to himself. *Maybe he's going to have me arrested so I can't resign tomorrow, ha ha.*

Bill followed Vasily a few more steps.

Crap, maybe he is going to have me arrested so I can't resign tomorrow...

Bill tamped down a wave of panic that threatened to overpower him, and continued to follow Vasily, hoping Vasily would defend him from the arrest, rather than participate.

As they continued to walk, Bill began to realize that they had walked in a large circle, and felt a wave of calm wash over him as they turned another corner and headed through the cafeteria doors.

"SURPRISE!"

The room was on its feet, all clapping for Bill. He was stunned for a minute, then overwhelmed by the show of support and aplomb from the assembled team of almost all of the engineers and technicians. Bill then saw Heinrich, Karla, Keith, and M'Bulu standing at the front of the crowd, all clapping and laughing as well. As Bill turned to look behind him, he saw that Vasily was also clapping.

Bill was at a loss for words, and just stood for a moment, trying to keep his composure.

After what seemed like too long to Bill, the applause subsided and Keith called for a speech. The room agreed with Keith, and Bill waved for them to all quiet down.

"First, I am grateful beyond words for all of this," Bill began. "Thank you, thank you, thank you. I know that I have had at least one heated argument with every person in this room, but I never doubted that we had the same goal. The crushing weight of the Imposter Syndrome that I have carried with me throughout this project was never more strong than this very moment, and I thank every one of you for giving me the remarkable opportunity to lead you all."

Bill let his words linger in the air before continuing.

"Doctor de Boer, I know this was your baby, and your life's work," Bill looked directly at Heinrich while addressing him. "As much as I still believe this project will one day kill us all, thank you for allowing me to witness the culmination of your life's work."

Heinrich laughed then responded.

"*Tusen takk*," Heinrich said, intentionally letting his facade slip and speaking in his native Norwegian.

Bill understood the depth of Heinrich's response, and nodded once, accepting the gratitude.

"Doctor Vanderzhen," Bill continued, looking at Karla. "Thank you for letting me sit in your chair for a few months. It never really fit me, and I'm glad you'll be sitting back down in it tomorrow. I can't think of anyone else more deserving of it."

Karla nodded her gratitude.

"Doctor vanGreig and Minister Mabusa," Bill stated, turning his attention to Keith and M'Bulu, who were both beaming at Bill. "You two bastards have dragged me through a path I could never have possibly imagined. After our first meeting, I kept asking myself, 'how can this get any crazier?', but then I finally stopped asking myself that question after a couple weeks, because the Fates seemed to interpret that as a challenge each time I asked. I don't know if I should thank you or curse you for these past many months of my life, but in the spirit of remaining positive, thank you both for an amazing experience."

"You're welcome, mate!" Keith hollered in response.

M'Bulu just bowed slightly to Bill.

"And one more person," Bill said, turning to Vasily, who showed a hint of surprise. "Vasily, I know that you literally risked your life every day that you have guarded me, and the debt of gratitude that I have to you can never be fully repaid. *Spacibo, muy drug.*"

Vasily raised an eyebrow, then spoke.

"You do understand Russian. I knew this."

Bill laughed hard.

"*Da, ya ponimayu.*"

Now Vasily laughed hard, and patted Bill on the shoulder, then yelled to the room.

"We eat now!"

The room erupted in laughter and applause briefly, and everyone walked toward a row of tables holding an array of different foods and dishes. Bill realized what he was looking at.

"Wait, is this…"

"I believe you called it a 'potluck'," M'Bulu answered with a laugh.

"I love potlucks!" Bill exclaimed.

"Your friend Kyle told us this," M'Bulu answered. "What better way to celebrate this event than one of your potlucks?"

Bill had a great lunch, eating way too much of his favorites, including a few dishes that could only have been known to the chefs if they had contacted Bill's mother. Then he spent the rest of the afternoon taking time to chat with each team member that wanted to chat. He didn't leave the cafeteria until well after 7:00 pm, and he was still stuffed from the meal.

As the room finally emptied out, Bill took his leave from Keith and M'Bulu.

"Oof, that lunch was a belly buster," Bill jokingly complained, "but thank you for that. I didn't realize how much I missed those meals. And, did you call my mom for the beef stroganoff recipe?"

M'Bulu laughed quietly and only answered with a wink.

"You are welcome, my friend," M'Bulu answered. "We will miss you. Doctor Vanderzhen and I will meet with you in your office tomorrow morning at 10:00 for the hand-off, then we will have a brief lunch, and then you will take one last blue light brigade to the airport."

"I'll be in your office at 9:45 to take out my things," Keith added, "and if you don't mind, I'll tag along on your ride to the airport."

Bill looked to Vasily, who nodded once.

"Works for me," Bill answered. "See you both in the morning."

They all left the cafeteria, and Vasily escorted Bill back to his quarters.

"Vasily, I know you're on duty, but I'd like to do a shot of vodka with you, since I'm leaving tomorrow" Bill said to the back of Vasily's head as they approached the door.

"*Da*, doctor," Vasily answered. "We will drink vodka tonight, but I will still be with you after tomorrow."

"Why will you still be with me after tomorrow?" Bill asked, entering his living room and heading to the liquor cabinet.

"I escort you back to Arizona, and ensure safe transition to team there," Vasily explained.

"I won't need an escort to Arizona," Bill answered, slightly surprised. "And besides, I'm not staying there. I just have a few things to gather, and a bunch of stuff to sell, then I'm going traveling."

"You need security," Vasily repeated.

"How about this then," Bill suggested, not wanting to drag out the argument. "You remain my guard until I'm done in Arizona, which won't be more than a couple weeks, then you escort me to my first destination, and then you can retire. Will that work?"

"Where is first destination?"

"Well," Bill began his sales pitch, "I wanted to find a pristine, undisturbed lake in the mountains of northern Russia somewhere, and just experience it and take pictures for a few days. Then, I'll probably want to go to Red Square and take pictures just like every other tourist through Russia since the end of World War II, and then I don't know after that."

Bill saw that he had caught Vasily off guard, and handed him a full shot glass, then held his own up for a toast.

"*Na zdorov'ye*," Bill toasted Vasily and downed his vodka.

Vasily downed his vodka as well.

"I know perfect lake," Vasily answered, not showing any signs of the burn of the vodka.

"That sounds great," Bill answered hoarsely.

Vasily laughed and handed his glass back to Bill.

"I return to work now, we have busy day tomorrow."

"Thank you," Bill answered, his voice almost back to normal.

Vasily left, and Bill spent a few minutes packing up his belongings for the journey the next morning.

Bill went to bed, feeling slight warmth from the vodka, and slept well.

Bill awoke before his alarm sounded. He lingered in bed and just looked out the window, watching the horizon begin to lighten and the sun eventually touch the tips of the peaks of the Alps. He wanted to savor the view one last time.

Eventually, he got out of bed and cancelled the alarm on his phone. Except for his toothbrush and deodorant and the outfit he was going to wear today, he had packed everything the previous night.

Bill got dressed and headed down to the cafeteria for breakfast. The hallways were deserted this early in the morning, but the cafeteria usually had more people by now. As Bill ordered his breakfast, he chatted with the chef, since no one else was present.

"It is strange," the chef said through his thick accent that Bill had never been able to place. "No one has been in here since yesterday afternoon. We did have a lot of orders to the control room. It is as if the engineers never left that room."

They're all as bad as Heinrich, Bill thought to himself.

When the food was ready, Bill took it to a table and sat and ate. He noticed that Vasily seemed on edge today.

"Vasily," Bill started. "You seem on edge today. *Shto eta?*"

"Is too quiet," Vasily answered.

"Well, everyone is down in the control room playing with the machine," Bill thought out loud. "Let us just enjoy the quiet."

Vasily spoke quietly into his headset, then shook his head when he received the response. Then he walked to the chef and spoke to him briefly before walking back to the table.

"You are correct, doctor," Vasily said when he returned. "I check with all teams, everyone is at control room."

"Good, then you can join me for breakfast and relax a bit," Bill answered, taking a bite of his Denver omelet.

"*Da*, I join you for meal," VBasily answered, unhooking his weapon and setting it on the table in arm's reach before sitting down.

Bill eyed the gun for a moment before shrugging and returning to his omelet. He heard Vasily chuckle once.

They sat in silence until the chef brought Vasily's meal to him. It was a bowl of something that smelled awful.

"Ugh, what is that?" Bill complained.

"Borscht," Vasily answered, stirring it and smiling.

Bill perked up.

"Really? I love borscht!"

Vasily looked surprised, but then hollered something to the chef that Bill couldn't understand, and the chef responded in perfect Russian, saying something else that Bill couldn't understand.

After a moment, the chef brought Bill a bowl of the borscht, and brought a fresh loaf of pumpernickel bread, still warm from the oven for the two men to share.

Vasily still did not believe Bill, and looked at him suspiciously, so Bill tore off a piece of the bread and began eating the soup as fast as the temperature would allow. Vasily looked impressed, and began eating as well.

"I have only had borscht maybe three times before," Bill said through spoonfuls, "and it was good. but this is by far the best I have ever had."

"*Da*, is very good," Vasily agreed.

After the men had finished their soup, Bill decided to discuss the plans for the day and the rest of the week. He was happy to hear that Vasily would be escorting him to Phoenix. Once Bill was safely in a hotel, Vasily would be meeting with the head of the security team at the GlobalForce office, and turning in his rifle and security badge. Once that was complete, he was officially retired.

"Any chance I can hire you to be a guide to show me a few spots in rural Russia to take pictures?" Bill asked after a few minutes of contemplation.

"*Da*," Vasily answered with a smile, "but you must pay for hotel room in Arizona and plane ticket to Russia."

Bill smiled and extended his hand. Vasily laughed and shook it.

Bill felt much better about the next few days.

Bill was sitting at his desk when M'Bulu, Karla, and Keith were escorted into the office. Bill rose from the desk to meet them halfway. They made small talk for a moment, then Bill decided to get it over with.

"Doctor Vanderzhen," Bill began in his most formal voice, "I hereby turn over this entire project to you."

Bill then motioned to his desk, and Karla walked to it, then stood in front of the chair.

"Doctor Fibulee," Karla said, matching Bill's formality, "I accept. You have my deepest gratitude."

Bill nodded, then turned to face M'Bulu.

"Minister Mabusa," Bill continued in his most formal, "I have learned much on this project. If there is nothing else, I will take my leave of you now."

"Doctor Fibulee," M'Bulu answered, maintaining the formality, "you have performed exceedingly well, and you have my gratitude, and the gratitude of the people of South Africa. You are always welcome in my country, and in my home."

M'Bulu extended his hand, and Bill shook it. Then M'Bulu pulled Bill in and hugged him.

"Never be a stranger, Bill," M'Bulu said after finally releasing Bill.

"I will take you up on that, M'Bulu," Bill answered with a laugh. "I'd like to see South Africa through the eyes of a tourist for a change."

M'Bulu chuckled.

"A tourist with the highest levels of access anywhere in the nation."

"Thank you, my friend," Bill answered quietly.

Bill turned to face Keith finally.

"Any time you're in Durban, mate," Keith said before Bill could speak, "you have a room at my place."

"This has been a hell of a ride, Keith," Bill answered. "Thanks for leading me through most of it."

Keith laughed and shook Bill's hand.

There was an awkward silence. Bill turned to look at Karla, who was seated, then back to M'Bulu and Keith.

"Well, before this gets any more awkward," Bill said finally, "I'm out. Catch me later."

Everyone smiled, and Bill walked to the door, followed by Keith and Vasily. Bill stopped and took one more look at the scenery beyond the window, then walked out the door.

Vasily led Bill to the main entrance, where a full motorcade was waiting. Bill chuckled and shook his head.

One more spectacle, huh M'Bulu? Bill thought to himself.

CHAPTER 87: NO LONGER THEORETICAL

"Where is it all going?" Amir screamed at his team again.

The trillions of Euros that were supposed to be in the accounts in Mauritius are dwindling quickly. Over the past three weeks since the connection to Switch 3 had shown there was no longer any traffic, not only had Amir's team been unable to get past the obvious block and see the traffic again, the money in their account had been going out, without them initiating any of the transactions.

Worse, Amir had been unable to get any new theft transactions to validate. With each passing day, his leadership grew less and less hospitable.

Amir was desperate to recover control of the Switch 3, and to stop the outflow of funds from his accounts, and to start replacing the lost transactions, but he seemed to be completely blocked.

Amir's cell leader entered the room.

"Little brother, I would speak with you."

Amir stood and walked to the front of the room, standing in front of the man, hoping to find a good way to explain his lack of progress.

"Yes, brother?" Amir greeted him.

"We have news," Amir's leader began. "The reason you stopped seeing transactions three weeks ago is because the Large Hadron Collider project has gone live, and there is no longer any processing going through your box in Pretoria. You are unable to confiscate any more funds from anyone, because the system you were controlling is dead."

Amir was stunned.

"No, that was still theoretical," Amir said as much to himself as to his leader. "That system can't be on for another two years."

"Well, it is on now," Amir's leader continued. "The funds in our account are dwindling because our brothers at the bank were apprehended, and those funds are being returned to those from whom we took them. Your project has turned out to be a failure."

"No, we can recover if…" Amir began to argue, just as his leader shot him in the head.

CHAPTER 88: BUY GOLD

In the many months following Bill's departure from the Q'Loud project, GlobalForce, and everything else related to that chapter of his life, Bill did exactly what he kept promising himself that he would do: travel and take pictures.

He spent almost two months traveling across Russia with Vasily after he got home from the project in Geneva. After the trip was over, Bill realized that he had spent days, and taken tons of pictures, in each of the eleven time zones that encompassed Russia. When the trip was over, Bill and Vasily parted ways, and Bill went home to Arizona to store all his photos in his cloud drive and edit a few of them.

His "home" was really just a room he rented from a friend of his mother's. He paid for the high-speed internet in Margaret's house, so he would have high-speed connections when he was there, but really only kept a bed and a desk in the room, except for his Doctorate diploma, propped up on the desk, leaning against the wall. When he was home, he would connect his laptop to the wifi in the house, upload all the new images to his cloud storage, and do some laundry. Margaret apparently kept the room clean for him, because it was never dusty when he showed up. It worked well for both of them.

After the trip through Russia, Bill decided to just spin a globe and close his eyes and point to a spot. The spot ended up being relatively near Uluru in central Australia.

He spent nearly a month on and near the great, red rock, not really wanting to leave, but knowing he needed to see more of the world. Since he had been keeping in occasional contact with his former team members, Bill decided his next stop would be to see Eileen.

After spending two weeks catching up with Eileen and her mom and Matilda, and seeing that Eileen was absolutely thriving in her new life, Bill decided to stay in the southern hemisphere and head over to Durban to take Keith up on his offer of lodging and fishing.

Fortunately, Keith was home when Bill called, and would be home for the foreseeable future when Bill arrived.

————————————

On his third night in Durban, Bill and Keith were sitting on lounges, drinking strong drinks and watching the waves roll in onto the beach as the sky on the eastern horizon darkened. Bill had noticed that Keith was evasive about why he was home and not working, but he decided to let it sit and let Keith tell him when he was ready.

"I resigned the day after you did, like I said I would" Keith said, finally breaking the silence.

Bill considered the heavy significance of that act. He decided to keep his response light in hopes of encouraging Keith to tell him more.

"I knew that. But did you agree with me?" Bill joked.

"Yes."

Keith's answer stunned Bill.

"Wait," Bill answered, trying to keep the surprise out of his voice, "you actually do agree with me? On what part?"

"That new configuration and the usage of the LHC is going to destroy that facility," Keith responded without any hesitation. Then he clarified. "I don't necessarily agree with you that the 'debris', as you called it, that is being left behind in those artificial dimensions is going to suddenly fill up and explode back, but you were spot on with your concern about those packets disintegrating in the presence of the gamma and antimatter bursts."

"I fucking knew it!" Bill exclaimed without hesitation, and with a tinge of anger in his voice. "Then why didn't you back me when we were having those arguments in Geneva?"

"It wouldn't have mattered," Keith explained, shifting slightly in his chair to face Bill. "Mate, you need to understand that the project was going to happen with you or without you. The longer you stayed on, the more sanity remained in the way the project was managed, but the project would have been completed anyway, even if Mabusa himself would have had to manage it. There was nothing you could have done to stop it."

Bill pondered Keith's words. It bugged him that the entire team had just willfully chosen to ignore a potential threat such as this.

"Is there any way to shield the facility from the gamma bursts?" Bill asked, hoping that maybe he and Keith could make a case for it.

"No," Keith answered after a moment of thought. "You would have to encase the entire facility in a protective shell, with no openings whatsoever, while it was running. And even then, the shell would only be questionably safe."

"I mean, I understand how encasing the whole facility is not feasible," Bill tried to continue to spur brainstorming, "but what else could be done?"

"Well," Keith began, thinking out loud, "if they didn't run the Q'Loud processes during any thunderstorms, then they wouldn't have those antimatter and gamma bursts to grapple with. But the storms could not be anywhere within the view of the facility, completely below the horizon. And, there couldn't be any storms on any of the planetary magnetic lines that run near the Machine, because those bursts travel along those lines. So, in the rainy seasons, if there were any storms within a vast diameter around the Machine, it couldn't be used."

"But those transaction validation processes need to run all the time," Bill joined the thought exercise. "So, they can't just take the LHC and Q'Loud system offline whenever there's a storm within five hundred miles of Geneva."

"Correct," Keith continued the thread, "so they won't. And during storms, there will be antimatter and gamma bursts that destroy packets. Those packets will be handled by the exception engine in the process, so that's not a concern. The real concern is that those packets will be disintegrating in an unmanaged condition."

"Why is that the main concern?" Bill really wanted to understand the foundation of his fear of the unknown with the ruined packets.

"Bill," Keith began, "I think I remember you saying one time to Heinrich that no one can truly understand any of this quantum stuff. And you were right. There is a reason that bad science fiction writers use quantum as a crutch, and that's because no one can argue with them or prove them wrong, because there just is not enough understanding to call bullshit on the fiction writers, nor on the scientists for that matter."

"Yeah, I said almost exactly that to Heinrich," Bill agreed.

"Then that's the thing, isn't it?" Keith continued. "None of us, not you, not me, not any one of those madmen in Geneva, can possibly know what actually happens when those packets are destroyed. You were right to worry that any of the packets were snuffed out, because they don't know what is causing them to actually fall apart, nor what happens to the particles when the packet collapses."

"Wait, what do you mean 'they don't know what is causing them to fall apart'?" Bill was now more worried than he had ever been when he was in Switzerland. "How can they not know what is causing it?"

"That's just it," Keith clarified. "They know that when a lightning strike happens, and that gamma and antimatter burst happens at the cloud top, that the packet below may disintegrate, but they don't know why. There is no measurable gamma radiation in or near the reactor, nor any antimatter detected in range either. The bursts go away from the planet into space, either straight up, or following a natural magnetic line. So, they don't know. Heinrich speculated that the infinite size of the artificial packet may expand into a dimensional range overlapping part of the bursts, and that the particles in the burst are destroying the boundary of the dimensions or something. Again, they just don't know. Worse, since they don't know what the interaction is, they won't know that a fatal reaction has occurred until after it occurs."

"I was right, wasn't I?" Bill asked.

"*Ja*, you were."

The two friends sat in silence for a few minutes, the fire growing low a few feet away from them on the beach. They watched the stars fill the sky, the absence of light pollution allowing a dramatic stellar tapestry to be fully observed.

"How many of those stars are going to be destroyed by our project?" Bill finally asked, as if confessing to a sin orders of magnitude greater than genocide.

"No way to know," Keith answered after taking another sip of his drink. "Could be none of them, but it could be all of them. Chances are, we won't even know when it happens. If a singularity forms, we are so relatively close to it, we'll be destroyed before our brain is able to process that anything has happened."

"I'll miss seeing the stars," Bill accepted his inevitable fate.

"Ah, you won't have a chance to miss them," Keith countered. "You'll be gone before they are."

Bill looked at the stars for a few more minutes.

"You've given me the worst-case scenario," Bill continued grimly. "What's the best case scenario if something explodes?"

"The Q'Loud goes offline for many years," Keith began enumerating the possibilities, "and since the Switch network can't be brought back online, we go back to magstripe."

"Why would we have to go back to magstripe?" Bill was surprised to hear that. "We have the chips on all the cards."

"True," Keith explained, "but we don't have a system to validate the tokens from them, because all of the banks decommissioned the independent systems years ago when the Switch network came online."

"But humanity survives?" Bill pushed the point.

"Yes," Keith answered, "except for the people within a blast radius of about 75 kilometers or so from the collider."

Bill thought for a few more minutes.

"Buy gold," Bill said, mostly to himself.

"Buy gold," Keith agreed.

The two friends had no more conversation for the rest of the evening, and instead continued drinking, watching the stars swim across the sky, and letting the fire die.

Bill remained in South Africa for a few weeks. He and Keith flew over to Johannesburg to visit Taylor and Kyle and the old team. Bill was happy to see them both, and was thrilled that Kyle was thriving as well as Eileen was in New Zealand.

The National Secure Citizen project had been a success, and Kyle had received all the credit for that. He even won some kind of national award for the project, which was of course presented to him by M'Bulu in a big event. Bill chided Kyle for taking all the credit, and Kyle said that he thanked his entire team, not bothering to mention Bill's involvement with a hidden grin. Bill was happy for him.

After finishing his trip through South Africa, Bill headed home again to center himself and decide where his next trip would take him.

CHAPTER 89: NEXT JOURNEY

As Bill watched all of the images on the ninth chip from his camera load to his cloud drive, he let his mind wander as to his next destination. He remembered there was a contractor back at LookAtMe that had talked about a "Supernatural Tour".

The idea was to drive to Sedona in Arizona, and experience the vortices there, then head over to Jerome, Arizona and stay in the haunted hotel.

From there, head to the Meteor Crater in northern Arizona, tour that, and then to northern New Mexico to take in the landscape, food, and galleries in Taos and Santa Fe for a few days.

Next, the tour would head down to Socorro, New Mexico to the VLA facility, and go on all the guided walks around the facility and find out what they have heard while listening to outer space.

Once that was completed, the pièce de résistance was a week in Roswell, taking in all of the hype and pomp surrounding the UFO conspiracy there.

Bill had been intrigued by the idea of such a trip when he first heard about it, and decided then and there to make that his next journey.

CHAPTER 90: HYPE

The tour had lived up to the hype. Bill was refreshed by his time in the vortex, confused by what he experienced in the haunted hotel, enjoyed the crater, loved the galleries and food, was thoroughly impressed by the VLA, and loved the campiness of Roswell. He was happy that he had made the trip.

He decided to take the southern route back to Phoenix from Roswell, and he was surprised to see the signs letting him know he was approaching White Sands, New Mexico. He had heard a lot of stories over the years of the history of the atomic bomb program in the United States, and always found it interesting, so he decided to add a stop to his trip, and take a tour of White Sands National Park.

He arrived near dinner time, so Bill decided to get a motel room and grab some dinner, and then head up to the Visitor Center in the morning.

Morning dawned clear and comfortable outside, and Bill drove to the Visitor Center and began looking through the vast building, which seemed to be just a very large gift shop, with a few informational displays. Eventually Bill made his way to the help desk, and found a very friendly and helpful park ranger, who was happy to tell Bill all about all the different tours available to visitors, including a self-guided one. Bill chose the latter.

After walking for about an hour, Bill was marveling at the almost translucent color of the sand. Regular white beach sand seemed yellowish brown compared to this. Bill's phone rang, surprising him, because not many people contacted him lately. Bill looked at the screen and saw that the call was coming from Heinrich.

Weird, Bill thought, then tapped the ANSWER button.

"Heinrich, how the hell are you?" Bill asked happily.

"Bill!" Heinrich was shouting, and there was a lot of noise in the background. "There was a storm! A string of packets failed and caused a fatal cascade! The system shorted out! We are trying to shut it down now!"

Bill heard a lot of people yelling and alarms blaring in the background as he heard Heinrich's words.

Bill wondered to himself if he would even feel the gravity waves from the back hole that would almost certainly form.

"Heinrich? What's happening? Can you stop it?" Bill yelled in response.

"We're trying!" Heinrich shouted, followed by the sound of a very large explosion.

Heinrich looked around the room, watching engineers frantically trying to bring the reactor under control and cut power to it in an attempt to stop the chain reaction of explosive failures surging through the entire ring. The ground shook, and the overhead lights flickered. Heinrich looked up to the monitor that showed the external video feed in time to see one of the segments explode in a massive shower of sparks, lightning, and debris. After a few seconds, one of the segments next to that one exploded in a similarly impressive fashion.

"Bill," Heinrich yelled into his phone so he could be heard over the carnage, "the Machine is exploding! I don't know if we are going to be able to st…"

Erik Torssen's last words were cut short as he felt the blast of invisible radiation hit his body. His phone exploded in his hand, and just before his machine killed him with a stream of new, exotic, previously unknown radiation and massive blasts of blue and red lightning that tore the flesh from his body and shredded his organs, he was able to notice the irony.

"Heinrich?" Bill shouted again, then heard the call disconnect.

"This can't be good," Bill said out loud to himself, then started hiking back to the Visitor Center. As he was walking, he pulled up Keith's number and dialed.

"Bill! Where are you?" Keith answered quickly.

"I'm in New Mexico, I just got a call from Heinrich," Bill jumped right to it. "He said something about a string of failed packets feeding something back in a storm and causing explosions."

"*Ja*, Karla called me, she said there was a catastrophic failure," Keith recounted quickly, "then she said there were explosions in two of the segments, and then the line went dead."

"Yeah, that's what happened when I was talking to Heinrich," Bill confirmed.

"Do you remember that best-possible worst-case scenario we talked about?" Keith asked.

"Yes," Bill answered.

"Well, we are still alive, so there's a good chance a singularity didn't form," Keith continued, "but it's still bad. What else did Heinrich tell you?"

"He said that they were trying to shut it down," Bill recounted, "and that it wasn't working, and then two segments of the Collider exploded. Heinrich was telling me that he didn't think they could do something, but then the call cut off."

"Shit," Keith said after a moment. "Did you buy gold?"

"As a matter of fact, I did," Bill answered.

"Good," Keith continued. "If the LHC is damaged with multiple segments destroyed, it won't be back online for several years, if ever. Worse, we don't know what kind of exotic particles may have been created by those explosions, so we don't know what will happen yet anyway."

"So, what," Bill decided to ask, "we are going to have unimaginable angry life forms coming out of the smoking ruins?"

"*Ja*, possibly something like that," Keith answered. "We just don't know. Wait, hang on."

Bill was uncomfortable by the distraction.

"I have access to military communications," Keith stated when he returned to the phone. "Military channels are reporting that communication with most of Europe and Russia are lost. There is an incredibly massive storm moving out from where the LHC was. Cloud tops are at, shit, cloud tops are over a hundred thousand meters. Military is saying that the storm is expanding at Mach 1, and only supersonic planes in the air can get away from it. They have been watching civilian airliners explode in the sky as the storm approaches them."

Keith was quiet again for a moment as he listened to more communications.

"Bill, we may lose power for a bit. You take care of yourself, my friend. Hopefully we will talk again someday."

Keith disconnected the call.

CHAPTER 91: FORTY-FIVE MINUTE WAIT

Bill looked at his phone for a moment, then sat down in the brilliant white sand to process all he had just heard. The storm, the largest storm ever experienced in written history, had encompassed all of Europe and a good chunk of Russia in a few minutes. He wondered to himself if it would be large enough to reach him in New Mexico. And if it could, he wondered how long it would take to reach him.

Bill pulled out his phone to look up distances and the speed of sound. The internet was suddenly very slow, but he was able to finally get the distance and the speed, and using a little basic calculator math, he figured that, if the storm could reach him, he had about seven hours before that happened.

Now that Bill had an idea of how long before the result of his former project reached him, his mind turned to his deceased friends in Geneva. Bill felt the worst for Heinrich. Erik, Bill corrected himself. There was no point in maintaining the cover name.

The poor bastard let his own arrogance get away from him, Bill thought to himself.

Then he wondered about Vasily, and hoped someone warned him before the storm got to him. Bill figured he probably had a good warning from his military contacts.

Bill checked the clock on his phone. It was still over six hours before the storm would arrive, if it kept at the pace that Keith had discussed.

Bill considered his options. He could hurry back to the car and not quite make it home before the storm hit. He could try to take shelter in the Visitor Center.

Neither of those alternatives seemed like they would be safe anyway.

Since safety didn't appear to be an option, Bill decided he'd set up his camera on the tripod and film the storm coming.

Maybe I'll be able to sell it to a news organization after the power comes back on, Bill thought to himself.

Bill went back to his car and got his tripod, a sandbag, and a couple water bottles from the trunk, then headed back into the middle of the monument.

The weather was still nice. 76 degrees, gentle breeze.

Bill found a spot with a nice, flat rock for him to sit on, and began setting up the tripod. He hooked the sandbag to the center post in hopes of keeping it from blowing over when the storm hit.

Next, he tried various lenses to see which one would give the best view of the storm coming across the horizon and eventually enveloping him and his camera. Bill settled on a 85mm prime lens, turned on the camera, made a few adjustments to the settings, then turned it back off to conserve the battery.

Bill sat back down on the rock to wait, resting his eyes for a few minutes to gather his strength for a potentially long night.

Bill awoke with a start. He hadn't intended to sleep, because he wanted to start filming as soon as he saw the beginnings of the storm on the horizon. He checked his phone to see what time it was. Bill figured he had about an hour before the show started. The sun was low on the horizon behind him, and he wondered if he would see another sunset, so he grabbed the camera and took a few shots before turning it back off, and turning himself to watch the eastern horizon for the beginning of the storm.

About twenty minutes later, Bill thought he could see a strange

431

disruption in the far distance, so he stood and connected the camera to the tripod, checked his settings and focus one more time, and pressed the button to begin rolling. Then Bill sat back down to watch the storm approach.

It took almost forty five minutes for the storm to fill both the horizon and the sky as it approached Bill's location. Bill just continued to watch the storm, his awe growing every minute. Bill noticed that the colors of the clouds, the sky around the storm, and even the lightning were unusual, a combination of blues and reds, rather than the grays and greens of the severe storms that Bill had encountered around the world.

The wind picked up suddenly. It battered him and the tripod, but the sandbag held it in place. Bill decided to check to see how the footage in the camera was looking, and opened the viewer to watch. He wished he had used a smaller lens, but the pictures were as equally stunning as the live view.

Bill felt as much as heard the thunder from the lightning strikes, which were constant as the storm rolled across the desert.

Bill could no longer see the sky above him, as the storm had obscured it. He saw that the lightning strikes were hitting and damaging every piece of metal that he could see, and eventually several struck the Visitor Center, destroying it, as well as several cars in the parking lot, and on the highway in the distance.

I wonder why all the metal is getting destroyed, Bill thought, turning back to the camera and closing the viewer.

At that moment, Bill's camera exploded, as it, and Bill, were hit by a massive bolt of lightning.

EPILOGUE

Bill was not aware of how long he had been unconscious, but his whole body hurt. He became aware of more pain in his thigh, and looked to see a burned hole in his cargo shorts where his phone had been, his leg red and blistered.

He was able to sit up, and looked around to see what had happened. The wind had died down significantly, but the storm was still overhead, and was still rolling across the horizon to the west of him. He looked back to where his camera had been, only to see a smoking crater where the tripod once stood. He saw a piece of the canvas from the sandbag several feet away, but no sign of the camera or the tripod.

Bill finally stood and walked to inspect the crater closer, but as he stood, he noticed that the sands around him now were sparkling with a blue light. The light wasn't a reflection, but was actually coming from within the sand.

That can't be good, Bill thought to himself, then decided it was time to get away from whatever strangeness was happening in this sand. He looked at his camera bag, and saw that the lenses and accessories inside, along with the bag, had been shredded by the explosion, so he grabbed his water bottle off the rock, and started walking back to the parking lot.

As he approached his car, he noticed that some of the cars were still smoldering, and some appeared untouched. Bill then realized that the cars that were damaged had charred human remains in them, and appeared to have been in the process of being driven out of the lot, while the parked cars appeared to have no damage.

Bill opened the door of his car, and the handle shocked him as the overhead light in the car popped and sizzled. Bill quickly reached in and pulled the trunk release, then jumped away from the door.

He grabbed his gym bag, filled it with water bottles, and left the car, walking towards the highway, away from White Sands, while keeping a wary eye on the storm still roiling in the western sky.

ABOUT THE AUTHOR

Jeffrey Flaat is an independent film producer, photographer, software engineer, and writer currently living in Arizona. Jeffrey has collaborated as an editor on several other works of fiction as well as documentaries and scary software.

Made in the USA
Middletown, DE
08 September 2021